THE AUTHOR

Matt Ritson was born in 1957 and raised on Britain's north-east coast. As a youth he studied Art and Architecture at 'A' level, along with Ancient Greek and Roman history then worked his way through his education, which added to his design skills and instilled in him his entrepreneurial spirit. After gaining a Master's Degree in Industrial Design Engineering at London's Central St. Martin's College, he returned to his native north-east where he spent the first part of his career both as a conceptual design consultant and a prototype manufacturer, before side-stepping into property design and development.

His hobbies include painting and sculpture, travel and hiking and he has a particular passion for the Greek and Caribbean islands. Other hobbies include scuba diving and horology: the collection of timepieces.

He lives on the Northumberland coast.

THE HIPPO-TEMPUS

AKA The Alexandria Key

Book Two of the Time-Horse Series

MATT RITSON

Matador
9 Priory Business Park
Kibworth Beauchamp
Leicestershire LE8 0RX, UK
Tel: (+44) 116 279 2299
Fax: (+44) 116 279 2277
Email: books@troubador.co.uk
Web: www.troubador.co.uk/matador

ISBN 978 1780882 536

British Library Cataloguing in Publication Data.
A catalogue record for this book is available from the British Library.

Typeset in Aldine401 BT Roman by Troubador Publishing Ltd, Leicester, UK
Printed and bound in the UK by TJ International, Padstow, Cornwall

Matador is an imprint of Troubador Publishing Ltd

For

Nathan,

Matthew,

Grace and Olivia,

My past and future.

And for Hollie - my test pilot.

XXXXX

CONTENTS

Map Of Ancient Alexandria xii

Map Of Aegilia xiii

Author's Notes: 'On Memory' xv

'On Pronunciation' xvii

Prolegomenon: Part One - Wilusha xix

Part Two - Dead Bodies! xxvi

Reintroduction xxx

Part I: The World Is Lost 1

Chapter 1 The Refugees 3

2 Ptolemy's Secret 'Weapon' 13

3 The Tomb Of Alexander 22

4 'Caesar's' Secret Weapon 36

5 Total Loss 46

6 Lio's Odyssey Begins 58

7 The Image Of Youth 65

8 Colossus 74

9 Kidnapped 85

10 The Chase 96

11 Lio's Darkest Hour 109

12 A New Life 119

Part II: Softly, Softly, Catchee Monkey... 129

Chapter 13 Imperator Mundi 131

14 Plumbing The Depths 142

15	Plumbing The Depths Again	153
16	The Summer Of Bliss	160
17	The Premonition	168
18	Marmalade!	176
19	Led By The Nose	181
20	Dawning Realisation	191
21	An Old Friend	200
22	Another Old Friend	211
23	The Mother Of All Weapons	218

Part III: The Countdown — 225

Chapter	24	The First Arms Race	227
	25	Madness!	231
	26	A Ball Of Flame	239
	27	The Truth Will Out	249
	28	The Killing Machine	259
	29	Coming To Terms	265
	30	Gone!	274
	31	A Relapse Of Madness	282
	32	The Great Unveiling	288
	33	Boris And The Rabbits	299
	34	A Trip To The Farm	309
	35	A Final Audience	316

Part IV: Zero Hour — 327

Chapter	36	Trouble	329
	37	A Last Goodbye?	342
	38	A Trip To The Seaside	348
	39	A Trip To The Library	360
	40	The Hippo-Tempus!	372
	41	Carpe Diem	382

Part V: Aftermath   389

Chapter   42   Message In A Bottle   391
             43   The Rescue   398
             44   Eos   406
             45   Many Blissful Memories   417
             46   The Removal Of Evidence   423

Epilogue: 429

The Legend Of The Desert   431
In Homage And Apologia   437
Acknowledgements   443

The Future: 445

Hand In Glove   447

... AND THE NAME 'WILUSHA' WILL BE STRICKEN
FROM HISTORY

MAP OF ANCIENT ALEXANDRIA:
CIRCA FIRST CENT. BC

I   THE SERAPEION;
II   THE MOUSEION AND LIBRARY;
III   THE ROYAL PALACE;
IV   THE GREAT TOWER;
V   THE MOLE;
VI   PHAROS ISLAND;
VII PTOLEMY'S CAMP;
VIII PTOLEMY'S SECRET WEAPON;
IX   THE EUNOSTOS (ROYAL) DOCK;
X   THE GREAT HARBOUR;
XI   DOCKSIDE;
XII NAVAL BATTLE SITE;
XIII FRESH WATER LAKE;
XIV THE CANAL SYSTEM

    BARRICADE

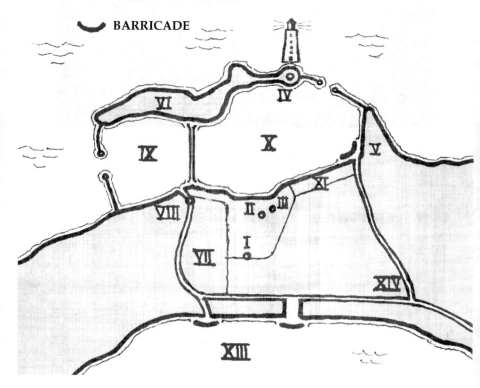

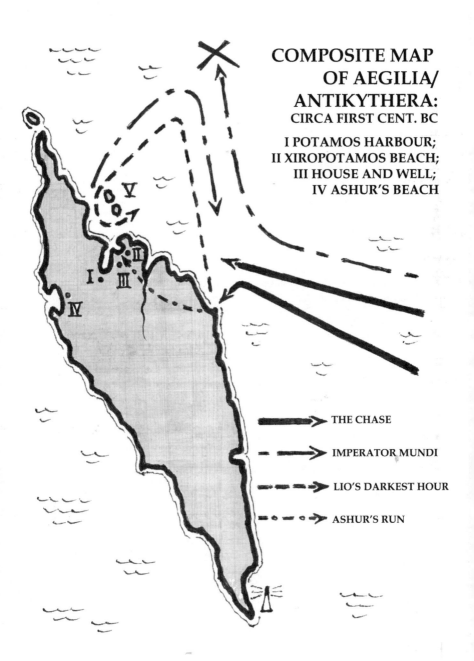

COMPOSITE MAP OF AEGILIA/ ANTIKYTHERA: CIRCA FIRST CENT. BC

I POTAMOS HARBOUR;
II XIROPOTAMOS BEACH;
III HOUSE AND WELL;
IV ASHUR'S BEACH

THE CHASE

IMPERATOR MUNDI

LIO'S DARKEST HOUR

ASHUR'S RUN

AUTHOR'S NOTES:

'ON MEMORY'

Since you're reading this, I assume you've already read the first book. If you didn't however, you could always go back and read the Hippo-Chronos as a prequel I suppose. Though, by changing the sequence of events, goodness knows what paradoxes you will open up and will now have to get your head around. Actually, on second thoughts, I'm not so sure it can be done – good luck!

One thing which I neglected to say at the start of the first book, *The Hippo-Chronos*, was that I met him once – 'Tom' that is. It is a remarkably short, but treasured, memory. It was years ago, when my own son was tiny, a babe in arms. It was a freezing cold winter's day, so I wrapped him up warmly and tucked him into one of those papoose affairs that I used to wear on my back when I was younger. Then I took him for an early morning walk - just the two of us - the proud father and his new son.

I was a relative stranger to Tynemouth then. We started our long walk at the fish quay and followed the riverside path of Hadrian's way, up to Collingwood's monument, before ending up on the promontory of the Spanish Battery. My son lay asleep as I took in the whole view from there, but, as tiny as he was, we were absolutely together. I was daydreaming in a world of my own when a rather shabbily dressed old man approached me, unseen at first.

Seeing me there at the edge of the cliff, obviously happy and content, he must have felt driven to speak. He nodded toward the baby: "*That...* is what life is about!" was the single phrase he uttered. I still remember his strange accent. I smiled and nodded back in agreement before turning to face the sea again in easy silence. By the time I looked back moments later, he had disappeared, just as mysteriously as he had arrived. That meeting was many years ago... or was it only yesterday? Strange how such a casual event can stay with you forever – affect your life.

Since then, whenever I meet someone new, I try to make a point of speaking. It seems such a simple thing to make a stranger feel welcome.

However – back to Tom's story. This, *The Hippo-Tempus*, is the second and concluding part of the tale. So, now, as I urged you at the beginning of book one:

PLEASE - DARE TO DREAM ON!

'ON PRONUNCIATION'

Once again, please don't lose any sleep about pronunciation; after all, this is only an adventure story, isn't it?

However, for those who still insist that it matters, I have added to the list of some of the more potentially awkward words and names together with accepted pronunciations. The words and names are mostly in Greek or Latin. Some other words in English and other languages are **stressed** as written. Most meanings or explanations are given, but again, as reminders only.

Agamemnon [Gk] – A-ga-**mem**-non
Arsinoë [Gk] – Ah-sin-**oh**-ee (sister of Ptolemy XIII of Egypt)
Athena Nike [Gk] – A-**thee**-na **Nee**-kay (all round goddess of wisdom, war and life)
Cassiterides [Gk] – Kas-sitter-**ee**-dess (mythical islands of tin)
Chiton [Gk] – **Hee**-ton (short male robe, or kilt)
Daedalus [Gk] - **Dee**-da-luss (the engineer father of Icarus)
Delos [Gk] – **Dee**-loss (sacred island, and supposed birthplace of Apollo)
Drodos [Gk] – **Droh**-doss (oak tree, sacred to Zeus)
Druides [Gk] – Droo-**ee**-dess (worshippers of the sacred tree)
Efkaristo [Gk] – Efk-harees-**toh**! (thank you)
Eolipile [Gk] – Ee-**ollip**-eel (ancient forerunner of the steam engine)
Herkoose odonton [Gk] – Erk-oos oh-don-**ton** (most secret)
Faces [Lat] – **Far**-chez (ceremonial axe surrounded by sticks)
Fascist [Eng] – **Fash**-ist (pertaining to fascism)
Fathom – unit of sea depth equivalent to 6 feet, or roughly 1.8 metres.
Foot/feet – Unit of length roughly equivalent to 0.3 metres

Gyrotourbillon [Fr] – Jee-roh-**too**-bee-on (superlative rotating timekeeping mechanism)

Helios – [Gk] – **Hee**-lee-oss (one of the elder gods or Titans, and bringer of the sun)

Helio – [Gk] – **Hee**-lee-oh (proper name – pertaining to the sun)

Herakles [Gk] – **Herra**- kleez (Greek hero, AKA Hercules)

Himation [Gk] – Him-**matty**-on (ceremonial mantle, worn over the arm or shoulders)

Horologion [Gk] – Or–oh-**lodj**-ee-on (public time-keeping machine installed in Athens)

Klepsydra [Gk] – Klep-**sid**-ra (water clock)

Kyrros [Gk] – **Kirr**-oss (philosopher, engineer and designer)

Menelaus [Gk] – Men-el-**ay**-us

Mouseion [Gk] – Moo-**zay**-on

Ne [Gk] – Neh! *Spit it, remember* (yes)

Ohi [Gk] – **Oh**-hee (no)

Poseidon [Gk] – Poss-**eye**-don (god of the seas)

Pila/Pilum [Lat] - **Pee**-lah (plural of **Pee**-lum – Roman spear)

Poseidonios [Gk] – Poss-id-**oney**-os (philosopher, athlete and noted traveller)

Potamos [Gk] – **Poh**-tammo (place name)

Ptolemy [Gk] – **Tol**-emmy (name of the dynasty of Greek Kings of Egypt)

Skandalopetra [Gk] - skan-dallo-**petra** (diving stones)

Strophion [Gk] - **stro**-fee-on (decorative headband)

Wilusha – Will-**oosha** (obscure ancient city in Asia Minor)

Xi [Gk] – Chi, like cry, without the 'r' and sounded from the back of the throat.

Xiropotamos [Gk] – Hero-**poh**-tammo (place name)

Yassou [Gk] – **Yas**-soo (hello)

Zeus [Gk] – Dzeeooss, *single syllable – like 'swish!' Go on, try it.* (Father of the younger, Classical Greek gods – and son of one of the earlier Titans)

PROLEGOMENON
Part One – Wilusha

On the Northwest Coast of Asia Minor, 1197 BC

It was not the gods' anger which caused the colossal thunderstorm above the heads of the warriors – it was natural science!

Inside the carpet of rolling clouds, as warm air rose up from the arid landscape, untold billions of atomic particles clashed violently into the freezing particles already there. This action generated massive friction and static electricity. Any time now, this build-up would discharge itself directly to earth in a superheated high-tension spark. As this happened, the heat would expand the surrounding air at such an explosive rate that it would cause its fabric to tear apart and re-form in a massive supersonic bang. It was *these* things which would shortly cause the next bolt of lightning and clap of thunder. However, this was not yet understood. Instead, in place of knowledge, man's fear and imagination prevailed.

Directly below, on the shores of the wine dark sea, the night sky boomed and crashed in unholy colour. Alarm spread throughout the Greek encampment as the rain lashed down and soldiers cowered in dread. Each of them agonised over the subject their leaders even now discussed, for wh   else could cause this Heraklean storm to be visited upon them?   njured up images of Zeus weighing his thunderbolts in his hand, choosing his next target. And each began to pray for the right decision to be taken, and for his very life!

Inside the bleak tent of the council of war, a deathly silence hung in the air. Only the sound of the heavy rain pounding the canvas was heard. Nobody spoke. In the gloomy torchlight, Agamemnon stared-down each of the disgruntled kings in turn. No one except himself would dare speak again. Now, he shouted angrily, "As the commander of this expedition, I invoke Zeus himself to visit a thunderbolt upon *any* man who would turn and run now... when victory is so close at hand."

The anticipated bolt of pure white light illuminated the Greek camp for a full second. A moment later, as the inevitable clap of thunder crashed out, Agamemnon's perfectly timed fist smashed down onto the meeting table. Pausing for added effect, the thickset commander of the combined Greek armies rounded on the council. "Not now, before avenging the death of our hero, Achilles!" He looked around for support. "Not now," he spoke passionately through moistened eyes, "when the rescue of the poor wife of my brother, King Menelaus is so near to hand! And... not now, when brave Odysseus has almost completed our weapon of stealth!" He stood fully upright again. "It may well be the end of the battle season, but we will not break our long siege. In three days, Priam and his line will be wiped out. We will rescue Helen of Sparta, and the name of the city of Wilusha will be stricken from history. This is my solemn promise!" With that, he stood upright and stormed out in deathly silence.

The king's accomplished act over, he walked hurriedly through the downpour, back to his own larger and more comfortably furnished tent. He wiped the rain off the top of his balding head, then wiped away the crocodile tears. Taking off his spotless quilted battledress and girdle, he threw them at his waiting Persian slave. Then, breathing a sigh of relief, he sat heavily in his chair beside the log fire at the centre of his quarters. He stroked his well trimmed grey beard and, not for the first time, cursed his fate. This time, he had barely survived the meeting – but only with the help of the weather. There would be no more chances. There could be no more broken promises. It would not be long, he knew, before they would all turn on him. He had demanded a few more days, and that was precisely what he been given – entirely grudgingly. This time, if *this* plan didn't work, if the new siege machine failed to give the troops access to King Priam's city, he would be both ousted from power and penniless.

Menelaus followed him in from the driving rain to stand beside the fire. He clapped slowly and dryly. "The performance of a lifetime, brother," he smouldered, "but what if she's escaped?"

"By then we'll have the city," answered his older sibling coldly. "Anyway, why would you suddenly care?"

The younger of the two jabbed casually at the fire with the tip of his sword. "Care? Did *I* say I cared?" he asked cynically, "though, I would like to pickle her head and bring it back with me. Just to silence the wagging tongues of course. Not that she's that beautiful," he lied. "So, what do we do now?"

Agamemnon gazed into the flames. "*Now*, it's time to get on our knees to the gods and pray – if you believe in any of that rubbish. Pray that Odysseus gets it right. In the meantime, I suggest that we prepare to make a hasty exit back to Sparta. I have no intention of returning empty handed to Mycenae. Something tells me," his eyes narrowed, "that after the sacrifices I've made, penniless, I would not be at all well received in my own home."

Since the outset of this strict business venture, it was the royal brothers themselves who had engineered the convenient excuse to attack and invade the wealthy Persian city. 'Love' and 'honour' had precious little to do with it. Agamemnon squirmed at the worthless sentiments. Bronze – the alloy of copper and tin – defined this age of sophisticated weaponry; and tin was what the war was really about.

Agamemnon's intention was to break Priam's stranglehold on the tin trade and in doing so, break Persia's growing power. *Cassiterite* – tin ore – could be found all over Asia Minor, but there was much fuel and effort required in the smelting process, especially on the industrial scale in demand. Vast swathes of trees had been felled over many centuries to make the necessary charcoal it required. The land was increasingly denuded and, as a result, tin was scarce. This scarcity gave it such value that it had allowed Priam to vastly increase his standing, and in-so-doing, amass a fortune.

The true reason for the Greeks' invasion then, was to seize not only Priam's treasure coffers, but more especially, to capture his city intact. This was a must, in order to dominate the tin trade themselves, and forge ahead in the arms race! The excuse that Agamemnon had needed to persuade the Greeks to support the venture, or at least legitimise their already overwhelming desire, had been unwittingly provided by Priam's young son Paris. The fifteen year old adult had been invited by the two calculating brothers to meet Helen, the youngest concubine of Agamemnon's brother Menelaus – a pretty girl of the same age as Paris himself. The rest was already history.

But since it was Agamemnon who had rallied the Greeks to invade Priam's city and had since failed to break its defence walls, it would be he who would also bear the inevitable blame for the Greeks' likely defeat. Many of the Greek kings had invested their fortunes in this campaign, including Agamemnon himself, and each had been promised massive rewards by him. However, the logistics of the venture – keeping and feeding the armies so far from home – was not cheap and the long period of the siege had been especially underestimated. If defeat was allowed to happen, the loss of this business investment on top of everything else would not be taken lightly. Dissent at his continuing rule was rife, and he'd known well before the meeting that the others would not let him continue for much longer. Everyone was ready to quit.

On top of all that, his days as overall commander had been especially numbered since the Greeks' own hero the 'invincible' Achilles had been killed. From the top of his boar-tusk covered helmet, down to his toughened bronze body armour and the greaves on his shins, only one place had been left bare. But it was his overinflated ego that had been the real chink in his armour. He had once again boasted his invulnerability, dancing in the black rain of his enemy's poisoned arrows – and it was that overconfidence which had been his downfall. After ten long years of siege, the ageing, out of condition warrior was no longer what he had been in his youth, and he had finally let his concentration slip. In fairness, he had seen that very arrow coming, but was no longer quite nimble enough to side-step the speeding missile. The slight graze against his heel was enough to finish him.

Not that Agamemnon cared particularly. The two had squabbled almost from the onset of battle. Besides, without Achilles, he reasoned, the avenging Myrmidons – the dead hero's own crack troops – would be reinvigorated – and far easier to control.

A messenger walked into Agamemnon's tent, drenched to the skin. "Commander," he barked. "The troops are all assembled."

"Really, in this downpour… they *are* keen," Agamemnon mumbled sarcastically. "Then let's get on with it." The king threw on a dry, more comfortable garment. "Perhaps," he sneered, "we should indeed pray for a miracle!"

Menelaus followed his brother out into the rain, pulling his cloak tight around him. The vast army knelt in the mud, waiting for their leader. Agamemnon climbed up the few steps to the wooden dais and studied the almost completed wheeled siege machine; the front half of a heavy, upturned boat now painted with an oddly stylised horse's head on both sides. Not for the first time, he wondered if this strange weapon was indeed strong enough, as his general had promised it would be. Strong enough, that is, to force the pointed bronze battering ram on its bow, through the huge bronze-clad gates. He remained unconvinced. Agamemnon had *had* to promise something to end the war spectacularly – but this was all he had come up with. After ten long years, the writing finally seemed to be on the wall. If this, his ultimate hostile takeover bid failed, it would be all over for him, and no doubt reprisals would be taken against him personally. Each of his fellow investors would undoubtedly in turn, make a grab for compensation.

The commander-in-chief carefully got onto his knees, waiting for Menelaus to catch up. Flames crackled in the small fire basket while he addressed his troops by its flicker. "With the help of the gods, the right decision has now been made." He raised his voice to a bellow: "FATHER, ZEUS... WE BESEECH YOU FOR HELP IN CRUSHING THE NON-BELIEVERS OF THIS LAND... LEND US HELP TO DO YOUR WILL!" He fell prostrate.

Behind him, Menelaus snorted and murmured under his breath. "Brother, you might as well ask Zeus himself to show up."

The king stood up to pour just enough of his cheaper oil onto the dying, spitting fire, to revive it and make a small 'flash' for the benefit of those watching.

Then, without warning, the earth started to tremble and shake below him. Gradually the powerful shaking grew more and more – into something akin to an earthquake. He grasped his brother's shoulder to steady himself, covering his ears against a screaming, screeching wail that filled the air with the noise of the Sirens. In the next instant they saw a ball of lightning and mist hovering overhead. Then they felt, rather than heard, a thunderclap. The mist expanded into a cloud which obscured everything. From within the terrifying, voluminous cloud of orange flame and the billowing black smoke, what appeared to be the vaguely familiar silhouette of a gigantic horse's head, neck and flanks appeared. With an enormous crash, it landed directly on the painted timber contraption in front of the king, smashing it to smithereens. As this happened, a blast of wind blown by the Furies knocked Agamemnon over and scattered the rest of the camp to the eight winds. Four enormous polished metal hooves bedded heavily down into the deep mud. The king's eyes bulged. Exposed ribs at the core of the beast displayed a furnace within. He watched as a metal barrel whirred around and around in its flames; steam, visibly turning to water vapour and rusty water spewed out from its long nozzle as it slowed. Now, as the mechanical monster settled, a carpet of weird blue sparks wiggled their way down the mysterious object's frame and slowly fanned-out in all directions. Before the Greeks' eyes the sparks fizzled out into nothingness.

Agamemnon didn't know which way to turn. Looking around, he saw his troops run to stand behind him as they stared up at the monolith. The 'great warrior king' reluctantly decided that he had no choice other than to stand his ground. Whatever it was, clearly it was not a living entity. Already, hatches had opened all around its upper wooden half. What were obviously weapons – horizontal metal bows of a sort – were levelled around them. Another, far larger, manned weapon of similar design – a ballista – pointed down at him from its back. Then, another hatch opened. A soldier dressed in black uniform and boots, and wearing a helmet crested with a purple and white horsehair plume poked his head out and looked around. He stepped through the hatch and began to descend its rope ladder. Reaching the ground, he stared out around himself. Still wearing his helmet, the interloper looked at the most elevated person there and saluted Agamemnon formally. He beat his right fist against his chest, while his left hand clutched the hilt of his gladius – his short sword. He spoke boldly, reading the three Greek phrases previously translated from his native Latin tongue. "We are mercenaries for hire… soldiers from your future… where is your commander?"

Agamemnon looked from the soldier's unfamiliar uniform to the huge animal, fire and brimstone still pouring from its nostrils. He stared at the monstrosity before him, scarcely able to believe his apparent good fortune. He looked out to address his troops, and in particular the other kings. "AND THIS… IS THE *REAL* SECRET WEAPON I SPOKE OF…" he lied in relief.

As soon as the commander had finished bragging, his servant immediately sneaked past the transfixed troops, on the way to warn King Priam himself. The Greeks had a new weapon of stealth which might give them their longed for strategic edge!

Part Two – Dead Bodies!

Just off the Greek Island of Antikythera: 1900 AD

In the sweltering heat of mid-day, the steam paddle-boat Eleni bobbed up and down at anchor on the indigo swell. For the second time in an hour, the wind changed direction and began to pick up. The North wind – *The Boreas*, as it had been called locally for thousands of years was now threatening to drive the sponge-diving boat onto the treacherous and lethal razor-sharp rocky coastline. It was time to begin packing up to get out of the small bay before the sea became too rough.

The leathery-skinned master of the vessel had spent the whole of his long life diving for sponges and thought he knew the best sites in the whole area, but this site was new to him. It was only by accident that he and his small crew had found this morning's site, having been blown off course from where they were originally headed – across the channel to the island's nearby larger neighbour, Kythera. Drifting back across the channel and down the coastline with the strong current, they had stumbled upon this place and had already collected many of the big sponges – the reason why they'd made their way from Crete. In these extremely deep and rarely visited waters, sponges grew much larger than those in shallower waters.

He looked at the reasonable day's haul in the open stern, assessing the value of everything that had been brought up to the surface. Since the old methods had died out – free-diving to incredible depths, clinging to the heavy 'skandalopetra' or diving-stones, wearing only a pair of shorts and a pair of rubber goggles – his fortunes had changed in many ways, and not for the worse. Gone were the days when a dive lasted three to four minutes, sometimes five at the very most, with the exhausted divers being heaved rapidly back to the surface by the long diving ropes. Now, a dive could last much longer; no more did they have to just scratch-out a living. The new diving equipment manufactured in England and sold worldwide by Messrs Siebe and Gorman: the canvas suits, the lead weighted boots and the copper diving helmets, had revolutionised underwater exploration. True, it was all very expensive and the weight of it all had necessitated him, even this close to his well earned retirement, to stretch his finances to purchase and convert his new boat. But the new technology had proved a worthy investment.

The equipment had also been a revelation. It had opened up much more of the hitherto mysterious sea-bed to him and there were many, many new things to be found down there – five thousand years of sunken cargoes, to begin with – the supposed earliest beginnings of travel by ship. Now fed from the surface by air pumps, the divers' only decision was how long it might be safe to stay down and explore. This factor seemed, to those who had the most experience, to be a combination of safe dive-depths and the duration of each dive. Sadly, those pushing this new technology too deep or too long had paid dearly, as a recurring phenomenon began to grip many a diver which had previously been experienced only by those working in deep mines, or building deep tunnels. Too many divers, once back on their vessels, had been lost in agonising paroxysm – now known as 'the Grecian bends' – or more simply, 'the bends.' This captain though, had no intention of losing any of his men. They were all like family to him.

Now working at a depth of forty fathoms – the latest recommended safe limit of the equipment – he would allow his divers only another five minutes to complete this, their third thirty-minute dive that morning. After that, he would tug gently on the air hoses, giving the signal for them to make their way back to the open cage before being raised to within a few fathoms of the surface where they would take a compulsory, short safety-stop.

On their first dive, once down on the bottom, both men had

worked hastily together, filling several of the large net sacks with the valuable soft sponges. They had collected a goodly amount, given the swirling currents down here, but just then, the more valuable chance find of an ancient lead anchor had halted the job. They'd tied the anchor to one of the salvage ropes and had it hauled up – the scrap value would supplement their income. Although the sunken wrecks they'd found on previous occasions were always treated with respect – they were a superstitious lot and who knows what sea-graves they might be disturbing – any valuable metal objects found were thought of as treasure trove and therefore fair game. Underwater archaeology at this time was unheard of; it was all simply salvage. Perhaps someday soon, the captain dreamed, they might even stumble upon something that would allow him to retire earlier than planned.

On their second dive, in the poor visibility of the now kicked up sand that their movement had caused on the seabed, one of the divers had spotted the second extraordinary find of the day: a huge upturned old bell of sorts, covered in crud. However, this was unlike any they'd found before. Half-buried in the seabed, this was much, much larger – taller than a man. It was in fact, almost the size of a modern diving bell, the kind used mainly in the underwater building industry, for constructing underwater bridge pilings. When they'd raised it onto the boat and a patch of the concretion was chipped off, the object had turned out to be solid bronze, identifiable by the multi-layered surface patina of green and brown. Presumably, this was very old then. Obviously it could not have been designed for the same purpose, could it? Not that any of that was of consequence to the captain. The lead and the bronze objects would be melted down within days anyway. Such was the often cavalier attitude of these first marine explorers toward history and science.

Now, on this, their third dive, an early tug on one of their air-hoses had indicated that they'd found something else – another lead anchor perhaps. But that was when, for the third time, as they'd hovered over what was now clearly an ancient wreck site, the wind had changed again.

As the crewmen continued to crank the twin air pumps, the

mate held the boat chugging steadily, keeping its stern from swinging toward the rocks. The captain wondered idly to himself how the sunken ship could have found itself in dire straits here. It may have been anything of course – the changing winds blowing it out of control as they had themselves experienced. Perhaps it had been a warship of some sort, or a cargo vessel, or possibly even a pirate vessel. After all, since the time of the fall of Troy, over three thousand years earlier, the sea had been plagued by pirates from this very island. The captain ran his calloused fingers over and through one of the four holes pierced through the rim of the rough surface of the massive bell, his imagination ticking over, but then the crew raised the sudden alarm and broke him from his reverie.

The repeated urgent tugs meant only one thing – get them up immediately. Forget safety stops; they were throwing caution to the wind and abandoning the dive right now. Something was wrong!

Within three minutes, both divers were back on the boat and were sat on the bench as the crew unfastened their helmets. As the first helmet was removed, the elder diver blurted out hysterically, "Dead bodies! A hundred of them – their hands up – beckoning to be rescued." The master had never seen the normally unflappable diver spooked like this before. Another of the crew grabbed the bottle of ouzo and poured him a medicinal glass to calm his nerves. Now, the second helmet came off and his younger buddy-diver grinned broadly in contrast.

"Statues!" he said – "lots and lots of them." Clearly it wasn't he who had given the alarm. "And, I found these!" From behind his back he handed over an untarnished, solid gold trident. The captain's face cracked into a broad grin as he planted the end of it on the deck as Poseidon, god of the sea. Then, the diver flicked a single large gold coin high into the air toward the captain. Ironically, it was the one coin which, from its solo portrait of Cleopatra, experts could have later allocated a true date for the shipwreck – 48 BC. That is, if it had not been immediately sold. The captain caught it in his hand. "Tonight," the mariner bit the piece delicately, testing its authenticity, "we will all celebrate!"

Reintroduction

It was midday in Tom's small kitchen. Alex, Conna, Maddie and Bex all took their places around the plain round table and the wide copper tray, the couscous dish, which covered its centre. Arranged on it was a wide outer ring of the moist yellow grains, and inside that, a smaller, concentric ring of grilled vegetables. In its middle was a large bowl of thick broth. The smell of the simple food was intoxicating. After helping Tom prepare everything, they were now all ready to 'dig-in' to lunch, as he had earlier prompted. Now, without speaking, they followed his example and sat quietly, eyes closed in contemplation – although, to be fair, each had sneaked a look at least once.

So far, they had listened for two days to Tom's *Tale of Eos* and each of the four found it quite entertaining in his or her own way. But to date, after much soul searching, that was all they thought. The only one to actually begin to believe any of the tale was Alex, but that was for good reason – to find out what Tom knew of his dad's whereabouts. It remained to be seen whether anyone else would be persuaded. Doubtless, over the length of the story, each would in turn be forced to decide.

Breaking out of his silence, Tom readjusted the green sunglasses, and immediately beckoned each in turn to help themselves from the tray. The couscous grains were not something that anyone other than himself was familiar with. The girls watched politely while Alex went first. Only Conna eyed it suspiciously.

"So, Tom, is this some sort of Greek food?" Alex asked curiously.

"Actually," answered Tom, "I would call it Eastern

Mediterranean food, although it has evolved over time."

Alex took his bowl to the centre and half-filled it with the serving spoon.

"Now try some of the roasted vegetables," Tom coaxed, as the boy chose from the seven various sorts. He took a few carrots, red peppers and sliced aubergine.

"And pour over some of the lentil broth," he advised.

Alex did so and then tasted it. "Actually, this is really good," he sounded a little surprised.

Maddie smiled, immediately recognising some of the more 'exotic' vegetables. "Okra and sweet potatoes… it's ages since we've had these."

"Mum used to give us these at home in the Caribbean," Bex added. "But it's difficult for her to cook much now, what with being in her wheelchair most of the time. And dad's a hopeless cook – 'cept he thinks he's good at it." The sisters rolled their eyes at the amusing thought.

Conna looked forlornly at the food; it was *all* strange to him.

Tom tried to encourage him. "Conna, please try it for yourself. It may not be the pizza or the burgers but it is just as nutritious… perhaps more-so. Won't you try?"

"Is it spicy…?" Conna turned up his nose, "'cos I don't like spicy."

"Ordinarily, it would be," Tom advised, "I prefer it that way. But today, this is simply aromatic – it has an exotic aroma. I was not certain of what everyone's preferences might be."

"It certainly does smell nice," complimented Maddie, "What is that?"

"Only a little nutmeg and cinnamon," Tom answered, "and lots of saffron of course – the spice of Alexander. It's the most ancient and expensive spice in the world – more expensive than gold!"

At the mention of the famous name, the four looked at the meal anew,

Tom went on, "It is the saffron which also gives that wonderful golden yellow colour to the food."

Conna took the smallest amount of the grains and put it in the bowl then sniffed it. "So what does it taste like – rice or pasta or something?"

Bex chirped up, "no, it tastes just like couscous," she said sarcastically.

"Har-har," mumbled Conna, before deciding to get adventurous and cover the single plain potato with a small spoonful of the lentil broth. He tried a tiny bit on the tip of his spoon. "Hey, it's not bad after all…" he admitted. Then, realising, he offered, "…even though there's no meat in it!"

Tom smiled, "I am not a vegetarian, we are, after all, omnivorous animals – whether or not we wish to be – but I do not eat meat or fish more than a couple of times per week. And then, it is only in small amounts."

Suddenly it dawned on Conna. "So is this the sort of stuff that Lio might have eaten all those years ago?"

"Very similar," Tom smiled. "It is strange how certain things – clothes, gadgets and the like – have changed over the years and yet how so many simple things like toddler's toys and good food have remained just the same. Now, please continue, it has been so many years since I have been able to share this simple pleasure with friends. Such a basic pleasure that I now realise I have missed."

Now, everyone dug-in with gusto. Only Boris, Alex's dog, stretched out quietly in the corner, didn't seem impressed at the lack of meat.

After half an hour, everyone had finished. Together, they chatted as they joined in tidying up, washing, drying and putting away the dishes. Bex went off to the bathroom so that she could wash her hands properly, but returned straight away. "Tom," she asked, "where do you keep the soap, there's none in the bathroom?"

"I don't use the stuff," he replied, "I use olive oil instead. It's what keeps me looking so youthful." He raised an eyebrow over his sunglasses.

Conna snorted and whispered to Alex, "If this is him looking young, goodness knows how old he'd look without it!"

"I heard that" smiled Tom. "Here, use a few drops of washing-up liquid if you insist, but it'll dry your skin out."

Alex narrowed his eyes at Maddie, both wondering again just how old he might be.

"Finished?" asked Tom. "Then, let's skip reassembling the component parts of the horse for now – let us just return to where we left off our story." He stood up unsteadily and Maddie and Bex helped him into the laboratory. Not for the first time he mumbled, "I really should like to find that old walking stick." Settling into his chair, Tom looked across at who he now regarded as his friends and hoped that *this time*, he had at last found the key to saving the world from the mysterious Roman machine he referred to only as 'The Hippo-Tempus'. Each of the four resumed their seats, this time, to everyone's amusement, Boris jumped up onto Maddie's lap to settle. Alex smiled and patted the dog, then took out his note pad and pencil as Tom summed-up the story to date:

"I have spoken so far of how it came to be, that in the year of 595 BC, the son of a courageous tin-trader and the daughter of a tribal chieftain from the Cassiterides islands – Britain – was orphaned on Rhodos. Of how the boy, Lio was brought up by the man he knew as his grandfather, the High Priest of the Temple of Helios. But of how this short, idyllic life was devastated by the man who took the title: High Priest of Zeus. Of how this self-styled 'Zeus' was both responsible for the death of Lio's young friend Marduk, and for cruelly mistreating and ruining the life of Marduk's sister, Ashur. I have told of how, on the occasion of a solar eclipse, as a result of the way this Zeus had played on the ignorance and superstition of the population, Lio was very nearly sacrificed. And how, by complete coincidence, the boy was rescued on 'The Hippo-Chronos' – the Time-Horse – the world's first time-machine – although the boy subsequently lost his memory.

I have told of how the engineer and designer known variously as Andronicus of Cyrrhus, Andronikos of Kyrros, or simply Kyrros, had built the said Time-Horse that had been dreamed of by many philosophers, for many years. And, of how Lio had been transported by his rescuer to Alexandria in the year 50 BC. How Kyrros borrowed from Lio's grandfather's sundial design, and incorporated its ingenious features into the Tinos sundial. And how in turn, Lio helped Kyrros build the first public time-machine – or public clock – the Horologion of Athens.

Importantly, I have told next of how, after Lio was visited by the face of Ashur in a dream, the boy 'borrowed' his father's Time-Horse and went back to rescue the traumatised little girl. But in doing so, he inadvertently caused the beginning of a time-paradox that has continued until today. This, even though he and Ashur would not admit to themselves the possibility of what might have occurred – that they might also have transported a most unwanted visitor!

And finally, I have spoken of how Lio's 'father', Kyrros, married his 'mother' Miriam. Of how Lio was formally accepted into the ancient and most secret Chronology Society of Alexandria, and of how they retired to Kyrros' farm at Drodos hill, near the pyramids and the Great Sphinx at Giza. But, of how that retirement was now rudely interrupted by the eruption of the Alexandrine war: the civil war between the rightful King Ptolemy XIII and his elder sister and wife, the ruthless Queen Cleopatra, now aided by her new lover Julius Caesar.

After news was brought to the small family that war was on its way, they had no choice but to move on. No one could risk being captured by either side – that would inevitably lead to the secret of the Hippo-Chronos being extracted from them and doubtlessly used to no good. And despite both keys to its use being separated from the Time-Horse – the first key, the Chrono-key, or time-computer, being already sent to the far northern edge of the known world – the discovery of their joint whereabouts could still be cataclysmic for mankind's future. Now, all the small family could do was flee the farm and the country, and try to prevent the secret from falling into the hands of *anyone* who might seek to use the machine for their own military ends.

Together then, Kyrros, Miriam, the just turned thirteen year old

Lio and the nearly twelve year old Ashur, all sat in the cart that trundled past the Great Sphinx and back to the River Nile. The refugees carried with them only a few precious belongings. Kyrros, of course, had with him his stash of gold coins and his prototype time and distance keys – the Chrono-key and the Cosmos-key. Miriam had the precious gold torc around her neck, and Lio had his precious sun wheel symbol – given to him by the old athlete, Poseidonios – around his own neck. Sitting with their legs dangling over the back of the cart, the boy held the girl's hand in comfort, and each tried not to dwell on their growing fear. It was perhaps inevitable that within a short time they did, but thankfully the journey was not too long and soon their unhappy thoughts were broken. In the meantime, each of them prayed or meditated in their own way to a god, gods, or the scientific universe, that they might escape the ravages of war.

However, each, of course, was sadly unaware of what the future actually held for them. And, that their nemesis, the self-styled High Priest of Zeus, had indeed managed to follow them from the past, determined to get his hands on the Greek Hippo-Chronos. He would then use it to create a superweapon more appropriate to the rapidly expanding Latin world – The Hippo-Tempus!"

PART I:

THE WORLD IS LOST

A GOOD TRAVELER HAS NO FIXED PLANS,

AND IS NOT INTENT ON ARRIVING.

Lao Tzu: Father of Taoism 6th Century BC

CHAPTER 1:

The Refugees

East of Giza, December 48 BC

Tom resumed his story: "It was not long before the air became thick with the muddy smell of the "life blood of Egypt." Reaching the Nile and this time picking up a passing felucca, Kyrros negotiated to hire it to take them downstream in the direction of Alexandria, but past it to one of the many mouths across the river delta. There, they would have to transfer to another seagoing ship if they wished to set sail into the Mediterranean and reach any of their chosen escape destinations, but Kyrros would handle that particular problem when they met it.

Last month, on their way upstream from Alexandria to Giza – only what now seemed like a few days ago – the recovering Ashur had slept exhaustedly through the whole thing. This, then, sailing consciously on any kind of vessel, was a whole new experience to her. One after another, both Kyrros and Miriam failed to get her to step into the wobbling craft, until Lio took her by both hands and stepped backwards into it himself. Ashur took his cue and at last followed. Once on board, as it pulled away from the shore, she quickly settled. For now, there was nothing to do but steady themselves for the journey.

The first two hours were uneventful, save for reaching the point where the boy had remembered previously seeing his first living crocodile, the Fort of Camels. Ashur's eyes opened wide as he pointed out the sleeping reptiles along the river bank and she made a hand sign that Lio recognised from their distant shadow plays. Placing the palms of her hands together she tilted them to one side, one raised forefinger forming the loop of an eye on top. She opened and closed her hands twice quickly, then she signed in the language that their father had made up for them, 'do you remember?'

'Yes,' he signed back silently, practicing for fun, 'I do'. But then, perhaps because it had reminded her of things that she wished not to recall, she suddenly looked away from him and sat down in the boat again.

To all intents and purposes, Lio had himself managed to put all of those bad memories to one side, often visiting them in dreams without trauma – except for the few times that he had seen the face of Zeus! But he wondered sometimes if Ashur would ever recover from those deeper and more painful memories. At the farm, she had often let out a scream in the night and jumped into his bed to throw her arms around him. Lio hoped at any rate that some day she would finally be able to set those memories aside.

A couple of hours later, the vessel owner, who stood by the stern, paddling back and forth easily, began to mumble. Lio noticed that they were effectively beginning to travel in a slow queue. No river traffic was sailing *up* the Nile. Instead, boats followed only the flow toward its many exits across the river's wide delta.

Before long, they passed a few people. A young family was walking south, beside the riverbank – the opposite direction to their boat – and away from Alexandria. In the absence of a father figure, the mother led with an ox-cart full of their precious belongings, a few pots and bowls clanking as it passed. A little while later, a few more women and children came along pulling hand carts, piled up as high as they could balance everything. Miriam looked on in dismay as the thin line of refugees became heavier, smaller children and toddlers walking at the feet of their exhausted mothers and aged grandparents. They held onto each other as they trudged south and hopefully out of danger.

Now, the clanking of a few pots and pans grew steadily into a

4

clamour of banging and clashing of the mixed belongings of what seemed like a whole city on its feet. The line had swelled massively as first hundreds, then thousands and even tens of thousands passed by with nowhere to go. With it, there came a growing moaning sound – the unmistakable noise of untold misery and hardship. It was composed of the cries of hungry children, mothers weeping, animals of burden bellowing under great toil, and a few men – those disabled and not pressed into army service – shouting out in their growing frustration at the situation they had been thrust into. All through no fault of their own, but instead, the squabbling of their leaders, their peers: King Ptolemy; his queen and sister, Cleopatra; and the Roman general, Julius Caesar, who had been invited by Cleopatra to 'help' the country's situation.

Miriam turned to Kyrros and spoke into his ear, and he immediately nodded his consent. She stood up in the boat, holding her husband's hand to steady her as she called over to the riverbank. 'Make for Giza,' she shouted, 'there is a small farm there at the hill of Drodos. Tell them that Kyrros and Miriam sent you – you'll be safe there.' A few desperate faces nodded in reply. Of course not all of them would, or even could follow their advice. The eldest of them, both old men and women, already looked hardly able to move along any further; they had walked for days now. Some, stopping to sit there by the road, would never stand again. However, some of them would make it and would hopefully set up a temporary camp at the farm. Miriam repeated her message at steady intervals, until she had lost her voice, then she sat down, saddened and in floods of tears at the distress they'd witnessed.

By mid-day, still watching the steady stream of displaced humanity, they had caught up with another line of slow moving boats upriver. Now the entire Nile was becoming congested – there was another delay. Very quickly, the various boat owners called back and forth up and down the river to each other, enquiring about the hold-up. What was the cause of it, refugees in boats? At first, no one knew, but it did not take long before the call came that threw them all into panic. The situation in Alexandria was worsening. Ptolemy,

5

it seemed, was about to make a final push – to drive his wife and her new lover, Caesar into the sea in an attempt to save the country. The Egyptian troops of Ptolemy, stationed out of harm's way in the desert, had been ordered to head to Alexandria by any means possible – commandeering river vessels to get there quicker. Any boats carrying lighter cargoes were now having the same cargoes thrown into the Nile to make more room for the troops.

No sooner had Lio and his family been told of this, than they saw the soldiers wearing the white sash of Ptolemy's allies piling into the shallows around them and making for their boat. Kyrros prompted Miriam to hitch up her scarf to cover the torc around her neck, while the boat owner immediately stopped his vessel in fear of what would happen if he did not.

The felucca was not large, nor did it sit high in the water, and as the troops clambered aboard from the larboard side, all of the increasing occupants thought they would be swamped. Then, there was a sudden short, but agonised scream. Behind the boat, a soldier who had been wading out to it waist high desperately lunged toward them, trying to pull himself on board. Lio looked into the terrified face as he was dragged powerfully down. His blood curdling scream changed to gurgling as he slipped below the muddy green waters. Miriam covered Ashur's ears and buried her face in her bosom, trying to shield the girl from the sickening attack, while Kyrros looked at his son and shook his head briefly. No one needed to say what had taken him, everyone knew about the dangers of the Nile. The reality could not have been more different to the children's shadow game.

Now, surrounded by soldiers, Kyrros would have been perfectly comfortable in their company if it was not for the fact that they began to pick up and kick around their belongings. Though even now, he refused to take sides, declaring under his breath that each of the protagonists were equally stupid. Before he could protest, his tool chest had been picked up, smashed open and thrown overboard, the two soldiers responsible now each picked up one of the bags of clothes, weighing them in their hands in a hopeful attempt to see if

6

there might be food inside – few of them had been able to eat properly for weeks, save for the few dates which they'd managed to scavenge from the palm trees that lined the river. Wearing the most stupefied expression, Kyrros flew to his feet: 'STOP!' was the only word he shouted in Egyptian. By his reaction, Miriam at once realised just what it was that had been hidden in the chest. Now one of the other bags was ill-temperedly thrown overboard. It floated briefly, before disappearing, while the other bag was dropped back into the boat. The soldier who had siezed it pushed his way toward Kyrros menacingly, pulling out his short, curved sword as he did.

Lazily, the officer in charge, already seated in the boat owner's own chair and looking rearward from the bow of the boat, held up his hand to stop the proceedings. 'You,' he addressed Kyrros roughly in Persian, 'old man, what is in the packages?'

Kyrros glared back at him, ruffled by the tone and the manner by which he had been addressed – he never did think of himself of being an 'old' man. 'My name – FOOL!' he boomed, fixing him with his almost maniacal stare, 'is Andronicus of Cyrrhus', he dropped easily into his childhood Persian tongue. 'I am the engineer to the court of His Royal Majesty King Ptolemy the Thirteenth. And this, soldier, is the property of your king. It is strictly herkoose odonton – most secret.' Kyrros paused to let the message sink in. 'I trust you will guard what is left of it until we reach Alexandria.'

'Engineer!' The buzz went around the soldiers, whispering, in awe of who he was. Who knows what designs for new weaponry might be contained in the packages – something to help beat back the Romans perhaps?

Mollified by the way he had been spoken to, especially in his own tongue, the officer immediately capitulated. 'Yes sir, of course,' he acknowledged stiffly, his hand slapped against his chest in salute. 'We didn't know'.

Kyrros almost crashed back down beside Miriam, shaking his head in exasperation, mourning at the senseless loss of his precious tools – and almost his entire stash of gold coins which had been rolled up in papyrus and stained to look like spare wooden tool handles. 'Didn't think, more like,' he muttered. *At least though*, thought Lio, *we are all safe, and won't now be touched.* Miriam was just glad that his outburst hadn't got them all run through – even though the money had been enough to retire on. She patted him lightly on the knee in sympathy and support, comforting him in his loss. All of the money he had made, for all of the work he had put into the Tinos sundial and the Horologion of Athens was all gone. Kyrros and she would now have to find work again, or find somewhere to live cheaply. At least she still had the gold torc in reserve. Throughout the remainder of their time in the boat, apart from a few smouldering glances from a few of the soldiers – each time faced down with Kyrros' glare – the rest of the journey would at least be safe. Lio's father had a very commanding way about him.

The boat once more got under way, the river reaching perilously close to the top of its sides as everyone settled down silently. The soldiers glared at the boy and girl occasionally but said nothing. They were approaching battle and were concentrating on that eventuality.

After a further four uneasy, not to say painfully silent hours, the boat reached the turnoff – the entrance to the Great Canal of Alexandria. Kyrros' escape route lay straight ahead, although from the moment the soldiers had arrived on the boat, all four of the small family had realised that they would not now be taking it. To ask even to be put ashore instead of going on into Alexandria would be to admit that the King's Engineer and his precious cargo were not returning to the King's aid after all. There was nothing they could do. They would reluctantly have to return directly to Alexandria. Uneasily, the fully laden boat took the channel slowly toward the city.

It was the thin, cloying veil of smoke that greeted them first, plumes of which arose into the damp winter night from the hundreds of small camp fires that lined the canal. It was not long before the evening came, creating a dark red backdrop to the Great City. The troops were building up steadily, awaiting the command of their king.

Witnessing it for himself for the first time, Kyrros now began to realise the scale of the catastrophe that had already begun to befall Egypt. Until that moment, he had professed little interest in the political affairs which he had no control over. Now, even he feared for the future of the city, his precious mouseion and library. Alexandria, it was always said, was virtually fireproof, because of the completely tiled roofs of the city – not straw, as other places. But, he worried, having all of those fires in such close proximity to it, could not help but be potentially disastrous.

'Here will do, set us down,' the officer commanded. Then he stood up and silently saluted the King's Engineer warily once more as he ushered his troops to disembark far more easily this time, directly onto the top of the low canal wall. With that, Lio and his family were once again alone and moving on their now short way toward the familiar royal dock at Eunostos.

Lio remembered the first time he had made this journey, filled with wonderment at the sights and sounds of the city sleeping peacefully. Now, by contrast, even to him, the city was obviously on the brink of a disaster. Something awful was about to happen here, he was certain. This feeling was not born out of superstition, but out of the all-pervading air of malevolence that he had started to pick up from the soldiers on the boat. It continued here in the faces of the men around the camp fires – a primeval tension that he had sensed only once before on the night of the distant eclipse. And now, as then, it was destined to lead to bloodshed.

The felucca made its way silently along the waterway, and Lio looked at the disturbing scene of the city under siege. Where once everything had been neat and tidy, or at least in a way shabbily friendly, now the overshadowing impression was one of extreme duress. Most of the larger buildings that he could remember were now gone, although he could now see quite clearly the whole of the end of the Serapeion which had been obscured before this night. A broad band of flattened masonry, almost a roadway, or at least a rubble filled track fifty feet wide, separated the Roman and Egyptian protagonists.

When the Romans had first moved into place, Caesar had hoped for a swift victory before Ptolemy had time to assemble a large army, or cavalry against him. The Romans had therefore flattened most of the larger buildings to form this pathway and leave a clear space in front of their defences. This would in turn allow Caesar to train his weaponry onto his enemy through the shuttered windows of the buildings that were left intact. It also allowed them to use their cavalry to harry Ptolemy's few assembled Egyptian troops that kept on trying to get to their walls – the horses more able to cope with the bad terrain. But the Egyptians had realised their plan and had immediately punched holes through any buildings that backed onto that path, so that they could fire back at the Romans. They then flattened any remaining smaller buildings that stood in their way, so that they could further expose the Roman cavalry to their own growing numbers – stalemate!

But, unexpectedly, the Romans again outsmarted them and had then widened the path from their own side – now to their own advantage. The wheeled siege towers that the Egyptians had brought to scale the walls of the inner city, now stood uselessly in front of the widened rubble path, unable to reach the Roman held territory. Again the Egyptians had been thwarted by their enemies.

Now, every time the Egyptian infantry had attempted to slowly cross the broken terrain, which to Lio looked impossible, the Romans had filled the sky with arrows from their many expertly drilled Cretan mercenary archers. Despite this, when the Egyptian foot-soldiers tried to clear a path through the rubble – which the Romans had allowed them to do several times – as soon as they did, the Roman cavalry would appear through the many doorways of the remaining buildings backing onto them from the Old City and cut them down. If the Egyptians rushed at them all at once, the Romans would simply open up the window shutters and bring their catapults into play, lobbing jars full of Greek fire – the sticky incendiary liquid – together with rocks wrapped in sacking and soaked with the stuff. Alternatively, following their stumbling across the ingenious

10

weaponry plans of Archimedes in the Great Library, their newly constructed ballistae and machine-ballistae would mow down hundreds at a time by arrow.

It was all an impasse. Unless, of course, Ptolemy was prepared to raze the whole of the Old City with fire – the whole palace quarter – the Serapeion, the Mouseion and the Great Library included. But mercifully, he was not callous or stupid enough to do so. The king, it seemed, had at least in a way suitable to him, learned the true value of the wealth of knowledge contained in the library – especially with regard to military tactics and engineering technology.

Instead of taking the Romans head-on on land, given his vastly superior naval force, Ptolemy was more confident of a resounding victory at sea. The king's own ingenious plan was therefore simply to continue to pollute the Old City's drinking water supply, as he had done so from the outset of the Romans' occupation of it. Thus, the Romans' fewer ships had been forced to leave the captured Eunostos dock in order to collect drinking water from other sources along the coast. In the meantime, Ptolemy had been waiting for adequate weather before bringing his own fleet of gargantuan ships into play against the Romans' far smaller fleet.

Now, nearing the end of the canal, on the right bank – the city side – the felucca started to drift past the area reserved for the generals – itself almost a city under canvas. Here, the tents were huge. Even in war, it seemed to the boy, the generals still felt obliged to out-do each other – to show off their self-importance. Past the tents, there was even an unnecessarily large 'V' sectioned drinking trough of fast flowing water running through the encampment – toward the end of the canal. Though, quite why they needed so much fresh water was anyone's guess.

Rounding the last part of the curve in the canal, the small family's hearts sank. Just a few hundred feet from their goal, the whole canal width had been blocked by a low rubble and earth dam. On either side of it, taller rubble walls stood cutting off the Roman occupied Eunostos harbour from the Egyptian sector. A massive wooden structure, a fort, or tower of some sort that had looked from the distance to be another siege engine, occupied the whole width of the canal to the rear of the dam. There was no way to reach their second goal and the open sea. Now, they realised together – they were trapped in Alexandria, on the eve of war!"

CHAPTER 2:

Ptolemy's Secret 'Weapon'

"Only when their boat had stopped at its base, was it apparent that the thing that blocked their way to the Eunostos dock was in fact, a vast, disguised waterwheel. Or rather, one divided into four, lying end to end like so many barrels.

Looking at it head-on, no one could make out its true form, but from the perspective of the boat, it was clear. Kyrros had seen many pumps before, had even written about their various designs, but nothing he had seen before even approached the size of this behemoth. He and Lio got out of the boat, clambering onto the canal bank to take a look at it from the side. Each of the four waterwheels sat on four submerged load-bearing wheels set within a frame. The diameter of the machine was thirty feet or more, the width of the whole installation, incredibly, three times as much. The reason for its size was quite obvious. Inside the wheel, across its width, five rows of forty slaves and convicts clambered around it, driving it heavily around. Spanning the outside diameter, fixed every three feet or so around its circumference, were one hundred rows of four long, square-bottomed buckets. As he watched, a vast quantity of water was being picked up and deposited into the water trough they'd seen running through the camp. The idea was simply brilliant. Many had missed it, but Kyrros realised the deception within seconds.

Unknown to the Romans, the end of the canal had been stopped up by a low wooden dam just in front of the wheel. Seawater had then naturally filled the blocked end of the canal. Then, a deep sluice had been cut into the opposite bank, allowing the fresh Nile water flowing down the canal to exit through this concealed diversion. Thus, the Nile water directly bypassed the harbour and was delivered straight into the sea. From a distance, the wheel may have looked as if it was standing in the fresh water of the canal, but it was in fact, standing in the sea water of the harbour. Therefore, the water that the wheel was pumping toward the Egyptian camp on the city side of the canal was in fact all saltwater. This undrinkable water was in turn immediately re-channelled *through* the Egyptian camp and into the city's main underground aqueduct – not *into* the camp at all.

Here was the thing that, even as they spoke, was poisoning the Romans' water supply. It was happening right there under the Roman's noses – in full view – and yet they had assumed, not unreasonably, as had Kyrros and Lio initially, that the wheel was the freshwater pump for the supply of the Egyptian troops. So this was the most powerful weapon in Ptolemy's arsenal – a waterwheel! Kyrros smiled to the boy as he explained it all to him:

'Trudging forward, with each revolution, thousands of gallons of water are being lifted out of the deep, salt-water basin – the Eunostos harbour – and used to completely pollute the Roman water supply. If only the Romans had done their arithmetic', said Kyrros, 'they would have realised that the amount of water being drawn off was out by several orders of magnitude – thousands of gallons per minute instead of tens of gallons – and this would have then exposed the trick.' Both Andronikos the engineer and Lio the apprentice were mightily impressed."

Tom paused to pick up his glass of water. He looked toward the cloth covered bench, recalling more of the things it covered. "Over there", he said, "if you wish, you will find a simple model of Ptolemy's waterwheel, which I made from mem…" he stopped abruptly, "I mean… *for*… my amusement." Alex looked back at him remembering to help clean it only a few days ago.

14

The model, along with the cut-away section of the earthworks, the dam and the sluice, were exactly as he'd just described. "It is, as I previously said, the only model of a 'weapon' that I ever made!"

The old man sighed. "Unfortunately for Ptolemy though, due largely to his inexperience, ultimately he would not win the war. Since his father's death, the new king also had the problem of massive corruption to deal with. His generals constantly pocketed the maintenance money from the king's treasury which was meant for the navy especially. Caesar already knew the state that Ptolemy's poorly maintained ships were *really* in. It was one thing to simply position a less than properly maintained and watertight ship on the Nile Delta in order to intimidate pirates and black market grain traders. But without enough proper oars to propel them in battle, what good was a trireme, a quadrireme or even the massive quinquiremes that Ptolemy possessed? Besides, the Romans had a new 'secret weapon', re-built from the fanciful designs of Archimedes of Syracuse that they'd purloined from the library. No one truly believed that it might work, least of all Caesar, but tomorrow would tell!"

Tom looked around especially at the girls, the corners of his eyes crinkling again. "While Kyrros helped Miriam out of the boat, Lio, Ashur and the master of the vessel carefully hauled their remaining belongings onto the side of the canal. After the boat owner had been paid, they all stood and looked on, while once again Kyrros rather *foolishly* attempted to explain it all for the benefit of his wife and daughter."

Maddie, but Bex in particular's eyes narrowed, but this time she didn't bite. Tom's lips were pursed. "I use the word *foolishly*, not because the ladies were unable to grasp the concept – they most certainly were – but because they were all being watched."

The girls' eyes crinkled too, knowing that Tom had again been baiting them. Bex poked her tongue out at Conna who had turned innocently toward her. He shrugged. Alex permitted himself a smirk, while Tom continued.

"From around the back of the largest tent, not far away, the young man that Lio would never now have ordinarily recognised looked on distractedly, as two of his generals argued over tomorrow's battle plan. Each was totally absorbed in the secret. It was far safer to discuss these things out in the open – who knows what spies might be lurking outside a tent? As his father pointed at the water sluice, Lio sensed the stare of the boy king and turned to meet his gaze. He gawped at him, recognising him immediately despite his changed countenance, possibly through his ornate white and gold dress, but more unmistakeably from the blue and gold striped nemes on his head. The vulture and snake, the insignia of Upper and Lower Egypt, now glinted in the moonlight. In the short while since Lio and he had previously met, necessity had transformed the boy into the man that now stood in front of him. Every part a real pharaoh, Ptolemy XIII stood watching Lio and his family. In turn, Lio stood silently transfixed – rooted to the spot.

During the short, tumultuous period since Lio's previous meeting with Ptolemy in his palace, the king's own personal life had been turned upside down. Firstly, now fifteen years old, the birthday celebrations that had gone on in private while Lio had been living at Kyrros' farm near Giza, were meant to mark his passage from boyhood to manhood. His royal sister, however, had used the event to ridicule and humiliate him in front of the entire Egyptian court. But Cleopatra had underestimated the strength of those there, if not their loyalty to the king. The next morning she had been ousted by those who had witnessed the unforgivable spectacle, not only by his steadfast supporters, but those with more selfish motives – seizing the opportunity to ingratiate themselves with the young rival. However, the king knew this, and knew he could trust no one. He had personally taken charge of all battle plans – he had for years educated himself in the art of war using the resources of the Great Library. Also, he quickly learned that his generals in particular had to be watched. For instance, he had only just learned that someone had been skimming-off funds from the various equipment maintenance budgets.

Now, the generals looked up casually from the wheel to the small group of 'spies' below it who were looking intensely at its design. They were astounded at the audacity of them, to be stood there in the moonlight, pointing at it for all to see. One of them called to two of the guards who stood at the entrance to the king's tent. They immediately started to approach Lio and his family. Together, the two lifted their heavy machete-axes, ready to lash into the four. Then, at the same time, Ptolemy held up his own hand to halt them. He walked slowly, and a little clumsily, toward Lio himself. The metal platforms on the soles of his shoes, both to make him look taller and to keep him out of the dirt, made him wobble on the uneven surface. When he eventually spoke, it was not with the loud voice of authority Lio had expected, it was the voice of the child that had been buried somewhere still deep within him. 'I know you,' came the soft voice, 'you are the sun haired boy... Helio... I remember you.' He smiled, a tired smile.

Ashur tugged at her mother's skirt, eyes wide open, trying to interrupt her and her father.

'Yes,' answered Lio simply.

'Then this is?' He pointed at Kyrros' back.

'My father,' Lio translated the man's self-introduction to the soldiers on the boat. 'This is Andronikos of Kyrros, he is the engineer to the court of His Royal Majesty, King... you... he trailed off as Kyrros turned to see him for the first time. As these things were said, for the first time she could recall, Miriam suddenly fainted in a crumpled heap.

Not long afterwards, now inside the king's vast tent, Miriam sat recovering in Ptolemy's own chair, a little out of breath but none the worse for her fall – which was in any way partly caught by Kyrros. Ashur sat at her knees, while Lio and Kyrros spoke separately to the King. The king had recognised Lio instantly. He had often thought of the boy, and especially of the second time they had met, the day when the resourceful Lio had bluffed his way into the palace just to offer to 'talk' to him – perhaps share his worries. It was an opportunity Ptolemy sometimes regretted not taking, realising that the boy had been trying only to offer his genuine friendship. The king was instinctively aware that Lio could be trusted – a rare quality – almost unique around him. This was why, now, within this vast tent, none of his generals were present. This was the fulfilment of the long awaited private audience that Lio had once proposed.

Ptolemy's apparent air of arrogance had now gone. He at last looked and sounded settled with his own self and was comfortable with his command of the situation – even though he was on the wrong side of the city wall from where he should have rightfully been. *His* Egypt, he was convinced, should remain independent of Rome – the country which he knew had coveted the land for years. Now speaking honestly, he also let it be known that Cleopatra, on the other hand, was willing to do anything to grasp sole power from her brother – even to the point of effectively giving away the whole country for personal wealth and status. It seemed, from the way Ptolemy spoke, that he was well rid of his treacherous sister and wife, and was at last confident that he could stop her and the Romans.

Before he'd had to flee, he had raided his own library, looking for plans of imaginative weaponry. Now, he was as certain as he could be, that the plans he held could bring him victory – soon. It was, he realised, only the might of the Egyptians that could possibly stay the ever increasing power of Rome. They were the last great independent Mediterranean power to hold out against Caesar's new fascist state. Ptolemy certainly had a bigger navy and far greater numbers in his own army, especially with the addition of his allied foreign mercenaries. It was only a pity that Cleopatra and her own armies were not willing to stand with him. But she had now proven that she was quite willing to capitulate, or frankly do anything to sell the country out from under him.

Lio and his father listened as the boy king confided this to them both, glad that at last he had found someone to share his worries with – to simply talk to. Lio especially, felt a great empathy for him.

In his turn, Kyrros congratulated the king on the deployment of the water pump. It was, he said, a most inspired move. When he suggested that the Mouseion workers had excelled themselves though, the king raised his eyebrows. It was entirely his own design, he assured the engineer. Kyrros was entirely pleased to know this, even though he had never previously been told of the young king's interest in these subjects, and would willingly have taught him personally. The Romans had seen the wheel of course, but despite the two hundred slaves and criminals that it took to power the device, they had, Ptolemy assured them both, assumed that the naturally wiry Egyptians were simply physically much weaker than themselves. It was this arrogance that led them to dismiss his secret weapon as an unnecessary waste of resources.

When Kyrros next asked about the safety of the museum workers, all Ptolemy could tell him was that he was aware that as soon as he had been ousted, Cleopatra had let it be known that she had reinstated the ancient torture chamber. Rumours abounded about what was held in this subterranean pool built by one of their ancestors into the palace foundations, the threat of which alone had forced those remaining to help her. Those of the Mouseion workers unable to escape had similarly been 'allowed' to keep on working. Although, they were now forced to work for the Romans, searching out and constructing imaginative weaponry for them – on pain of death if they would not. The weapons the Romans chose though, were far more fanciful than his own water pump, and were, Ptolemy knew – he had a spy – untested in battle for many years. He doubted in fact if the weapons they were currently working on could even work at all – especially in winter!

There were still, however, a few in the library who were especially loyal to the king and even now were working on one last, more peaceful commission. This secret work was in honour of the friend of his earliest traceable forebears. And it was with this, the king hoped, that Lio and his family might now be able to help him. He could not, would not, command them to do so. This was something that needed to be carried out relying only on implicit trust – and personal honour.

As the oldest male descendant of Ptolemy Soter, the king was the only person who knew the true whereabouts of the body of Alexander the Great. It was the one secret passed-on by his father to him, the eldest son alone, with the mission to keep the mortal remains safe at all costs. Still determined that more than two hundred and fifty years after his death, the relic could not be allowed to fall into Cleopatra's and the Romans' hands, Ptolemy the thirteenth was now about to change its secret location one last time.

Over the past weeks, the workshops had been working on a suitable storage vessel to protect the mummified body. The moisture-tight, lightweight sarcophagus was crucial – to allow Ptolemy to remove Alexander from his current position and into the desert, out of harm's way while the battle for Alexandria raged. The vessel was now complete, he knew. A note had been received telling him so. It was now just a matter of passing a message to the Head Librarian – his spy – and the container would be handed over at the secret entrance to Alexander's true, underground tomb – as opposed to the bogus body which was on public display in the building directly above it. Lio, but more especially Kyrros, was understandably taken aback at the revelations about the tomb, but more especially about the librarian. Hitherto, he had thought of him as only interested in his precious books.

Regardless, passing the exact details of the whereabouts of the location of the secret entrance would now be the price of Ptolemy's favour for smuggling Kyrros and his family back into the city. If Kyrros and his small family would swear on their personal honour not to reveal the tomb's secret location to the Romans, then in return, he, the king, would show them a way through the Roman line and into the city. Once there, after passing that message, they could either head for the Eunostos, or even the Great Harbour. There, they might still be able to find passage from the country and therefore escape the impending battle for the capital. Of course, for many reasons, Kyrros, Lio and all of the family readily agreed.

After the short meeting ended, Kyrros spoke to his wife. 'Are you well now?' he enquired.

'Yes,' Miriam assured him, 'I am fine, it was just the suddenness of seeing the king right there in front of me, and after the worry of the journey, I'm sure.'

'Good,' he said, 'then if you *are* sure – and if you are fine too Ashur,' he looked down at the little girl's sleepy face, 'we would be best to continue our journey immediately.'

'Then follow me,' said the king, 'I will show you the way myself. There are many spies on both sides and this is, after all, the sacred duty given to me by my ancestors.'

At that, he bade his two bodyguards stay, while he led the way outside. After a short walk through the camp, following the gushing water channel, they came to an enormous tent – a stable for the swelling number of horses. Keeping to the line of the channel which continued through it, they then came to a wall where the channel disappeared almost noiselessly through a hidden aperture. 'This is it,' whispered Ptolemy, 'the only way through. Please climb into the channel!'

Kyrros looked at the now terrified face of Miriam.

Ptolemy cautioned them: 'The channel discharges directly into the main city water supply – a network of now sea-water polluted cisterns, or water tanks which led beneath the city and to the Royal Palace and Mouseion quarter. There, it is pitch black, but quite safe. You'll be able to stand up and walk – after the first deep stretch. Keep walking past the well, then you'll know that you're nearly there.'

Kyrros looked at the king worriedly. 'But… neither my wife nor myself can swim,' he delivered the bad news.

'What!' Ptolemy was taken aback.

The five stood there looking at each other in silence, wondering what to do now."

CHAPTER 3:

The Tomb of Alexander

"'I have an idea,' said Kyrros finally, looking at the water channel. 'We need some goat skins, eight should do it. We will empty them and blow them up to make floats, it will be sufficient, I am certain.'

Within a short while, Lio and the king had retraced their steps to find the goatskins and had returned. Tying two of the inflated skins together end to end, they were passed around Miriam's back and under her arms. She took no persuasion to clamp them in position. Kyrros similarly held two under his own arms. A fifth and sixth goat skin was attached to each of the two wooden boxes, and another two were attached to the remaining bags. 'Alright,' said Lio, 'I'll go first, give me a few moments to swim clear, and then follow.'

'As I said, it will be very dark,' warned Ptolemy, 'but just keep to the left side and you will be safe. It will carry you all the way, but be quiet at all times – especially at the exit point. It is very public, perhaps even at this time of night. And at the end…' he suddenly remembered '…push the centre of the letter Xi.'"

'X' *marks the spot!* thought Alex. He winced visibly at the obvious notion, fearing to look around at the others. Conna narrowed his eyes suspiciously, also recognising the Greek letter. Guessing, Bex pursed her lips. Even Maddie blinked. But whatever their thoughts, nobody actually spoke up. Tom noticed though. He cleared his throat noisily before continuing:

"At that, Lio climbed up and into the freezing sea-water channel. As he pushed himself firmly back against the torrent of water, the sun-wheel symbol pendant that hung around his neck popped out of the top of his tunic. Ptolemy smiled, recognising it from the colourfully dressed philosopher with whom he had often spoken in the old days. 'Goodbye Lio – my trusted friend – and good luck,' he wished. Then, without further ado, Lio let go of the sides.

Immediately, the enormous force of the water shot him through the gap in the wall and briefly into the air before he landed on his back in the vaulted cistern. Within moments, he was clear of the bottom and could see again – though only just – entirely by courtesy of the tiny shaft of moonlight that shone through the gap where the water spout entered. Next through was Ashur. Lio called out at her to let her know where he was. She swam toward him and together they began to tread water, waiting for the third person to come through. There was a single masculine cry as the engineer splashed heavily into the water, clutching the goat skins that projected from beneath his arms. Lio and Ashur grabbed an arm each and led him down the body of water out of harm's way. 'I'm alright,' he said, 'get Miriam.'

Above, Miriam gripped the sides of the water channel as she climbed into it. As she sat down, the weight of the cold water pushed her forward and her hands suddenly slipped. Lio and Ashur were just about back to the spout when they were hit with the panicked, echoing scream of their mother flying through the air. As she landed in the water, the cord tying the goatskins together snapped. The floats shot into the air, and she disappeared below the surface, the full force of all those gallons pushing her down. Unseen, she swirled around and around, not knowing which way up she was. Lio and Ashur scrambled and dived around her, trying unsuccessfully to grasp her. Consternation sounded in Kyrros' voice as he constantly repeated his single question, 'Miriam, are you alright?' But there was no reply.

They continued to scramble around, looking for her. Then, at last, after precious minutes, Kyrros felt the heavy bump of something hitting his knees. He grabbed at Miriam as she started along the waterway past him. Taking a deep breath, he stooped down into the water and grabbed her by the shoulders, dragging her to her feet. There was a short, echoing clamour of gasping and coughing as they began to sort themselves out again, Kyrros attempting to calm Miriam's panic. 'I will be fine,' she gagged on the brackish water, starting to regain her composure. Then, hearing the clamour, Ptolemy called-out through the gap – 'is everyone safe?'

'We're fine', Lio called back.

'Then let good fortune guide you on your way,' the king wished finally.

Lio called back a last goodbye.

Slowly and calmly then, they waited for their eyes to pick out the left hand channel in the sparsely lit chamber. Without further ado, they retrieved the floating packages and began to walk: up to Lio and Ashur's chest in the cold water, through the pitch blackened channels below the city.

The journey was thankfully fairly short; their main channel narrowed in stages and only forked twice as it flowed into several smaller cisterns and channels beneath the larger houses. 'Keep left,' reminded Lio, who had assumed the lead position from the start. Once or twice they all had to duck, as the stone-lined channel became shallower and its ceiling lower. But the changing echo always gave warning. For a short while, the channel became lighter as they passed below a circle of moonlight – the deep well in the old market place – just as Ptolemy had advised. At one point, they all stopped, listening to a faint growling noise of sorts. It was followed by a short, agonised scream. However, as disturbing as it was, they decided that whatever the source of it, it was too distant to be of immediate concern. Nevertheless, it immediately filled Ashur in particular with dread. The girl threw her arms around the boy, and he hugged her and stroked back her hair, whispering to her that he had promised to keep her safe. It seemed to comfort her and he took her hand as they moved on again. Then, after feeling their way along for fifteen minutes more, eventually it opened up into another cavern. Still unable to see, the four stumbled into what was clearly a rough staircase cut into the bedrock.

'Shh…' Lio reminded them, creeping up it alone. After a minute he came back. The way seemed to lead to the basement of a temple, like the Temple of Zeus on Rhodos. He spoke to Ashur in particular, 'Follow me,' he said taking her hand. True enough, they had been guided into the basement of a temple. But from there, there was no obvious way out. After feeling their way around the walls in the pitch blackness, no one could seem to find a trace of the thing that they'd been told to look for. Realising that there was no way back – even if they could make it against the flow of the water – it would be impossible to climb up the sheer wall and to the source of the spout. Consternation started to set in. As for the clue, 'Push the centre of the Xi', no one could feel any obvious X feature. Again they felt all around the walls, Kyrros and Miriam reaching up to the low ceiling and Lio and Ashur taking the bottom. But the only thing anyone could detect was a line of what was possibly etched script which no one could make out.

'Wait a moment,' Lio suggested, trying once more to feel the shallow carved figures, 'let me try again.' He closed his eyes in concentration, letting his fingers drift across the indentations once more in an attempt to read the inscription. Slowly and surely he read out what was written there in capitals. 'His soul long ago released… here rests only the mortal remains… of the greatest soldier that the world has ever known… Alexander, King of Macedon… conqueror of the world.' Without waiting, Lio pushed a small, raised metal button in the centre of the Xi in the illustrious name. As he did, one of the large stones in the wall moved, illuminating the edge around it in a golden light. Lio and Kyrros pushed their fingers into the crack and heaved at it. Gradually, it moved a little more, though as if it had not done so in many years. The light grew steadily brighter as the gap opened up into a doorway and Lio and his family were able to file through singly into a small room bathed in a soft, warm glow. The place also smelled of peculiar fumes.

The plastered walls and roof of the low burial chamber were

lined throughout with gold-leaf. This glow was reflected from a single, small flame, which burned at the head of the open-topped granite sarcophagus standing in the centre of the floor. Kyrros and Lio looked at the deep, foot-wide channel cut around the perimeter of the white marble floor. It was filled with some kind of mineral oil, the source of the fumes and an almost endless supply of energy for the single flame. No one made a sound while they all lined up at the feet of Alexander himself – gazing.

Inside the heavy coffin, the perfectly preserved body of the conqueror of the ancient world lay in state. All exposed skin was stained with saffron and lightly dusted with gold. On his chest, he wore a broad, muscle-embossed, breast plate and he had a purple cloak draped around his upper arms. The cloak was held by a golden brooch. It depicted the Greek world and the extent of his conquests. His arms were crossed over his chest, and in his left hand was the ceremonial blue and gold crook of the Kings of Egypt. In his right, a ceremonial depiction of a scroll, once again in gold, was inscribed, 'Achilles' – the name of his own boyhood hero. His lower half was clothed in a short, leather battle kilt, trimmed with gold. His bare, golden thighs exposed, and his shins covered with golden greaves, gold sandals adorned the soles of his feet. Now in awe, the small party split in two. They moved along each side, toward his head, each one finally gazing upon the countenance of the man himself. Alexander, his distinguished face and head propped slightly off the base as if in uneasy sleep, wore a single golden headband – the *strophion* – to hold his long black hair in place. His ringlets were extended onto his shoulders. His face, again glowing with saffron and dusted with gold, wore the ceremonial blue eye make-up of the pharaohs.

No one spoke. For a moment, they just stood and stared at the sight before them. Then, each tapped the other lightly before moving on silently. They filed past the coffin and the spiral staircase that led directly to the temple above the Serapeion – and to the more bejewelled and publicly presented, though entirely fake, remains of Alexander the Great.

They made their way toward the door on this basement level – another concealed entrance – and cautiously followed each other through. It led directly to the street beside the temple. Ptolemy's caution about the possibility of witnesses was thankfully unfounded – no one was there. Undoubtedly there was a curfew in place – all people banned from the streets. Quickly and silently therefore, the four, still saturated and now shivering, made their way with their few belongings to the library, leaving behind them a watery trail.

Kyrros and his family found the door he was looking for. In the early hours of the morning, he banged urgently on it. The librarian answered the call with a look of shock. 'Help us.' Kyrros whispered. 'If the Romans find out we're here, we'll be taken to work for them, then who knows what will happen!' Standing back, the librarian's reaction could best be described as one of continuing astonishment. When all of those who could, had already fled, he found it difficult to fathom why Kyrros had made specifically for the city. That is, until it dawned on him that the real reason for the visit might not be to bring the secret location of the delivery point of the sarcophagus, as Kyrros had gone on to tell him, but to plan how to remove his precious Hippo-Chronos.

The librarian was an intellectual: knowledge, to him, belonged in books. However, once that pure knowledge became physical, it then became immediately sullied. The Time-Horse had been a perfect demonstration of why some ideas should remain as ideas only and not be pursued practically. It had, after all, caused nothing but bother since the project's live testing – although he would never have said as much to Kyrros in front of Lio and Ashur. It was the same reason why, since he had come to the library years before, he had not left it again. Never again had he ventured out into the real world. What was the point, he reasoned, in spending all that time, effort and money in visiting other places? Not to mention taking risks, real risks. For instance, the risk of being taken ransom by robbers or pirates, or a ship sinking.

No, instead, all he had to do to visit these places was read about them from the austere comfort of his own world in the library. Even

27

wars could come and go. The librarian longed only for the day when he could settle down to normality again and continue in his task of cataloguing all of the knowledge in the world. Try as he might though, even now, he couldn't convince Kyrros to destroy the machine. Kyrros insisted that they continue with his earlier plan, a more practical approach, to prevent anyone getting their hands on the Time-Horse.

Exasperatedly, the librarian confirmed that all that Kyrros had earlier asked the messenger – his trusted technician – to convey, had already been carried out in accordance with his wishes. All three parts: the horse; the Chrono-key; and the Cosmos-key had been duly been filled with wax, ready to be transported. In fact, the librarian confirmed also that he had taken the opportunity to despatch the first key already – to the furthest end of the world. An Arab trade vessel had left earlier that evening, calling in at Porphyrusa – the island of purple – before heading out to what was likely to become the next extension to the Roman Empire – once known as the largest of the Cassiterides islands.

Lio listened intently to the conversation as the librarian described the furthest settlement northwards along the eastern coast – to a place just at the edge of the Scotos lands. A trusted courier would carry the Chrono-key personally and deliver it to the port. From there, it would be taken across the river that was guarded by treacherous, hidden black rocks. The librarian himself knew about the place from one of the old travel accounts of a trusted writer; he held a finger to his lips. There, the key would be finally deposited at a very specific place: *'within a crevice in the rock – in the promontory which overlooks the river'*. If ever it was required again, assured the librarian, it could be found there. It would be in the same deep crack where the accompanying Roman guide of the Greek traveller and account writer had long ago deposited a gold coin: the coin which had been placed in sacrifice and dedication to his own gods – in prayer that his ship might avoid those moving black rocks on their way home.

The second of the keys, the Cosmos-key – or what the librarian preferred to call the armillary sphere – would be duly despatched that day, now that he knew where to deliver the sarcophagus. As for the bulkier Time-Horse itself, that was more difficult to move. Later that morning, it would be put back in the crate to be stored in the concealed chamber of the library. Now filled with hard wax, it simply looked like any other sculpture. If it was discovered, confirmed Kyrros, and even cleaned out thoroughly, it would still not be of any practical use or be of real benefit to anyone. Kyrros reassured him, without the keys, the Hippo-Chronos was useless. He reminded him: without the Chrono-key, the worst that could happen was that it could only be sent or taken into the future, never to return. Without the Cosmos-key it could not move under its own energy from its present geographical location. As soon as the Cosmos-key was off the premises therefore, the horse could not even be used as a stealth weapon to slip behind enemy lines unnoticed. Everything, assured Kyrros, was still in-hand.

Finally that evening then, it was agreed that they would spend the night at Kyrros' old house. The four would be able to sleep there overnight and at last be able to dry their clothes and warm themselves by an open fire. Lio and his family duly left the librarian with a promise that they would stay no longer than necessary before seeking passage abroad, but also that they would meet again in the morning – to finalise the plans for the horse and the delivery of the sarcophagus. Since yesterday, the Romans had also deserted the museum workshops, their own secret weapon now finally completed. Borrowing a firebrand from the librarian, Lio and his family made their way across to their old quarters.

After Kyrros lit a fire in the hearth, they all eventually dried off, and Lio made his way sheepishly upstairs. Kyrros followed more confidently. From their vantage point in Lio's bedroom, they could see fairly clearly into the Great Harbour, though not all of it. It was crammed as never before with the ships of the Egyptian navy. Also, clearly, out to sea behind the safety of the harbour walls and ranked closely together, were what looked to be about eight to ten smaller Roman galleys. Later, as it turned out, they were a contingent of galleys from Rhodos that had been hired to Caesar under a mercenary agreement. It could not have been comfortable on board though, the winter sea was picking up again. They would either have to enter the harbour by force, or disperse to find safety themselves in the Eunostos dock. Both Lio and Kyrros turned away and retired to bed.

For what was left of that night, Lio tried to sleep, but only managed to in stages. Throughout, Ashur clung to him, her arms around his waist. Though, she herself remained awake all night, waiting for the dawn to break through the open shutters of the window. Eventually, although still pitch black, the boy sensed the time, his body-clock reminding him to get up and greet the dawn. Ashur had finally fallen into a deep sleep, so he slid her arms from around his waist and got quietly up to creep to the window.

As he watched the dawn's breaking yellow light, he caught the spectacle of the Roman fleet moving forward in line, one by one, towards the harbour and himself. Perhaps the two sides had made peace, he hoped innocently. But as they came nearer, two Egyptian ships – both larger quinquiremes – the water glinting with the early sunlight off three of what should have been five rows of oars, moved off to block the entrance. The Egyptians had no need and no intention to meet them on the open-sea just yet, and they would certainly not allow them to enter the harbour. Then, gradually, more and more Roman ships sailed into sight – much larger quadriremes and quinquiremes.

The boy's father came into the room. 'I see you're watching,' he murmured.

'Yes,' Lio whispered, 'what should we do now?'

'Sit and wait,' Kyrros suggested, 'who knows who will be victorious after today.'

Or, what will happen to us as a result, thought Lio.

'We can only hope,' said Kyrros.

'And pray,' Lio's mother offered, entering the room.

'We will know soon enough.' Kyrros murmured.

Unseen by them, a mile or so away on the landward side of the city, the Roman troops had been steadily building up with each day. They had busily strengthened their grip on the encircled old city, pushing the line of defence gradually further out. The land defences now formed a long line from a point just to the east of that where the Great Harbour began, punctuated by the short pier – the mole. From there, the line continued around the palace, the temple area and the library and museum, to where it cut off the smaller Eunostos dock. Thus, the Romans had left the canal, but not the smaller dock, to the Egyptians. The Egyptians had then, as Lio and Kyrros had already seen, seized on the opportunity to poison the water supply from that exact spot.

Simultaneously with the start of naval movement in the harbour, the Egyptian army had also decided to test the resolve of the occupiers elsewhere in the city. The designs of other ancient war machines found in the library were brought into play – machines which were supposedly first used at the long since siege of Wilusha. At each end of the occupied area, two squat, ten-wheeled vehicles, each resembling huge, hard-shelled beetles, were brought into the light of day for the first time. The thick, barrel-topped timber carapace of these *Scarabs,* named after the sacred dung-beetle of Egypt, were wide enough for fifteen rows of ten men. They all faced rearward in order to be able to heave it forwards, pushing their way gradually through the rubble – its metal 'V' shaped plough forcing the building debris to both sides as it did. The combined effort of three hundred feet and legs strained to clear pathways, to allow the massively armed siege-towers to follow. Each tower had five wooden hatches on its front, each of those having a repeating ballista behind it. Probing Egyptian soldiers also began to attack where they could. The action would last twenty-four hours – but it would be to no avail. Neither side would win the land battle for the city that day.

Lio and Kyrros' attention though, and, to begin with, Miriam's, was on what they could see from the windows of their house – and that centred squarely on the Great Harbour. They looked out as an old man and a boy much taller than Lio walked away from the dock gates and toward the library. Both people had been looking curiously at the distant tower on the Pharos Island."

Tom continued to his guests, "As a spectator, it is difficult to know what is happening when one is watching a sea-battle. Unlike a land battle, I suppose, never having witnessed one, I would presume that the observer might see whether a line is moving forward or backward, whether a skirmish is successful or whether one side is about to be outflanked by another. The sea battle before the pair though, appeared to Lio, more like a slow dance of courtship.

To begin with, seven Roman ships neared the western side of the Great harbour from the royal, or Eunostos, dock threatening to enter beneath the tall, seven arched bridge that joined Pharos Island to the city. But then, they slowed down and stayed just off from it. When the Egyptians sent ships to block the same arches, within minutes, the Romans sank each of them in turn with heavy ballistae – their massive catapults – thus blocking the exit completely. The Egyptians were now locked-in from that side.

The Roman ships then sailed around to join the main fleet, which now numbered fifteen larger quadriremes and quinquiremes – although it was very difficult to see which was which at their further range – together with around thirty galleys and smaller vessels. They drew themselves out into a thin line, opposite the mouth of the harbour. The Egyptians' far greater number of larger ships: twenty or more quadriremes and at least five quinquiremes sailed to face them.

With the line of the bulk of their own ships now appearing westward of the Nile Delta – about to arrive shortly – the Egyptian fleet commander now decided to take the Romans on in battle. One by one they poured out of the harbour to face their foe, but did not move toward them. Kyrros presumed that they were hoping to draw each other into the shallows and sandbanks to cripple them, but the Romans knew of the shallow waters. They had prepared themselves for battle by surveying and charting them previously with plumb lines – lead weighted ropes. Then, as they approached, each Egyptian ship moved off and appeared to dance in line with its Roman partner. It was a bizarre, almost surreal sight to behold, as they sailed for hours to and fro. First the Egyptians, then the Romans fired various flaming missiles, rocks and arrows at their dancing partners. Next, their powerful ballistae fired huge bolts at each other's hulls. It was all very bemusing to the boy Lio, who watched the silent spectacle. But the man Kyrros, knew full well what was happening.

In fact, the battle out there at sea couldn't be more noisy, vicious and bloody. Oars were being smashed to cripple each other's ships, before they were lined-up for attack, their crews quite conscious that they were about to suffer the consequences of being outmanoeuvred. Few seafarers in those days knew how to swim; superstitiously, it was considered to be tempting fate to learn. They would be out there, waiting in gut wrenching fear, thinking of those loved ones whom they would never see again. Each waiting to be rammed below the waterline with the enormous three pronged spike designed to send their adversaries to the bottom of the sea. And, if it made a difference, they were not manned by slaves, as everyone seems to think now. They were highly motivated and trained citizens. Citizens, who had between themselves, willingly paid for the construction, equipped and manned their own ships – to help defend their own country's interests personally. People who knew that if they lost a battle, their wives and families would be left alone to defend themselves, their freedom and their homes. These things could not be trusted to a mere slave. Neither the lash, nor the threat of it, could force them to do something that the citizens themselves were most willing and able to fight to the death for.

On deck, other crew – sailors and marine soldiers – were being shot at and pierced, burned and killed, blinded and limbs torn off. Many more hundreds of troops risked their lives wielding grappling hooks, leaping across gangplanks or falling off to drown in their armour.

Whether slicing into one-another with sharp swords, cutting and hacking each other like slabs of raw meat, or being reduced to use their bare hands to strangle and gouge, all had the same goal: to kill each other – to take each other's very lives at the command of their leaders. On many ships would come the inevitable moaning of men who knew that their end had come, as their vessel blazed out of control or rolled over and sank.

Lio watched all of it, but obviously could neither see nor hear it in any more detail than that distant elegant dance. His father did not explain any of what he knew. Instead, he left the boy alone at the window.

Halfway through the day, Lio watched as the Romans – later, as it turned out, commanded by Caesar himself – took the long island of Pharos. They swiftly landed cavalry and troops on it from a few of their reserve vessels. Next, they cut off access to the connecting bridge over to the port, no doubt to rob the Egyptians of its further use as a secure mooring point. As this part of the battle happened more closely, Lio caught a few blood curdling screams and had decided to stop looking. It was not right, he knew, to watch the last moments of men's lives like this. This was not intended as entertainment. However, it was at that point that something else caught Lio's attention.

One of Caesar's ships moored on the island had begun to offload many packages. A long chain of soldiers was then set up to pass the same packages along toward the Pharos tower itself. Lio watched intently now, wondering what the relay-chain might be transporting in the middle of a battle. What was so important – so urgent? It was mid-day now and the sun, almost at its brightest, was behind the boy's head. Now there came larger packages, flat sheets of something. Whatever they were, they were covered in sacking. He saw a bright flash of reflected sunlight as the sacking slipped from one of the polished objects, but was none-the-wiser. Like ants, the line worked deftly until they had delivered their cargo into the tower. A few minutes later, figures began to emerge on the roof: one or two soldiers, but then more figures, dressed in bleached white. It was a civilian uniform that

34

the boy recognised immediately – the museum workers' uniform.

Just as his curiosity took hold, Kyrros called for Lio and Ashur to come with him, if they wished, to visit the workshops. They would all be permitted to accompany him one last time before they had to leave Alexandria."

CHAPTER 4:

'Caesar's' Secret Weapon

Tom looked fleetingly at each of his guests in turn. Gathering his thoughts, he said, "It was at this point that the fortunes of Alexandria would be forever blighted. Never again would the city be held aloft as a place of learning – and all presumably caused because of the secrets held in the Great Library." He shook his head regretfully.

"Kyrros, carrying a large bag with him, led the way to the museum workshops. Miriam, Ashur and the boy followed in his wake. The doors to the library were open, so the four passed freely through the completely deserted space and into the almost equally deserted workshops.

There, Lio recognised three of the faces of the eldest workers who had attended the wedding not long ago. Each one looked tired and weary, but each smiled in relief at the familiar young faces of the boy and girl, and each in turn recognised the pendant that still hung around Lio's neck – Poseidonios' old athlete charm. They were all that was left of the museum workers, the others now drafted into working for the Romans. They were paid, of course, so that they would not be tempted to make deliberate 'mistakes' in their work for their new bosses. Nevertheless they were without choice in the matter. Even the recently returning technician that had been the messenger to the farm had been taken prisoner as soon as he'd got back. All that remained were the three elders which the Romans assumed would not be able to keep-up. The others were at that very

36

moment inside the Pharos Tower. For the past weeks, most had been working on the Romans' own secret project. Whilst unbeknown to them, now working in isolation, were the few remaining highly experienced elders. Just the three of them had managed to construct the object on the bench in front of them – the Sarcophagus of Alexander.

The empty, dull-silvered, slim-line coffin was in the classic Egyptian mummy shape. It was caringly decorated across its entire surface with a depiction of battle armour. The metal was electrum, a mixture of gold and silver which was resistant to tarnishing. It was the same metal that had been used in antiquity to cap the top of the pyramids as a lightning conductor. Three features marked this coffin out in particular though. Firstly, the six heavy loops that were on each side of it, designed, when the long timber carrying poles were introduced through them, to both hinge and lock the case shut. Secondly, there was a rounded, shaped flap, hinged over the face. The technician in charge opened it to reveal an almost perfectly clear, blown glass panel beneath it. The third feature was less noticeable. Alexander had been tall for his time, around the same height as Kyrros, six feet. Lio had seen this for himself already, but this sarcophagus was over a foot longer again than the man, and the bulbous, foot shaped end was more rounded than usual. As Lio looked at the extraordinary handiwork before them, the librarian walked in carrying the box which contained the wax filled Cosmos-key. Thus, he confirmed Kyrros and Lio's suspicions of the appropriate resting place of the last component part of the Hippo-Chronos. Alexander himself would carry the armillary with him. In death, he would have the world at his feet.

The engineer was entirely happy with the plan. As the librarian handed the armillary to Kyrros, the wax covering it made it slip from his hands. Both tried to catch it, but the holed sphere bounced heavily off the corner of the bench and landed on the stone floor with an ugly clang. The librarian was devastated. Kyrros picked it up and looked at the big ugly dent, but said nothing. Instead, he calmly picked up the largest axe he could find within the workshop.

To the astonished faces around him, he raised it high above his head and brought it heavily down on the object, almost severing it in two. The shock and the noise of it threw Lio and the others, but it was obviously to the great relief of the librarian especially. Next, however, Kyrros revealed what was in his own bag. He took out the working prototype armillary and put it into the coffin instead. Now, the horse would finally be prevented from being used against them all. There was dead silence in the room until Kyrros spoke. 'I think, gentlemen – and ladies – that the time has come for us all to put to sleep the Time-Horse.' With that, Kyrros and his family bade farewell to the technicians and the librarian, and they left toward the library. Kyrros carried with him only the axe. Now, no one was as shocked as Lio.

Along the corridor, stood there in its own chamber, the Hippo-Chronos was a pitiful sight. Hardened wax squeezed out through the web-like holes of its entire exo-skeleton. It was, to all intents and purposes, dead. Lio held Ashur's hand as the pair stood and looked at it for one last time – into its hollow, dead eyes. Ashur started to weep silently for the animal that had rescued her. Tears rolled down her face and onto her chin. She began to sob softly, now comforted by Miriam. Lio, the boy himself hurting inside, led the horse on its castors into the packing crate.

'May we have a moment alone with him,' asked Lio, 'so that Ashur and I may say farewell?'

'Yes,' agreed Kyrros, himself now choked with regret for what he had to do, 'we'll wait outside,' he took Miriam's hand and led her away, the least emotional of the four.

Ashur and Lio stood in silence, before Lio was moved to say something to his horse. Hand in hand with Ashur, he said, 'I know that you are only a machine, but for the brief moment you were alive, you did wonderful things for us, Ashur and I – so your own short life was not in vain. Perhaps sometime in the future, when mankind has learned not to make weapons from peaceful creations, you may live again.' With that, Lio stroked the machine's muzzle and stepped back from it. Ashur stepped forward next and crouching down, pressed her face to the top of its front leg, hugging it to her. She stood up, then seeing a small bowl of oily red pigment on the floor beside it, dipped her finger in it. She walked back to the crate and carefully began to mark it. When she had finished, the pair looked at the handiwork that Lio didn't want to correct: this was Ashur's own personal tribute. The letter 'Rho' was the wrong way around, but the single word of thanks quite clear – 'EFKARISTO.' She dipped her whole hand into the pigment and sealed her work with a handprint, then offered the bowl to Lio. Lio signed it with his own handprint.

A few moments later, as Miriam, Ashur and Lio walked down the corridor and out into the library, all three shivered as a heavy, dull clank came from the Hippo-Chronos room. Miriam comforted her son and daughter as she led them out of the mouseion and toward the house.

Once more upstairs in his old room, Lio watched intently, trying to blot out what was happening in the library. Over the next hour, the sea-battle in the Great Harbour of Alexandria raged on below. During the time they had spent in the workshops, at the top of the Pharos tower, a large timber frame had been fixed around the short, circular colonnade at its top – borrowing from its strength. There was still no clue as to what they had been constructing, but the white uniformed figures seemed to beaver away urgently. Now at the point of the frame's completion, the next phase of the construction began immediately.

Slowly, one by one, five, square polished copper mirrors, each as wide and as tall as the outstretched arms of a man, were fixed to it. The bottom row first, then building to the top row, another five, and so on, until twenty-five gleaming mirrors sat glaring and reflecting the sun's bright rays all over the harbour. Just this construction phase in itself took a further hour. Then the ants scurried around to fix what appeared to be a series of ropes and pulleys to the back of each of the mirrors in turn. Finally, Lio watched the whole mass of mirrors focus as one, until the single pool of reflected light flashed momentarily across the harbour and into his face. As it did, he had to avert his eyes. Even with his sun-protectors in place the glare was frighteningly strong.

By now, a few of the Egyptian vessels started to return to port. Without enough decent oars, they had become sitting targets – better to return to dock, than lose their vessels. Many of the larger ships especially had already been lost; unable to move fast enough out of the Romans' way without their full complement of oars.

A few Roman galleys were trying to put out fires of their own, one blazed-on unsuccessfully as it followed the Egyptians. Most of the Roman ships had now pulled back, all except that one in flames, and obviously, to Lio, completely out of control. Instead of rejoining its own fleet, it kept coming faster toward the slowing Egyptian fleet, making to pull in amongst them all. *If the master can't control his ship,* thought Lio, *it will be suicide.* But still it kept on coming. Then, protecting the harbour, the last Egyptian ship dropped its anchors and stopped abruptly. From his window, Lio could, for the first time, hear the splintering crash of two ships collide. In that collision, fire spread from mast to mast, but thankfully not to any of the rest of the fleet. Now realising that this had been a failed incendiary attack thwarted by the single Egyptian ship's commander's self-sacrifice, Lio began also to realise for himself the devastation that could have been caused by a fire in the harbour.

However, his attention switched abruptly. He saw the large bright spot, flash across the sail of one of the retiring Egyptian ships, now well inside the harbour. The reflected pool of the sun's rays that shone out from the tower flitted briefly back and forth, until it became fixed in one large spot. Lio called to Kyrros to see the strange effect, and his father arrived in time to witness the weapon that the tower had now become. The mirrors being focussed further together now, the bright spot grew smaller and more intense. The ship's master, unaware of what was happening, carried on unhurriedly for home. Then the spot grew smaller still and after only a few more seconds, it began to turn yellow – then brown. Smoke rose from it as the sun's heat began to raise the oiled canvas to its flashpoint.

Kyrros recognised the contraption now. It was none other than a reconstruction of a device he had seen and discussed in the library years ago: *The Burning Mirrors of Archimedes!* This was one of the devices reputed to have been used against the Romans over two hundred years ago at their siege of Syracuse. With a mixture of awe and horror, the pair watched as the Romans now turned the power of the sun's gift of light against the Greeks. The spot on the ship's sail suddenly blackened and burst into flames. The instant it did, the beam was switched to another Egyptian vessel, then focussed more and more tightly to perform the same lethal task. Caesar had waited till the ships had sailed between the tower and the sun for maximum effect, to destroy as much of the Egyptian fleet as he could – in one clean sweep. Kyrros turned and walked away in regret and bitter disappointment. It was all but over for Ptolemy's fleet. The boy king, it seemed, was sadly destined to lose.

The wind being behind the fleet, flames now licked from each of the targeted ships in turn. Then, effortlessly, it spread to the next ship in line. Lio realised why Caesar's first move had been to block the arches of the bridge. It had been the fleet's only line of escape – but now it had been removed.

Within fifteen minutes, it seemed that the whole of what remained of Ptolemy's fleet was on fire. Again Lio called for his father to come and see the rapidly developing conflagration unfold, although himself not realising its full significance. Kyrros' reaction was entirely different though. The buildings lining the harbour were the only ones in Alexandria to be made entirely of timber. The fire was spreading rapidly and now one of the wooden roofs of the dockside warehouses, an empty grain store on the harbour-side, caught alight. The wind continued to pick up steadily now; the fire leapt across the rooftops, gradually catching another and another. Slowly but steadily, it spread toward their own house. 'Quickly...' Kyrros called out, 'the fire may easily spread into the city – grab our belongings and get downstairs. Run – everyone!' There was little time to argue. Each of them carrying a bag, Lio took Ashur's hand and ran down the stairs into the square outside. No one ran past them, it was entirely deserted. Then, Lio remembered, everyone had already fled. Momentarily, the pair waited for their parents to come. But at that, the librarian ran past their house – in the wrong direction!

'Where are you going?' Kyrros called out.

'The library, I must save the books,' came the distraught reply as he kept going. 'Help me – PLEASE!' he begged.

Of course, the enormity of the full task made it impossible. *But*, Lio thought, *perhaps a small portion of the most precious works might be removed for safety.* It was Andronikos the philosopher that seemed to look into the boy's eyes; he could not abandon the library either. He did not have to tell the boy, but neither would Lio have guessed Kyrros' own overriding reason for returning. 'Miriam, take my bag. Go to the Eunostos harbour…' Kyrros said at once, 'all of you. It will be safe there. I will meet you later.'

'But Kyrros', his wife started to protest.

'Don't worry,' he raised his eyebrows. 'Now go, before we are all trapped.'

Lio started to go with his mother and Ashur but then stopped. 'Go on,' he called out, dropping Ashur's hand, 'take my bag too. I'm going with my father.'

His mother shouted after him, but Ashur was already running towards the safe area and Lio was heading in the opposite direction. Miriam stood fixed in the centre.

'Go, mother… stay with Ashur,' Lio called over his shoulder, 'we'll be alright.'

Reluctantly, Miriam turned and ran after the girl, while the boy followed his father and the librarian into the empty building, calling out as he did so.

'Go back.' Kyrros demanded.

'No,' Lio refused flatly.

'Go back… Now!'

'No, I have come to help.'

He looked at the boy exasperatedly before giving in. 'Then hurry, we do not have long, follow me.' The three ran into the main library, Kyrros formulating the rescue plan as they did. He shouted to the librarian, 'Find blankets, sheets, anything to carry the papyri away in.'

Out of breath, the librarian began to panic. Head in hands, he replied: 'We're not going to have time to do it all alone – I'm going to find help,' then he disappeared toward the area of his private study.

Next, his father cried out to Lio, 'We will start at the top. Quickly, up the ladders. Throw everything into the centre of the aisles.' Kyrros ran to the ladder opposite him and together they began to hurl down the scrolls as fast as they could.

As fast as Lio worked, pulling himself along with the ladder, he called out, 'there is still something I don't understand. Why did you have the Hippo-Chronos filled with wax and the two keys sent away if your intention was to destroy it anyway?'

'What?' asked Kyrros, 'why would you think I destroyed it?'

'But we heard you swing the axe.'

'You most certainly did, but I would never harm the beast!' Kyrros assured him, 'the horse was merely crated-up, ready for removal. I nailed the top on it myself.'

Lio's heart leapt, 'really? But that means it can still be rescued from this library.'

Kyrros sighed with exasperation. 'We haven't the time,' was the pained reply, 'It doesn't matter now and we don't have any choice in the matter anymore!'

Lio emptied another section onto the marble floor. Again he pulled himself along, unable to come to terms with the man's attitude, leave it – to risk its destruction by fire. 'Then it will be lost forever,' he said incredulously. 'Why have we protected it all this time?'

'To prevent anyone else re-enabling it; many people here could do that. The plans still exist – right... *here!*' he said, finding what he had hidden there years ago. 'EUREKA!' He pulled out a heavy roll of papers and slid down the ladders with them. Kyrros stood in the centre of the pile of fragile papyrus rolls. 'Come along, let's go.'

Lio was shocked at his sudden lack of care for the precious writings surrounding him. 'But what about all of this work?'

'Leave it,' Kyrros said, 'Doubtless it will all be rediscovered some day. Quickly, in this confusion we may be able to get onto a boat and slip away.'

The boy slid down his own ladders to join him just as the librarian arrived, followed by a full cohort of Romans – ten soldiers – swords drawn. 'This is the man I told you about,' the librarian said, 'the engineer of the Mouseion – the man who can bring you a swift victory and stop all this wanton destruction.'

Kyrros and Lio looked at him incredulously – at his staggering betrayal.

'Please, forgive me,' the librarian begged, 'It was either you or these precious works. They will look after you – they have promised me.' Tears welled up in his eyes. 'I am so sorry!'

Neither Lio nor Kyrros spoke. Instead, each was astounded at the treachery.

'Take them,' the officer called out, walking towards the couple. As they made to grasp Kyrros' right hand, from the left hand behind his back, he dropped unseen the heavy roll of dozens of drawings that contained the entire set of detailed designs for the Hippo-Chronos. They fell right into the centre of the pile of scrolls that lay in a heap where he stood.

Being frogmarched past their trembling, still apologising betrayer and outside onto the square, Lio and Kyrros looked back at the Great Library once more, wondering if it would survive the late afternoon and the approaching evening. It was to be the last time they saw it intact. Their hands were tied before they were marched off behind two of the soldiers, followed by another two together with their officer. The small group then turned toward the palace – and its dungeon.'

Tom cleared his throat. "Fire did indeed rage throughout that late afternoon and well into the night. However, the Romans, already prepared for the coming conflagration, quickly changed their duties to containing the fire and not letting it spill further into the Roman sector. Later, the fire got a little too close to the library for comfort. Flames licked at its roof, but the soldiers then formed five separate relay-chains. Perhaps one hundred or more legionaries had assembled to douse the building in water from right there in the harbour, using ropes to pull leather buckets up onto the roof. The water was then handed to a small group of soldiers who were stood on its top, wetting the tiled roof to prevent any chance of sparks taking hold. At least the Romans had been true to their promise, no doubt to the joy of the librarian. The Great Library of Alexandria, it seemed at that time, would be forever safe."

Boris yawned and looked up at Tom, briefly deciding that nothing exciting was happening. Tom couldn't help but react. "It appears that I am boring someone," he said. The dog's head dropped easily back into Maddie's lap. Alex reached over and patted him on the head. "Hey Boris, are you bored?" he asked. The dog didn't budge except for moving his eyes towards his owner. He was quite content. Alex shook his head. If the dog was bored, he would now be the only one. Everyone else was riveted.

CHAPTER 5:

Total Loss

Tom again scanned the pensive faces. "I hope none of you will ever have to spend a night like theirs: Lio and his father. To begin with, the cell where they were held was both damp and cold – freezing cold. Kyrros and Lio both shivered together until the early hours of the morning. The man reached out to his boy and pulled him closer to him. Then he wrapped his arms around him so that they shared their body heat.

It seems a curious thing to say, but as long as Lio had known him and had grown to respect the man, never, in all that time, had he directly and physically demonstrated any direct love or affection toward him. Now Lio knew his genuine feelings, and he was sure that this sudden gesture was meant to comfort and reassure him, as well as keep him warm. Subconsciously, Lio clutched the comforting symbol of the sun wheel, although he was quite conscious that they were in dire peril. And, he wondered if Kyrros' gesture did not inadvertently communicate to him the depth of his own fears. The boy presumed that like himself, his father was deeply worried at what had become of Miriam and Ashur. Separately, they hoped that they had managed to find and board a boat, or better still, had somehow already slipped through the Roman blockade. Perhaps even now, they were en-route to somewhere safe in the Aegean or the Mediterranean. At least, that was what Lio and Kyrros jointly willed them to do, no matter what was about to become their own peril.

Before first light of dawn, they were together marched out of the cell, now by two different guards. They were Egyptian jailers: one fat, one thin, but both shorter than the same middle-aged centurion that had led them in last night. The scruffy guards prodded and cajoled the prisoners along the corridor, up the stairs into the palace and finally into the one room that Lio recognised from his visit months earlier. There, they were again prodded and poked to stand in front of the now lightly curtained-off bed. The centurion called out smartly: 'Caesar, we have brought two prisoners for you.'

'What! Isn't it a little early?' came a no-nonsense voice from behind the curtain. 'Come back later.'

The centurion's voice carried on uneasily 'Emperor, in light of the events overnight, we thought it best to alert both you and the queen.'

'What events?' returned the yawning voice, 'What has happened?'

The centurion, unable to fathom out how the General of the Armies was still unaware of it, picked up his courage to deliver the news. He prayed to Jupiter that he would not lose his head for it. 'The library, Emperor...' he hesitated, 'it has gone.'

'What?' came the confused voice, 'What are you talking about, gone!'

The soldier cleared his throat, 'it has been subjected to a serious incendiary attack.'

'What? *My* library?' The shrieking voice of the young queen was instantly recognisable to Lio.

Within moments, the figure of Cleopatra wearing a long nightdress burst through the curtains. She fastened a cord at her waist as she did so. 'What has happened?' she demanded, 'how serious, explain!' For all she had herself never visited the library – preferring instead to send one of her many assistants to find something interesting to read to her in the palace – politics, the histories of past power struggles and such – to her it was a prize, a possession unequalled in the world. It was one of the few

47

achievements that *her* city and *her* direct ancestors could be justifiably proud. Although she was herself not unintelligent, in fact displayed quite a gift for intelligence of a sort – perhaps more akin to cunning and subterfuge – to Cleopatra the library was a status symbol. Even if she herself did not fully understand its true value, she could at least flaunt it in the faces of other world leaders, and offer its secrets for sale.

Lio and Kyrros were both as eager to know what had happened to it as she.

The centurion stood to attention. 'Your majesty,' he explained, 'last night the Royal Library was subjected to a most devastating attack by fire.'

Cleopatra looked genuinely shocked. 'How bad is the damage?'

'Very…' confirmed the officer fearfully. 'Very, serious your majesty,' he said at last.

Lio and Kyrros were confused. At the last glimpse they'd had of it, there had been no sign that it would be touched.

'What do you mean "very" serious?' interrogated the queen angrily. The centurion steadied himself ready for her reaction.

'Your majesty,' he wondered whether to string out his reply further, then decided not to. He only hoped Caesar would protect him, a loyal soldier, reluctantly delivering the devastating news. 'The library was engulfed. It has been totally destroyed.'

All mouths dropped open, Lio's, Kyrros' and the queen's. *That can't be*, thought Lio, *surely!*

'A total loss?' Kyrros himself began to question the story. 'But…'

'The prisoners will be quiet.' A voice hissed from behind them in an oddly familiar and silky tone. Lio did not dare turn around, hairs prickling on the back of his neck.

'What!' Cleopatra shouted in disbelief. 'My Library – gone! And what of the works?'

'Also gone,' the centurion confirmed.

'Was nothing saved then?' She spat.

'No, majesty, the building and its entire contents were entirely consumed by the fire – along with all of the Mouseion buildings.

There were many volatile things there – papyri, wood, wax, oil…'

Lio could not believe it. And judging from the expression on his father's face when they looked at each other – neither could Kyrros.

'Gone! the Great Library! Just like that!' Kyrros said aghast.

The boy began to re-think the events of last evening.

Yesterday, when his father had casually told him to leave everything, and after which they had been arrested, Lio had assumed that the librarian would go on emptying all of the works, or at least saving some of its contents. No one had really dared to imagine this! He thought of all the great works regretfully, all of those great philosophers' lives works lost. But most of all the boy thought of the Hippo-Chronos – his own very special horse. A pang of regret that he might have felt for the loss of a real animal or pet surged through him but he refused to show it. He also remembered the plans – *had even those been lost?* he wondered. He stood stolidly, watching and listening only.

Cleopatra spoke to the figure behind the bed curtain. 'You told me that the library would be protected from accidental fire,' she accused petulantly.

'And so it was,' Came the exasperated and clearly exhausted voice.

The centurion spoke up again. 'Your majesty, my Emperor', he tried to ingratiate himself before he somehow got the blame, 'the fire was not started accidentally – the man who started it was killed at the scene.' He called out a command and a body was dragged in by two soldiers and dumped unceremoniously, face up on the floor – the librarian!

There was a dried patch of dark red on his chest. Kyrros gasped, unable to take it in. For all the librarian had betrayed them, he had understood why. Even if he didn't agree with his motives, he certainly wouldn't have wished this on him.

'These two were also at the scene!' Kyrros looked around to see who the centurion was referring to, but there was no one else behind him other than the two guards who had marched them in, and another shadowy figure now standing in the furthest, darkened corner. He was dressed, Kyrros noticed, in the purple trimmed, black uniform of the Praetorian Guard, the black horse-hair plumed helmet covering most of his face. These soldiers, Caesar's own troop of bodyguards had a fearsome reputation. *The elite officer,* thought Kyrros obliquely, *looks oddly on the small size for the post, he is obviously well connected – or very skilled at his craft.* The delivery of this last spoken sentence now distinctly troubled Lio's father. He placed his hand on the boy's shoulder and gripped it. Things had just gone from bad to worse.

The long, intelligent face of the man who appeared from around the curtain looked in every way a commander of men, even as he was now, dishevelled, yawning and wearing a purple trimmed nightdress. Neatly trimmed grey hair covered most of his head. Though, as he bent down to retrieve a belt that he must have dropped earlier, strands of much longer hair fell down his face from the sides. Lio noticed that most of the top of his head was quite bald. As he stood up, he combed it across and forward with his fingers. Nevertheless, despite the absent-minded gesture, he was not at all a comical figure.

'Who are you,' he cut straight to the chase.

'My name is Andronikos of Kyrros,' he preferred the Greek, more elite version of his name in the present company, 'I am the engineer of the Mouseion. This', he squeezed Lio's shoulder again, 'is my son, and that', he pointed downward, 'is the head librarian – alive and well when we were brought here last night.'

The centurion spoke again. 'Sir, they were caught red-handed, building a bonfire from all of the library's works, piling them in a heap, ready to burn them.'

'Were they indeed,' it was not a question. 'And why would the engineer and the head librarian – men whom I would suppose to have spent all their lives in the quest for knowledge – suddenly take it upon themselves to destroy the greatest body of recorded works in the world?' The question was levelled at the centurion and at the owner of the voice that had hissed from behind them earlier. 'I think you will find that you have the wrong men,' Caesar proposed, shaking his head. 'Wouldn't you agree gentlemen!'

'Might I suggest a reason why they would?' came the voice from the dark corner behind Lio. Lio winced.

'Go on,' accepted the Emperor.

The boy began to wonder. Should he have earlier mentioned the attempted interloper – the time he'd rescued Ashur? His stomach began to churn.

'Perhaps they are spies. Perhaps they were attempting to deprive us of the many plans and drawings for machines that we might have used ourselves in our quest for glory? Perhaps one in particular!'

Lio stiffened instinctively – not daring to look behind him – now wondering if he really did recognise the high pitch and the silky intonation of the voice. But, fighting against the thought, he relaxed slightly. He knew, or at least prayed, that five hundred years later, it was, after all, clearly impossible.

'A weapon?' Caesar raised an eyebrow. Now, after the unlikely success of the earlier ancient invention – the burning mirrors – he was prepared to consider any possibility.

'Effectively, yes,' the voice answered. The boy still could not look behind him, still naggingly frightened that his worst nightmare might be true. The voice certainly sounded like the one he most feared.

'Is this true? Have you such a weapon?' Caesar asked Kyrros.

'I know of no such *weapon,*' answered Lio's father truthfully.

Caesar sighed deeply and then yawned. 'Then this is mere speculation.' He held up his hand to stop the conversation. 'Let them go, I'm tired – am I the only one who remembers what a busy day I had yesterday?' He yawned again and turned to retire through the curtains.

Cleopatra looked at Lio, narrowing her eyes – 'Wait! I recognise you from somewhere,' she said, 'that hair – that strange glass jewellery!' she nodded at the eye-protectors and the athlete pendant hanging at his neck. 'What is that sign?'

'It is a most ancient good luck sign – a token' – Lio answered, 'given as a gift.'

At the words 'good luck' and 'token', Caesar also took an interest

51

in it. He stepped forward to look at it. He reached out to thumb it curiously, obviously taken with it, consigning it to memory. Then he dropped it again and turned away.

Lio's father looked down his nose at the boy, wondering what else he had failed to tell him previously. Still, Lio did not speak. After a few moments the queen spoke up. 'Don't worry – I'll remember soon,' she smirked. 'Lock them away till I decide their fate.' She gave the royal double-clap, then she too disappeared behind the curtain and the prisoners were led away back to the cell. Before Lio had a chance to see who the silky voice belonged to, the figure that had stood behind them had already left. Lio shrugged to himself; obviously he had been getting carried away. He tucked the disturbing thought to the back of his mind.

On their short trip back to the corridor, the centurion breathed a sigh of relief. That had been a close call. At one point, he thought he'd end up in *the other room:* the cell that he regularly delivered prisoners to. Cleopatra had an unnaturally vicious streak in her. He had witnessed it personally over the past few days. One of the first things she had ordered him to do on her return to the palace was that the number of her *pets* be topped up in that *special room*. It was not without reason that the guards referred to her as 'Queen of the Niles.'

The centurion locked the prisoners back in the cell, dreaming of making enough money to get out of this place. *This wasn't soldiering.* He turned to head outside, to settle his nerves. He only hoped he could make it to the door before he was too late!

As he ran, the two guards began to laugh. The queen wasn't the only one with a cruel streak. Taking out his short knife, one of them stroked the blunt tip along the bars of the door, humming the lullaby he had been taught as a child. He looked the boy up and down, 'Such a shame, and so young,' he taunted.

'But tender as a baby,' finished the other guard sniggering. He continued to hum the rhyme.

Kyrros recognised the flat tune, 'Be quiet!' he attempted to shut the guard up.

'I'll sing if I like!' he continued, grinning cowardly. Turning to walk toward the other guard and the seat a little further up the corridor, he broke slowly and intimidatingly into his well rehearsed ritual 'comic' song, dwelling on every phrase. *'She sailed away... on a pleasant summer's day... on the back of a croco-di-ile, you see said she... he's as gentle as can be... I'll ride him down the Nile...'*

Alex and his three friends looked at each other incredulously at the thought of the child's rhyme – the crocodile song – being known back then. This time Alex cringed visibly. Conna closed his eyes, embarrassed for his friend. Maddie looked almost pitifully at Tom. Again, no-one commented, but, now Bex blew out her breath in a thin stream.

"Of course," admitted Tom, reading the look on the surrounding faces, "sadly, I have never been able to carry a tune. I cannot swear that either the rhyming translation or the tune we know today are one and the same – but it is close enough, and the sentiment was similar." He shifted a little in his chair.

Still no-one else spoke.

"Nevertheless, Lio and Kyrros sat uncomfortably in the cell, trying to ignore the guard, separately contemplating what might have happened to the library and its contents, and trying not to speculate on their fate. *Could it have been a lone spark?* the boy wondered. Perhaps it was, certainly the whole city being ringed by fire made this a distinct possibility. The alternative was unthinkable. Surely, it could not have been deliberate, could it?

As for the librarian being the culprit, he knew only too well where the man's loyalties lay and that was entirely with the body of work. It was preposterous that he could be held responsible. No, concluded Lio, whatever had been the cause, the library was no more. What was done could not now be undone. The world would be a different place without all of that stored wisdom, but all scholars would have to learn to accept the fact. As his father had said only last night, 'someone would inevitably rediscover all of those things,' but even though this much was true, little did either one dream that it would take mankind almost one and a half thousand years to even begin that process of rediscovery. Regardless, together, they sat and contemplated their own likely joint fate.

The second guard joined in '...*The croc winked his eye, as she waved her hand goodbye...*'

Lio and Kyrros tried not to listen. Miriam and Ashur were their joint concern now, not that they were in any position to assist them in any way. They could only go on hoping that they had escaped. Kyrros wondered morosely if they would ever see either of them again – there was, after all, no way that he and Lio could escape from this place. Inevitably, Lio's own mind drifted back to the machine. What had become of it? He imagined it lying part-incinerated, part-crushed in the rubble of the library. Its beautiful polished skin now blackened and covered in dust, its hollow eyes crying out to him to come to its rescue. Regardless of the loss of the library, it really was quite sad that such a magnificent creation could have been lost to the world. Still, even now – even though he would be most reluctant to have admitted at the time – he knew that the horse's destruction was quite necessary. Now, he finally, really, understood the full danger it would have threatened in the wrong hands. Following on from that thought, and remembering the silky voice he'd thought he'd just heard in Cleopatra's chamber, he also wondered whether he should at last tell Kyrros about his fears as to who might have followed them from the past. Was it time to tell him about his suspicions of the high priest Zeus possibly making it here?

'...*wearing a radiant smile...*'

'Stop it.' The centurion had returned. 'There's no need to taunt; you're working under my command now.' Feeling much better now, he began to dream again of going home. At least it wouldn't be long now he inhaled, suddenly feeling buoyed up. By incredible chance, his luck had just changed.

The guards sneered at what they perceived as the weakling Roman. *No stomach for it*, they thought. The centurion marched the guards away.

Who knew how long later, the centurion once more approached the cell with the guards. 'Stand up,' he commanded. The two obeyed without question. One of the guards unlocked and opened the cell door wide, leering at the pair.

'Follow me,' the centurion barked. Lio and Kyrros got stiffly to their feet; they looked into each other's faces. Both turned and walked in silence behind the Roman, flanked by both guards, who once more began to mumble the same tune: '... *By the end of the ride...*'

Lio's mind raced. *Now what was about to happen, had the queen remembered him?* And if so, was that good or bad. He had only tried naïvely to make friends with her brother, where was the harm in that...? *Her brother,* he reflected, realising now... *the deposed king.* And she had witnessed Lio as he had attempted to befriend him! Maybe she would forgive his insolence, as it seemed to him now. Although, from her demeanour on the two occasions that the boy had now seen her, that seemed at best unlikely. As if in answer to Lio' thoughts, the centurion announced: 'bring the keys to the wet room.' Now they both knew.

The corridor could not have been longer for both of them. His father once again put his hand around Lio's shoulders. In return, Lio could not let him go into the room without letting him know how sorry he was for the trouble he had brought upon the great man from the instant they had met. It was too late to mention Zeus, but at least he wanted to tell him belatedly how much he thought of him. Only now did he realise that he had never thanked Kyrros or told him of his affection. Finally, he decided that this was the time – before it was too late. He swallowed as they reached the door. 'Father, I am sorry for everything...'

Kyrros cut off his apology. 'No, need,' he assured the boy, 'no need!'

The centurion stopped sharply, but this time not at the stairs. Now he stood at a heavy wooden door. Kyrros looked down at Lio with a pained expression on his face, dreading what might await them behind it – for himself, but especially the boy. Of all the things he wished to say to him, all he could think to say was, 'Lio, I have enjoyed the time we have spent together, you have helped make my life whole…and for that, *my son*, I am truly thankful.'

The guards couldn't resist finishing off their version of the song, each whispering into their ears, '…*The – "baby" – was inside…*' one completed the other's lyrics, '…*and the smile was on the..?*'

Opening the door, the foetid stench hit them, making Lio retch. Behind the door was a set of wide steps that dropped steeply into a bleak, grey, chamber. Only a narrow stone ledge ran around the wall, separating the two levels. The space was not huge, but large enough to hold a deep central pool full of water. Alerted by the opening of the door, the dozen Nile Crocodiles hissed and writhed over one another, clambering menacingly out of the water. 'You two – inside! You first,' commanded the centurion. Lio looked for one last time at his father and began to walk forward.

'No, not you… step aside. You two,' he beckoned to the guards, 'check it over first!'

The guards looked at each other, puzzled. They had never been asked to do this before – but he was the boss. They shoved past Kyrros, pushing Lio roughly to one side. Together they stood on the top step, looking down into the pit.

'Is it clean enough?' asked the centurion.

The guards looked blankly back at him.

'Well, is it?'

The taller of the two scratched his head,

'Look man, look!'

The shorter of the two bent down, peering at the floor between the approaching reptiles, 'Well, I think I can see a bit of bone…' It was the last thing he said, as the heavy door shut behind them.

Lio and Kyrros looked in disbelief at the centurion now removing his breastplate and helmet.

'Well – what are you waiting for? This is your lucky day – and mine.' He patted the dirty yellow-brown purse hanging at his belt and turned toward the door back into the world.

Behind the locked door of the dungeon, the guards stood still, spread eagled against the wall, praying to Sobek that crocodiles couldn't climb along narrow ledges.

As the Roman opened the outer door, the early sunlight streamed into Lio's face and he had to quickly put on his glasses. And there, unmistakably – standing in the centre of the paved area outside – he saw the twin figures of his mother and Ashur.

'You're free to go," said the centurion abruptly. "But I would put a move on if I were you.' He left them at the doorway and walked quickly toward the dock gate himself.

The boy's father opened his mouth – not to speak, but out of sheer disbelief. Their incarceration was over, the death sentence that they'd almost accepted, now evaporated. All four rushed to greet each other, and Miriam threw her arms around her husband whilst Ashur and Lio hugged each other gleefully and danced up and down in relief.

Behind them, the centurion now broke into a fast run through the docks."

CHAPTER 6:

Lio's Odyssey Begins

Conna snorted at Lio and his father's unlikely escape, his head still echoing with the crocodile song. "So, just like that, they were released?" he asked the room.

Maddie once more explained. "Someone had bribed the centurion, given him enough money to get home – quit the army!"

"Oh, right... you mean he deserted!" He wandered on, "he could've got shot for that, I saw a documentary about that – deserters..."

"Actually the punishment at that time was 'garrotting'," explained Tom patiently.

Conna realised, "Yeah... well."

"Garrotting?" asked Bex.

"I'm sure that one of the boys can tell you later," Tom spared himself the gruesome description.

Conna's tongue lolled out as he mimed being strangled.

"So who bribed him then?" Bex asked, "And why?"

"On the face of it, it was quite simple. On the evening before, Miriam and Ashur had fled back to the house, to store their belongings until they could meet up with Kyrros and Lio, they were not about to leave without them. Miriam had left Ashur briefly to check that the coast was clear. Miriam then went to see if she could find a boat owner ready to take them all – anywhere. But she was intercepted by a shorter than average Roman soldier of some sort, wearing a black uniform. Far from being the heartless troops that

58

they were thought of, this man seemed immediately to understand their plight. He took pity on her, wanted to help, and offered to help her and her husband – the King's Engineer – and his family. He knew someone, it seemed, a rich merchant who was leaving the next morning with a valuable cargo: statues that had been 'rescued' from the temples and the Great Library. The merchant would no doubt be grateful, he assured her, if he and her important and obviously trustworthy husband would accompany the cargo to Rhodos – for its safety. If they all met this merchant there later, he would be sure to sort the whole matter out.

However, returning to the house and to Ashur, Miriam had learned from the young girl that she had seen Kyrros and Lio being marched away in the direction of the palace. At that disastrous news, she had later run quickly back alone, to meet the soldier's colleague. The merchant, who was waiting in the place exactly as described, stood by himself. She wished only to tell the well dressed, though quite drunken man that they could not now go. But as she had explained why, the merchant's soldier friend emerged from the shadows after all – he had just arrived back, he said. He then spoke up, telling her that early next morning he would, on her behalf, make enquiries with the palace guards. He was sure they would all eventually be able to come to some financial arrangement to cover his costs.

Bex stepped back into the tale. "So it was this mysterious soldier and his colleague that rescued them all?"

"Yes," answered Tom, "by bribing the centurion on their behalf. Of course, Kyrros was a man of honour and promised to repay this debt.

"Weren't they all a bit suspicious?" challenged Alex.

"Of course", Tom continued. "They all more than suspected that they were being used. Used, that is, as a convenient decoy to cover up, or legitimise what was an obvious looting operation. When Miriam told Kyrros the tale on his release from the dungeon, he was only too aware of what they were getting into. He assumed that he would at some point be called upon to vouch for the excuse that the prized statues were indeed being rescued. It became patently obvious, he knew, when later that morning, they found out what the 'cargo vessel' was. Though ultimately, at that point in time, he was only too willing to play along – to get his family out of further danger."

"So then what happened to Lio's family?" asked Maddie.

"Ah, then," said Tom drifting back: "Lio and his small family began the long journey back to the island of his birth!"

As bizarre as Tom's tale had become – with the mention of the Crocodile Song especially – everyone listened on as the old man continued:

"It was at this point, that Lio and his small family continued their escape from the Alexandrine war. However, their hope to find a safe haven was eventually to be dashed.

Miriam told her family that they all had to hurry if they were to make it on time to their vessel – back to the main dock and then across to the Pharos Island where the galleys lay. At high tide, two hours after first light, it would leave – with or without them. Time was pressing.

'We must retrieve whatever we can of our belongings,' Lio's father reminded them, 'they may not be much, but they are all we now have.'

And so, they ran quickly back from the square, to their old quarters, before starting to carry their bags for the mile or so to the harbour. Within minutes, they were hurrying – hopefully not too conspicuously – across the square, with the four bundles of their belongings. Lio's giveaway coloured hair was covered with his hood. Kyrros also carried Miriam's doctor's bag past the still smouldering ruin that had been the library.

Thin wisps of smoke rose from its ashes as they passed by the place where it had stood. A few people were already scratching around amongst the broken roof tiles and clumps of plaster to see what they could salvage. A thick-set man heaved at a bronze handle that he had wound a rag around – obviously still hot – trying to salvage the huge pot that Lio had hidden inside just a few months ago. But the man looked crestfallen as only half of the broken pot emerged. The boy, Lio, clambered briefly up and across the wreckage as the others walked around and past it. Where the Hippo-Chronos chamber had been, there was only a pile of rubble. Nothing remotely identifiable remained of the room itself – and there was no sign of the machine. His horse, his friend that had saved both himself and Ashur, was evidently buried deep beneath the high piles of marble and granite. Lio almost wept with despair at the thought of never seeing it again. But then his father's shout of urgency shook him from his mawkish thoughts, and Lio ran to catch up.

Although a battle had been fought only the day before, the atmosphere in the harbour was extraordinarily calm – eerily quiet. All signs of normal commerce had long stopped. Still, it was no easy task gaining access to the bridge over to the island. Roman guards were posted all around and continued to slow them down by asking the same repeated questions. 'Who are you, and where are you going?' It was only for the fact that word had been left and bribes already paid out, that the family were able to get across at all. What had remained seaworthy of the Egyptian fleet of the night before had long since fled. All that was left were the half-sunken vessels which still blocked the arches of the bridge below. Those others that had sunk in the deep harbour had almost vanished from view. Victory really did belong to Caesar, although the land siege of Alexandria and the war for Egypt would last a little longer. Until finally, only weeks later, still only at the age of fifteen, Ptolemy would himself be killed – betrayed by his own generals' reckless stupidity as the Egyptians fled from their defeat at the decisive Battle of the Nile. By now, the sleep deprived four shuffled along as fast as they could, slightly out of breath. They trudged toward a line of low galleys that were tied up to the dock – the Rhodian fleet. Of course, Kyrros realised as soon as he had seen the line of ships from the bridge, that their task here was complete.

Being mercenary forces, they had been retired from action. It was not in Caesar's interest to go on paying their wages without reason. Obviously then, it was time for them to return home. And, as they were leaving, each of the masters of the vessels now had an opportunity to supplement their wages by taking on cargo. Accordingly, the vessels were all packed with boxes and crates of various shapes and sizes, and, of course, the many statues and sculptures. Some ships were still packing extra cargo that was even now lying on the dockside. Clearly no one was returning empty-handed. The commander of their own particular galley greeted them perfunctorily – this was not kindness, it was business. 'Get on board quickly, my cabin is now yours,' he looked only cursorily, 'you have a generous benefactor.'

'Where is he?' Lio's mother asked.

'He's travelling on the first boat,' he nodded toward the Pharos tower at the farthest end of the dock. He left a message for you: 'If he doesn't see you until you arrive, he said that he is grateful to have been of service to fellow Rhodians.' Lio's father looked intrigued, as they all did.

But how did he know that they were from Rhodos, Lio wondered. *Perhaps he'd previously known or worked with Kyrros?* Nevertheless, the boy couldn't believe his luck. Despite everything that had happened to him there years before, he was about to go home. *Perhaps,* he thought, *they may even settle there.*

Ashur looked less happy.

Kyrros also looked intrigued. 'Miriam? He really must be very wealthy, this merchant friend of yours. You must have made quite an impression,' he raised his eyebrows teasingly.

His wife smiled back, 'perhaps he is just a kind-hearted philanthropist like you,' she joked. Kyrros never had been loose with his own hard-earned money.

As Lio followed the others down and onto the deck, coaxing Ashur once more, he looked toward the Pharos Tower. The strange equipment – the burning mirrors – were now removed, packed away, no doubt, for possible use at another time. *At least,* thought Lio and Kyrros both, *the scholars and technicians who had been collected from the Mouseion would now presumably be freed.*

Unnoticed by them, in the distance, the last piece of cargo was being hoisted off the dock. The particularly large and heavy looking wooden crate was being loaded onto the second of the galleys, along with other last minute boxes and packages. One of the crew looked down at his hand as he manhandled it onto the deck. He cursed under his breath, thinking he had cut his hand, but then realised it was not blood. He wiped the oily pigment onto his backside. Soon it would be time to cast-off.

Lio followed the others on board their own ship, last in the line. Within a few minutes of getting into the cabin in the stern, the ship had disembarked and the rowers below deck headed out of the harbour. Above them, Lio and his family each looked out of the four opened hatches and back to Alexandria. At the sight, the boy's head became filled with all the jumbled up memories he had of the place – good and bad – and he became suddenly melancholy. The galley's sail was unfurled, the oars shipped, and the vessel now moved with the wind. They briefly turned to the north-east. Again last in line, passing the Pharos tower. And again Lio looked up into the sky in wonderment at the lighthouse. Despite everything, already he hoped to see it again someday. 'Perhaps when I am older', he mumbled under his breath,' and wars are over!'

With that, the sails were trimmed to carry the line of ships north-north-west – directly en-route to Rhodos. The boy looked over his shoulder at Ashur and she smiled sheepishly at him for the first time in days, instantly brightening his spirits again. He tried to guess what it might be like to be in her place – how this adventure was so new to her, and how stressful it must have all been to her. She was in a new place and in a new time. She was part of a new, loving family, but now there were new threats. Lio smiled back happily, trying his best to reassure her.

Then, from nowhere, a low, thick, sea-fret began to roll into the harbour. The combination of this, together with the midday sun shining brightly down for one last time, silhouetted the great city in a misty, dove grey outline against the clear blue sky. Only the Pharos tower was fully visible, reaching high into the heavens. Now, Lio realised, they were all simply refugees, awash at sea. No plans of what they would do when they reached Rhodos, but happy to be together again. Something would turn up, reassured Kyrros, it always did. It would take two to three days of favourable winds, and Lio looked forward to it.

Ominously though, as they passed into deeper water, the ship started to plunge deeply forward into the rolling black sea, and dark clouds began to gather in the distance. Then they heard the unmistakeable rumbling of thunder.

CHAPTER 7:

The Image of Youth

That night, their first at sea, the sky was black, the blackest that any of them had known in a long time: not that anyone in the cabin actually noticed. Kyrros was ill, Ashur was not so well herself on this, her first sea journey. But with Miriam keeping an ever watchful eye on all of them – and after the sleepless nights they'd each had since the distant evening the messenger had visited the farm – they nevertheless got quickly and soundly to sleep.

The next day, the rain began to hit the ship from all sides. The ever-changing direction of the wind made heavy work of the journey, forcing the master to constantly re-trim the mainsail. He also stowed the directional foresail completely so that he had to steer with the heavy larboard at the stern. The trouble with sailing by the wind, Kyrros complained in the cabin, was that the vessel would always be at its mercy, and yet, between that and being propelled by man-power – oars – sailing was at least the most efficient way to get about.

'How so,' asked Lio?

'Each rower has to be well fed, enough at least to give them enough energy to pull on the oars, which takes a lot of resources', he offered academically. 'Whereas, if someone could devise a machine to propel them through the water: something like the paddle wheels that were used to lift water from a river, a smaller version of Ptolemy's wheel… possibly even driven by an engine…' he began to get carried away. 'I recently read about a new device called an eolipile – a nozzled pressure vessel that spins around on a central axis. Part filled with water, and heated by fire, it produces steam. And as the steam escapes from the nozzle, it is this in turn that produces the device's rotating effect. It is worth investigating, don't you think Lio?'

'Don't you think we've been lucky enough to escape as it is?' asked Miriam worriedly, 'without you bringing more attention to ourselves?'

Kyrros looked huffily back at her.

'Instead of filling their heads with these fanciful ideas, why don't you tell them another story more appropriate to children?' she turned to face Lio and Ashur.

Kyrros pulled a face at her behind her back. 'Alright then,' he conceded. He suddenly grinned before turning to Lio and Ashur both. 'How about one of the greatest stories in the world – and oldest?'

They both nodded.

"Then I shall tell you a story that was told to me by my own father – the story of the Greeks' return home from a long war in the eastern Mediterranean – Homer's Odyssey, just like the one we seem to be on ourselves!' At that, to the delight of all of the occupants of the cabin, Kyrros began to recount the full and highly exaggerated tale of Odysseus' return to his homeland of Ithaca – the story packed with Cyclops, Sirens and witches. It staved off the boredom for the remainder of their journey.

On the third day at sea, the weather grew worse – dangerously so. The wind tore at the sheets that had been drawn over the statues on deck, and the master and crew began to fear the weather would not let up. Through the tiny cabin window, Lio and his family watched as the master and a few of the crew 'sacrificed' one of the largest marble sculptures. Appropriately, it was Poseidon, god of the sea – now re-named Neptune by the Romans.

The statue was dragged from beneath one of the loosened sheets which flew away in the wind. The crew heaved at it, but as it moved slowly, its massive weight only made the bow of the ship list menacingly to the starboard. Frustrated, the master ordered his crew to push harder. Then, as they did, it suddenly slid along the wet deck and crashed through the side-rail on the same side, plummeting overboard. Satisfied, the master prayed for better weather. The senseless, superstitious waste left Lio's family astounded. Also, dangerously, it left part of the handrail missing on that side. Now, half of the ship's cargo was uncovered and would be open to the elements for the rest of the journey. Nevertheless, the rough weather continued until well into the evening, when Kyrros continued telling his version of the Odyssey. Thereafter they tried to sleep again. Thankfully, overnight, the weather started to turn. The master's sacrifice, he was certain, had worked.

In the morning, the sea was much calmer – although the wind was icy and the sky was still grey. More importantly for Kyrros, his nausea had subsided. Gradually, after wrapping up well – thankfully their heavy winter clothes had not earlier been ditched into the Nile with Kyrros' tools – one by one, each of them ventured to go out on deck. As they emerged, the master warned each in turn not to stray too near his cargo. It was, he said, too valuable for words. Kyrros snorted at the idea, recognising most of them as the copies of statues he knew from other places. But, there again, he was not yet aware of to whom the cargo belonged. They were images that were familiar to all of them, from around not only Alexandria – images that Kyrros recognised from his travels, especially to Athens – quite famous statues by the classic sculptors. They were mostly full sized, though some were head and shoulder busts. And some of the statues were, of course, headless, ready to have replacements – the heads of their new owner grafted onto them. Gods and men all mixed up, all tied together on the deck. All of them fake of course: good fakes, but mostly student copies from the Mouseion workshops. Kyrros and Miriam strolled arm in arm around the deck, whilst Ashur and Lio strolled behind. Each one of them looked in admiration at the artistry of it all. However, they all studiously avoided the gap in the temporarily repaired, splintered handrail where the statue of Poseidon had been ditched, now tied only with a rope.

It wasn't until their parents had started to go back inside that Ashur began to giggle at one particular statue, the head and face of which only she could see from her slightly shorter perspective. There, in the front row, just beneath the remaining covering sheet, stood the bronze statue of a naked young man. She looked at Lio, pointing to it and giggling harder, until Kyrros turned back to look at what had caused this merriment. Although neither of them had seen the finished works, both Kyrros and Lio had seen the wax proofs before they had been taken to the casting foundry. Now, gently folding the sheet back from the face and head, Kyrros looked onto the recently completed twinned works that had not even made it to their destination inside the library entrance lobby. They were though, unmistakeably, the faces of Kyrros and his assistant – Helio – to give Lio his proper title. If final proof was needed, there it was on each base. Two name plaques struck in lead, read: 'Andronicus of Cyrrhus, Philosopher and Engineer'; and 'Sculpture of a youth with the world at his fingertips'. As Ashur giggled on, Lio shrugged his shoulders but he himself began to smirk at the likenesses of them both, and the probable source of Ashur's mirth.

The head of Kyrros could not have been more lifelike, his unsmiling face and the uncompromising look beneath the heavy beard looking out in his no-nonsense way across the deck. The pale glass irises of his eyes even gave a good approximation of his well known maniacal stare. The finished statue stood as tall as the great man himself, clothed formally from his sandals, up to the chiton – the thigh length kilt, and his himation – the symbolic mantle draped across his right arm, posed scribe in hand.

The other portrait was far more idealised than Lio looked, at least at present. The bronze boy looked more like eighteen years of age – or even older. The look on his face was in every detail Lio, but a much older version of it. Lio's boyish good looks had been expertly and uncannily transformed by the sculptor. His face was slightly longer and more mature than it was at present, his nose equally more elegant and his eyes, the irises picked out like Kyrros', in glass paste. This time though, everyone noticed, the wrong colour –

hazel, instead of green. He had however, retained the tousled hair, although trimmed a little. The statue represented a well built, athletic figure with 'everything' in proportion for an older youth and the hair on his head, along with an extra, triangular, area of bodily hair picked out expertly in gold leaf. This was, no doubt, the reason for Ashur's giggling. He stood with the weight being carried on his left leg, his right bent at the knee. His left arm hung down easily while his right arm was outstretched. In that hand, he delicately held by the tips of his fingers what looked like a large apple, but was on closer examination, a small solid golden version of a globe. It really was expertly done. Lio looked from Kyrros, to Ashur, then to Miriam, saying nothing.

It was Miriam who broke the embarrassed silence. 'Someday you're going to make someone very happy Lio, I wonder who it will be?'

Kyrros smiled broadly and led Miriam into the cabin, leaving the two young friends to play.

Slowly but surely, before too long, the winter skies turned grey again, and though the wind and the sea remained reasonably calm, the sound of distant thunder began to roll once more. Flashes of lightning lit up the horizon, so they returned to the cabin themselves for more of Kyrros' retold Odyssey. Later that evening, the weather changed dramatically and the transition from reasonably calm, to extremely rough was not gradual. It was as swift and as sudden as the crack of a whip.

Lio's father had gone up on deck again to take the air, but it was not long before he came back to the cabin, ashen faced. 'Prepare yourselves for a bumpy ride,' he warned, before lying face down on his bunk. Curious as to what was approaching, Lio sloped off outside. Ashur preferred to stay in the cabin with her mother. All around, white horses were picking up on the peaks of the waves. The icy wind that was driving them forward was also driving them into heavy weather. Four of the crew were checking the lashings of the cargo, to ensure the ropes did not break free. While another, ran a rope from their cabin to the mast then forward to the bow – a lifeline – in case the crew needed to grasp it. Dead ahead, not more than a few minutes away, a huge, low black cloud loomed up on the ship – just visible against the cloud-filled, dark grey sky. Lit up occasionally by lightning above them, the rolling, crackling thunder now boomed out close by. The boy stood and looked in fascination at the dark patch below it. Mesmerised by it, he wondered what it might be, only realising as they drew closer that the patch was rain – torrential rain.

The sailors had now all disappeared below decks and Lio was left alone in the face of a squall. One moment he was fine, in the next he was hit by the blast of a cold sheet of rain. The shock of its suddenness stiffened him as though he had been slapped in the face. At once, the ship began to pitch and roll ever more wildly as the low depression made the waves surge around them. And yet, throughout all this, and despite the obvious danger, Lio realised that he was far from scared, he was in fact elated by his lone-ness in the extreme elemental event. Each peak and trough that made the galley buck, dropping bow first, then slowly rising up again, was to the boy, a most exhilarating ride.

All at once, as it was struck by lightning, he saw the mast of the lead ship lit up as if in daylight. Then, something that the boy had been told was impossible, within a split second, the lightning hit it again. At its stern, he saw the larboard itself – the rudder – drop into the sea. Gradually the leading ship struggled to keep its course, and it began to veer off to the larboard and to the west. As Lio stared, the ropes around the statues on their own deck started to grow slack and the cargo lurched from starboard to larboard, from fore to aft, until it appeared obvious that some of the statues were about to break free. Of all the ones not to be tied down properly, they were those which he and Ashur had tugged at to get a better view, that of Kyrros and the youth – Lio.

Who knows what the boy was thinking of? He should at best have alerted the crew somehow, and at the worst got out of its way. But, stupidly, and acting from bravado, he decided to rescue the bronzes. Making his way slowly forward along the lifeline, not more

70

than ten paces, he balanced himself on the rolling deck. There, he attempted to tighten the rope that should have held them firm. But it was at that point that a high wave crashed into the side of the galley and over the deck – catching Lio off-guard. It swept him away from the lifeline and sent him reeling into the splintered broken end of the handrail, gashing and breaking his left arm badly, although cold and now fear temporarily numbed any pain. He grabbed the rail with his right hand and waited for the ship to pitch the opposite way. As soon as it did, he let go of the rail, then ran back to the lifeline. Still not realising the peril he was in, nor the extent of his injury, the boy stooped to pick up the end of the rope that had fallen between the statues. Shoving his right leg into a small gap, he tried to steady himself. But as he did, the ship again lurched, moving the statues and this time crushing and bruising his leg at the knee. The pain was searing. Lio cried out in agony and panic as another wave covered him. Coughing, he took a mouthful of salt water into his stomach. Again the ship pitched and the statue moved, enough at first to let him retrieve his leg, but its sudden release only served to send him tumbling over, hitting his other knee. He tried to stand as another wave caught him full in the face for the second time, though this time it drove him backwards to the gap in the broken handrail.

Now, at last, he realised what trouble he had caused himself by his witless display of bravery. Again the waves hit. Now the boy coughed and spluttered, trying to catch his breath as the rain and waves were lashed into him by the wind. He stumbled backward and then spun around out of control. Now facing the blackened sea, he realised this time that he would be lost. Lio managed to let out a single yell of 'help', and then grabbed the rail again. Teetering on the brink, as once again the ship went up and over a wave, he slipped head first over the edge. But as he fell forward, he felt a hand grab him from behind and pull him back. Exhausted, and now suddenly feeling the full pain in his arm as well as his knees, he collapsed into his father's arms. For the second time, Kyrros had rescued the boy from certain death.

Lio awoke later in the cabin, his arm bandaged from elbow to wrist, his knees covered in some sort of thick green ointment that his mother had prepared from the strange things in her bag. Miriam looked relieved as the boy came around. The squall had passed – or rather they had passed through it – within not more than five minutes. Realising at once what had happened, he immediately apologised to his father who was sat beside his bunk. Kyrros was again magnanimous and simply shook his head. 'Someday boy, you will learn the perils of the sea,' he said simply. His mother was less forgiving.

In her release of tension she remonstrated with him – entirely needlessly – that either he or his father might have been killed. Only too aware of the stress he had caused, all the boy could do was apologise again and promise not to do anything as foolish ever again. It seemed to pacify her and the girl who was stood at her side, tracks of dried tears on her face.

Later, as Kyrros retold more of Homer's tale to Lio and Ashur… and Miriam, the pain throbbed mercilessly in Lio's arm and knees, weakening him, and so he slipped into a deep sleep for most of the way 'home'.

It was finally only two days later when the weather had this time properly broken. Lio lay alongside Ashur on the rear of the deck. Their legs again dangling down, his arm now in a sling, they sailed solidly and comfortably up the coast of Rhodos Island. His mother had given him something to counter the pain, although there was still the dull ache to try and put out of his mind. It was the first time they had spotted land for days and Lio became buoyed-up at the thought of seeing his old home – officially this time. He couldn't wait to show off the sights to his mother in particular. Not far off the starboard side, but too distant for the crew to catch, a rainbow shoal of flying fish skipped across the top of the flat-calmed sea. The boat neared land, but not closely, keeping to their straight course for Rhodos Town at the north-east tip of the island. They would be there by the end of the day. So, in the meantime, after listening to Kyrros' conclusion of Homer's account of the tale of Odysseus, the boy and the girl enjoyed basking in the warm winter sunlight.

Looking towards the ancient acropolis of Lindos, Lio spotted the lead ship that had veered off during the squall, struggling to steer properly. It had at least made it to the island and safety, though it now sat squarely on the beach. He overheard the master of their own vessel saying to one of his crew that it would obviously need repairs before going on – they would at least have to replace the larboard. Without it, it would be too dangerous to attempt to negotiate the small and restricted harbour at Rhodos town. For the life of him, Lio couldn't think why that should be so, *what restrictions?* he wondered. The harbour had always looked open enough to him and Ashur. Now, so near to the home of his childhood, Lio's excitement again began to mount. But unnoticed to him, Ashur's face registered something entirely different.

Elsewhere on deck, Miriam and Kyrros wondered how long it would be before they would meet their mysterious benefactor again. *Still, if the vessel's master thought it safer to beach the galley below acropolis, that was his choice,* they each thought disappointedly.

'There goes your saviour,' shouted the master, and now each of the family of four wondered between themselves if they would ever again be able to see him in order to thank him for his kindness.

Meanwhile, on the beach of Lindos harbour, whilst the 'rich merchant' sat around once more in his ordinary and quite scruffy sailor's clothes, the soldier stripped off his breastplate. Now that the sun was out, he was overheating in the black uniform. All he could do was watch frustratingly as the line of galleys passed-by. He stroked his pock-marked face and wondered just how much longer it would take before he would eventually catch up with his precious cargo in the second ship – and the machine's designer in the last."

CHAPTER 8:

Colossus

Conna's face at last registered the sub plot of Lio's voyage. He narrowed his eyes at Alex first, still scribbling, then he looked at each of the girls in turn, but still no-one spoke. Instead, Tom carried on.

"For the rest of that morning, the ship followed the island coastline more closely, eventually turning around the northernmost point of the headland, to sail directly for the main town of Rhodos. From a distance, it did not look much different than it would have appeared five hundred years earlier. But now, as they rounded the long, rocky sea-break and approached more closely, it became immediately apparent to both Lio and Ashur that the town had become a place that neither of them would have recognised even in a thousand years. The harbour was vast, crammed all over and around with cargo ships and boats. They were amazed at how it had grown, but the most amazing thing to them was the sight that greeted them at the harbour entrance. Although Lio had heard the whole tale from several of the museum workers – on several occasions – he was still taken aback at the sheer scale and enormity of what still remained of the Colossus of Helios.

The colossal statue that had once stood over the entrance to the harbour – each foot planted on one of the solid piers – had long since collapsed into the sea. All that remained intact was the partly clad structural metal archway that had been its legs. Separately, propped upright at the harbour entrance, was the part submerged upper-torso and head of the god, his left arm still balancing the vast fire bowl that had been a beacon to ships trying to find the harbour in the fog. *And yet,* thought Lio, *his face still managed to look beneficently out at them all.*

As they negotiated their way past the now partly blocked harbour, the reason why the damaged lead ship might have struggled to bring their own cargo safely back home, Lio's father now gave his own commentary for the benefit of Lio and Ashur:

'In the days since you were last here,' he addressed them, 'and perhaps even precipitated by the very, very public and most shocking events on this island – in which all three of us were involved,' he looked down his nose conspiratorially – 'the worship of Zeus was diminished greatly, especially against the more tangible benefits of the god Helios, or at least of the natural sun. Truthfully, for who knows what reason, here, the worship of Helios became accelerated far ahead that of Zeus. However, a new temple was built and dedicated to the joint deities of Athena and Zeus – further along from the old temple – which still remains. In turn, the old temple was re–dedicated to Apollo – Zeus's son. It is now run by priestesses, and specialises in forgiveness – without which, the penitent cannot enter Hades.' Kyrros raised his bushy eyebrows. 'Of course, this forgiveness is always granted – for a fee! From that day forward, Helios has remained the leading god of the island. That is, until after the death of Alexander the Great and the wars of the diadochi – about two hundred and fifty years ago. These were the wars which Alexander's claimed successors waged against each other.

In an effort to boost his war funds, one of Alexander's generals, Antigonas, had sent his son Demetrius to take this rich island on his behalf. Demetrius brought vast amounts of siege engines and weaponry to help him do so – at absolutely staggering cost. However, after a series of successively disastrous mistakes, and after Alexander's friend Ptolemy the first of Egypt sent troops to help the Rhodians fight the siege, Demetrius had to abandon the island quickly. Two things happened as a result. Firstly, Ptolemy was honoured by the island of Rhodos and was bestowed with the title 'Soter', or Saviour. From then on, he would always be known simply as Ptolemy Soter. Secondly, the successful Rhodians sold Demetrius' machines for a vast fortune, spending some of it in thanks and praise to their patron god Helios by building the hollow structure known as the Colossus of Rhodos.

The statue once towered above the harbour twenty times taller than a man,' Kyrros continued. 'It was one of the tallest statues ever built in the world; his high beacon beckoning ships to pass safely beneath.' Kyrros faithfully quoted the inscription on its plinth:

"To you, oh Sun, the people of Rhodos made this bronze statue reaching to Mount Olympus, when they had pacified the waves of war and crowned their city with the spoils taken from the enemy. Not only over the seas but also on land, did they kindle the lovely torch of freedom and independence! For to the descendants of Herakles belongs dominion over the sea and land".

Alas though, it was not to be for long. The Colossus of Rhodos was not able to withstand the power of the earth itself. Just over fifty years after it had been erected, the statue was toppled by an earthquake and it plummeted into the harbour. All that remains is what you can see in front of you now, testament to the over-ambitious designs of man and the vastly superior forces of nature.

Two generations later,' he finished the tale, 'Ptolemy III offered to pay for it to be rebuilt, but the island's rival religious pilgrimage centre, Delphi – at the hub of the Cyclades islands – warned the island that if they did so "Helios himself would be offended!" The tacit threat paid off, the statue itself was never rebuilt. Thus, no doubt, more pilgrims were persuaded to visit Delphi and therefore enrich their coffers instead.'

The ship sailed closely past the collapsed monument, and though now less than half its original height, it still soared taller than the top of the mast. As the family looked on, a small boy, not more than ten years old, jumped from its head with an excited yell to land with a splash amongst his waiting friends. Apart from now defending the harbour from swift attack, the statue still at least provided another useful purpose!

Heading into the safe haven, they disembarked. All were thankful to the master, but still aware by his expression, of his suspicion that the boy had been entirely the cause of the damage of some of his precious cargo. He did not give so much as a rearwards glance to the odd looking boy with the eyeglasses. Within seconds of leaving the ship, the family was pestered, jostled and cajoled by half a dozen guest house owners to stay with them. Finding accommodation would never be a problem on the island. Behind them, all of the ships' cargoes were being taken quickly along to a vast warehouse. They were mostly statues – and one large crate."

Tom looked knowingly at the faces that surrounded him. "Even after everything that had happened to him on that island, Lio really was looking forward so much to taking that walk. It is difficult to imagine is it not? But after all, it was the place that he was born. And, as it is often said, 'There is no place like home'.

Next morning, having rested well in the guest house by the port the previous night, Lio was eager to see what changes had been made in the town, and especially on the Acropolis. In remarkably little time, his knees especially appeared to have healed – at least enough for him to walk well enough – albeit with a slight limp. Miriam again changed the dressing on his arm before they all made their way into town.

Although the line of the main street had not changed, there was now a beautiful amphitheatre cut into the hill, an open air 'gymnasium' for athletes. This 'place of nakedness', had a huge, seated hippodrome where even now, riders thundered past on their horses. But it was the density of the crowd that was the most noticeable of all changes. Only once before had Lio seen such a sizeable crowd on Rhodos – and that was on the long past day of the eclipse. The boy pushed the memory to the back of his mind as they were swept along with the crowd and into the agora and marketplace. Now he was filled only with renewed excitement. Lio took Ashur by the hand as they threaded their way through – just like years ago for him – but only months ago for Ashur. He had sadly forgotten this fact – together with his promise that he would take her away from this island forever. In his excitement, he had not noticed the look of dread on her face. The girl was being led back by the hand: to revisit the place of her enslavement and brutal mistreatment – and the scene of her brother Marduk's death.

Ashur reluctantly tripped along behind Lio, to where they had expected to find the marble ramp up to the Acropolis; but even that had changed. Instead, there stood a wide marble staircase, making ascent to the higher level much easier. The boy stopped to allow the others to catch up while the girl sat cross-legged at the bottom. Head down, she absent-mindedly looked at a small lizard poking its head out from a crack in the wall in front of her. When it decided that it was safe to come out, the lizard crawled uneasily across the low marble wall and stood over the fossilised indentation of a seashell. After a moment, Ashur's hand shot out quickly and grabbed it. Then, slowly, she brought it up to her face to examine it just as she had tried to do on the same spot a short while ago – the time that she, her brother and Lio had been returning from their swim in the harbour. That had been over five hundred years ago – but it was still almost yesterday for the girl. Ashur did not cry, but a deep sadness overwhelmed her as she was transported back in time. She remembered that rare day away from the temple, the last day before the new, young high priest had arrived. A day when all three, Ashur, Lio and Marduk had stopped there to play, seeing if anyone could catch one of the lizards, but no one could. Today, her brother would have been proud of her small victory.

Now, Ashur opened her hand gently to let the reptile's head peep out. She looked directly into its golden eyes. If anyone had been near enough to her, they might have sworn that they heard her murmur something to it, perhaps whispering a boy's name. Then, without showing Lio that she had at last caught one, she held her fist back over the fossil and let the defenceless creature go. She watched it jerk its tiny head nervously. It nodded up and down, not moving from the spot, then suddenly it shot into a deep crack and was gone... and with it, so was Ashur.

Kyrros and Miriam finally caught up, but when Lio looked down to where Ashur had been sitting, she was nowhere to be seen. Miriam called out as she thought she saw her disappear in front of them, up the steps. Exasperatedly, without rest, the married couple started upwards while the boy again weaved his way in front more easily. He stopped at the top, straining to see if he could see the girl. But if it had been her, she had now vanished completely.

Lio continued to look out around him, ignoring the spectacular open sea-view that now enthralled Miriam and Kyrros – they were not overly worried for Ashur as yet. Every single temple that the boy saw had changed. Yes, the same religions, variously Egyptian, Persian, Egyptian and Greek, were still represented, and on the very same sites. Though now, the old buildings had all been knocked down and rebuilt, bigger and bolder. Even now, there were still the moving statues, but now, Lio knew, unlike in the days of his early childhood, they were not powered by children. Instead, they were moved by a myriad of complex temple machines – the new and ingenious machines that his father, Kyrros, had told him about. The three walked steadily along the top of the hill, both parents now calling out in increasing alarm for Ashur. Lio looked behind him, at his mother and father as they neared his old home. *Where was she?* he thought idly, at first wondering whether it was a game of hers, but becoming increasingly annoyed. Although he had not realised at the time, come to think of it, last night at the guest house, Ashur had seemed a little subdued. *But she had seemed alright this morning hadn't she?* Ashur had, he supposed, been a little introspective, but everyone assumed that she had only been recovering after the long sea journey.

Finally approaching the crowd outside the Temple of Helios, Lio consciously averted his gaze as they passed the temple beside it. It was the single remaining original temple – the Temple of Zeus – the temple now re-dedicated as the Temple of Apollo. With his back to it, Lio stood and gazed up at the newer temple of Helios beside it.

On its rebuilt front stood the original statue of his grandfather's god, Helios and his four horses. They were mounted against the triangular frieze above the six fluted marble columns at the front. Temporarily, he pushed Ashur to the back of his mind, although Miriam and Kyrros now started to worry, and continued to look and call out around them. *Now*, Lio thought selfishly, *Ashur is spoiling things.* This was his big opportunity to impress his parents with his knowledge of the place. He began to get exasperated. Without further thought, the boy let himself get deliberately carried away in the presence of his father – and especially his mother. 'Look,' he said, 'this carved image is the same one that stood here over five hundred years ago? The very same god that had the eyes of green emeralds – now "lost",' he said smirking at the open secret between them. Both Kyrros and Miriam shot him a dark look in return. A few others stopped to listen to him. 'This is the god who transports the sun across the sky.' Miriam and Kyrros looked clearly more worried now, looking around them. 'And there,' he pointed, 'are his four horses, Pyrios, Aeos, Aethon and Phlegnon, who pull the chariot for him.' Kyrros gripped the boy's shoulder, shaking his head in sudden annoyance, a small crowd beginning to gather.

Belatedly, Lio realised what he had said to annoy his father and stopped dead in embarrassment and guilt. There was, after all, nothing remotely amusing to him or any of them about the emeralds – or more especially, how they had been lost. Lio had been showing off. Momentarily elated at being home, he had failed to remember that it was Marduk who had been killed in removing them – his best friend – and Ashur's brother!

The boy was suddenly ashamed at his own callousness. He looked around expecting Ashur to be beside him, so that he could beg her forgiveness. But now he realised, too late, that her quiet manner since they had landed had been masking her fear and loathing at having been effectively forced back here to face her demons. And Lio very much doubted Ashur would ever be ready to do that. Of course, it now began to dawn on them all why Ashur had disappeared and what they'd done in bringing her back to this very spot – the scene of all her horrors. Between themselves they made a quick search plan. Without delay, each ran off in opposite directions in near panic – to find the girl before anything could happen to her.

For over an hour they scoured the entire area. Lio pushed his way painfully through the crowds, though being careful not to break his repairing arm again. Then, eventually, from sheer desperation, he went back to the one place that he would have never imagined her to go. Not being able to find her anywhere else he could think of, he found the still usable secret doorway into the Temple of Apollo – the old Temple of Zeus. He crept through the subterranean passageway and stumbled warily into the inner sanctum.

It was the last place he would have normally expected to find her after all. But to his eternal relief, he found the girl in there. Ashur stood shaking bodily. She was all alone in front of the same old line of sacrificial bowls – though now gold ones – and the same huge statue – though now fully clothed again and with its new, younger head. She stared up at the face of the god, a clean shaven face, unlike the bearded god that had terrified her as a child, but still an idol that epitomised all she hated and detested. Now, as Lio watched from behind, there was only a look of dogged frustration and anger on her face. That under the pretence of being a priest of these gods, a man had chosen to mistreat and beat her so savagely. And, he had so cruelly mistreated her brother that he had been killed. Now she could do no more than shake her tightened fists in vexed frustration that, even after five hundred years, these monstrosities were still here. Tears ran silently down her face.

Lio crossed the small space and stood quietly behind her, knowing only a small part of how she felt, but finally realising that the silly, even naïve ambition that he had held secretly for the past few days, could never be. Their small family would never be able to settle here on his home island. There were simply too many painful memories here which would never leave the girl. He stepped forward and gently took her clenched fist. 'Ashur,' the boy said softly, 'Please forgive me. I am sorry that I forgot my promise so soon. I will never, ever forget again.' Ashur looked for one last time at the idol, then turned and sobbed quietly into the folds of Lio's clothes. Just then, a woman's voice shrieked out, giving them both a start. 'How did you get into my temple without paying? Get out, get out at once!' *So much for forgiveness*, thought Lio, *some things never change.* With that, the boy led his charge silently back into the light, to find Kyrros and Miriam. It was time to get away from there.

If Lio had ever entertained the notion that the little girl he had thrust upon Miriam and Kyrros had not been a much loved part of the family, the elation shown by them – and Miriam in particular – when he brought her back to them, left him in no doubt that it was unfounded. Her mother, in particular overjoyed, hugged and kissed her as though she'd never expected to see her alive again. Kyrros' eyes similarly welled up.

No, they all agreed, after this, there would be no more debate. They would, at the earliest opportunity, head for Athens, just as Kyrros had suggested days ago. More to the point, although the island of Rhodos was truly wonderful in many respects, they would get off it as soon as possible.

Miriam, Ashur and Lio returned directly to their guest house to prepare their belongings. Miriam washed and hung out to dry their single change of clothes, whilst Kyrros went back down to the harbour to see if he could find them a passage off the island. Within the hour, he had returned – they were in luck. That very evening a large cargo vessel with a cabin below deck – no doubt nothing more than a store room – was to sail from the harbour, around to the port of Heraklion on the island of Kriti – or Crete. Then the ship was to pick up another cargo and take it directly to Piraeus, the port of Athens. Not a direct route then, though few were, but it would at least allow them all to get off the island of Rhodos without delay, no matter that the long and undoubtedly rough sea journey would be more prolonged. No one wished to see Ashur remain distressed for a moment longer than was necessary. And, in particular, Lio was determined not to let his vulnerable charge feel this badly ever again.

At six o'clock then, they boarded the heavy Roman corbita, a proper, safer cargo vessel. Miriam kept the scarf high around her neck, covering the gold torc, and they began to settle themselves in what indeed was a hastily cleared out 'store room', although it was used for many purposes, not least as a brig – a jail – and for occasionally transporting a few slaves. The passage was permitted, the master said, on expressed condition that they would not be allowed to leave their 'cabin' throughout the voyage – 'for safety reasons' – he explained. The four filed into the dark and dingy interior. Spare coils of various sized and rather smelly ropes lined the walls, hastily covered by some old sails. Two tiny, double-decked bunks were each tied to the walls using the high line of dozens of heavy metal securing loops. A single, small window hatch through the stern gave the only light, apart from a single, tiny oil lamp.

Outside on the dock there was a clamour as one last large and heavy part of the cargo was being loaded into the hold. All eyes followed the red daubed crate that was suspended in the air – not that Lio's family could see it from their restricted hatch. The Roman master shouted and cursed especially noisily, waving his arms animatedly at the thought of it crashing down onto the many statues he'd just finished loading from the dockside. The hold was already crammed. Repeated shouts of 'faster', mixed with 'careful… watch out…' were exchanged between the master and those who were responsible for loading the ship. Until, without too much fuss, they heard the clunk of it landing close next door, in the hold. Once loaded, It did not take too long before they pulled away from the dock and headed out of Rhodos harbour. They sailed past more children splashing around the earthly remains of the Colossus of Helios and turned to head east-south-east, in the direction of their port of call, Heraklion.

As he looked back across the sea and at his birthplace, Lio now looked upon the island with what he could only call bitter disappointment. All the good memories he'd ever held about it were now submerged by the bad. Sadly, unlike Alexandria, the boy had no ambition to ever revisit the town or the island of his birth ever again."

Unseen behind Tom's glasses, tears began to well up in his eyes as he said ominously: "However, as they headed for Crete, now began the final, tragic leg of the refugee family's very last journey together."

CHAPTER 9:

Kidnapped

Tom continued steadily: "In contrast to the mood of the strange looking boy in his hold, the middle aged Roman master was both happy and proud of himself, not to say smug. In the past forty eight hours, no doubt due to his last promise of an offering to Neptune, his luck had finally changed. As soon as he had secured the contract, he had then prised the golden orb from the outstretched hand of one of the bronze statues and thrown it overboard.

He had been waiting in the harbour with an empty vessel, no cargo forthcoming, when the fleet of galleys had arrived. Seeing the cargo, and guessing where it might be eventually headed, not only had he managed to secure the transport of the most valuable cargo he had ever transported, he had also been assured that Caesar himself would be personally delighted to reward him if he delivered the emperor's statues safely.

Then, an hour ago, when the hapless Greek idiot who had turned up at the docks and offered to pay for himself and his entire family to be transported off the island, the Roman could not believe his good fortune. After all, selling travellers into slavery had been a sideline of his for years – and, they were always completely oblivious to it until it was too late. Finally, seeing no one around to guard the last piece of cargo – the only piece he was warned not to take – he had managed to get it quickly on board. He had then got out of the harbour before he could be caught with it. The contents of that extra crate would now be his. Whatever the value of the weird looking bronze sculpture, it was certainly heavy. At the very least, he could melt it down to yield the precious metal. Now, all he had to do was get the entire cargo to its destination, and on top of the gold coins he had already received in part payment, he would be worth an absolute fortune. He flipped one of the largest gold coins back and forth between his fingers, smirking again at how he was going to repay the old fool who had given it to him in payment for his family's journey.

The corbita rolled slowly away from the broken Colossus and away from the sound of laughing children perched on it. It made its way around the north coast of Rhodos this time, hugging the island on their larboard side. As they passed, despite its obvious hurry, a lone ship stood well off – to let them through the narrow gap. It had taken two days on the beach at Lindos to get the damage to the leading galley mended – a replacement larboard being the least of the master's worries. In beaching the ship, he had managed to hit the only large rock there, and they had been forced to repair and re-caulk the hole in the hull as well as re-fix the damaged ship's bronze ram that had been dangerously slackened on the same rock. In future, the Greek master would be careful to make a bigger offering to both Zeus – to avoid another bolt of lightning being launched at him – and to Poseidon – in thanks for him not being taken to the bottom of the sea.

At the bow of the galley, the short, black uniformed soldier was now desperate to get to his own single part of the entire haul that had been looted from Alexandria. As the corbita passed, and his own ship turned to slip into the harbour, the soldier put on his distinctive, plumed helmet and made sure he would be first onto the dock. It was only a matter of finding where the entire cargo had been stored before he would finally get his hands on what, until now, he could only dream of!

For Lio's family, the three and a half days journey to Heraklion, the port of Crete was this time uneventful and the four settled down to the drudgery that they'd shortly become used to. Never having been there before, Lio was intrigued to be going to the legendary island of King Minos of Knossos. His imagination was fuelled by the story of the great king, the labyrinth built by Daedalus, and inhabited by the half-man, half-bull Minotaur. And of Icarus – Daedalus' overconfident son – who perished by flying too near the sun. Of course, most of the story had been dismissed as superstition by the storyteller – Kyrros – except to say that, perhaps buried deeply somewhere and covered by the mists of time, the tale might have been sparked by one obscure event or another. *'Behind every fanciful story and legend,'* Kyrros told Lio and Ashur, *'there is nearly always a spark of truth!'* Not that there remained any traces of the ancient places now. Unlike the great city of Wilusha – or Troy, the place where one of the greatest legendary heroes, Achilles, had perished – which was now a popular Roman visitor attraction. To Kyrros, Knossos was simply a fairytale if you will, but one which fascinated everyone all the same.

Nevertheless, even after returning frequently to discuss it all with Kyrros – perhaps a little too often – Lio grew restless. Both he and Ashur took it in turn to stare out of the tiny hatch hour after hour, to see if they could see anything other than the sea, which they rarely did – and then it was only to watch as unidentifiable islands seemed to drift by. Bit by bit, hour after hour, the journey began to bore them all, and Lio began to wish for something more exciting to happen. However, with the benefit of hindsight, the boy would come to forever regret that wish.

It was on the fourth morning that Lio awoke to the heavy repeated bump of the ship's hull against the dock. They had moored in the busy port of Heraklion. It was not as busy as Alexandria of course, but at least the noise and clamour was as great. Lio grappled around for his glasses and looked again through the window. Hundreds of people milled around on the dockside, loading and unloading the various vessels there.

His mother and Ashur were still asleep, snuggling against each other in the lower level of one of the bunks. His father was nowhere to be seen. Before long, the bumping eventually woke Miriam. She immediately asked if the boy knew where Kyrros was.

Lio was explaining that he didn't, when the door opened and his father walked in with an air of disappointment. Instead of being able to get off for a while and at least allow Lio to set foot on the island of the legendary King Minos, he had been told that they still had to wait on board again 'for their own safety' in the cabin. At least, Kyrros said, it would be without delay that they would get under way.

It was 'without delay' then, that after a further frustrating four hours of being cooped up in the overheating 'barrel', as Lio's father now openly referred to it, he complained noisily that they could all have all been for a short walk into town by then – if it was not for the intransigence of the Roman master of the vessel. Kyrros, now plainly refusing to stay locked up and bored in their cabin without reason, decided that they would at least stretch their legs on the dockside after all.

The master stood not far from his ship, on the verge of doing a deal over his 'slaves'. He waited for his contact to return. But then his attention was grabbed by something else – a notice of some sort. A Roman soldier was busy nailing a papyrus to the harbour office. He browsed the few words he could personally read and instantly decided to cancel the sale of the family. Then he surreptitiously tore the notice down before anyone else had time to see it.

That was when he turned back toward his vessel. To his immediate horror, he watched as the four began to leave the ship. They started down the gang-plank, then headed through the small, mixed crowd. He ran over to remonstrate furiously with Kyrros for disobeying his instructions, but his protestations to the engineer were drowned out by a barrage of offers of accommodation – and many more things. The happily married engineer dismissed some offers politely and some darker offers quite sharply. Kyrros blanked the Roman master, who danced around him animatedly – but now, curiously, no longer angrily. Instead the Roman was quite charming. Nevertheless, Kyrros continued to ignore him. The family of four stood on the solid harbour side, resting momentarily from the perpetual motion of the sea and taking in the busy atmosphere.

Many huge and thin looking open-net bags, each one the size of a small cart, were ranked along the dockside. Each of them contained curious pale grey rocks. As the family looked on, one of the tall wooden joists or cranes on the dockside began to hoist one of the bags toward the already overloaded vessel.

Kyrros again became exasperated, wondering how much the master thought he might squeeze in his ship's hold before the vessel would sink. He was on the point of abandoning the ship in favour of finding another one, when Miriam had to remind him that he had already paid the master. They had precious little chance of getting their money back if the master's abrupt attitude in visiting their cabin to bring the sparse meals was anything to go by – and the gold coin bearing the lone head of Cleopatra had been almost the last of their money.

The big bag now swung directly over their heads; they all looked up at it. Then it snarled against the yard – the cross-member that held the top of the sail. At that, the net tore open, spilling the rocks directly down onto them. There was no time to dive for cover. Instead, each of the figures instinctively covered their heads with their hands and arms. Bizarrely however, the rocks simply bounced off them and onto the dock. They then splashed lightly onto the surface of the sea, where they remained floating. All four looked at each other astounded, laughing in relief at what had happened. Relieved, and realising what it was, Kyrros picked up one of the strange lightweight rocks that had landed beside him. The cargo was evidently bags full of pumice, found in abundance on the north coast of the island."

Tom took time to explain to Alex and his friends: "although it was unknown at the time, the pumice – a volcanic rock – was formed naturally in the distant past. Super-heated steam passed through it in its molten state as it cooled. This had then formed its frothy air-filled structure of solidified 'sponge'. Ideal for cleaning, washing and bathing, it was prized across the Mediterranean. But now it was especially prized in Rome – where their culture of bathing and scrubbing their bodies at least once a day made it a must. This now pushed up the demand and therefore its value." He switched back to the tale.

"Lio watched, as one of the strange rocks bobbed up and down, floating on the surface of the water. The master though, did not share their amusement. Now back to his former ill-tempered mood, he ordered the family immediately back to the cabin – if they wished to continue to their destination! Kyrros reconsidered. Perhaps, he admitted, the lightweight pumice wouldn't sink the ship after all.

The rebuke accepted, to the obvious relief of the Roman, they duly turned toward their wooden dungeon – as Lio had himself come to think of it – though not before he had decided to take a little tour en-route. Of the two gang-planks fore and aft, Lio's parents took the closest, the aft. As they did, the Roman next began shouting and swearing at the dockers, blaming the spillage of his precious pumice on them. Lio, on the other hand, followed by Ashur, walked quickly up the dock and took the forward gang-plank.

Yet again, for no other reason than his resurfacing curiosity, which until now he had been forced to keep in check, the boy crept slowly through the darkened hold – just to see what he could see. Ashur fumbled warily for his hand. In the scant light, they could make out around them only the silhouettes of many silent and unmoving figures. As their eyes became accustomed to the dark, it became apparent that they were surrounded by some of the same statues that had been on the galley. However, this time they had been joined by more, especially larger ones. Obviously these were all of the same ones that had been smuggled out of Alexandria on board the other galleys. Lio gave a start as he almost walked into a solid gold trident pointed directly at his face. It was being held by an enormous, seated figure of Poseidon. This one was even bigger than the statue that had just a few days ago, been pushed overboard from the deck of the galley in sacrifice to the storm. The large cargo hatch above him was just being opened, ready to take on more of the bags of pumice, so he led Ashur quickly through the hold, and on their way back to the store room.

Just as they were about to go in, Ashur stopped and then squeezed his hand. Turning back to see what she wanted, he saw her grinning at two of the collection of bronze statues in the far corner – those of Kyrros and Lio. Lio dropped Ashur's hand to peer at it. Since his accident on the deck of the galley, everyone had assumed that the bronzes had gone overboard, but obviously they had been rescued after all. And, by the look of them, they were perfectly intact. Except, he noticed, for the absence of the globe. Lio was sad to discover that his future self had seemingly lost the world!

'Let's go and tell Kyrros his statue is here' he said to Ashur. Then he turned around to see the girl dangling in the air.

The Roman master had his thick forearm around her throat. 'Stand still!' he said, 'otherwise I'll snap her neck like a twig.'

Then, without warning, Lio felt a dull blow to the back of his neck and he slipped silently to his knees, unconscious.

It was an hour later that the boy awoke. The ship was rolling gently; they were obviously at sea once more. His head swam as he came-to in the lamplight. The back of it throbbed and he felt as though his ears might be full of cotton wool. He lay quite still, flat on his back on one of the top bunks, staring up at the low wooden ceiling of the storeroom. Both his arms and feet were tied – extremely painfully. His recently broken arm hurt so much that, – even if he could have – the last thing he would have wished to do was move. Slowly, he watched as the dark wooden planks that made up the roof of the store room came into focus. He realised exactly where he was, but not why. 'Father,' he called, looking to where he should have been sitting on the wooden bench, 'what is happening?'

Kyrros attempted to calm the boy's growing fears. He called from the bunk opposite. 'Lio, you are alright my son, don't worry.'

'Why am I tied-up?' Lio asked, as calmly as he could. 'What's happened? I wasn't doing anything wrong this time. Where's my mother, where's Ashur?'

'Please don't fret Lio, we're all here,' he heard her reassuring voice, 'it's not your fault.'

'Try to keep calm,' Kyrros said, 'but it seems we've all been tricked.' Lio's father broke the news to the boy as to what had happened earlier in the cabin.

When he and Miriam had returned to the store, they hadn't been especially worried when Lio and Ashur had not joined them straight away. Within a few minutes though, as soon as the ship cast off from the dock, the master and several of his crew had barged into the cabin and had thrown the boy onto the bunk. They next threw the girl at Kyrros' feet, declaring that now they had left the port of Heraklion, things had changed. 'What is the meaning of this outrage,' Kyrros had demanded loudly.

'Justice,' came the reply, 'You're a wanted fugitive, aren't you!'

Kyrros was about to repeat his performance to the Egyptians from only weeks ago, 'Do you realise who I am?' when he began to wonder.

'This is you, isn't it? – I can read,' the master boasted. He shoved an unfurled scroll in front of him, which Kyrros now scanned quickly:

By order of her majesty Cleopatra, Queen of Upper and Lower Egypt, Queen of the Nile… and by the order of Julius Caesar, Emperor of Rome… let it be known that the following fugitives from justice are to be detained and handed alive to the Roman authorities, wherever they may be found…

There followed a list of Egyptian military commanders who were accused of 'deserting' to Ptolemy. Below that was a separate list of those who were to be detained for various other crimes within Alexandria, including fire-starting and, in particular, the burning of the Great Library. The names that stood at the top of the list were "Andronicus of Cyrrhus and his son, known as Helio". Two short descriptions followed: "A tall man with pale blue eyes; and a pale-faced, red haired boy". Beside their names, a reward was offered of five thousand denarii for each one – ten thousand days wages for both – enough for the master to retire on comfortably – and that was without the money from the cargo. Along with it was a warning.

That failure to detain the above people on sight would result in an immediate death sentence being passed upon the head of those who had failed to hand over the wanted criminals.

Kyrros looked directly at the ship's master. Instantly, he offered, 'I will pay you more – twice as much – if you take us to Athens.'

The master didn't falter, 'Where is the payment then?'

Miriam clutched at the scarf around her neck, but Kyrros shot her a glance. 'I do not have it here, but my friends in Athens will pay, just take us there.'

The master smiled cruelly. 'I am a Roman citizen, if I take you to Rome, I know I will be paid, and, I will not have to risk punishment for helping you escape. Besides,' he added sardonically, 'there is another reason.'

'And why is that?' Kyrros asked in exasperation.

'Because I don't like you! I am a citizen of Rome – and a patriot. I don't like people who think they are better or cleverer than me or any other Roman. And I don't like your family either – an old man, a freak, a Hebrew and an African. I hope you all end up being executed – you'll be crucified on the Appian Way – all of you.'

Kyrros tried to protest his innocence, but the master wasn't having any of it. Instead, he immediately had his ankles manacled and chained. He didn't bother to chain either Miriam or Ashur though, so they were tied like Lio.

Once again, Lio could hear Ashur sobbing. He was immediately worried for her.

The worst of it though – Kyrros continued his account of what had happened – was that the master did not trust the authorities other than in his home port – he'd said so. There, they would be less likely to take his passengers away from him and claim the reward from themselves. Accordingly, they would be going directly to Rome.

And another thing, the master had argued, when he got to Rome they would have to take it very seriously that he had brought in the right man. By sheer luck he had a perfectly captured image of them right there in his hold. He *knew* that now, since he'd caught Lio and

Ashur looking at the brand new statues. And, they even had the names of the most wanted man and boy on them.

Lio, still dazed, only half took in the tale. He followed what his father had said, but naïvely thought, and said, that they would just have to prove their innocence and everything would be alright. Before long, the pain in his arm and head started to overwhelm him. So despite his worries, he drifted back into deep unconsciousness.

"Of course," explained Tom again, "whether or not Kyrros was wanted, there had never been any prospect of them ever getting to Athens. The Roman master's real destination had always been Rome. When Kyrros had asked the master of the vessel for passage to Athens, he had simply seized on the opportunity to take his money and, in time, take them all as slaves.' Tom looked up. 'As I have already said, he'd done so often enough before. The old man continued:

All of that day, and all of the next, all the family could do was try to rest as comfortably as they could and attempt to keep their spirits up. But Lio was once again in trouble. The pain from his broken arm, still tied up, was enough to keep him in a fitful sleep, but he was in danger of running a fever. Realising this, the master loosened his ropes off. He didn't want the boy to get too ill, or worse, die. It would half the reward on him.

Again, all of the next day and night, the ship slowly bobbed along the remainder of the north coast of Crete, heading gradually toward its westernmost tip. There, it would pass into the fathomless waters between Crete and mainland Greece. At that point, the master would then attempt to take his vessel to Rome. He would sail through the channel between Porphyrusa and the tiny island of Aegilia: the very island which, for centuries, had been used amongst other things as a regular base for the Cretan Pirates – the scourge of the Mediterranean Sea.

Although the master had sailed all over the world, he had never attempted to pass through the strait before. But this time it made little sense to sail all the way back around Crete, just to take the safer route along the southern coast. Time was pressing, the boy still didn't look too well, and, he wanted the full reward for both of them. Anyway, he gambled, even if he was stopped, no one would dare take a cargo belonging to Caesar himself!

Rounding the cape to turn north-west and head through the channel, before the corbita's sail could be trimmed, the north-east wind – the Kaikas – caught the ship side-on. It lurched ominously. The heavy cargo shifted in its hold, and it began to list to one side. If there had been anyone present in that hold, after that jolt, they might have heard a sound like breathing coming from a large wooden crate tucked away in the opposite corner to the statues.

Nevertheless, after a few leagues, the wind also began to carry with it the ammoniac stench of the purple dying process of Porphyrusa. The distinctive rotten, fishy smell of boiling sea-shells and urine – part of the purple dyeing process – now let Kyrros know exactly where they were. Lio was awake. He sat silently, nauseously, simply concentrating on breathing in slowly. Miriam had taught him to do this, to concentrate as best he could to control the pain while she tried to calm his and Ashur's fears. The Roman master returned to the cabin.

Kyrros again complained at their incarceration, and this time, seeing the ashen pallor of the boy's face, the Roman grudgingly, finally conceded in fully untying him to let the boy out on deck. Then he untied Ashur's feet and told the girl to go with him – to lead him and prevent him from falling overboard. Now, for a change, it was she who led Lio by the hand, up the staircase to the deck. Then, just to make sure that neither of them tried anything, Miriam was finally, though grudgingly, also allowed out of the cabin. The master waited alone with Kyrros to make certain he didn't follow."

CHAPTER 10:

The Chase

Tom held his audience captivated. "It was the dead of night: a fine, clear, moonlit night, but Lio and Ashur were bitterly cold. There, in the stern, being watched-over by one of the crew, the pair lay shivering on their backs, looking up at the stars. Miriam had already returned to the cabin. Gradually, although he was far from well, the cold returned the colour to the boy's grey face and he started to be able to think properly. Each of the pair was worried sick, yet neither one cried, nor otherwise let the other know how frightened each was. Instead, Lio just kept whispering to Ashur that they would be fine – just wait and see!

High above them, there was the thinnest layer of stationary cloud, but through it, clearly visible, were the stars. Lio kept Ashur occupied by continuing her education as he had done so many times before, pointing out each of the constellations in turn. As his grandfather had done so many years ago for him, he started with each of the thirteen signs of the zodiac, including Ophiuchus, or Serpentarius – the snake. Then he named dozens of the stars, even translating some of them into the other languages he'd learned: Egyptian, Arabic, Latin… all just to keep her mind off their situation. 'And there,' he nodded, describing the line from the two pointer stars from the plough to the North Star, 'is where my grandfather lives,' Lio smiled. He wondered whether the tale made sense to Ashur.

'When we get out of this,' he promised her, 'we'll find

somewhere safe to live and grow up and never leave – a place where everyone knows each other and is friendly and looks out for one another. And no one will ever hurt you or bully you ever again – you'll see.' Ashur understood and appreciated every single word and every sentiment. She squeezed his good hand to let him know how she felt.

Suddenly there was a shout from the crew member who was supposed to be watching them: 'Vessel approaching from astern!'

The master went to look back from his boat. In the distance, he could clearly see by the moonlight that another boat was gaining on them – and gaining fast. No cargo vessel could achieve that speed – it must have both sail and oars. *Was it one of the Rhodian galleys*, he wondered? Maybe he had been seen taking the extra crate and they had finally caught up with him. He wasn't sure, but he was not going to take any chances. Agitatedly, he shouted, 'More sail.'

Lio was no experienced sailor, but he knew that it was dangerous to sail perpendicular to this heavy wind, threatening to tear the sail or capsize the ship. It was then that the ship's list to one side began to worsen. The boy sensed something was very wrong, though what, he didn't know. He wondered why they were trying to put extra distance between themselves and the following vessel. The other crewmen were scurrying around under orders.

'Get up,' the pair were ordered, 'get below deck.'

'What's wrong?' Lio chanced his luck. 'Who is it, pirates?'

The master glared at him and decided to frighten him into doing what he was told. He leaned down towards him, 'get out of my sight – or go overboard!'

Stumbling toward the steps, the boy looked ahead of the ship. In the distance, he could see the clear outline of an island rising from the sea, their ship heading straight toward it. Ashur and he stumbled quickly down into the cabin, to tell the others of the new danger. 'We're being chased by pirates,' Lio blurted out breathlessly, 'at least – we're definitely being chased.'

Kyrros knew the waters. 'What?' he exclaimed, 'Will we outrun them?'

His mother and Ashur listened hopefully to the short conversation.

'I don't know; there's an island ahead. If we can get there in time, maybe we'll be safe.'

'What size island, large or small?'

'Fairly small, I think – I can't tell.'

It didn't take Kyrros long to guess what was happening or where they were. If it *was* a pirate ship, they were indeed in trouble. It was one thing to argue the case for his innocence to Caesar, but pirates would simply sell them into slavery and pocket the instant money. Their corbita, sailing at five or six knots was no match for a lighter vessel, probably a galley. It would be gaining on them at around eight or ten knots. Even if they could make it to the island and find a safe haven, would they indeed be secure, they wondered? Surely they would be followed there. The situation looked hopeless. 'Go back and see if you can see what's going on' Kyrros prompted Lio.

Finding new energy and ignoring the pains in his arm and knee, the boy tried to run as he picked his way forward through the packed storage space, now thoroughly congested by the settling bags of pumice. The strange rocks had spread out in the bobbing motion of the ship, almost filling the walkways. Someone had opened the hatch above him, and every time the listing Corbita rolled, the light sea-spray splashed over Lio. The boy picked his way carefully through.

This time, as he picked his way between the bags, he looked again at the various statues. Then he noticed a large, canvas covered crate in the furthest corner – presumably the last cargo loaded at Rhodos. Suddenly, Lio was struck by the strangest, but most familiar sensation. Even in this urgent situation, it was not simple curiosity that beckoned him to reach over and lift the corner of the cloth – it was something else entirely unexplainable. It was as if a living thing had whispered to him, calling out to him as he passed. The boy could have sworn that he heard the breathless sigh that took him back years. The hairs stood up on the back of his neck.

As urgent as the situation was, Lio had to know what was there.

He stepped forward and delicately pulled back the canvas that covered the crate. Below and to his mixed surprise and shock, he recognised the object instantly. There, in red, on the end of the crate, was the single word that Ashur had daubed on it in Alexandria: 'EFKARISTO' – the 'rho' around the wrong way, signed with both of their handprints. Then, as he peered through a narrow gap in the crate, Lio could see the distinct face of his horse. His head swam. How it could have possibly survived the burning of the library? And what was more, how had it got here? But just as suddenly, his face dropped. After losing it and now finding it again, he realised that he was about to lose the Hippo-Chronos again, perhaps forever.

There was another yell from the deck, and he snapped out of his thoughts. No time to think about it now, he ran forward and popped his head up on deck. The crew ignored him in their state of clear panic.

The master himself now began to worry; it was he who had opened the hatch. He thought about the stolen crate again. *What if it was indeed the owner? What if he had followed them, knowing he had taken it.* He tried to anticipate what he would offer as an excuse. Then he shouted a command and six of the crew clambered instantly into the hold. Within minutes they re-emerged, manhandling the lightest of the bronze statues on board, a beautifully sculpted half life-sized bronze statue of a horse and rider. If he could get rid of it overboard before they were seen, the ship's manifest – the list of its cargo – would show amongst other things that everything was accounted for and that they had only three bronze sculptures. *Wrong bronze horse, sorry!* he rehearsed in his head, *a genuine mistake – please just take it back with my apologies – take these female slaves too for your trouble,* he continued in his head, planning his way out of trouble. Anyway, the money was in the two wanted men.

As he planned it all out, the horse and rider went into the sea with a splash – and a scream – carrying with it one of the hapless crew who had got his loose garments tangled around one of the rider's feet. *No need to outrun it now,* thought the master. He would heave-to and allow them aboard. The master was now quite confident that he could talk his way out of the 'misunderstanding'. He breathed a sigh of relief as the galley gained more and more on them. But then, he realised gradually that the vessel was in fact his own worst nightmare.

'Cretan Pirates!' The shout went out from one of his crew. He stiffened, not believing his evil luck. Instantly he lost faith in the fact that the cargo belonging to Caesar might save them. He looked to the ship's bow and at the growing black silhouette of the island in the distance. It was at that point, that the master dimly recalled something – a story that he had been told years ago about the smaller of the two islands – something about twin pinnacles and a hidden beach? That was it: he would beach the ship on the shore and fight them off – if they followed his risky move. Or, run away and never come back, one of the two. Hang the reward and his retirement, this was now only about survival!

Lio also watched ahead. In the moonlight, the island had grown much larger by now. He could just about make out the outline of small buildings on top of a high promontory which overlooked an inlet. Behind them was what looked like the entrance to a natural harbour. It was protected by two tall rock pinnacles near its mouth – *thank goodness*, he thought. To the stern though, the other vessel was still gaining, pulling toward their starboard. It was still perhaps a couple of hundred paces away – this was not good. What were they trying to do? They were not close enough to board them. *Are they trying to pass us*, he wondered? Briefly, he began to hope that they might not be pirates after all – that they might be just heading for the same harbour. But then he clearly saw that twenty or thirty men had already collected on the deck. And, just as clearly, even from this distance he could see the silver glint of moonlight on their weapons and the grappling hooks swinging from their hands. The distance from the island began to lessen. They began to move in close to the shoreline and follow the coast around to the inlet and the rock pinnacles. But then it dawned on him what the other ship was doing.

It was not trying to pass them, it was threatening to block them

– drive them into the pinnacles if the master didn't yield to them. They had no chance of skirting the coast and the rock pinnacles safely, they would surely run aground if they tried. The distance began to close between the two vessels as the pinnacles loomed closer. Was their corbita going to try to manoeuvre through the gap after all? Lio ran down to the store again and told his father that they were getting close to the shore. 'Something else,' blurted out Lio. 'The Hippo-Chronos is on board!' Everyone stared at him incredulously. 'Could we use it to escape?' Lio asked. Kyrros' eyes immediately lit up. Then, without wasting time on wondering how it had got there, the engineer began to wonder if they could indeed use it. However, the hopeful expression that had illuminated his face now faded just as quickly. He had personally ordered its body to be flooded with the wax! 'I'm afraid not,' he said, 'it's too late, there's no time to prepare it... get it out of the crate... clean out the wax... wind it up and set it – it would take days. No, I am afraid that it is to all intents and purposes useless. Even if it could be achieved, only one or two of us could get away.' The idea that had lifted each one's heart briefly now left them in despair.

Then, Kyrros remembered something. 'There is however, one part of it that you can take with you, if you wish. It is over there, in that bag,' he beckoned the boy to it. 'Take it out.'

Lio quickly found the single familiar remaining package, the long wooden box. 'Take it with you,' prompted Kyrros, 'you never know, it might come in useful some day!'

The boy took it over to his father and offered it to him. 'No, you carry it', he nodded back, tucking it into the front of the boy's loose garments, above his waist cord. Then he re-tied it tighter for him, to stop it falling out. 'Look after it for me' he asked. 'Now, quickly, once again, tell me what's happening on deck.'

Lio again ran up to look around. Now a volley of arrows flew toward him – one narrowly missing his head. They were trying again to force the ship to heave-to. Another volley of arrows stuck into the timber deck and he ran back to the cabin. 'They're gaining on us... only a few hundred feet away... they're starting to fire arrows at the crew to get them to stop…' he ran to the hatch opposite, 'but we're making straight for the island – there must be a beach.'

'How far is it?' Kyrros called.

'Much closer now, perhaps only half a Roman league, the master must be going to beach the ship, he's turning to head straight for it.'

'Perhaps,' Kyrros agreed, remembering from the report that Poseidonios had given him years ago – the account of his being chased by pirates when he had been testing the armillary. Now he knew precisely which island it was, and guessed that they might be heading for the concealed pebble beach, 'then get ready to jump off and run!'

Miriam was on her feet. Seeing the look of apprehension on her children's faces she hugged them briefly to her.

'Miriam,' called Kyrros, 'take care of them. Quickly, both of you, collect the things up into the bag again, you may need it.'

'But what about the horse?' asked Lio again hopelessly, 'is there nothing we can do?'

'Alas not,' sighed his father.

'Then what else should we take?' asked Miriam.

'Just your doctor's bag… Ashur,' he called out, 'pass the bag to your mother, and pass that bag of my belongings here to me.'

'Now what?' asked Lio.

'Nothing,' said Kyrros to his family, 'nothing at all but sit and wait, and when we land on the beach, jump off and run fast and far away. Now, get your shoes on everyone, and prepare to run.'

Miriam immediately found their shoes and she helped Ashur tie them on. Then she helped Lio with the laces that he couldn't manage with his single uninjured hand.

It was only when she'd finished the small task and the three stood up expectantly that Miriam looked quizzically at Kyrros, still sitting on the bottom bunk. He hadn't moved at all. Miriam frowned at him. He met her look with a shrug. His eyes dropped down at the manacles, still around his ankles. A long chain led from them, disappearing beneath the bed. Miriam's eyes traced it back up to eye level. Suddenly she realised – he was chained to one of the securing hoops! When she had been allowed out of the cabin earlier, he must have been secured so that they would not all be tempted to try and escape.

'Why didn't you tell us?' She rebuked him, 'quickly, we'll have to remove them,' she said matter-of-factly.

'And how will we achieve that without any of my tools?' he probed gently.

'But we must, we can't just... leave you behind,' she stared, starting to realise what this meant.

'What's wrong?' asked Lio.

Kyrros looked at the boy he'd rescued and had grown to love as his own. 'Lio,' he said simply, 'it looks like I'll not be continuing the journey with you. My fate is now joined to this vessel.'

The boy too began to realise, 'Ashur,' he called fearfully, 'help me to find something to break the rivets off these manacles. Come on, quickly.'

'Lio, Ashur, stop!' Kyrros called, 'my tools lie at the bottom of the Nile. And there's none in here, you know there aren't.'

The boy turned to explain to him, as if the man had any choice, 'But you can't stay, anything might happen... the master... the pirates...' he trailed off.

Kyrros raised his thick eyebrows in resignation – 'No choice,' he said simply.

'Then we'll all stay,' Lio tried.

'NO YOU WILL NOT!' Kyrros boomed. 'You, my son, will look after the women – take them with you.'

'But I...' he protested.

'No buts, promise me you'll look after my wife and daughter for me... on your word of honour!'

Lio nodded. Then his eyes began to fill up and he struggled to keep his composure.

'Now, one last time Lio, are we far away? Look for me – be my eyes,' Kyrros prompted, keeping the boy occupied.

Lio again popped his head up on deck, returning only a few

seconds later: 'We're only a few hundred feet from a wide, sandy beach.'

'And where is the pirate ship?'

'Slowing down, it's not coming after us, they're turning. I think we might have lost them,' he said hopefully.

Miriam did not share his optimism – she looked worriedly into Kyrros' eyes. He stood up and opened his arms to embrace her briefly one last time. 'Now, go over there,' he said, 'sit with your back against the bulkhead, and as soon as we strike the beach – run!' He sat back down and looked for something to grasp, when a look of shock suddenly flashed onto his face. 'How close are the twin rock pinnacles?'

'I can't see them anymore,' replied Lio.

Kyrros' brow furrowed deeply: 'wide, sandy beach?' The man finally took in the significance of the boy's description. 'Not a narrow, pebbled beach – with a small temple?' A sickening feeling grew in his stomach. Lio shook his head as he and Ashur ran hurriedly to embrace him, 'no father, there is no temple,' he advised. The long box again poked into Lio's ribs before he re-shuffled it behind him, then he sat down quickly beside his mother. Ashur was about to sit down just the same when, all of a sudden, they felt the harsh, painful impact. There came the splintering crunch of the ship's heavy wooden hull colliding not with a sandy beach but with solid, jagged rock!

On the aft deck, the Roman master who'd stood at the handrail with his entire, crew had been jeering at the pirate ship. Obviously they were too cowardly to follow them onto the gently sloping sandy beach that he'd finally spotted at the last moment. But it was only after fleeing as fast as they could toward it, with the wind now fully behind them, and when it was far too late to turn, that the forward lookout realised their mistake. Far from being a soft sandy beach, they were heading for what looked clearly like rock. Paralysed with shock, he said absolutely nothing.

The pirate ship master in turn, could not believe that the corbita was speeding straight toward the shore. Disappointed that after the long chase from Crete, the fool of a master had decided not to yield and hand over his ship, but had instead decided to crash it into the most treacherously razor sharp rocks of any coastline in all of the islands. He could only watch and listen, stupefied.

In the bright moonlight, the Roman corbita crashed hard into a rocky outcrop. The bow shot briefly into the air, before almost bouncing back down. In a whiplash effect, this instantly catapulted most of the crew backwards into the sea. The ship then seemed to lodge itself there for a minute or two. Then, by degrees, it slipped slowly sternward, disappearing under the water with the rest of the crew. After watching it all, the pirates turned reluctantly but immediately for home. Just then, the night's changing wind chanced to turn again, and the Euros blew from the south-east.

Those two minutes were a lifetime. Inside the cabin, Miriam held Ashur's hand as she began to sit, when the sudden impact made all three of them hit their heads against the solid bulkhead – Ashur's heavily. Kyrros was catapulted off the bench like a sling shot. Tied by the long chain, he flew into the centre of the room to land face down. After its initial, splintering crash, the ship slid partly down. Inside the hold, the heavy cargo was forced forward by the momentum. This temporarily shifted the balance point to the forward half of the ship. It locked the vessel onto the viciously sharp outcrop. Instantly, Kyrros' fears were confirmed. He couldn't believe the stupidity and ignorance of the master. The island of Aegilia was notorious throughout the Aegean for many things, not only its stronghold as a pirate base, but also for its reputation as having been formed from the most treacherous, sand coloured rock. It had only one saving grace, one worst kept 'secret'. That beside the entrance to its hidden harbour, there was a second, hidden entrance. There, a narrow, smoothly pebbled beach had been used over the centuries to save fleeing vessels by allowing them to be beached there: hence the tiny Temple of Athena being built right there in thanks. And yet, it had been Kyrros' ill fortune to be on the one ship whose ignorant or arrogant and brutish Roman master hadn't known the waters. *And now, he had got him – Kyrros – drowned, for surely that was about to happen.* These thoughts flashed through his mind in the instant before he called out, 'quickly – RUN!'

Lio was already on his feet, Miriam just after him, but Ashur sat dazed between them. Each grabbing a hand, they helped her to her own feet as she blinked her eyes around her, trying to focus. Miriam looked shocked, but almost relieved to be on dry land, as she thought; though at least she was alive. Then, the ship began to rock back slightly again.

Within moments, cold water poured through the gaping hole in the bow, into the hold and thence into the stern. Kyrros looked at his family. 'Please Miriam, run, while you still have the chance. For their sakes… look after them.' He smiled briefly and sat down at the stern to watch his wife, now in control, grab her bag and walk quickly to the door. Miriam knew what had to be done. There was no more time to lose. She hesitated briefly for one exchange of glances and to let her husband have one last pained smile, but then she was gone. In a daze, she led Ashur through the door and into the storage hold, and there the girl waited as her mother clambered up the steps. Lio watched at the door of the cabin as Miriam and Ashur managed to pick their way cautiously over the wreckage.

That wreckage, which had until a few moments ago been the precious cargo of sculptures, was now strewn all over the place in a broken heap of parts. The head had broken off the disintegrated bronze statue of Kyrros and lay in a pile of arms and legs. The broken marble torso and arm of Poseidon, still holding the gold trident high, also lay there as if to guard the door. Whilst at the far end of the hold, the Hippo-Chronos had broken free from its now smashed crate. It now lay on its side amongst the sacks of pumice that had cushioned its impact. The moonlight streamed through the still opened hatch, illuminating its strange head and muzzle as the horse lay on its side, lifeless.

Kyrros sat waiting on the bunk, resigned to his fate. Lio looked back at the man who'd saved his live twice. 'Goodbye father,' he said proudly, 'I will never forget you.' Suddenly bursting into tears, he ran toward the man he had come to love and respect and threw his arms around him. Kyrros stood up again to hug his boy tightly, but being careful not to hurt him – the box still tucked in the boy's clothes. He whispered into Lio's ear, 'and I will miss being in your company Lio, but now go. Live-on for me – live to grow into an old man – as I am', he finally accepted his own age. Then he sat himself back down patiently.

As Lio turned back to face the hold, he saw Miriam's hand come back down the stairwell to take Ashur's, to pull her quickly up. But as the girl disappeared through to safety, without warning, the Roman master dropped through the cargo hatch directly in front of Lio. He stumbled on the rubble, then got to his feet. Two broken-off arrows poked out of his bare chest, and his mouth oozed crimson. 'Come here you,' he coughed, producing a short sword. 'If I'm dying, so are all of you – painfully!' He began to walk slowly and deliberately toward the boy as, once more, the ship lurched suddenly sternward, sending some of the cargo back to slide down the hold. Lio's eyes fixed on the figure of the Hippo-Chronos sliding fast toward the Roman. The boy was transfixed – dumbstruck. Hearing it too late, the Roman didn't turn to see the horse collide heavily with the arm of Poseidon. Instead, he stood staring at the boy as the horse sent the arm and the trident to hurtle into his back. Still looking at Lio, he seemed at first not to notice the three red and gold objects which appeared to poke from his chest. The Roman looked down in amazement at them, trying to brush them away. Then, perplexed, he looked into Lio's eyes. Finally, he crumpled forward to the floor. Kyrros, who had seen it all from his bunk cried out: 'Good, now at least I'll have company.' The water began to pour down toward him rapidly, sweeping the body from view.

On deck, Miriam stood with Ashur, trying to pick the least dangerous part of the rock to leap to. The ship lurched heavily again, opening up a growing gap. So without waiting, she threw the bag high onto the rocks, then she herself jumped. Her foot luckily found a relatively flat area; though on impact she rolled over, slicing her hands and knees. 'Quickly Ashur, hurry!' She cried out, but there was no way that she could catch the girl. Alone, Ashur weighed-up the chances of making it to the rocks.

'Ashur, jump... please!' Miriam called in desperation, but to no avail. The girl didn't move; not until the ship moved under her feet. And then she leapt right out into the sea – away from the rock – and away from where Miriam stood. As Miriam climbed down the few feet, Ashur started to swim back to meet her as fast and as strongly against the tide as she could. A few minutes later, she carefully clambered onto the sharp-edged rock where her mother again grasped her by the hand to pull her out of the waves. And as she did, the ship finally slipped from view.

CHAPTER 11:

Lio's Darkest Hour

At the very same moment that Ashur had jumped, and the corbita had suddenly lurched heavily, the stern dropped toward the bottom of a slope that grew steadily more steep. The sea surged-in even deeper, starting to submerge Kyrros as he smiled brightly at the boy. 'Go!' He prompted one last time.

The water around the boy was freezing. Lio knew that he had to get out. 'I promise I'll never forget you father...' he repeated. A spark of pride, if not something else, blazed briefly in Kyrros' eyes and he raised his brows almost hopefully. Then, the water covered his head and he disappeared from view.

It was then that the ship began its steady roll onto its side. Lio instantly turned back to climb toward the doorway into the hold. There, he headed quickly for the stairway. Going down heavily at the stern, the ship began to slide, picking up pace as it did. Losing his grip on the floor, the boy tried to part scramble, part swim up towards the bow, but now, the net bags of pumice were swirling around in the water. They blocked his progress to the forward stairway and the open hatch. The gaping hole in the hull allowed the moonlight to spray in and around it, illuminating the contents of the rapidly submerging hold. As he struggled on, the boy could see only fleeting shafts of blue-white light coming through the opening. Briefly, the ship lifted with a large wave, but then it dropped again and began to bump down the slope faster, filling the hold with dull wooden echoes. Pieces of wood from the empty crate floated up towards the bow along with the open-mouthed, staring face and body of the Roman. The air pocket was growing smaller as air steadily escaped, then the incoming water surged over Lio's head and he began to choke on it before he managed to catch a last breath. He saw the Hippo-Chronos again as it slid heavily past him to disappear below and in the direction of the cabin. Even as it did, his heart felt a pang, but this was hardly the time for regret.

That was when he realised that he could hardly move, let alone swim free. His thrashing around had now got him firmly entangled in the net bags of pumice. The ship was sliding fast now, almost upside down. Fragments of statues rained down in slow motion around his ears as the ship bumped steadily toward the brink of an underwater precipice. Unknown to him, Lio was headed over with it. Unable to breathe, he began to grow desperate – he was entirely submerged. Overwhelmed by hopelessness, he began to lose focus, but that was when he felt the sharp corners of the box digging into his back. The pain of it brought him back to his senses. The added weight of the Chrono-key inside his billowing garments also began to drag him down. He tried briefly to get rid of it, to reach it in the back of his tangled clothing, but he couldn't. He pulled at his rope belt, but now saturated, the knot wouldn't move either.

As the boy took a gulp of water, the ship finally rolled over entirely, launching itself over the edge. It plummeted downwards, now pitching forward, bow first. At that, he caught a flash of light sparkling on something. Hurtling back down in the moonlight, now heading the opposite way, the head and flanks of the Hippo-Chronos again tumbled heavily past him. The horse trailed a rope behind it that caught around the boy's leg. And with that, the machine unravelled itself and finally fell through the upside down cargo hatch. Losing consciousness, Lio watched, unfocussed, as the bags of pumice burst through the hatch. As he began to pass out, one net bag dragged the same loose rope behind it, and Lio felt a tug on his leg as it pulled him roughly through the hatch and upwards. For one last time, the Hippo-Chronos had managed to save his life, and all he could do was cling to the rope as it carried him to the surface. His head bursting above the waves, Lio coughed and spluttered while the net bag bobbed feebly around. There was nothing but the noise of the wind on the moonlit sea as the ship carried Kyrros and its cargo, to follow his incredible invention to the bottom.

An age later, Lio bobbed up and down. He was not cold any more. It seemed curious to him as he drifted out further and further to sea, how he had passed through that stage and was now only tired – dreadfully tired. The Euros wind blew strongly, whistling painfully around his head and ears so that he couldn't hear a thing. He had been cold for the first few hours of course, shiveringly cold, icy cold, but now he was just numb. Though, even that was a blessing in disguise – it had at least stopped his arm from hurting. From the time the ship had gone down and he had shot to the surface amongst the other floating debris – mostly loose pumice – he had clung to the one intact net bag that still contained plenty of it. He'd been almost ashore when the wind had changed, but with his weakened arm, he hadn't chanced to swim for it. Now he had missed even that chance.

It was a strange stuff pumice, he thought idly. It seemed, like him, to be desperate to be on the top of the water but was not quite able to achieve it. Like he, as strong a swimmer as he usually was, he knew it was too weak. As soon as it had hit the surface, the bag fanned out across it – not on the surface – but just below it. It was not quite buoyant enough for him to climb on top of and be saved, but at least enough so that if he held onto the net, it would stop him from going under again. He had tried to climb out several times of course, more and more exhaustedly. Especially in the first hour – only to fail – once shouting out in agony as his repairing broken arm was snapped again. But now he was resigned to the fact that unless a ship happened along – and of that, there was no sign – it seemed that he would not survive the night.

For the umpteenth time, another small wave hit Lio's face and he took another mouthful of salt water. It made the back of his throat burn, which made him cough and retch in turn. Recovering his composure, he thought it ironic that the one thing he had wished to save from the ship – other than his father of course – had been the Hippo-Chronos, and that he'd effectively managed to rescue a part of it. But that was now the thing that was dragging him down. And unless he could release it, it would probably get him drowned.

Hours ago, when he finally realised his predicament, he thought he had nothing better to do than simply let go of the pumice and swim to the nearby shore. But each time he let go of the net, the weight at his back pulled him steadily down. Not that the key was especially heavy. It was the combination of the key, his weakened arm, and the stiff wind that was blowing him further away from the now distant rocks. *I am not afraid of dying,* he thought almost idly. It was a strange thought to him that faced with the hopelessness of the situation, he had, after the first hour, resigned himself to the fact that it was most likely that he would not make it.

His emotional state was more of a deep sadness at the loss of Kyrros, mixed with disappointment; a deep, overwhelming disappointment such as he had never before known – not even on that long past night of his near sacrifice. It was a disappointment that he would never see Kyrros, Miriam or Ashur again. His mind wandered-off – back to when he and Ashur had played games together, pitching rocks at a target. He remembered his friend Marduk, Ashur's brother, smiling and laughing with them. Then he remembered his grandfather, and now his father – all happy thoughts. There was no time left for sadness.

His head bobbed under the surface as he nearly fell asleep, but as he snorted in a nose-full of saltwater, he was jolted a little and he tilted his head back to see the night sky. *It truly is a marvellous moonlit night,* he thought. The thin, high cloud was still there, but again he could easily make out all of the constellations. That was when even that thin cloud cleared, leaving a perfectly visible sky entirely filled with stars. For a short while he struggled to twist around to see if he could see his grandfather's star. He nearly lost his grip, and took in another mouthful before he managed to twist even his broken arm around into the net, desperate not to lose it again. The wind dropped for a moment and his face was instantly much warmer. Again he tried to reach the Chrono-key with his free hand, but couldn't. That would be his last attempt.

The water seemed to swirl, turning the pumice slightly around. Now way out into the channel between the island and its neighbour, the current began to drive the floating mass toward the east, spinning it further around as it did so. Lio looked up at the sky again, craning his head. Yes, there at last, he could make out the plough. There were the pointing stars, Merak and Dubhe. His eye followed them, and there at last was his grandfather's star – the North Star – Polaris.

Unable to speak aloud, he thought a prayer to his grandfather, the old priest. He asked him once more to look after everyone, either alive or that was no more: Marduk; and now his father Kyrros; then Miriam. And, of course, Ashur. *Help her,* he asked, *if she is still alive… if she managed to escape… to find the special place which she deserves. So that at least one of us will make it and live out a happy, peaceful life.* Low clouds began to fill the sky again, moving from the north and blocking out the moonlight. His face grew cold again as the wind began to pick up – stronger this time as it blew the thin stream of pumice and himself once more. This time though, he lay on his back, managing to keep his tired eyes fixed firmly on Polaris, trying not to close them.

On the shore, a short way up the coast from where Miriam had pulled Ashur out onto the rock, the pair stood hugging each other against the chill wind, looking carefully around to see if they could see any survivors. At first they had stood for half an hour, calling out for Lio into the dark, windy night, trying to see if there was any trace of the boy. But the only thing visible had been the stream of pumice which made its way slowly up the coastline, moonlight reflecting on its dirty white surface. They had been about to quit when a single weak cry had sounded out to sea – and Lio's arm had broken. There was nothing to be seen though, just a bigger clump of pumice within the rest of the stream. Then they realised that he must be amongst it.

They had started to follow the trail of debris and as quickly as they could across the sharp rocks, but couldn't move nearly fast enough. Now, it was too late to save him. The wind had by then carried all that was left of the ship well off the coast, and although they couldn't see him, they knew that Lio was being carried away with it. It was, to Miriam and Ashur, almost worse than not finding him at all. He was there, by then half a league away, but they couldn't reach him. Miriam couldn't swim, and it was far too far, and the currents far too strong for Ashur to swim out – although Ashur herself did not appreciate this. Once the young girl had realised Lio was even likely to be there, she signalled frantically that she wanted to go to him, but Miriam wouldn't let her. The distance alone was enough to get her killed – there and back was at least a league and she wouldn't be able to carry Lio with her, or tow the bag. And that would only make things worse – a double tragedy. Miriam had forbidden her to try to save him, so now all they could do was watch as the boy disappeared into the distance, around the headland and out of sight. Now the debris was no more than a memory. Low cloud had moved across the sky and blotted out the moon so that its light could no longer be seen reflecting off the pumice. Standing there watching this was now too painful, it was time for them to turn and leave.

Ashur looked at the clouds following them from the sea. She tugged at Miriam's hand as they walked, beckoning her to look. 'Not now Ashur,' Miriam chided softly, 'please. She thought about Lio and her husband, but the girl was determined, tugging again at her arm. Through the distant cloud cover to the east, she could just see the faint glow of pre-dawn. The sun had begun to rise almost imperceptively, slowly beginning to illuminate the distant horizon. Within a few short minutes, its own golden light had just started to spill out onto the surface of the sea. Then the clouds seemed to move southwards across the island while Miriam and Ashur picked their way over the rocks, trying to reach more solid ground to walk on. Again Ashur tugged at her.

'Please Ashur, not now.' Miriam begged.

Ashur stopped dead, refusing to move. The sunlight was gaining as she pulled at Miriam, pointing back to the sea. By now, the wind had begun to blow harder, chasing the low clouds along and chilling their backs. It was the coldest wind – the north wind – the Boreas. The wind direction had changed almost completely, from southeast to north. Ashur's face was stone. She pointed silently but repeatedly to the sea. Miriam finally looked in realisation.

She strained her eyes in the thin light, trying to pick up a sign. Yes, there it was – the pumice. Very far away, no more than a thin golden thread reflected in the sun's rays... but moving closer. Not straight toward them, but on a tangent. The slick moved steadily south, back towards the narrow tip of the island – behind the headland. Keeping an eye on the golden line, the pair began to walk steadily up the coastline toward the high, jagged rock promontory and the concealed harbour – the same promontory that Lio had told them he had seen from the deck of the ship. The ground here was better, still very rocky and covered in thin undergrowth: wild rosemary and gorse. But it was better underfoot. Now the pair began to run. The pumice wasn't moving fast, but it would pass there within the hour. Though now, from their present vantage point, they could see also that there was no way around the steep and jagged cliffs that guarded it. They would have to go over the top of the promontory.

Miriam started up toward the hill that obscured the harbour, Ashur following in tow. A herd of feeding goats bleated on their approach, the bells around their necks sounding out gently as they scattered away. On, the mother and daughter went, not quite running, but stumbling as quickly as they could over the loose rocky soil, their legs bleeding and scratched by the rough terrain and especially the sharp thorns of the gorse. Looking over their shoulders while they ran, they kept watch over the sea's surface. There *still* was the pumice, not much closer, but growing steadily more-so.

Reaching the top of the slope, Miriam was at once devastated. The goat track did not lead straight over to the harbour as she had thought, but instead it led way back down toward a trickling rocky riverbed. Only then did the track go up and over toward the harbour. They had to keep going though, there was no choice. Miriam stumbled and skidded on down the loose slope, trying not to fall, while Ashur ran faster ahead, now already at the bottom. The mature woman, normally quite fit, was falling behind – out of energy and breath. As Ashur reached the shallow river she didn't stop to look behind. She ran straight through, up to her knees, and started straight up the second slope. Now, Miriam in turn reached the bottom, but the young girl was already half-way up the steep incline and on her way to the other side of the headland and the harbour.

Ashur stopped on the highest ridge that overlooked the now visible harbour, a little out of breath but determined that she was not about to quit. She could see the pumice coming in fast now. But then, just before she'd committed herself down the slope, she noticed that the thin line had begun to change direction yet again. This time she watched as the floating mat skirted its way back down the coast and swirled almost back out to sea. It moved only briefly into the harbour mouth before the channel currents took over from the wind. From there, the current would take it back into deep water, past the twin pinnacles, where it would be lost. Ashur's own path headed to a short, pebbled beach right beneath her – another tiny, concealed entrance with a small temple. That, she guessed, was the last point Lio would pass before heading out into the wide sea again. Without waiting further, she tore down the slope as fast as her feet could carry her.

In the channel, Lio could hardly keep his eyes open any longer. If it had still been dark, he would no doubt have gone to sleep by now and that would have been the end of him. Since the sun began to rise however, he had managed to rally a little, but only because he had realised just before Polaris faded in the daylight, that he was heading away from the star now and therefore back toward the island. If he could just stay awake, perhaps there might be a last chance? He managed to turn, painfully, to see the harbour getting closer. He wondered how near he needed to get to it before he could chance letting go of the bag one last time. He also wondered whether he could make it at all, swimming with only one arm. *Soon enough I will know*, he thought.

In some respects, it was easier for Ashur to run across the rough ground than the big, smooth, rounded pebbles on the beach; she stumbled and fell several times, bruising her legs and knees. This didn't stop her though, each time, she picked herself up and ran resolutely toward the sea. The line of pumice grew thicker now, swirling around in the mouth of the harbour. It drifted past the entrance to the pebbled beach and headed back toward the pinnacles – just as Ashur had anticipated. Reaching the water's edge, the girl stopped to take off her shoes and dress. She watched for the biggest clump heading towards her, following it along the beach, her breath now almost sobbing in her chest. But still she couldn't see him – there was no sign of him. Tears began to well up again for the second time since the sun had risen that day. But just then, she heard a shout. It was a weak shout – but she did hear it! Without waiting, Ashur ran onto the furthest and highest part of the surrounding rock. Without hesitation, for the first time ever, she dived headlong – and expertly – into the deep water. Now she swam as fast as she could before the net bag could get past the narrow inlet.

Lio could see her clearly gaining on him, now only a short distance away on the other side of the pumice, but what was she going to do when she *did* reach him? Surely she couldn't hope to drag him with her. Then she disappeared, and the boy began to panic for the first time since being in the water. Not for himself, but for what might have happened to Ashur. But just as he had begun to despair, her head popped up beside him – she had gone right under the bag. Panting as she looped her arm through the net herself now, she then grabbed both sides of Lio's face and stared purposefully into his eyes. Then, letting go, with her back to the shore and the back of her head resting on the bag, she began to kick furiously. Realising what she was trying to do, Lio swung around onto his back like her and began to do the same. At first, they didn't seem to change direction; the current was too strong. Then, gradually, the bag started to move slowly toward the shore and the beach. New energy filled him as the warm sun shone on their faces. Lio looked into Ashur's wide eyes while they kicked furiously, determinedly, getting slowly closer to the beach.

Before long, Miriam reached the shore. She waded in, fully-clothed, up to the neck toward them. Finally, between them, she and Ashur managed to drag Lio out of the water.

The brave boy" said Tom, "had been saved."

"By the brave girl!" reminded Bex.

No one had interrupted Tom's story for ages until now.

"Indeed," the storyteller smiled satisfactorily, "by the *very* brave girl."

CHAPTER 12:

A New Life

"But Tom," asked Alex, "what happened to the Chrono-key – the Time-key – if Lio still had it when he managed to get ashore?"

"Ah," Tom answered, "despite its short immersion in the water the computer dried out, perfectly well."

"But he managed to hang onto it – it wasn't lost?"

"I don't get it," chirped-up Conna, "I thought the key was found at the bottom of the sea… that is what we are talking about aren't we… the Antikythera device?"

"It is," admitted Tom, "the Antikythera device, as it is now known…"

Conna had remembered correctly that the ancient name of the island, Aegilia, had in fact changed – though many times since – before being eventually known by its modern name, Antikythera.

Tom continued. "In fact, the machine was lost to the world much later. For the duration, Lio simply held onto the key as a kind of… relic! The device became a tangible reminder of his father and, in itself, a useful enough piece of equipment for converting various calendars, setting dates and many other things. The boy kept it and studied it for a long time before eventually he had to 'let it go'. But for the time they spent together on the island then known as Aegilia, at first overcoming their considerable grief at what had happened to Kyrros, they worked hard to settle into a new but rewarding life.

Despite everything that had happened to them, they were happy together. There had been no other survivors from the shipwreck, the vessel had gone down so quickly that only Miriam and Ashur had been quick enough to jump onto the shore before it had disappeared. And as it had run aground in the dark, there had been no witnesses to their appearance on the island. It was assumed therefore, that the new faces had come to the island especially – simply to live there. And that, they did – although even their new life was not without a shadow.

Life on the island was hard for the few, mostly farmers, who had inhabited it. The island was effectively just a large rock. Its lack of good topsoil made it difficult to till and grow sufficient food for profit other than through keeping goats. But since the latest resurgence of the Cretan pirates who had menaced the area for years – and who raided them whenever they wished – most islanders had reluctantly left for Kriti or the Greek mainland. The entire island was littered with abandoned terraced gardens and small houses. Many owners had simply had enough of struggling to scratch out a living, only for the small profits of their yearlong efforts to be stolen from them. They had packed what little they had left, and gone.

Very few people were to be seen around; most were now suspicious of all strangers. And yet, from the outset, Miriam, Lio and Ashur were well received. The now sparsely populated island had not seen a doctor for years, and a few of the locals had witnessed how she had 'miraculously' saved the boy's arm. Miriam's interest in medicine therefore gave her an instant means of supporting Ashur and Lio. So, Miriam worked as doctor and nurse for those with ailments and injuries, and her gentle, caring demeanour made her instantly popular with those few hundred locals who remained.

Not that either Ashur or Lio was given a free ride. Ashur worked alongside her mother. Men in particular hated to show pain in front of the young girl and so were far happier to deal with it quietly. Their lack of shouting out aloud quickly added to their mother's reputation as a 'painless' doctor – much to her family's amusement.

Lio on the other hand, began to use the computer, once he had stripped and cleaned it thoroughly. He drew charts for people who, for various reasons, wanted to know about the movement of the stars and planets. Some for agricultural reasons, some for navigation, but most, he guessed, for superstitious reasons. However, because he had never had proof positive that either the gods existed or did not, he held in the same way the constellations of the stars. The signs of the zodiac may have seemed irrelevant to him, but, nevertheless, he accepted their importance to anyone of another persuasion. Accordingly, he was able to charge – though not too much – for his time in making up each chart scientifically. However, he was never persuaded to take this any further in the form of interpretation, 'reading the future', if you will. That would have been a betrayal of both his father's and grandfather's principles. They were principles that Lio had inherited and would never sell out.

And so it was that, in a very short time, they were able to buy back the gold torc that his mother had 'pawned' on the first day that they had arrived there – albeit for a lot more than she had sold it. Although the interest and more was repaid to her in time, when she was able to help with the moneylender's ailments.

Before long, the three moved out of the one shared room in the guest house in the small, elevated settlement of Xiropotamos overlooking the pebbled beach." – Tom pronounced it Hero-**poh**-tammo – "Instead, they resettled themselves in an abandoned cottage on the edge of the village. It was a semi-derelict property, not a farm exactly, but a smallholding with a small area of rocky, terraced land around it. Though in a terrible state at first, after a while, and a lot of back-breaking work that took the whole of the spring, the family started to grow their own food. Of course, the work of planting, mainly vegetables, was done usually at the hands of Lio, whose arm had mercifully re-set without too much permanent damage.

After a few early failures, Lio even became quite adept at building dry-stone walls. In fact, he spent much of his time rebuilding the broken down enclosure walls and terraces around their house. He even rebuilt parts of the old house itself. Also, he walled-off a small area around the house, and this garden became especially spectacular in his hands. The boy even found and successfully transplanted a small apple tree. For days he hacked out a huge hole in the rock to put it in, so that one day they would have another fruit in addition to the meagre few grape vines they'd managed to establish. After another while, they even kept a goat that had arrived as payment for treating an ongoing and painful back injury over many, many weeks.

It was very satisfying for Lio to be contributing to their simple way of life, it made him realise that the ancients had been quite right in their condemnation of excessive wealth. *Happiness,* he thought, *is little to do with money.* For Lio, it was more to do with being creative or productive. Just as happiness could not bring money, money could not, he was certain, buy happiness and contentment.

What little spare time Lio had then, was spent walking in the hills and climbing crags. And of course, swimming: off the beaches both at Xiropotamos and at another unnamed sandy beach on the west side of the island. Now that his health and strength returned and he was back to being the strong swimmer that he'd always been before he'd broken his arm, he and Ashur went swimming most evenings before dusk. Of course, the girl still always trounced him. And so, the place became known to them all simply as Ashur's beach.

After a short while, the family learned that, unlike much of the ancient world, they were quite safe there. But whilst the full-time resident population was honest, it did not take a genius to work out that the whole island was prey to constant pirate attack. These attacks were seldom vicious. Or, at least, they were only as vicious as the Roman tax collectors on the mainland, but it still paid to store valuables away. Accordingly, within a day of moving to the new house, Miriam began to look for a hiding place for anything that she may have of value – especially the gold torc.

One day, quite by chance, when he was quarrying new rock to rebuild the walls, Lio stumbled on a natural underground fresh-water supply. His banging caused a narrow fissure to open up in front of his eyes. He chipped away at it until it was wide enough for him to crawl inside. It led to a room-sized cavern. The clean water supply was of course an immediate boon, but Miriam also realised that it was the perfect place to stow her valuables, unknown to the boy – or so she thought. Thereafter, every time she was paid in coins, rather than by barter – eggs, chickens, vegetables etc – she insisted on personally collecting the water for the household. Before long it became obvious to both Lio and Ashur that the water cistern had also become the bank. Remembering Kyrros' secret hiding place at the farm, it was for that reason – and not as Miriam and Ashur thought, because Kyrros had dug the well on the farm – that Lio suggested they call the natural spring: 'The Well of Andronicus'. Miriam and Ashur liked the name, but Lio never did betray what had been the secret of Kyrros' bank.

Over the next two years, life was idyllic for the family, who made many friends on the island. Between building, helping create their home, keeping animals, using the machine to make charts and generally being the odd-job boy, Lio was extremely content. The boy grew taller, and began to fill-out, especially through his constant daily swimming and other physical toil. He reminded Miriam of the now sunken statue of him that they had once giggled at. Perhaps he was not fully grown yet, not quite yet a man, but at fourteen years of age, his voice changed and his body along with it – his chest and shoulders broadening. He was certainly at least on the way to becoming a fine young adult.

And as Lio grew over the years spent there on the island, so Ashur grew along with him – her own body and personality changing just as dramatically as his – although she did not grow as tall as he. Until gradually, although he often denied he'd noticed, Ashur started to become what was an undeniably quite beautiful young woman. And, of course, the young woman did not notice at all that Lio had changed!

Still, both of them were the pride and joy of Miriam."

Maddie and Bex glanced sheepishly at Alex and Conna. The boys looked back equally sheepishly. No one spoke, but everyone now felt entirely at ease in each other's company.

"Oh!" Tom remembered, "There was one other thing that I almost completely forgot to tell you about. Not long after they had settled, Miriam had a child of her own – Kyrros' child."

"What!" Conna almost choked on the apple he'd just helped himself to. He started to cough as various other comments were voiced.

"But, we thought."

"But how?"

"But who?"

The clamour settled as Tom went on to explain.

"Of course, since they had arrived, Lio and Ashur noticed that Miriam had gradually started to put on weight, although no one, including Miriam, guessed the cause until she had been carrying the baby for about four months. She had even shrugged off Ashur's own direct hand-signed question. "Are you having a baby?" At her age, she had assumed that the various signs were something other than what would have been obvious to another woman. *Perhaps,* she thought, *they might even have been caused by all of the obvious stress that they'd undergone.* But the bump at her abdomen very definitely began to confirm the woman's greatest wish, to have her husband's child. Now realising it, it explained the other clear signs that in retrospect had been plain to the physician in her: the fainting in Alexandria, her breathlessness and her recent dizzy spells. It really had been quite obvious all the time.

Perhaps it was simply that her own mind sought to deny everything subconsciously – in case it was not true – and in which case she would be overwhelmingly disappointed – not to say devastated. Nevertheless, it was indeed true. Although, Miriam did not stop practising medicine until one month before she gave birth, when the bump became too ungainly for her to move about properly.

Already, in her short time on the island, Miriam had delivered several other babies. She knew the signs and what to expect, and yet on the evening of her child's own birth, she was still caught out. On

124

that day, Lio had gone to the other end of the island to make up a chart for a rich merchant who had arrived from Syracuse. Such was the reputation for success he had gained within the time he had been there, that the merchant had asked for him specifically on the recommendation of another sailor. Mapping charts out and using a machine to demonstrate their accuracy were absolutely unique, and news had spread rapidly of the 'boy wonder' and his machine as he became known once more. For that reason, and for the simple reason that their neighbours were too far away for even Ashur to alert in time, it was the young girl, Ashur herself, who delivered the baby – perfectly."

"Was it a boy or a girl?" asked Maddie, desperate to know.

Tom teased a little more, rubbing his eyes before insisting on going for a short 'comfort break'. There was a short breath of exasperation from the girls as he left the room, heading for the bathroom.

"What difference does that make?" asked Conna.

"Everything," said Bex. "If it was a boy, we've got a second candidate for who Tom might be. He could either be Lio – Kyrros' step-son – or this new baby, Kyrros' birth son."

"Oh yeah!" Conna hadn't considered that possibility, although he was the only one who hadn't. "So Tom's saying he might either be Kyrros' adopted son or his real son."

"Quite possibly," confirmed Maddie.

"Of course, neither one is actually possible." Bex interjected quickly, keeping everything real – we're still talking two thousand years ago, aren't we. No one could actually believe it?" Then realising, she shot a look of either apology or contrition at Alex. Alex remained silent.

"Well, yeah, obviously," mumbled Conna.

Tom re-entered the room and sat back down to continue. "Where was I?"

"The baby," prompted Maddie urgently.

"Oh yes, the baby," Tom repeated. "When Lio returned later that morning, he was instantly delighted to learn from Ashur, even before he hit the house, that they had a new baby brother. And, of course, his first name would be Andronikos. The real surprise to Lio was that his second name would be Helio, in honour of his big brother and in his father's belief in the natural power source of the world – the scientifically constructed world."

The four friends exchanged knowing glances.

Maddie looked curiously. "Tom, how did Ashur tell Lio they had a brother?"

Tom shrugged: "she signed it of course."

"What's the sign for boy then?" Conna smirked cheekily, "this?" he dangled a chubby forefinger.

Maddie looked straight past him to Bex, who kept her face straight whilst dangling her little finger instead.

Conna folded his arms huffily.

Alex shook his head, grinning at the pair.

"As I started to say earlier then," Tom continued, "Lio grew up into a fine young man, bringing up his baby brother, Andros, as he shortened his name, until he had turned eighteen months old. Lio, now fifteen years old, and Ashur, at fourteen, made him toys. Miriam made the simple smocks that all babies wore at that time, until the boy could almost walk quite reasonably on his own, and they were all happy together.

Then, one morning, quite unexpectedly, an urgent message came for 'the boy with the machine' to come quickly to the enclosed harbour at Potamos. He was to be sure to bring the device with him. He was not requested to attend the heavily escorted vessel that had just docked. He was commanded to attend the ship – belonging to Emperor Julius Caesar!

The shock of the sudden communication chilled them all. Lio was, of course, horrified. Instantly, they all thought of the reward still on his head. Their first idea was to pack immediately and to attempt to flee to the other end of the island – try to catch a boat to Crete. But Lio quickly rejected the idea as being fraught with danger for everyone, including especially his baby brother. Other plans were quickly dreamt up only to be equally hastily rejected.

No, thought Lio, *I have not been asked for by name. Perhaps this is not about the burning of the Great Library, but simply the machine.* It was well known that Caesar himself was extremely superstitious. It followed then, that the purpose of the passing visit would most likely be to have Lio make up a chart for him – at least, this seemed the most logical explanation. Though unfortunately, as it turned out, this was not the case at all.

Over two whole years had passed since his brief last meeting with Caesar, and Lio himself had grown. If he covered his bright hair, perhaps he would not be recognised – unless Cleopatra was with the emperor – then he was less sure. Nevertheless, Lio duly took one of Miriam's broad himations – the mantels – and folded it in half lengthwise. Then, with her help, he wrapped it around his head in the manner of an ancient mystic he had once seen as a child in Rhodos – from the lands beyond Persia. His hair tucked carefully into the 'turbanos' and Miriam's scarf wrapped around his neck to complete the effect, he said a nervous goodbye to Miriam and his brother Andros and went to look for Ashur.

At the door, the girl stepped out in front of him carrying the wooden case that he was about to forget in his nervousness. His mouth turned suddenly dry. 'Goodbye Ashur', he croaked, 'don't worry, I'll be back soon,' he hoped to himself. Ashur worriedly handed him the computer box. He took it in his hand and let it swing at his side. Then she suddenly flung her arms around his back and buried her face in his chest, squeezing herself to him as she'd never done before. Lio was taken aback. She really was a young woman now – there was no further denying it. As she freed him from her grip, he looked into her pretty face, not knowing what to say. So as most boys – he said nothing.

The messenger from Potamos now urged Lio to follow him quickly. Then, after a last look at his mother and his brother, Lio looked once more at Ashur, knowing now that she was not simply his friend's sister to him anymore. Nor was she just a friend, nor

127

even a sister – but something else that he couldn't quite fathom. The opposites had truly begun to attract.

This realisation however, seemed to settle his nervousness over the whole urgent meeting as he repeated his promise into her eyes, this time more believingly. 'Please, don't worry Ashur, I *will* come back, *I promise.*' For a brief moment they looked at each other again, wondering what had just communicated itself between each of them. And with that, Lio pulled up the sun-protectors and began to jog toward his appointment with the most undeniably powerful man alive: Gaius Julius Caesar, Dictator Absolute of the Roman world.

PART II:

SOFTLY, SOFTLY, CATCHEE MONKEY…

QUINQUIREME OF NINIVEH FROM DISTANT OPHIR,

ROWING HOME TO HAVEN IN SUNNY PALESTINE…

…DIRTY BRITISH COASTER WITH A SALT-CAKED
SMOKE STACK,

BUTTING THROUGH THE CHANNEL IN THE MAD
MARCH DAYS,

WITH A CARGO OF TYNE COAL… FIREWOOD…
IRON… AND… TIN!

John Masefield: 20th Cent AD

CHAPTER 13:

Imperator Mundi

The specially finished trireme that lay at anchor between the two escorting vessels in the harbour of Potamos was built both to fascinate and intimidate. In the bright spring sun, the gold-leaf which covered much of the carved surface decoration across the ship's sides, dazzled. Its rich light scattered across the surface of the crystal clear sea. And, at the bow, what was now Caesar's own personal good luck charm gleamed – Lio's running cross. The boy noticed it and tucked his own pendant into his tunic.

Walking down the steep hill to stand before the ship, Lio noticed a shoal of small fish sheltering beneath the hull of the big fish that was waiting for him. Hoping again that he would not be recognised, he took a deep breath to calm his nerves. He pulled down the glasses from his eyes and let them hang around his neck, covering them up with Miriam's scarf. Then he stepped forward past the two black-uniformed Praetorian guards who stood at either side of the bottom of the gangplank. He passed a dozen more at the top and another dozen along the deck before he was ushered to the door of Caesar's cabin. 'Enter,' was the one word uttered by the Emperor. At that, Lio was patted-down lightly by two more guards, before being finally shown in by a last guard. Thankfully, he recognised *none* of their faces.

The interior of Caesar's cabin was gloriously cool. The fabulously decorated interior in black and red, with the inevitable purple trim, somehow managed to fit in with the gold, silver and

131

black cushions, couches and the curtained bed within it. It was a richly colourful interior, designed to astound the emperor's visitors as much as it was designed to be comfortable for its owner. Caesar lay on one of the couches, propped-up on one elbow. No one else occupied the cabin. There was no sign of Cleopatra; and that, for now, was at least good news for Lio. Caesar looked much as he had done the last time they had met, but now he wore a crown of gold laurel leaves – presumably to keep the long side strands of hair in place.

'Hail Caesar,' barked the guard, saluting smartly, hand outstretched.

'Any news yet?' Caesar enquired of the guard.

'Not yet Emperor,' came the short reply.

'The moment we hear then!'

'Yes sir,' he saluted, again and left promptly.

Caesar turned his attention to Lio. 'So you're the boy who foretells the future with a machine? Your reputation has spread even to Rome.'

Lio did not agree with the term. 'Emperor,' he answered, 'I can only show the positions of the stars and the planets in the heavens – I cannot predict the future.'

'If that is your belief…' Caesar considered. '…I wish my augurs in Rome were quite as truthful. Tell me, what is your name?'

Lio stumbled over the simple question; not wanting to give his real name on the off-chance it might still be remembered. 'My name sir…?' he replied.

'Yes boy, come on. What is it, what is it?'

'Erm… my name is Lio… of Aegilia,' he almost stumbled again.

'Leo,' Caesar repeated, 'that is a good name. And do you fight like a lion?'

'I'm afraid not sir, I have no interest in fighting.'

'Hmm', considered Caesar, looking directly at the boy. 'But every man needs to be able to handle a sword – at least in self-defence. Lio did not answer back, content to avoid the argument.

After a short pause, Caesar continued abruptly. 'Tell me, how does this machine of yours work boy? In fact, show me.'

Lio took the computer out of the long wooden box and approached Caesar's couch. As the Emperor looked on in fascination, the boy began to explain what the ingenious machine could do. Lio showed him: how it converted the calendars of different countries; how it tracked heavenly bodies; showed the phases of the moon; and calculated both the solar and lunar eclipses. Then, at the end of the short demonstration, Caesar asked, 'And do you claim to have made this machine yourself?'

'No sir,' replied Lio, 'it was made by my... by one of the greatest minds in history. He is not with us anymore.'

'I see, but plainly you know how to operate it well.'

'Yes sir,' replied Lio.

'Good, then I have a proposition for you. I have long considered that throughout my empire there still operates many different calendars besides the official Romulan calendar which has been used since the founding of Rome itself. However, even this Roman calendar is inaccurate and leads to certain "nuisances". The organisational problems this situation causes are a source of constant aggravation. Instead I propose to replace them all with a single calendar to be used throughout the whole world. Perhaps in future, when I am gone, the world will remember me,' he said wryly.

'Sit down,' he beckoned the boy to the couch opposite. 'Indeed, part of the reason I have made this journey is to organise such a change. It may take some time of course, and it will involve many astronomers from around the empire who are gathering as we speak – so that I may consult with them. I require someone to help me in this task, someone who understands all the intricacies of the mechanics of the heavens. More especially, I need someone to work entirely in *my* favour – keep all of the other astronomers in check.'

Lio didn't quite get the idea. 'But surely Emperor, there are many greater people in the world...'

'Yes, quite. I'm sure there are, but none that I might... "trust". They are all obsessed by serving one or another god or king. This problem needs someone young enough to think decisively, know when the religious festivals are – when the stars and planets are in conjunction, et cetera – but cut a swathe through it all. Someone to set definite dates so that in future, as far as it is practical to do so, the same date each year will become known for a certain event. This is the proposition I have for you. You are young enough to realise that it is in your interest not to dare displease me, and obviously, on this tiny island, completely unconnected with those who would seek to discredit me and my efforts to establish a single calendar once and for all'.

Lio shrugged.

"It occurs to me that you will be well placed to help me in this task, someone whom I know will not to give me excuses as for why certain religious festivals cannot be changed, et cetera, et cetera,' he waved a hand dismissively into the air. 'I need someone who will report directly to me in the strictest confidence and report how these negotiations are continuing."

A spy, thought Lio.

"I propose,' Caesar went on, 'that the Egyptian, or Sothic, calendar be used as the basis of the year, with three hundred and sixty five and a quarter days in each year – which will be divided into twelve months. Furthermore, all festivals are to be standardised wherever possible. It has been tried before, I know. But these religious leaders always sow dissent and gradually they return to their own calendar again. This time they will not dare. I will not tolerate another incident like Athens.'

Lio wondered mildly what incident he was referring to, he had not been aware of anything. 'Incident in Athens?' he floated the question curiously.

'Hah… apparently', Caesar explained, 'over a year ago, the Roman calendar and clock tower there – the Horologion – the Tower of the Winds – was the subject of a major riot. Religious leaders from the city stirred up and orchestrated a mob reaction to the mechanical marvel which, amongst other things, showed that the earth was round and it revolved around the sun – something that, in particular, the priests objected to.'

'And what was the outcome?' asked Lio warily.

'Mayhem,' came Caesar's reply. 'The governor was powerless to stop the riot. The doors of the tower were smashed in, the contents trashed completely and major parts removed and melted down. And now, since the destruction of the library of Alexandria and the dissolution of the Mouseion, there is no one who has the knowledge to repair it. The designer, Andronikos, long ago fled – his whereabouts unknown – after being implicated in the library's destruction. A point of view which I cannot agree with Cleopatra, but who nevertheless issued the arrest notice and set a reward.' Caesar raised an eyebrow. 'There is little point in arguing with the queen. She can be a little… stubborn!'

'So what has become of the Tower since?' enquired Lio.

'Oh… not everything was lost,' Caesar snorted. 'The High Priest of Jupiter has turned it into a ritual bath house!'

Lio was staggered. He could have cried at the ignorance and stupidity of it all. All of the hard work and genius of the Horologion – the most amazing machine that the ancient world would ever know – gone, only a year after it was built. And yet, the boy could not let his vexed reaction show for fear that it would reveal his true identity. *Miriam will be devastated,* he thought. To think that her husband's lasting monument to science and technology was already no more than a bath house!

'Coming back to the subject then, that is the reason I wish you to keep an eye on the proceedings in my absence. As young as you are, now with the personal ear of Caesar, you will be able to speak with authority on all of the proceedings regarding the calendar. You will secretly report by letter to me regularly until the task is finished, and then you will return home. For this, you – and your small family' – he said calculatingly, 'will be generously rewarded. And – they will be "protected" from the threat of harm.' At the mention of family, Lio's face dropped.

'The Emperor of the world knows many things,' Caesar pointed out.

Lio understood the implied threat, though he began to wonder why the Emperor had not simply commanded him to come to Rome rather than travel here himself to collect him.

'Well, what do you say?'

'May I have the time to consider?' Lio dabbed his scarf against his sweating forehead. The turbanos was making him hot.

'Yes you may, until my ship sails,' Caesar levelled his eyes directly at the boy's neck.

Of course Lio had no choice, he knew, but while he started to come to terms with what would happen to the others if he did not capitulate, Caesar looked him up and down more fully. 'Where are you from – originally?' The Emperor asked, 'You're not Greek, not with white skin like that. You're from the north lands aren't you?' The older man looked long and hard at him. 'Take off that headdress.'

Lio started to worry, but he removed the turbanos anyway.

'I've seen that hair before, somewhere...'

The boy was about to capitulate, when Caesar almost shouted smugly, 'I know... Britannia... there are many tribes there which have blonde, red and brown hair colouring – all natural!'

Lio caught his breath again.

'I'd wager money on it that your parents came from there. Am I right?'

'I don't know sir,' Lio answered. 'Both parents died before I knew them. My grandfather told me I was from the Cassiterides.'

Caesar recognised the old name. 'Anyway,' prompted the emperor, 'what's it to be?'

As Lio made up his mind to agree to the 'choice', so the guard came back in and saluted. 'Caesar, the pirates are fleeing,' he barked out smartly.

It was then that Lio began to realise the emperor's other reason for his visit to the island.

'Good' replied Caesar pointedly, more to the guard's news than Lio's decision.

Lio gulped in the air. 'Yes sir,' he agreed formally, 'I will help. May I inform my family?'

'No, no time, I'm afraid – they will be notified for you. I'll send a messenger. And later, you can write from Alexandria.'

'Alexandria!' Lio's head began to swim. 'I had thought I'd be taken to Rome.'

'No,' said Caesar, as the ship weighed anchor and got underway. 'You will be taken to work with the main organiser of the task of bringing in the new calendar, Sosigenes of Alexandria. It will take perhaps three years at most,' Caesar reassured him.

'Three years!' Lio couldn't help his shocked outburst.

'I need you to stay there well after the calendar is started – ensure a smooth transition period – inform me of any problems which may occur – remember Athens.'

Panic began to set in. Things were going casually from bad to worse. Three years – he would be eighteen years old by the time he returned! On top of that, he was being delivered by Caesar personally, back to Alexandria, possibly to work with some of the people who knew his full identity. Surely it would only be a matter of time before he was found out by Cleopatra.

As if reading his mind, Caesar then delivered the blow to his solar-plexus. 'I Remember, I met Andronikos once – although only briefly. It was a great pity he didn't survive the shipwreck... but at least your father went down with some of the greatest treasures I have ever collected.'

Lio's jaw dropped.

'It was your good luck charm that gave you away – bad luck!' he smirked. 'Don't worry, you are now under my absolute protection, no one will dare harm you. Besides, the queen, together with our son, now resides in Rome. Doubtlessly, she's enjoying her newfound wealth as usual, while I am busy.'"

Tom looked at the four. He inhaled, "It seemed that, at first, although no one knew exactly where the corbita had gone down after leaving the island of Crete, it was fair to assume that the Cretan pirates had played a part in it and its much valuable cargo going missing. When, over a year later, rumours began to emerge about a stranger on the island of Aegilia – a red-haired boy who wore strange glass sunlight-protectors over his eyes, and who had an ingenious mechanical device that he was able to use to make star charts – it became obvious to one or two at least, that the two stories were linked. Now, at last having the spare time available to him, Caesar had resolved to take his revenge on those who had deprived him of his spoils from Alexandria. He would also clear out the pirates once again into the bargain. They had now become more than just a nuisance anyway – they were also a constant threat to absolute Roman supremacy on the seas. Besides, on eventually finding out that the missing corbita had been delivering cargo for Caesar himself, the master of the pirate vessel who had run it ashore had also begun to brag foolishly that, since then, even Caesar had avoided his part of the sea. That was his fatal mistake. He had gone too far now – and that would be the final nail in his coffin. It was that, rather than Caesar's speech about ridding the seas of the Cretan and Aegilian thieves, which was the key issue to the man.

'Put on your eye-protectors and follow me on deck,' Caesar smirked, 'I have a personal score to settle. You can watch me take revenge on behalf of your father. This time though, the solution to the pirate problem will be more permanent. I'm sick and tired of the way that everyone seems to think we have to put up with them.'

As much as he knew the pirates were all of the things that Caesar said they were, constantly raiding the islands unopposed, the boy had a sense of foreboding about Caesar's permanent solution. At first, Lio had thought that the pirate vessels would be held captive whilst, yet again, a deal was struck to 'never again' dare to attack Roman ships. This was, after all, how these matters had been settled for generations. Not long before his beheading at the hands of King Ptolemy's generals, Pompey Magnus – Pompey the Great himself – had 'conquered' the pirates in just this fashion. Now, Lio felt uncomfortable in having to stand on deck to watch. Furthermore, he did not like the way that Caesar had implicated his father in what he was about to do. Revenge, he knew, was not something that

Kyrros would ever have contemplated or approved of.

Emerging from the concealed harbour, and flanked by the other two quinqiremes, Lio watched from close quarters as, only a hundred paces away, the Roman fleet pursued the five pirate vessels that they had chased there from Crete. In the flat, sunlit sea, a second column of his fleet had driven another five ships toward them from around the other side of the island. Now, rather than avoid colliding into themselves, the pirate ships had heaved-to in the deep water of the channel between Aegilia and its larger neighbour. The pirates knew when to quit, corralled as they were by the far greater number and far more well-armed Romans. This time however, if Lio had thought that this was going to be either a battle or a negotiation, he was mistaken. It was to be a private humiliation, a retribution for ridiculing the reputation of Caesar himself.

The boy stood on deck behind the Emperor and watched in growing horror as the whole plan unfolded before his eyes. These were people who had for countless generations preyed on innocent merchants and their crews. Their greed and cruelty was renowned throughout the Mediterranean. Some had indeed been indirectly responsible for the death of Kyrros – and, unknown to Lio, generations before, his genetic father, the tin trader. Nevertheless, what Lio witnessed that day would sicken him – the image of it haunting him for the rest of his life.

One of the Praetorian guards produced a large copper megaphone and stood beside Caesar with it. Then, Lio heard Caesar, the supreme commander, give the guard an almost casually spoken command, 'Phase I.'

The guard repeated the command in a loud shout – the predetermined plan to the other Roman vessels to squeeze the pack tighter together. The pirates had surrendered – had no intention of trying to fight or escape – they were merely waiting for the bargaining to begin again.

'Phase II.' The guard called out, repeating Caesar's command. The ships were boarded by soldiers, some carrying barrels. The crews were one-by-one, firstly disarmed, and then their hands tied behind their backs – about five hundred souls in all.

'Phase III.' The women were separated from the men – about two hundred – and children – a further hundred or thereabouts – aged four to fourteen were all taken on board one of the Roman Triremes.

'Phase IV.' Lio dared not interfere he knew, but what he saw disgusted him. The children were lined up on deck. Roman tradition dictated that, being under age, they could not be executed by one of the standard methods of garrotting – strangulation with a tourniquet – or else crucifixion. Instead they were, to the screams and wails of all the witnesses – mothers and fathers included – ritually strangled from behind: ten at a time by bare-hand. Their bodies were then thrown immediately overboard. Only a small white boy and a black girl were singled out and allowed to remain alive.

'Phase V.' Next, the women were lined up and again, one at a time, their throats unceremoniously cut and their bodies thrown overboard.

'Phase VI.' Caesar, not bothering to watch the end of the slaughter, ordered over his shoulder: 'make sure both witnesses are delivered home safely and intact. We wouldn't wish this to be forgotten, would we? And tell them to deliver a message from the Emperor; his eyes suddenly died. 'In future, piracy is *permanently* forbidden on this island.'

Lio could not turn away, but the tears that had welled up as the children had been dispatched, and had continued into a flood as he'd witnessed what had happened to the women, now dried up in shock at Caesar's final solution to the pirate problem. Not even the ships, now tied together, were to be salvaged. This really would be a demonstration of the sickening but absolute domination of Rome. The sticky content of the barrels was spread across the decks of the pirate ships before the soldiers retired and the Roman vessels pulled back. Then, at the final pre-organised signal, archers lined up on their decks and shot flaming arrows into the sky and into the pirates, still on their own decks. Within minutes, fire fully engulfed the ships' masts and hulls until, one by one, the vessels began to drift apart. Only after half an hour did they start to keel over and sink, scattering their remains across the entire area. Men screamed and moaned as they were either shot, burned alive or jumped overboard to drown. Any surviving swimmers – not many – were then picked-off with arrows.

Lio hung his head in shame at what he had witnessed."

Alex and his friends looked at one another, for the first time inclined to truly believe Tom's eyewitness account of such a massacre.

CHAPTER 14:

Plumbing the Depths

"Caesar sat silently in his cabin, eating, whilst once more Lio was ushered in. 'Does my justice disturb you?' he asked casually. 'It had to be done for the sake of free trade across the world. You do know that don't you.'

Lio didn't answer.

'No matter, before we leave for Alexandria, I have one last task for you. I'd like you to show me where my cargo went down – just out of curiosity. Can you do that?'

'Yes,' Lio answered blankly. Traumatised by what he'd seen, he turned to follow Caesar almost dizzily back up on deck.

As Caesar's ship was rowed gently along the coastline and past the various treacherous rocks, the oars constantly pushed through the thick stream of bodies – those that had preceded them by way of the natural current from the death site. In only a few minutes, the boat hove-to, the rowers sculling lightly to keep the ship over the precise spot that Lio had only visited twice since that fatal night on the anniversary of Kyrros' death. The constant thin stream of bodies passed by as he looked out.

In the daylight, and from the seaward perspective, the place now indeed looked like a low sandy beach as they approached. But now the rocks looked as jagged as Lio remembered. And there, in front, was the distinct single rocky outcrop that the corbita had struck. The boy indicated that they had arrived.

'This is the precise spot? You're sure?' Caesar asked for confirmation.

'Yes, it is,' Lio confirmed, still in a daze.

'Good.' He turned to the master of the vessel, now stood beside him, 'Take soundings.'

'Yes, sir,' the master ordered one of the crew to drop the plumb line. He threw the end of the knotted rope, twenty fathoms long, over the side to see how deep it was. Then he let out the line carefully.

'Nothing sir – fathomless.'

'Tie on more rope then,' ordered Caesar, 'it can't be that deep.'

Another twenty fathoms of rope was tied on and paid out gradually. 'Almost spent,' the master advised the Emperor. Then, at the very last knot, the crewman felt the distinct slackness in the line that he'd been waiting for. He pulled it up and down twice to confirm it and each time felt a slight clonk as it touched the bottom, 'Forty fathoms.'

Caesar closed his eyes and gritted his teeth. Forty fathoms and everything had lain there for two years. He wondered about the effort. 'Well boy, do you think I might find some of my treasure if I fish here?'

Lio could only think of his father down there. Entirely subdued, he ventured, 'I doubt it. In any case, some of it was smashed to pieces when we hit the rocks.'

'Hmm', Caesar turned to the master. 'Well… mark the site on your charts and remember it exactly, just in case. 'Now,' he said disappointedly, 'set sail for Alexandria.'

Caesar's Sicilian advisor had been right so far, this *had* been the island. Perhaps as a result of the advances made in technology that had been made recently, it would indeed allow some form of salvage attempt after all – even though it all lay in water much deeper than expected. He remembered being personally handed a particularly ancient account on the one occasion that he'd visited the Alexandria library. It was written by the ancient philosopher Aristotle himself. It described a salvage technique using an inverted iron cauldron designed to help in these situations. And regardless, the Murex shell divers from Porphyrusa did have a reputation second to none.

Drifting off down the coastline, just as the pumice had done years before, the garish slick of bodies parted to let the boat through. Disgusted at the cold blooded actions of the Emperor, Lio asked to be led to the cabin that he would stay in alone for the rest of the journey.

Below decks, the boy looked again at the machine – the computer – knowing that it was its use that had got him into trouble. He knew also that while it survived he would be unlikely to see peace in his own lifetime or that of his family. Picking it up, he held it out of the hatch. Just for a moment, he was tempted to drop it overboard – give it back to his father – but then he realised he could not. No doubt he would be executed for disobeying the Emperor. And then he shuddered as he thought of what might... no, *would* happen to Miriam, Ashur and Andros. He retrieved the device, lay down on the bunk and resigned himself to the task that lay ahead of him. Shocked, horrified at what he'd seen, and now that he was effectively captured, he concentrated on the one good thing he still had in his life – his family. And, the person who in particular he realised had become – probably always was – his soul mate, Ashur.

Caesar only once contacted him again whilst on board. He demanded that Lio calculate a three year chart of his own 'life stars'.

Of course, Lio began to, but still refused to comment on it other than scientifically. At that, Caesar became impatient with him and lost interest. So, after that short journey, Lio handed over only half of the chart. It mapped the heavenly bodies for eighteen months of Caesar's life, and then it stopped midway through the month of Mars – or March. To his immense relief, after that meeting, he would never have to set eyes on the Emperor again.

As the ship eventually passed the Pharos tower and made its way into the great harbour of Alexandria, Lio began to wonder about making that distant wish to return. All he could do now was plan to spend his time away from his family in absorbing himself in study at the once great seat of learning."

Tom stopped to recover from the disturbing downturn in his story.

144

Conna hadn't grasped the enormity of the harrowing scene Tom had earlier described, struggling to see it as a depiction of a real event. To him it was just a story. He decided to speak up, once again belatedly. "Tom," he asked, "weren't the pirates robbers and murderers themselves?"

"Certainly," he answered, "some of them were, but by no means all of them – I make no case for them other than they did not deserve to be eradicated in such a disgraceful and cold blooded manner, no peoples do. This was simply genocide – although that particular word was not invented until the twentieth century AD."

"But if they'd been warned for years… they couldn't be allowed to keep on getting away with it, could they?"

"It is a dilemma, I agree," Tom returned. "But the world did not actually ever belong to the Romans; they just stole it, as some peoples attempt to do from time to time. The pirates had a different philosophy – a different way of looking at the world. To them the world was a goat, and the people living on it merely quarrelsome fleas. To argue who owned the world was as ridiculous as the fleas arguing over which one of them owned the goat, no more than that. And doubtlessly, they had their own moral code as such."

"But they still had to be stopped, didn't they," argued Conna.

Tom paused deliberately. "Perhaps… but if you had actually witnessed the faces of those people… heard the pleading and begging, the screams and wails of those mothers and fathers forced to watch… believe me Conna, you would not be as quick to judge who should be allowed to live or die."

Conna looked subdued, beginning to realise.

"Tom, were the Romans always really that cruel?" asked Maddie innocently.

"Without a shadow of doubt," Tom almost growled. "They had a well-earned notorious reputation, from the time of the Spartacus revolt in Caesar's youth, the organised slave revolt named after their leader which ended in every defeated slave being crucified along the Appian Way – the main road leading from Capua to Rome. Six thousand bodies were left to rot in the sun – *six thousand souls!* They were left for weeks, until even the Roman citizens themselves campaigned to get them removed – such was the disgusting and unhygienic stench – and the flies!

Later, there was the Romans' callous treatment of the peoples of the Palestine, and the Christians in particular, making 'Roman candles' by binding them alive to poles, wrapping them in oil-soaked cloth and setting fire to them so that the fat on their bodies fuelled the flame. Or by feeding them to wild animals: lions and panthers, purely for the mob's entertainment. You all know this from your books, and movie films, and your TV machines, but no one now can imagine what it was actually like to see, hear – and smell – these sickening events. Even this country, Britannia, did not escape their moral outrages.

At the siege of Mona, the Druides knew that they were more than likely about to lose the battle at the hands of the vast surrounding Roman army that had rounded them up onto the now Welsh island of Anglesey. Heroically, they bade their own families to leave the besieged wooden fenced citadel – 'the pale'. At this last stand of the warriors, the Romans watched the thousands of women and children walk out in their long caravan 'beyond the pale' to cross through the enemy lines, as was the honourable way – the long established etiquette of 'barbarian' war. But the disgraceful Romans reneged on their given word and penned them all between the circular fenced battle lines. They then waited for the Druides to reopen the fortress gates to allow them back in. Knowing that the Romans would win instantly if they did, they were forced to watch for weeks on end as their own wives and children were starved, beaten and worse. Then they were slaughtered one by one. The demoralised warriors, who could not take it anymore, were then eradicated in the Druides own final solution.

To the Romans, genocide was just another strategy that led to world domination," Tom finished in disgust. "Such callousness for the wasting of human life as witnessed by Lio paled into insignificance against this." Tom's anger grew as he continued. "There were no depths which the Romans would not plumb.

Historians often make me wonder if they know about humanity. Often I have heard or read of how 'great' the Romans were, how 'strong' and 'single-minded' they were against 'the barbarians'. Remember this: they are the heroes of their own histories only because they systematically eradicated the truth about these so called barbarians." He thumped his fist on the arm of his chair. "Thankfully, this callousness would not be witnessed on such a scale for another two thousand years, until once more, the fascists rose – this time in the self-styled Third Reich. Tell me," Tom asked, "if that disgrace to humanity, Hitler, had won the Second World War, how do you think the history of his world would now be recorded? Would it mention the five million innocent men women and children that he slaughtered? The Greeks, the Poles, the Russians, the Catholic priests, the travelling peoples, the blacks, and of course, the additional six million Jews, amongst many, many missing others. Would it tell of the Nazis' unspeakable wickedness, their cruelty and contempt for the lives of their fellow human beings – men women and children? Or would the history of a victorious Third Reich simply have dismissed them all as 'sub-humans that had been victoriously eradicated for the good of the Reich!' This is the way history is written by the victors. Hitler's fascists did exactly the same as the Romans had before them. All of the Romans' vanquished foes became simply 'dead barbarians'. "

There was deathly silence in the room as Tom's anger subsided with his sobbing breath. The four began to appreciate why he had dismissed the Romans as wicked from the start. To him these were not simply stories, or history, but the real horrors – of real wars.

Calming down, Tom concluded "I wonder sometimes if these evils are destined to be repeated endlessly, just as Kyrros' toroidal shaped universe was thought to spin around and around." He left the four to briefly ponder this last oblique thought while he returned uneasily to his story. "I am sorry I lost my temper, but I get sick and tired of listening to those who admire this side of human behaviour – just because it all seems now long ago! Perhaps if they had been there to witness these atrocities…" Eventually, calmly, though a little out of breath, Tom began again:

"In Alexandria, for the past two years, the Nile had risen again and flooded the land with its life-giving mud. Crops again flourished and life for the ordinary population of the city had returned to some semblance of normality. Since Ptolemy's death at the battle of the Nile, and the introduction of Roman rule, admittedly, life in the city seemed stable. But sadly, the city was a much watered down version of its previous self. All hope of rebuilding the Mouseion or Library in anything like its previous grand style had gone, at least in all but name. There were simply not the funds available – mainly siphoned off by Cleopatra to fund her lavish lifestyle in Rome. Even years later, after Mark Antony succumbed to the temptations of Cleopatra and he replaced it with the contents of the library looted from Pergamum, Alexandria did not bear any resemblance to what it had once been. The city had become a hollow shell – without books, and especially without scholars to use them.

The moment that Lio arrived, as the personal representative of the Emperor, he was moved immediately into the royal palace – directly opposite the flattened area that had once been the Great Library. In fact, ironically, Lio was allowed to live in part of the opulent quarters previously occupied by the late king, his friend, Ptolemy XIII. This was because although Cleopatra's even younger brother was now declared Ptolemy XIV, he lived in virtual captivity – as a hostage in Rome. So, all the time that Lio was destined to stay in Alexandria, he lived in the lap of luxury – though this life of purely material wealth was entirely lost on him. More importantly, he was forbidden to leave Alexandria, even to *visit* his home. He was further forbidden to invite any of his family to travel to see him, though he regularly sent letters of course – always addressed to his mother. It took him months to pluck up the courage to write to Miriam to tell her of what had befallen the Horologion. Though, no matter how he thought of her, Lio always studiously avoided mentioning the subject of his private feelings toward Ashur –

whatever they were. That, he told himself, was something to address face to face – if ever the time came. At least though, to his great relief, Cleopatra did not return to Egypt. Despite what Caesar had promised about his safety, such was her unpredictability that he was certain he would no longer be safe if she did arrive – he was, of course, still officially on her wanted list!

There, in Alexandria, Lio did indeed get to meet and work with the great Sosigenes the astronomer, who was already quartered in the royal sector. In fact, despite the great differences in their age, they became good friends. Even though he was still only fifteen years of age, Lio was able to discuss with him what would be the most appropriate numbers of days in each month – although they would later be changed by successive Emperors almost upon a whim. Together, they set when important anniversaries – for instance mid-winters day would be fixed – around the solstices and equinoxes – and the dates of annual games etc. Though, as predicted, there were many arguments about fixing 'holy' days, like the various gods' celebration festivals and games. However, between Sosigenes and Lio, both having the Emperor's authority in these matters, they ensured that no one strayed too far from the desired track. Within that first month, the 'Julian Calendar' was agreed in full, and Sosigenes was well rewarded by the Emperor. He bade Lio farewell, and retired from the task immediately afterward, to live out the rest of his life in his villa by the shores of the Red Sea.

From then on, Lio was bored for most of the time. As grand as his job sounded, there was no value for him in being a minion of Caesar. All Lio could do was begin to fill his time as best he could, waiting for the day when he could return home."

"What year was that then?" Alex checked.

Tom looked surprised. "Why, the year zero, of course."

"No," asked Alex, "in our modern calendar."

"Ah," Tom considered. "It was adopted for use in the year 45 BC."

"So that's the same as our calendar today?"

"I'm afraid not, our modern calendar was adapted one last time by the Pope, Gregory XIII… in the year 1582, sometime after the Church finally accepted the assertions that Copernicus and Galileo had made regarding the heliocentric principle – with the sun being at the centre of the universe. The Church's 'Gregorian Calendar' is the basis of our modern calendar. It is strange to think of how much time and effort has gone in to marking the passing of our days on earth, is it not?"

Alex smiled as he again recognised the distant sentiment of his own father. He kept it to himself.

"The main task completed, still, it was Caesar's desire that Lio stay on for another two and a half years – albeit in this gilded cage – 'in case of any unforeseen problems'. Eventually, as the calendar was rolled out within the whole empire, it was Lio who stayed on hand to settle any claimed dispute.

Of course, as he grew over the next year, as the personal representative of Caesar, Lio's life experiences began to change. He was invited to many official functions by those who assumed he was in Caesar's particular favour, but that was not to say that he was happy. All the while that Lio lived in Alexandria his mind was focussed on one place – home. And on one person in particular.

Then, one day, on the last day of the month of Mars, in what we would now call the year 44BC – just into Lio's second year in the Emperor's service – news arrived that threw the palace into disarray. It would also simultaneously split the Roman world and again threaten Lio's future safety. In the middle of that same month, Julius Caesar had been brutally assassinated by the senate in Rome. News quickly circulated that, still in Rome, two opposing sides formed once again. On the one hand, the senate, led by Brutus and Cassius – two of Caesar's assassins – and on the other hand, the claimed new Emperor, Caesar's nephew Octavian, supported by Caesar's old friend and ally Mark Antony. The world was once again about to become embroiled in civil war. But this time, Lio hoped to avoid any part in it. Sadly, the young man's wish was not to be – and neither did it hasten his anticipated return home.

In the wake of these events in Italy, news also spread throughout Alexandria that the hostaged King Ptolemy XIV, Cleopatra's younger brother, had been mysteriously poisoned in Rome. Cleopatra and her son had immediately fled the city in the aftermath of the reported 'anti Egyptian' event. In the following days, a small anti Roman demonstration was quelled in Alexandria. Word came that all travel from the port was banned. Then, one afternoon, from Lio's quarters in the palace, he spotted an ornately gilded and decorated ship lying-off the royal, or Eunostos dock. That evening, as an 'emergency measure', Cleopatra's infant son Caesarion was proclaimed as the new King of Egypt – Ptolemy XV. He would reign with his mother. Fortuitously – or murderously – Cleopatra had at last won the throne effectively to herself!

The sixteen year old Lio was not about to wait to find out what was about to come next. As Cleopatra's royal barge landed next morning, Lio wasted no time in getting out of the city – though abandoning all of the payment owed him to date. First, sending a note to Aegilia to explain his actions, the young man fled inland, to the shores of the Red Sea. He made his way unannounced to the private house of Sosigenes the astronomer, where he was immediately taken under the wing of the scholar. Predictably, it was not long before the reinstated Queen Cleopatra found out that he had been living in her palace. She immediately reissued the warrant for his arrest. All Lio could do was lay low and hope that in time he would be able to return home to Aegilia without the risk of bringing danger with him.

For two long years after that, as the Roman civil war waged throughout the Mediterranean, Lio was desperate to head for home. But although he wrote whenever he could, the young man still felt that he could not take the risk of returning. In the meantime, as a cover, he worked at the private library of Sosigenes – in fact, he became its head librarian! There, he catalogued the works that the astronomer was busy trying to reassemble in an attempt to save the Greeks' knowledge for posterity in the aftermath of the fire in the

Great Library. Although, centuries later, even that small library would eventually fall – its scattered works ending up who knows where."

Tom looked down at his hands. Reluctantly perhaps, he admitted: "However, it must be said that whilst living there in self exile, as he grew through his mid teens, Lio enjoyed a full lifestyle. Although he did not often drink alcohol: wine, or even the watery Egyptian ale, as did virtually all others at that place. It never did agree with him and he was always prone to falling asleep with its effect. Throughout all of his time there, Lio still wished only to be in the company of the one girl uppermost in his mind. In fact, he dreamed of Ashur constantly.

For two years, no-one ever suspected Lio of being a 'wanted criminal', and so, one day, just after his eighteenth birthday, he decided that it was finally safe enough for him to leave. With the blessing of Sosigenes, Lio took the wage due to him, and bade farewell. Then he got his small belongings together and left across the desert, back toward the Mediterranean.

Finally," Tom announced, "Lio was going home!"

CHAPTER 15:

Plumbing the Depths Again

Tom clearly held the attention of the small group as he continued:

"Back on Aegilia, those same few years flew by. Since the destruction of the pirates, the island had become vastly repopulated in this now private island in the sun. After all, it was just far enough away from the rest of the dangerous Roman world, but close enough for all practical purposes. And, it was of course, at the crossroads of the business centres of Alexandria, Athens and Rome.

Along with this new prosperity, Miriam and Ashur's own fame as excellent physicians grew. Although they now had a very good living on the island, they had never moved from the house that Lio had rebuilt; and they had no intention of ever doing so. As regularly as he could manage, Lio would send a letter, of course telling them quite openly about his life in Alexandria. Ashur herself also had many friends – and had even gained one or two potential suitors. One Cretan Roman in particular often came to call. But the truth be told, although she was flattered by his attentions, her heart was never in the relationship. Ashur had long ago decided whom she wanted to share her life with. And she had concentrated on the anticipation of one event only.

One day, at last, Lio's long awaited letter arrived. He would be home within the month. Now everyone waited for his return.

However, a full year before Caesar's assassination, there had been one disturbing event happen on the island that neither Miriam nor Ashur wished to know about. The sea-grave of Kyrros had been disturbed.

That spring, after the rough winter seas had calmed, a huge ship, the like of which no one had seen before, sailed across the horizon. The ship, a twin-hulled barge, had a massive, flat platform that spanned the hulls, and which was filled with all sorts of strange looking equipment. Without calling at the island, it had sailed down its coast and positioned itself directly over the site where the corbita had sunk. Bracing itself off the rocks, it had stayed a few weeks only. Then it had sailed back to Rome. Witnesses of the event, and there were only a few, told of a huge bell of some sort being lowered through a hole in the platform. Tales circulated of many divers lost in agonising deaths and of broken statues being recovered, sorted, and many being dumped back overboard. Though thankfully, no one spoke of finding human remains. The rough winter seas had, no doubt, scoured that aspect clean.

In fact, although the salvage operation had taken only a few short days, it had been deemed a great success, if not by Caesar, at least by his advisor who had part-funded and organised the whole operation since its inception two years before. The strange vessel had been expensive to build and to operate. Many specialist Greek workers had been required to operate the equipment, and the divers themselves had been brought in from across the channel in Porphyrusa. Of course, these 'free-divers' were used to diving for the Murex shells that the purple dye was extracted from – sometimes up to twenty fathoms. Some were used to diving slightly deeper for the bigger sponges, but none had attempted to dive as deep as forty fathoms. This operation was entirely experimental – 'for military purposes' – they were told.

Three separate techniques were employed over the site:

The first, most obvious method was to attempt to employ the standard free-diving techniques – although strange glass eye-bubbles held with leather straps were provided to allow clearer vision. Clutching the skandalopetra – the roughly shaped diving rocks – the divers took it in turn to plummet as deep and as fast as they could –

but no one made it to the bottom. Each decided to let go of the diving rocks before they got too deep. It did produce the first casualty however, as one diver lost an eye when one of the carelessly damaged glass bubbles imploded. A few days later, when infection set in, he died. It was neither a painless nor pleasant death.

The second diving method was more experimental than the first. It relied on a different principle known to the Ancient Greeks – the same one rediscovered by the Romans in the Great Library just before its destruction – breathing underwater using upturned cauldrons – cooking vessels. This however, produced the first direct fatality. In pairs, the divers stood on a giant Roman concrete plumbum and clung on dearly whilst it was allowed to plummet instantly to the sea bed. Once there, they were supposed to breathe-in the naturally compressed air from the large cauldron each had taken with him – the buoyant cooking pot was tied directly to the plumbum. What hadn't been fully appreciated however was just how much the air would be compressed by the pressure of the atmosphere and water above. Breathing-in the tiny amount of air – compressed naturally almost ten times at forty fathoms – one of the two divers desperately held onto all of his breath during his assisted ascent. Using a huge rope and a geared pulley, he was winched up rapidly. As this happened, the air in his lungs expanded back to ten times its compressed volume. Obviously, this massively ruptured his lungs and, just below the surface, killed him instantly. However, the second diver, who had simply breathed out on his own ascent, was perfectly alright. Nevertheless, after a few more attempts, this method was finally abandoned. The divers' time on the bottom was rapidly diminished by the tiny air supply that could be carried to that extreme depth.

The third and final method was far more controlled. However it still did not stop the deaths. Based on the same cauldron idea, an ungainly and experimental bronze bell, one and a half times the height of a man, was lowered carefully into the water. This trapped the air inside it and allowed a diver to travel slowly to the bottom, also compressing the air to the said one tenth of its surface volume.

On the first occasion, the diving bell toppled over half way down in the current. The diver inside was drowned before he could swim back to the surface. To prevent the bell toppling over and losing the compressed air in future, four holes were roughly pierced through the rim of the bell. Extra weights, large rocks, were then attached to it by ropes, to keep it stable. By this method, two or more divers were able to stay down for ten minutes at a time, returning to the bell between breaths before the one foot of compressed air at the top of the bell ran out. This worked quite efficiently until it was decided that they should stay down longer, for up to an hour. But it was then that the 'screaming deaths' started.

At first, no one who witnessed the spectacle knew what was happening to the divers. Some guessed that the deaths were due to fear. That the shaking and convulsing bodies which were unable to speak as they were pulled out of the water were dying, clearly as a result of something so terrifying down there that they were simply unable to go on living. This, of course, led in turn to the myth propagated by the Roman master and the event organiser: that Neptune – formerly the Greek god Poseidon – had indeed sent sea monsters to protect the site for himself. All of the islanders kept away from the cursed place. It was only after ten of the original twelve divers had eventually been killed, that it was decided to go back to the shorter stays on the sea bed, and then only four times per day. At last though, even though many statues had already been recovered, it was, naturally on the last dive that the real object of the exercise had been achieved.

As the bell was lowered with the last two divers inside, a strong current swept it momentarily off course and its weights settled above the soft sand, well to the side of the battered corbita. One diver left the bell at the bottom and swam along the sea-bed, back to the stern where he had been on his last dive. He picked up the lightly rusted chains briefly before letting them drop. Then he noticed a pair of perfectly round diving stones, complete with some sort of looped handles. He presumed that they had been dropped in the previous weeks and no-one had retrieved them. Next, he turned his attention

156

to the area which had been the master's cabin before it had collapsed. Something glinted in the scant sunlight which had managed to permeate these extreme depths. He picked up the gold coin, rubbed it, and scratched around with his other hand to see if there were any more. He retrieved a dozen or so pieces before he returned to the bell. His diving partner, who had been exploring elsewhere, arrived at the same time.

Inside it, in the limited air supply, they briefly discussed how to hide the gold from those above, tucking it safely into their pearl pouches and into their loincloths. Intending to go back a second time, swimming across the sunlit bottom, the second diver passed another oddly geometric shaped rock that appeared to lie on the surface of the sand. He clutched at it but it didn't move, then he fanned away the loose sand that surrounded the object, realising that he had found what they had been sent to locate. Too late to do anything about it now, he returned to the bell and waited for his partner. Shortly after, he duly arrived with more coins, both gold and silver. Stashing the coins in the same pouch, the bell was hoisted slowly up. Then, at the top, the news was reported – to the enormous satisfaction of the master.

After a dangerously short rest, the two were lowered again, this time with a pair of shovels and one of the salvage ropes to tie around the mysterious sculpture. Having been offered a large salvage reward for the object's recovery, the divers were eager to stay a little longer on the bottom this time. With a little luck, they hoped, it would come straight out of the sand. Within seconds of the bell's four counterweight rocks reaching the bottom, the pair were out of it and digging around the rapidly emerging horse's hoof and leg. *There* was another hoof, *and there* its chest. They returned to the bell. After a few deep breaths, they returned to digging out the rapidly refilling hole. Another few minutes saw the majority of it uncovered. Now there was only the neck and head to go. Another few breaths, then more digging, and finally, there it was, falling onto its side as it came free. Now two of the horse's legs were lassoed and tied securely to the lifting rope. The second diver gave the three tug signal on the rope and watched the sculpture rise toward the surface while his partner returned for one last search for more of the coins. If he was expecting his partner to follow though, he did not – the other preferred to get back quickly to the bell. He was already exhausted and not about to risk the screaming death. Inside the bell, he gasped to get the air into his burning lungs. This day, having the goal right there in front of his eyes, he had pushed his luck further than ever before.

At the surface, Caesar's salvage expert yelled out as the horse snagged the side of the ship, the rope around it nearly tearing one off one of its front hooves and cracking the cast bronze at its fetlock. It was only when the sculpture was safely on deck that he was able to look at the amazing object he'd dreamed of for years. But finally, there it was. The horse was all still perfectly intact, having been buried deep below the sand all this time. The hardened wax still filled most of the odd-looking sculpture just as described; the exposed parts repairable. Only the same exposed hoof had been worn away slightly by the sea water and swirling sand, the iron castor badly rusted.

The crewmen in charge of the bell rope waited for the familiar thumbs up signal from the master to raise it. But this time the salvager made a thumbs down signal instead. The divers were no longer required, and the fewer witnesses that remained, the better.

On the sea bed, the first diver found dozens of heavy coins and crammed them into his pouch. Then, noticing something else, he grasped the prongs of what was a heavy trident poking out from below a nearby rock. With that in his hands, he swam rapidly toward the bell as he saw it being hoisted from the bottom. Just as the roped weights left the bottom and he was about to get inside the bell, it suddenly dropped, trapping his partner inside. The diver briefly tried to shove over the bell with his shoulder to get to the remaining air, but he quickly abandoned the idea, instead, heading straight for the surface. Struggling to rise quickly, he dropped the gold trident. He also realised just in time that it was the weight of the gold coins that was keeping him down. He scrabbled to ditch the contents of the pearl bag, spilling the heavy coins across the wreck and amongst the statues that remained on the bottom. But just below the surface, he began to encounter excruciating pains behind his eyes, then his ears and neck. Instantly, it spread to his joints, arresting his co-ordination – paralysing him – forbidding him to swim. His head burst above the surface and he at last took a breath, only to scream it back out as the death convulsions took his twitching body back down to the corbita.

Inside the now pitch black bell, there was only a little air left at the top. Now alone, it was enough for another ten minutes at the most. The second diver cursed his luck at ever taking the job. Despite his apparent wealth, he'd somehow known all along that the purple cloaked Sicilian couldn't be trusted."

CHAPTER 16:

The Summer of Bliss

The storyteller again took a deep breath as he pushed himself out of the gloom. Now, he looked especially elated as he glanced from face to face. "It was a glorious early summer morning and Lio's small sailboat sped across the last few miles of open sea from Crete towards Aegilia, the final leg of his journey home from Egypt. Standing on the bow of the vessel, the young man was surrounded by the few possessions he'd acquired in the three years he had been away. He looked again at the school of dolphins dancing in and out of the bow wave, now heralding his triumphant return. He marvelled at their agility as they playfully skipped from starboard to larboard and back again.

He was desperate to be home now – willing the boat faster towards Xiropotamos beach, the easiest point on the coast on which to land so that he didn't have to lug the heavy bags and the box up the steeper hill from Potamos harbour. Skirting the rocky coastline, somehow less intimidating in the bright sunlight, Lio recognised the headland that hid the pebble beach, knowing his long journey was almost over. It seemed a strange thing to him that the only time he had made that journey to the island before was entirely unplanned. It had cost the life of his father and nearly cost his own, but, despite all odds, this was the place he now dreamt of settling down. Also, finally, he had decided to resolve his dilemma with what to do about Ashur.

The master ran the boat carefully onto the smooth, round

pebbles and jumped into the water with the rope to pull it further aground. Leaping more athletically over the side and onto the deserted beach, Lio surveyed the small scene again. His eye led from the sea and up the beach – past the tiny chapel of Athena – and up the valley that ran toward the house. The ferryman placed the last of many bags onto the pebbles beside Lio and waited for his payment. Lio thanked him again for dropping him exactly where he had asked. He produced a silver coin from one of the bags and gave it to the astonished man. There was no change required assured Lio, elated only to be home. Now, with the long straps of two of the bags crossed over his broadened chest, four bags in his right hand and the other single wooden box in his still slightly weaker left hand, the young man carefully made his way back to the place where the turbaned boy had left in trepidation years before. The short journey across the pebbles was hard-going under his feet. It was only when he was onto the rocky dirt track, and a large herd of goats scattered away from him, that he began to look around the island once more. The picture had changed dramatically from the one of near deprivation that he'd previously known. The coarse, dry-stone walls and abandoned terraced gardens were all repaired and replanted now. The small houses were all rebuilt and occupied and, even at that time in the morning, people were out tending their land.

Miriam saw Lio coming up the roadway. Although he had changed dramatically, she at once recognised his bright red hair. She smiled, wiped her hands on her apron and called out to him. Leaving her young boy safely in the walled garden, she ran up to him. Lio dropped his bags at his feet and the both of them threw their arms around each other as he lifted her off the ground. She wiped away tears of joy to see how her little Lio had grown. They spoke a few words of welcome to each other while she looked him up and down, nodding approvingly at him. He was now much taller than her – almost six feet. He noticed the black haired boy playing in the enclosed garden. 'Is this Andros?' he asked in astonishment.

'Of course it is. You've been kept away from us a long time! Come Andros – this is Lio, your big brother. Do you remember all

161

of the stories we've told you about him – he's come home at last'
she cried out, 'to stay – haven't you?'

'Yes, of course, I *never* want to leave again,' confirmed Lio
bending down to hug the stand-offish child now hiding his face in
his mother's apron – strange toward the big brother who he had
could not remember. He stretched towards him, 'Hello Andros,' he
coaxed, 'I've come back to help look after you.' In time he would
make friends with him again, he was sure.

He stood up and made to pick up the bags again when he caught
sight of Ashur stood in the doorway of the house, only a hundred
feet away. His mouth opened, yet he couldn't speak, struggling to
come to terms with what he saw. She too was taller than he'd
imagined, but seemed even more beautiful. The young woman
smiled at his reaction – exactly as he'd remembered, and Lio took-
in a massively deep breath.

Miriam caught his gaze and turned to see the girl herself. She
smiled at Lio and shook her head, seeing that he'd finally noticed
her. 'Lio,' she said softly, 'Ashur has a surprise for you.'

'What's that?' he said absent-mindedly, still gazing at the girl in
the doorway.

'Go and find out for yourself,' she coaxed him. Then she bent
down to pick up Andros, and to wait there with the child at a discreet
distance.

Lio padded steadily toward the girl that he had dreamed about
for years, his mind racing across all the things he had longed to say
to her, probably since the long distant time she had looked up at him
from between the temples. Ashur stepped out confidently from the
door, drying her hands on a cloth. She stared at the young man
walking a little hurriedly toward her, now knowing that the boy, her
friend, that she had first met as a child of around Andros' age had at
last opened his eyes to her. As they ran the last few paces toward
each other and he squeezed her hard to him, spinning her around,
he pressed his face against the side of hers. Then she whispered into
his ear, 'At last you're home my Lio – my hero.'

Lio got such a shock he could hardly believe it. 'Ashur,' he looked into her eyes, 'you've found your voice again,' he said and they clung to each other and continued to spin around and around with joy. Miriam carried Andros past the pair and went into the house unnoticed.

It seemed, Ashur later explained, that it had not been long ago that her voice had suddenly returned. In fact, it had been precisely when Lio's last letter had arrived, telling them that he was going to risk coming home. Ashur had opened the letter and had begun to read it first, as she usually did, before handing it to her mother. Then, reaching the bottom, she rolled the letter up again and without warning said in a soft but crystal clear voice, 'Lio's coming home!'

Miriam couldn't believe her ears. 'What!' she murmured.

'Lio's coming home,' the young woman repeated, 'next month.'

As marvellous as the news was, Miriam still had to explain that that was not why she had exclaimed 'What!' It had been the fact that Ashur had spoken for the very first time since she had known her and it seemed, even the young woman herself had not realised it. Overjoyed, Miriam had kissed her face a hundred times in thanks that her daughter had finally managed to shrug off the 'curse' cast on her by the priest that Kyrros had described to her. Ashur was now back to her previous self.

All the rest of that day and well into the night, when Miriam and Andros had taken to their beds, Lio listened to Ashur tell of how she had felt unable to speak since the events in the temple. Now alone, Lio and Ashur wept together as she spoke of how Marduk had been handed the knife, and the pair had been thrown into the basement where Lio had last seen his friend alive. Despite the threats against him if he refused, her little brother had not cut off his sister's tongue as he had been ordered. He had made her promise never to speak openly again so that she could never give his desperate plan away, and to hide who's tongue it really was that he had silently handed to the priest later that afternoon. Once or twice since then, she had whispered in the dark to the stars and the moon to look after Marduk, but never until the letter had arrived had she felt safe

163

enough to relax her promise to him. Now, knowing she was safe on this island, away from everything bad in the world, and with her protector about to return to her, she had finally spoken up!

That summer was the most idyllic Lio ever knew. With the payment from Sosigenes for Lio's services, he had managed to buy presents for everyone, including a small, wheeled-horse for Andros, a bale of good quality woven cotton cloth for Miriam and Ashur and more things again for the girl. He bought her a pair of shoes that he'd correctly guessed the size of, mantels and scarves and, of course, a few clothes for himself. He'd also purchased tools: woodworking tools, drawing equipment, rolls of papyrus and coloured pigments. He would start whatever career he could right there, make a little money, then settle down in peace, forgetting his childhood ambitions to travel the world. All summer long the pair caught up on everything that each other had done in their time apart. Even talking about the other short romances they had both had, trusting each other implicitly now, promising that no secrets would ever be left untold.

Over that summer then, Ashur reintroduced Lio to the many friends they still had, and some she made in his absence. They often went out in company, but mostly Lio and Ashur were simply happy and content to be in each other's company, almost inseparable – though often with Andros in tow of course.

Each morning, they took Andros swimming at Ashur's sandy beach, half an hour's walk away. In contrast to their childhood though, now each a little self-conscious, each morning when they swam together, for the first time, both decided to wear something in the water. Lio wore a loin cloth and Ashur a short, lightweight cotton dress. This ritual continued for weeks until one evening, after standing at the top of the hill outside of the house, the couple moved their friendship further on.

Overlooking the sea, the pair watched the sun move steadily below the horizon, turning the sky maroon and the sea indigo. Taking her hand into his, still looking at the sky, Lio said aloud for Ashur to hear, 'Grandfather, father, thank you for the love and caring you showed to me and for helping to rescue this girl for me. I had thought for many years that I might love her, but now I realise I was wrong.'

Ashur looked at him, a little shocked and hurt. The young man smiled gently at the look of disappointment on her face and looked straight into her eyes. 'Now I *know* that I love you, and I always will.' It was the only time in his life that he ever said this simple phrase. As young as they both were, he knew he would never feel the same about anyone else. For the first time ever, Lio took her into his arms and kissed her properly, then, together, they tiredly strolled home hand in hand, though both still to their own rooms. After all, without proper means of support, it was too soon to begin a proper life together.

This loving relationship continued for another idyllic month, but then, a letter arrived on the island that would upset them both.

It was addressed to *Lio of Aegilia* and it would shake Lio, and cause a sudden and massive rift between Ashur and him. It was from Poseidonios of Rhodos – the athlete – the old man whom Lio had last seen at Kyrros and Miriam's wedding, when he had confirmed Lio's acceptance into the secret Chronology Society of Alexandria – the man who had given him his sun-wheel pendant. Lio easily remembered the old traveller standing with the spiral 'stick' that had long ago been mistaken for the lightning bolt of Zeus. He had thought him to be retired, but obviously, he was still going strong. Lio absent mindedly thumbed the pendant as he started to read.

The cryptic letter began worryingly:

Lio, forgive me. I have thought long and hard before involving you in the most diabolical state of affairs in which I and other members of our society find ourselves.

I have heard a rumour of your own illustrious career and I thought you might lend us your help. It is my painful duty to report that those of us taken "into service" by Caesar since the taking of Alexandria, have since been held captive. We are still to this day held in the fortified city of Syracuse – none of us able to convince our "leader" that we should be allowed to return to our

165

wives and families. I implore you, if you are able, as one who might still have some influence with the Romans, please help us – please come to our rescue – urgently before we are moved away from here. And be sure to bring Kyrros' computer.

It is not for our sakes alone that I ask – but the future of all humanity!

Lio let go of the athlete pendant. He could hardly believe the message. In the time he had spent in Alexandria and by the Red Sea, he had often thought fleetingly about what might have happened to the old philosopher and the other technicians since Caesar's siege of the city, but until now Lio had always assumed that they had all escaped the place. After all, the Romans had finally taken Alexandria with their forced help. Yet, all this time, it seemed they themselves had been held against their will. He wondered briefly about the reference to Kyrros' computer. *How did Poseidonios know he still had it?* But it was the last reference to the future of humanity which threw Lio especially. What could it possibly mean? He knew that he must somehow help. He discussed how best to do so with both Ashur and Miriam. The conversation was very short.

But, Lio,' Miriam coaxed, 'What influence you had with the Romans was only by the grace of Caesar, your authority has now gone – and you have told us of how you only just escaped the clutches of Cleopatra herself before she returned to Alexandria. Please, you must be careful before getting involved.'

Lio considered. 'Mother, I am already involved. I was and always will be a member of the Chronology Society – I cannot forget this?'

It was Ashur who sounded most upset. 'Lio, the society is no more. Please, don't bring danger to yourself, not again. We've waited too long for your return – I've waited too long.'

He looked into her eyes and stroked her hair. 'Ashur,' he smiled, 'how can I abandon those whose work helped Kyrros save me from sacrifice – and yourself from slavery – from that priest?'

Ashur knew.

'It is a promise I made – a debt of honour to the society – we would always look out for one another!'

'But Lio…' she implored.

Lio gazed into her moistened eyes as Ashur sniffed back the tears. Only very reluctantly did she seem to accept his decision. Whereafter, she immediately got to her feet and walked out to the garden alone. Lio thought it best not to follow."

Tom sighed deeply. "In retrospect, perhaps the young man should have followed – it might have saved considerable heartache."

CHAPTER 17:

The Premonition

Tom raked back his white hair. "For the next few days, as Lio made plans to travel to Syracuse, Ashur and he hardly spoke. Each time he had again tried to explain his decision, she had either changed the subject or excused herself from his company. At first, they were pleasant enough to each other to be sure, even if it was forced. But after a few days, the atmosphere in the house had turned cold. Within a few days more, as he waited for the boat that was due to leave for the fortified city on Sicilia, it was icy. Ashur had clearly turned her back on him, distancing herself from him. It was very obvious that there was now a very real rift between the couple. Each time the young man tried to speak to her, the young woman found an excuse to walk away from his company, until the situation between them became unbearable to both – and to Miriam especially. Finally, on the morning before his departure, the whole situation erupted into a full blown row.

'Lio, you can't go, you can't leave us,' Ashur rounded on him angrily. 'You don't know what you might be walking into!'

'But Ashur,' he tried to reason with her again, 'I've explained – we can't simply ignore their plea – you know it wouldn't be right!'

'Alright,' she lost her temper, 'but don't expect me to wait for you to come back – I won't! I've waited all my life for you, and now you're going to throw everything away – I've had enough!' She stormed out of the house. 'And don't wait up for me, she called behind her – I'm going to see my *real* friends!'

'But Ashur,' Miriam called out, 'Lio will have to begin his journey tonight. The boat leaves from the other side of the island.'

'I don't care,' she said disappearing down the path, 'tell him I don't want to see him again... tell him I never want to see him.' She broke into a run.

Lio was devastated. 'Ashur...' he called out, unheard, unable to believe the suddenness of what had just happened.

He was about to run after her when Miriam grabbed him by the arm. 'Leave her,' she cautioned. 'Let her calm down – maybe when she does, she'll return.'

Lio looked at his mother and the worried look on her face that betrayed her true concerns. 'I don't understand. Why is she acting like this? She knows I'm right.'

Miriam looked sympathetically at him. 'Lio, as grown up as you are, you have a lot to learn. Of course Ashur knows you're right – that's why she's running away.' She didn't say more.

Now Lio looked puzzled. He shook his head and turned away. With that, the young man began to pack the few things that he thought he might need while he was away. Now, he began to realise that all he wanted in the world – all he would ever want – had turned her back on him – cut him dead. He had lost her.

Later that afternoon, Lio stood outside. *It really is going to be a beautiful evening*, he thought distractedly; how he would miss the view from here when he was gone. In dead silence, her back to him, Miriam tended the vegetable garden he had helped to make as a boy. He was about to make his goodbyes to Andros and Miriam, when she sensed his approach. She stood up only to plead with him on Ashur's behalf. 'Lio, wait for one more night. There will be other boats leaving – you don't have to go just yet. Give her one more chance – please, for all our sakes.'

'Mother,' he shook his head, 'the letter says that it is urgent. I have to go – now! The boat leaves as soon as it is loaded in the morning. When I get back, I'll sort it all out.'

'An hour then – I'm begging you,' she looked more upset than ever before, 'One last chance?' In all the years they'd known each other, never before had she looked so devastated to Lio. Miriam broke down and cried tears of frustration. Without waiting for his agreement, she almost tore off her apron. She grabbed Andros by the wrist and ran through the house. 'One hour!' she begged again, knowing absolutely that she had to try – before it was too late.

It was mid evening by the time Miriam found Ashur talking animatedly to her friends and to one suitor in particular. They were all sat on the beach, in the same place she'd always sat before with Lio.

Reading the expression on her face as Miriam approached with Andros, Ashur's friends fell silent. They got up respectfully and gave the mother and daughter some distance. The Cretan boy looked at Ashur's expression knowing that he had finally lost the contest, as he somehow always knew he would. Although he was very fond of the girl, and, if he had had the chance, would indeed have married her, she had never been able to stop talking about the boy who had saved her life and whose life she had saved in return – her soul-mate – Lio. Smiling at Ashur, he graciously conceded defeat and wished her good luck, then he too left her so that she could talk to her mother. The women stood face to face.

Miriam's message was short and sweet. 'Ashur, in the limited time that I finally gained Kyrros for myself, I had the most wonderful time of my life. I still have him beside me even now, in Andros;' she patted the boy's shoulders. Tears of frustration began to well up in her eyes again. 'Listen to me – if you continue to turn your back on Lio now, you will regret it forever…'

'It's not my fault!' Ashur reminded her. 'It's Lio, he won't listen!'

'Nevertheless, that is the young man's decision. You know he's right – sadly, I know too.'

'But I'm frightened… I don't want to lose him – like Marduk – I couldn't stand it.'

Miriam took the girl's face in her hands. 'Ashur, if you go on like this, you *are* going to lose him,' she warned. 'You might never have another chance of being together again.'

'But he's going to hurt me, I know he is. He can't care about me if he would risk throwing our future happiness away on another adventure.'

'What!' Miriam gasped angrily, 'an adventure? This is a rescue! He is obliged. He has to try. And,' she reminded her, 'this is not the first time.'

The younger woman tried to look away.

'Ashur, in deciding to help rescue you all those years ago, the boy caused the loss of everything – his grandfather, his father, his chance at an education and a proper career as he wished – and all you want to do now is punish him. What do you hope to gain by treating him like this? Would you respect him if he broke his word? It would break him – and who would want a broken man?'

Ashur tried to speak but Miriam kept on. 'Ashur, this is the little boy who risked everything to go back and rescue *you*. Who, as soon as he remembered what had happened on Rhodos, cried himself to sleep thinking of you. For the sake of everything that's decent, wake up and realise who he is – this is *your* Lio!' She began to calm down. 'The boy who would never willingly hurt you… the boy who worships and adores you – his heart will never belong to anyone else – you know this!'

Ashur was shocked at the tirade, although she was still hurt. 'But it's *he* who has decided to leave *me* here again.'

Miriam tried to cut through the girl's stubbornness. 'My beautiful daughter, if you have any feelings for him, go to him now, before it's too late.'

Ashur looked at her mother, both Miriam's and her own eyes filling up again. Then Miriam delivered the real blow. Now fully calmed down, she warned, 'Ashur, Lio is packing his bags to leave right now as we speak. If you don't go now you may *never* see him again – I know this – *it is written!*'

Never before had Ashur known her mother to speak of the future being 'written'. The delivery of the message threw the young woman into shock, realising simultaneously how far she had tried to push Lio away, and how much she needed him. Sensing that there might be something else that her mother might be aware of, she looked at her askance and asked her softly. 'How do you know?'

Miriam avoided the question, 'please Ashur, just go – now. Hurry, before it's too late.'

Ashur looked one last time into Miriam's eyes in growing panic. Then, she turned and started off home. After a few paces, she kicked off the shoes that Lio had bought her. Then she broke into a sprint.

By the time Ashur had arrived home, the sun had begun to fade. Running into the empty house she called out frantically, checking the rooms, but Lio was nowhere to be seen. The young woman dropped, cross-legged on the floor of the main room. She wept to herself as a little girl, wiping the tears away brusquely. At last she began to come to terms with the gravity of the situation – too late.

Then, after a few minutes, in the fading light she noticed the bags and the long computer box in the far corner. Now she seized new hope. The young woman crossed to the back door to look out at the sunset, and there, with his back toward her was Lio. He was stood in his usual place, making his prayer of thanks for everything he had achieved – or at least had been given the opportunity to try and achieve – unlike some – unlike his friend Marduk. And, of course, in thanks for knowing for at least one, short, precious time, the love of Ashur.

As the young woman slowly walked to where he stood at the edge of the hill, the sun became wrapped in the night. Silently, she slid her arms around his waist, burying her face in his back as she had done so often as a child. Although the tension in his body relaxed, Lio didn't move. Instead, he took her hands in his and continued to look out at the huge red half-disc of the sun as it disappeared beyond the sea.

'I'm sorry this hurts you Ashur,' he said, 'but I have to go'.

'I know you do…' she finally admitted, 'and I'm sorry I've hurt you for it Lio.'

He turned around to embrace her, now never wanting to hold another girl in his arms ever again. Never wanting to be parted from her but knowing that, for one last time, they would have to be separated. For the sake of his promise to an old friend, to find out about this so called threat to humanity and, not least, for the sake of his own dignity. 'When I return,' he told Ashur, 'we *will* begin a life of our own. One day perhaps, we might even raise a family?'

Ashur smiled into his eyes, knowing that she was now happy to wait for him.

The young couple stood there on the hill, locked in each others' arms as the last trace of the red disc vanished. Then, at long last, the sun-haired boy, and the girl with skin black as night whispered into each other's ear a natural, solemn marriage vow. By its very nature their promise would never be broken: to simply give their hearts to each other and to try never to hurt one another again – for the rest of their natural lives.

At first light in the morning, Lio rolled silently out of Ashur's bed. The young woman slept on, her arms slipping from around his waist. After he'd washed and dressed, he stroked the scars on her naked back, kissed her softly on the neck, then he crept out of her room. Silently, he picked up his bags and kissed his mother and Andros who were waiting in the kitchen.

Miriam smiled warmly at him, 'At last,' was all she said.

'Thank you for helping us mother,' he replied, making his way outdoors and onto the track. 'But now, if I'm to still have a chance of catching the boat to Syracuse, I'll have to run!'

As he left home, Miriam called out to him, 'Lio, I've put something in the bag for you. You may need a reserve some day.'

Lio looked down, wondering.

'Don't worry, you'll return it in time,' she said confidently. 'And Lio – whatever happens – always remember how much you are loved right here and now.' Clearly upset, she wiped away her tears with her apron.

Not understanding why she was like this, he frowned exaggeratedly, pulling a sad face. Then he smiled broadly at her one last time and walked proudly on. He was about to break into a jog when he heard the sound of urgent footsteps behind him.

'Lio!' came the distressed call. He turned in surprise to see Ashur running barefoot after him with the box. Reaching him, she said happily, 'If you must go, then go with my blessing.' She handed the computer to him and threw her arms around him once more. 'But Lio, promise that as soon as you can, you'll come home quickly to me – my husband,' she said pointedly.

Grinning from ear to ear he replied, 'Don't worry! I promise – my wife. And when I return, I'll bring you back a wedding gift.' Then, still wary about the letter's reference to Kyrros' computer, just as abruptly, he gave her the box back. 'You keep it safe for me,' he said, 'better that it stays hidden, safe and secure on the island from now on.'

The young woman smiled deeply and ran her fingers through his hair. Then she smiled radiantly into his burning green eyes, trusting him absolutely to return as he had promised – within the year. Lio looked once again at her beautiful face, memorizing each wonderful detail – enough to carry the image of her with him forever. He squeezed her to him one last time, kissed her tenderly and then stood back. And with that, the naturally wed couple parted company – neither one knowing that this would be the last time they would ever see one another again."

Shakily taking a sip of water, Tom rubbed his eyes beneath his glasses and said, clearly choked. "I think I would like to stop there for today, I am suddenly feeling rather tired. Please, might you excuse me?" His head once again hung down.

The dog, sensing Maddie's concern, jumped down from her lap. "Are you alright Tom?" she asked. "Can I get you anything?"

"Perhaps you should pass my pills," he suggested a little breathlessly. "This has been a very long and stressful day."

Looking a little concerned as the others quietly filed out of his front door, Alex hung back. "Tom," he said quietly, "are you sure you're okay?"

"Yes, I'm fine," Tom said distractedly, swallowing the pill. He smiled bravely, now rallying around. "Sometimes... I forget how long ago it all was, and yet it seems like only yesterday. Go home Alex... Go home and I'll see you in the morning."

Alex crept downstairs with the others. Outside, once more they discussed Tom's mood. Then they decided who would check what on the list that he had carefully noted. That would take care of the rest of the evening, ready to compare notes over breakfast at Alex's place.

"Same time in the morning then," they agreed. Then they all left together.

CHAPTER 18:

Marmalade!

That night, Alex stayed up for hours, combing through the things that Tom had mentioned. Yet again, he confirmed everything in detail, but Alex was thinking about other things now.

Likewise, Maddie and Bex checked out their own details, it really was a very accurate picture that Tom had given them of life at that time. If it hadn't been so late at night they would have telephoned to tell Alex. Though secretly Maddie was actually quite worried about Tom again since he'd become suddenly quiet. It was this that she really wanted to discuss with Alex.

For Conna, however, that night was the worst night of arguing and rows that he had known at home. And once more, it was all apparently caused by him. It started as soon as his key rattled in the back door lock.

Conna had intended for Alex's sake to go straight to his room, and straight to his own computer, to check everything over again. He feared that ultimately, Tom was going to disappoint his friend. From nowhere, he fondly remembered he and Alex pretending to be time-travellers in Alex's back garden as a child. That was pure imagination, but this was different – more serious. He had been looking for something – not to discredit the old man, but to offer in evidence to Alex – so that when the time came, he wouldn't be suddenly devastated. He'd been racking his brain about the whole story, since Alex had first told him the short 'hypothetical' version, but to-date had not come up with a single thing. Then, from out of nowhere but the dim, distant memory he had of watching one of his documentaries – about watch making – he'd had an idea. It was a comment by Bex that had prompted the thought he had had about clock movements, and in particular, the one 'modern' – as in 'not ancient' – feature that all clocks shared, but he needed to check it first. He had been about to go upstairs to do so, when he heard the familiar shouting coming from the kitchen. It had gone on for years now – in fact, ever since he could remember. Since last year it had even quietened down, but then, since last month, things had flared up again.

Conna's mother's shrieking had sounded out as soon as he had walked in the door. "Here he bloody well is," she shouted, unanswered. "I can't bloody-well believe that useless boy, he deserves a flogging! Well…" she continued, "are you listening?"

"Yes dear," came the calm reply of his father.

"Then what are you going to do about it? Or are you suggesting that it's me who sorts it all out?"

Now what am I supposed to have done? Conna wondered. He'd been out all day, he hadn't gone into any of the rooms, except his own and the kitchen. He hadn't even dropped any crumbs today; hadn't touched anything. What had he done? He pondered awhile, and then came the answer.

His dad's exasperated, almost bored voice asked, "What is it this time then?"

"What's he done?" She sounded really angry this time. "What's he done… look at this!" She accused. "The one thing I have to myself, my one and only treat. The one thing I've asked him not to touch, and he's been at it. It's nearly a quarter gone – my marmalade!"

Of course, Conna knew that she was lying – she always did when she got like this. Not about him taking the stuff for himself, because frankly, last night he had. After all, once again there was nothing prepared for him to eat. He couldn't explain why he'd taken it; possibly he was just trying to prove a point to himself. But, it was that lie about the *one* thing that he particularly objected to. In fact,

177

there were many things Conna was not allowed to touch in the house. For instance:

Everything in the TV/ cinema room, including the sofas (he flattens the cushions); the smaller – still huge – TV in the 'family' lounge (he has his own); the polished furniture, or anything else in the dining room – and all windows – (he leaves finger marks); the polished granite bench tops in the kitchen (finger marks again); anything in his parents' separate bedrooms (not that he wished to go into either); and anything in the three immaculately prepared spare bedrooms.

Then there were the things he had to keep tidy if he absolutely had to use them: the 'family' bathroom (although no one else but he used it) including his three personal towels – always to be folded properly and replaced on the rack – but not to touch the perfectly neat and colour co-ordinated stack for guests – not that they ever had any; toothbrush and paste to be returned to tooth-mug (squeezed from the bottom only, and cap replaced properly); toilet seat always to be put down (including the top cover); the hand-basin to be rinsed and dried after use (cream cleaner and cloth provided); the glass shower enclosure to be rinsed and dried immediately after exit (glass cleaner provided); and the bath (hardly ever to use it at all – he leaves rings around it).

There were the other things too: all carpets to be kept clean, if anything accidentally trailed in – leaves etc – to be immediately picked up with the 'Handy-Vac'.

Next, there were his own things: all shoes to be tidied away, school uniform and all clothes to be kept in his room; all school books (other than the homework his dad sometimes helped him with) to be kept in his room; coats to be hung out of sight in the hallway cupboard – not on the rack, like his parents.

Lastly, there were the more spiteful things that were her personal property: *her* box of handmade chocolates; *her* real fruit smoothies; *her* expensive low-fat syllabubs (individual); *her* exclusive 'health' breakfast cereals; *her* 'skinny-milk' and of course, *her* marmalade – to name but a few.

If the TV programme 'Who's Home Is This?' had sent a crew into their house, Conna thought often, they would probably either deduce that it was occupied by a well heeled professional-couple; man obsessed with fast cars and woman with immaculate style; or, more likely, bachelor with overly fussy housekeeper. No one though, unless they had visited Conna's own bedroom, would have guessed that a child or youth of any description lived there. There were no photographs of him on display, nor any other evidence that he existed – anywhere.

"So, what are you going to do about it?" she continued screaming.

"Don't get upset again darling, its only marmalade – you know it's not important." He tried to calm her down.

"That's not the bloody point, is it?" she continued, "it's the principle of the thing!"

"What principle dear?" he returned. "Look, I'll talk to him at the week-end…"

"Weekend? Weekend!" And then Conna heard her start into the same familiar litany.

"Don't tell me that yet again you're going to attempt to take his side. That boy's ruined my whole bloody life. I could have easily taken silk now – I should have been made a Queen's Counsellor only last month. But, oh no, instead, I'm *still* just an ordinary bloody barrister – if it wasn't for bringing *him* up. He's ruined my career… ruined my life! We could have had that house opposite us by now – you know I always wanted the one with the tree lined drive. And all because *you* had to pack the bloody holiday suitcases: 'Yes dear, I've packed your pills… Yes, I'm sure'," she mimicked him mercilessly, ending in her favourite term for him – "you stupid… bloody… IDIOT!" Then came the inevitable crash as another glass hit the tiled wall above the cooker.

Of course, it wasn't the alcohol that made her say these things, as his dad always claimed afterwards. Conna knew that it was only that the drink made her able to voice the fact that she in particular had never wanted children – Conna! As for his father, in any disputes, he always seemed to automatically take her side.

Suddenly not hungry any more, the boy took a deep breath and walked upstairs to bed. Unable to concentrate, he put his TV on instead of going on the computer. Then he turned the volume up to drown out the noise below. Nearing the end of his tether, Conna sat there fully clothed with his hands over his ears until the early hours of the morning, rocking back and forwards, humming the crocodile song to himself and waiting for the inevitable visit.

CHAPTER 19:

Led By the Nose

Day Four of Tom's Story

At breakfast, Alex was quite 'chipper', as his mother was fond of saying. Really very much returned to his former self. Today was the day that he fervently hoped the end of the story would amaze and astound the others. All they needed was a little faith in Tom.

Maddie and Bex arrived bang on time again. Alex duly completed making the toast as they sat down in the same seats as the last couple of days. Again though, for some unknown reason, Conna was late. The three compared notes as Alex's mother busied herself in the kitchen, making the most of her daughter not being awake yet.

"So, what do we have?" asked Bex, playing devil's advocate.

"Well, I'm fine with everything," said Alex, "all the names and dates seem to be pretty accurate." He rattled through them for the sake of clarity.

"Well," began Maddie, "I think the same as you, everything still checks out pretty much accurately, wouldn't you say so?"

"Yeah, sure," confirmed Bex, still unable to get excited about the historical accuracy of the events and dates given by Tom. "But it's still not evidence of anything other than he's good at ancient history, is it?" She too had a nagging doubt about a few issues that she couldn't quite put her finger on.

When the knock came at the back door, Alex's mother opened

it to look at an obviously tired and dishevelled Conna. "Hi, Conna," she said, "come on in and join the gang."

Conna sat down heavily at the table, bags under his eyes. "Hi everyone," he yawned.

"What's happened to your eye?" asked Maddie – "is that eye shadow?"

"Eh… Oh, I was taking off my shirt and I caught it with my thumb. It's okay, "he reassured her.

The girls exchanged a glance.

Alex sensed Conna's discomfort. "Anyway, we were just discussing Tom's story. We've decided he's on the level so far," he volunteered. Bex frowned a little and Maddie shot her another worried glance. That wasn't quite the interpretation they would have put on it. "Well," Alex asked, "what do you think Conna?"

"Me, oh, yeah, if you say so," he said, his mind somewhere else.

"Well, help yourself to toast and marmalade," said Alex cheerily.

"Nah," answered Conna twitchily, "I'm not very hungry, anyway I've already had breakfast."

"Okay then," Alex continued, "Unless Conna's got anything to add, we'd better get going."

Conna nodded his head in capitulation.

Just then, there was a second knock, this time at the front door. Instinctively, Boris began to bark. Alex's mother went to open it. "Oh! Hi… you're a little early, aren't you…" she sounded a little put out. "Boris, be quiet, get down, don't grab his trousers like that. Well… I suppose we'd best get it over with – come on in."

The man in the suit carried his attaché case in. He looked down at the dog. "Hello doggy," he tried to sound convincing, "don't worry about it, he's fine," he shook his leg as the dog carried on growling at him, teeth clenched on the clearly expensive cloth. The man handed her a card. "Town and Coastal estate agents," he announced. "I'm Nigel, the property valuer."

Alex was taken aback. "Mam?" He looked astonished.

"I was going to tell you later…" she looked at him guiltily "… promise I was."

"When?" Alex was flabbergasted.

Sensing Alex's tension and discomfort, Maddie prompted the others to stand: "We'd best be going now Alex."

"Yeah, alright," he replied. "But you go ahead... I think *I'll* just hang back for a while first..."

Conna and the girls gravitated toward the door. At that, Boris finally let go of the house valuer's trousers and jumped up to paw at the door himself.

"Not today boy," said Alex, "not just yet."

The three left sheepishly. "See you later then," said Maddie, seeing Alex's alarm at what was appearing to happen around him. She stepped toward him and squeezed his arm.

"Yeah, see you later," replied Alex dazedly. Then, after closing the door behind them, he went back into the kitchen. Boris trailed along behind, still growling.

Together, the three others crossed to Tom's house, each locked in their own silent thoughts. They knocked once before letting themselves in. Upstairs, wearing his ever present sunglasses, Tom smiled to see the girls and Conna at the door.

"Where's Alex?" he asked.

"Oh, he'll be here later I should think." Conna guessed hopefully.

"Ah, well... I've told him most of the next part of the tale anyway," said the old man. He turned to make his way a little unsteadily toward his chair.

Although they were all taken aback at what appeared to be happening around Alex – though not so much Conna – everyone was at least pleased to see that the deep mood which had descended on Tom last evening seemed to have lifted. Once more he seemed as right as rain. Sitting in his armchair, he looked at the twins, and especially at Conna's black eye. He furrowed his brow, seeming to appreciate them each for themselves for the first time – not simply as Alex's friends. Miles away, Conna gazed once more at the lump in the centre of the room.

"Well then, shall we begin?" asked Tom. "I would like to try and finish sometime today – if you can spare me all day. After which, I have a favour to ask you." He did not expand on the subject any more.

"Fine," they agreed.

"Come on then Tom," Maddie urged. So without further ado, Tom resumed the tale in his familiar animated voice.

Once more, he closed his eyes before removing the sunglasses.

"Lio's voyage across the open sea from Aegilia to Sicilia was a short and uneventful one, although he did witness many warships of many sizes pass in the opposite direction. They were headed, he assumed, towards Egypt. Although who those ships belonged to, no one on this old corbita knew. Lio himself guessed correctly that they might be transporting part of Mark Antony's army. He had now taken up an almost permanent position in Egypt, the emperor Octavian and he having finally won the civil war. Of course, once more, Cleopatra had proven to be untrustworthy to the Romans. The ships had been sent to remind her that the Romans – and Mark Antony in particular – did not intend to relinquish their grip on the fuel store of their empire.

No matter, as soon as the ship docked in Syracuse, Lio was handed a second letter. It was another in the name of Poseidonios, which, by its content, had clearly been written after the one he'd already received. The short note devastated him personally and blighted the rest of his life.

A short while ago, it claimed, Poseidonios and his fellow workers had been moved on. They were no longer to be found in the city of Syracuse, nor anywhere on the island of Sicilia. They had been shipped somewhere as far from Rome as they could, somewhere at the darkest edge of the Empire.

However, the second part left him in no doubt that the choices he had left in his life had all been stolen from him. It went on to inform him that just before they were due to leave, the workshop had received a visit from one of the Praetorian guard, enquiring as to the whereabouts of Lio or, as the letter read, the boy known as

'Lio of Aegilia' also known as 'Helio, son of Andronikos'. According to the letter, the warrant for his arrest for his part in the destruction of the Great Library of Alexandria had been re-issued yet again. Anyone knowing the whereabouts of, or caught harbouring, or having any information whatsoever concerning this wanted criminal, was to communicate the same to the Roman authorities – on pain of death if they did not. Those failing to give such information would forfeit not only their own lives, but the lives of their entire families. Now, Lio's freedom had been finally taken away – for the one act he would never have considered.

The letter then went on to describe the exact location of their new lands on the faraway island to the north, on the edge of the Scotos lands. It begged him to follow, and offered him sanctuary there if he could make it. Poseidonios would leave word in various places along the route that he would, he trusted, be following.

Almost in panic, the first thing he did was write an unsigned letter – in case it was betrayed – to Ashur and his mother, warning them of what had happened and telling them to deny all knowledge of him to anyone who asked. Then he cryptically asked Ashur to remove the one piece of hard evidence that would link him undeniably to his small family. At the bottom of the joint letter, Lio wrote a short note of farewell to Ashur, it read:

To my beloved Ashur, my wife of one day, whom you know I would never again hurt willingly. The disaster that has overtaken me this time has now threatened your own life, which I will not suffer. I will follow my ancient colleagues, trusting that you will understand I have no choice in the matter – for all our sakes.

Accordingly, I wish that in my absence, you will finally return the property my father passed to me years ago, so that he may keep it and guard it forever from those who would use its existence against us.

For my part, know that if it takes me an entire lifetime to return to you, I will never cease from trying.

Do not weep for me, do not wait for my return and waste your own lifetime – make use of it instead. I implore you to live out a full and happy life

185

as you choose. As I release you now from your vow, know also that I will never break my own bond to you while we both live, and that I will never, ever forget you – the eternal love of my life.

L

As he initialled the letter, Lio never felt so utterly alone in this world.

Yet, there was nothing else to be done about it! No choice. With that, his heart now completely broken, Lio entrusted the letter to the master of the corbita returning to Crete via Aegilia, and then he himself made straight for the vessel that would bring him to Londinium and the island that was not yet, but soon would be, part of the Roman Empire. Hoping that some day he would be able to clear his name and return home, Lio followed Poseidonios' precise instructions with all due haste. Thumbing the pendant at his neck, he thought ironically of his childhood wish to travel the world. Now most reluctantly, it was about to come true.

Nearly three weeks later, wearing a brightly coloured turbanos, as suggested in Poseidonios' letter, and after calling in at the southern tip of Hispania and northwards along the western coast of Gaul, Lio approached his destination. Over five hundred and fifty years after his expectant mother and his warrior father had left that land to pray for the boy's safe delivery, Lio finally landed in the birthplace of his ancestors, Britannia. Never would he leave its shores again – at least, not for an unbelievably long time!

As soon as the letter arrived in the harbour of Potamos, the message was delivered – the only one being carried that day. The young boy to whom the harbour master had entrusted it was a good lad and did not stop on the way. Miriam was visiting a sick patient when the boy had knocked on the door of the house on the hill. He had been pleased to receive his usual reward, one of the apples that grew in the garden. Ashur sat with Andros at the small dining table. She instantly recognised the handwriting. Smiling, she opened the letter excitedly, only for the smile to disappear instantly.

She did not cry. After re-reading it for the third time – to make certain that she had not misread it or misunderstood any of its content – she rolled it gently and put it aside for Miriam. Then she got back down on the floor to continue the game of chequers she had begun with Andros an hour ago. Later, with Andros safely tucked-up in bed, the young woman walked out toward the setting sun. There was a chill in the air and perhaps a few spots of rain. She stared blankly out over the sea as Miriam approached her, just as only days ago, Ashur had approached Lio – her wonderful husband. Now, in exactly the same way, Miriam slipped her hands around the girl's waist. She had also read the letter.

'Do you believe him Ashur?' she coaxed gently.

Ashur sighed, remembering the vows that they had exchanged. 'Absolutely,' she patted Miriam's hand. 'I know him!'

'Then you must never give up hope – never forget him' – she advised. 'Even if it is meant to be that you will never see him again, at least you have known the true love of an honest man. Perhaps, my daughter, just perhaps, some day he may return to you – only time will tell.'

Still dark, very early next morning, they awakened Andros to come for a walk, despite the heavy rain. The well wrapped, bleary-eyed boy held the hands of his mother and sister not knowing where he was going. It took over an hour to walk slowly over the rocky, muddy soil and then stand on the sharp rocks that they had not visited since the last anniversary of Kyrros' loss. Ashur hitched the strap of the box over her head and stood with it in her hand. She didn't say anything. She didn't have to, Miriam had realised the same: the computer that had nearly killed Lio in the sea had betrayed him first to Caesar then to the Queen of the Nile. And now, it seemed her persual of him had ruined the lives of two of the most entirely innocent people that Miriam had ever known or loved.

The sky began to lighten, and just as the pale golden rim of the sun's edge appeared in the east, Ashur began to swing the strap to and fro like a pendulum, letting it pick up momentum. As it swung to its apogee, she let the strap go, lobbing the box high into the air. When it landed in the small waves, it floated briefly, to be carried out another ten feet. Then, with a single large bubble, followed by a chain of progressively smaller ones, the device disappeared from view – back to Kyrros. Now feeling a little faint, Ashur smiled at Miriam in relief, glad to finally see the back of it. Then she broke down and wept uncontrollably. Still unaware, as Miriam had been years ago when they had reached the island, that now, in turn, Ashur was carrying a child. And that child could only be Lio's."

Conna, though more especially Maddie and Bex gasped, but said nothing.

Without a pause, Tom carried straight on – almost too quickly.

"The small wooden fort and township of Londinium was a mass of boats that lined the muddy banks of the wide river. Most vessels moored there had delivered their various loads or were being loaded for a hasty departure.

It was ebb tide – the water still – almost stagnant. There was nothing of note in the rather smelly, cold place. Lio held his nose as the corbita pulled alongside an empty piece of river frontage. It wasn't since he'd been a young boy – in Piraeus, the port of Athens – that he's smelt worse. Lio began to disembark with his bags. Following the written instructions, the next part of his journey would be north, along the eastern coast. At a nearby Beer House – ancient fore-runner of the British pub – a dark, loud and obnoxious place, Lio took a drink of the bitter, watery ale that was produced locally – his first since he had lived by the Red Sea. He then began to circulate, listening for a familiar tongue. There were all sorts. Latin mostly, some Arab, Gallic and a smattering of the tongue he had only ever heard once or twice before – the Briton's rarely made it to the Mediterranean or the Aegean.

The Druides, Britons and Keltes, were already at that time frowned upon by the Romans, their many strange customs worried them. They were so foreign, so dangerous that these peoples needed to be watched. Customs like wearing long and plaited hair instead of the short, smart haircuts of the Romans. Like boldly covering their bodies in blue paint instead of wearing armour in battle, and in making annual willing human sacrifices in the woods – in contrast, of course, to the Romans who continued to capture then slaughter their own enemies as entertainment. But most dangerous of all – even potentially subversive – the Britons and Celts allowed women to take an equal and active part in running their society. There were even rumoured to be female chieftains!

As he listened to the completely alien world around him, Lio was finally spotted by the contact that had been waiting expectantly for weeks. The stranger approached the turbaned young man and asked him if he was the friend of the Greek – Poseidonios. Relieved at finding a more friendly face here, he was happy to confirm that he was. Good, the stranger declared, at least now he would be paid for his efforts. Without waiting, Lio was led outside and back down to the muddy track towards the river. He crossed the narrow wooden bridge that spanned it, and there, the stranger pointed him to the prearranged craft and bade him a succinct farewell. Lio thanked the stranger and got quickly into the boat, instantly more comfortable now that he could communicate properly with someone who spoke one of the tongues he recognised. The sailing boat would leave that evening, heading north along the east coast. Within a couple of days he would be at his final destination.

On the morning that the two day journey north ended, Lio sailed up the verdant coastline. It was late summer and the weather and the temperature, he had noticed overnight, was far colder than anything he had been used to before. Soon, he realised, it would be autumn here. From the vessel, he watched as cliffs rose from the sea and continued in an undulating line northward. Then, as the Arab master told him they were nearing the end of their journey, a single, towering outcrop of rock with what appeared to be a bear's head on one side passed by in the grey light of dawn. Finally, keeping a careful eye on the black rocks that seemed to move around just proud of the surface inside the river mouth, the Arab master sailed slowly into the great river. In front of them was another recent wreck of a ship still perched there, holed and unable to move. Slowly, the boat docked at the short mole, its draft too deep to pull onto the sandy beach as the few other masters who were already there had done.

Lio smiled to himself, looking around at the traders who were selling off their wares as he had seen them do as a boy on Rhodos. There, even, were the bright coloured robes and headdresses that reminded him of his friend the Persian trader. For a moment, he wondered fleetingly what might have become of the man who had passed away five hundred years before – the man that had helped save Ashur. Lio had to force himself not to continue with the train of these thoughts, knowing where they would inevitably lead, as they had done for weeks. With that, he disembarked for the second time in Britannia and walked upriver, making straight toward the place where he could see the wooden staith that was the cross-river ferry landing. Recognising the detailed description he'd been given, he realised that his journey was almost over." It was only then that Lio finally began to wonder why Poseidonios had suggested he wear, of all things, a turbanos as a sign of recognition. Was it because his normally recognisable red hair was more common here – or was it just *coincidence*?"

CHAPTER 20:

Dawning Realisation

Conna was delighted to have recognised the approach to the mouth of the Tyne from Tom's description of the long cliffs and the bear's head rock – though, throughout the past, rock-falls made it now resemble more of an ape. He also recognised the Black Middens, the south bank of the river and finally, even the mole. Still, from Tom's shabby description of the early beginnings of London, the boy had not grasped that Londinium was one and the same.

"Wait a bit," Conna said, dumbfounded. "What happened to Scotland in all this? You've been talking about the Scotos Lands – the dark lands – right from the start," he turned to look at the girls, "hasn't he?"

Maddie and Bex nodded, although they'd never been quite certain whether he'd been talking about this, or another river – black rocks and all. "Actually, I wasn't sure if you meant Scotland too," Maddie added.

Bex looked down her nose.

"Of course," Tom confirmed, "it is the Greek phrase 'scotos lands' which is undoubtedly the origin of that country's name. But, at that time, the 'dark lands' included all of the lands north of the wide river Tyne. Dark," Tom raised his eyebrows, "Not only because the winters got physically darker at these northern climes, but 'dark' as in mysterious. This, the north side of the river, may only be a relatively short journey from the south side, but it was inhabited by different tribes which were foreign to the people of Arbeia. That was why the Roman wall was built along the north shore of the river – a natural dividing line between the 'cultured' and 'uncultured' peoples! And don't forget: the modern dividing line for Scotland from England – the border – was set much, much later, and much further to the north."

Both girls nodded acceptingly.

Conna shook his head in wonder. "So Lio came right here, to Tynemouth – the north east of England – I mean Britannia – over two thousand years ago?" he said. *This really is a brilliant story*, he thought. It easily transported him from his own situation at home, as he now began to regret his impetuous actions early this morning before he'd left.

He listened on with Maddie and Bex as Tom told them of the ferry crossing from the south to the mysterious north side of the river. He described Lio's short walk along from where the fish quay would be now – a sparsely populated area consisting of a collection of a various bunch of mixed-use huts, cattle and pig pens, barking dogs and the mixed damp smells associated with it all. Regardless of Londinium, Tynemouth could hardly have been described as a wonderful place to live back then either.

"On, Lio strolled with his few bags, back eastward along the opposite riverbank. He passed beneath the open grazing land that was now the site of Collingwood's Monument and then climbed up the bank to the very spot where we are now all sat listening to his story. Finally, he looked across the grassy saddle that led from the promontory of the Spanish Battery and toward the unmistakable higher promontory of what had been called by various names and at various times: the Roman Acropolis, Benebalcrag or Pen Bal Crag – now the site of the ruined priory and castle.

The brightly turbaned stranger that had travelled across the known world walked past the tethered mule that grazed here, then he walked toward two thick-set men that sat on the damp grass. As he approached them, recognising the pre-described headdress, one of them picked up a rounded, hand-sized pebble and held it in his palm. Lio called out in Greek, then, when he got no response, in

Latin. 'Hail strangers, I am searching for the land of the Greek workers. If you will, please could you point out the direction for me?'

Without speaking, the smaller of the two made to take Lio's bags from him as the other knocked him to the ground in one fell swoop. Lio shook his head, dazed. Instantly, he assumed that he was being robbed. He tried to call out, but as he did, the pebble was forced roughly between his teeth, and his turbanos unwound from his head and then re-wrapped tightly around his mouth to keep it in. Within a couple of minutes he had been hog-tied at hand and foot. His clothing and bags were roughly emptied, leaving his clothing torn into shreds. Next he was kicked and rolled back down the hill to be followed and picked up again. Then he was thrown face down over the mule, and with a slap of the pack animal's backside, the three men made their way across the land-saddle and up the other side of the hill, to claim their reward. Steadily, they walked towards the top of the higher promontory, to what they knew as the Roman Acropolis."

"Right here?" exclaimed Conna.

"To be exact Conna," Tom stood up creakily, "Right there," he pointed, "right in front of Alex's house next door."

The girls didn't speak, whilst Conna still shook his head, gripped by the idea that the story had moved from the opposite end of the Roman world to right here. That they were now, two thousand years later, all discussing it and wondering about the improbability, or, even now, the possibility of it all.

"The only building on the top of that hill," Tom pointed to the priory, "was at that time a rather small, enclosed Roman villa. It was occupied, the locals knew, by a mysterious Roman who had arrived months previously. He had kept himself very much to himself, never leaving his 'fortress'. But then, it was known that he had been a close adviser and supposed one time bodyguard of Julius Caesar himself. He was known locally by the tribal chieftain who had been well paid for the land that the man had built his villa on. But he was known only as the man with the purple cloak: the Roman, who had arrived with two cohorts of troops and fifty other strange speaking men, all dressed in white. The Roman had paid further tribute in gold to the chieftain, to ensure his strict privacy and to pay for two of the chieftain's men to be posted at all times on the hill approaching his own. That way, he would never get embroiled in a local feud. Food and supplies were delivered every few days, but there was never any interaction between the Romans and the locals. Long after the time when the place would be eventually removed, all that would ever remain would be a few bits of broken pottery and tiles. No one today", pointed out Tom, "would ever have realised that at that time the Romans, let alone the Greeks, were secretly right here."

"Hang on "Tom," Maddie interjected, "surely that can't be right, there are Roman ruins scattered about all over here, what about the Roman Wall, what about Wallsend – Segedunum, fort number one – like Alex, and now you, just told us about."

"Ah, yes," Tom patiently sorted through the confusion, "but that was built much later, a hundred years later, in the time of the emperor Hadrian. No, at the time we are speaking of…" he sat down and confirmed in his head – "still 42 BC – even Arbeia was merely a trading outpost – not yet part of the Empire. The various tribes that ruled the land were still very much in control. The Roman who occupied the crag had not come here either to govern or to trade, he had come here for the raw materials that were in abundance here – coal, iron-ore and even tin from further south. He was also here to seek refuge from the warring Empire; so that he could complete his 'research project' away from the prying eyes of the new Emperor, Octavian; and without risking the danger of having the object of his obsession whisked away from his tentative grasp ever again.

Inside the walled villa were many workshops. There, for weeks, the imprisoned technicians and members of The Chronology Society of Alexandria had slaved away, completing the long task they had been working on in Syracuse. This, under pain of what would happen to their friends and families if they did not. At last though, their secret project was nearing completion. Now, all the Roman needed was someone to show him how to programme the machine that he had recovered from the sea bed of Aegilia. And with its inventor dead, the only person in the world who could now do so was Lio.

That was why Lio had been tracked down, and an elaborate trap had been laid around the boy. But it was only now that Lio was about to learn of the reasons why the prospects of his promising life had all been casually ruined.

When the mule was led through the closed yard and into the furthest workshop, Lio craned his head around, still with the rock tied in his mouth. Now upside down, he looked again, only in absolute horror at what he saw there. Through the pendant and goggles, dangling across his eyes, Lio recognised it at once – Kyrros' Hippo-Chronos! Now it began to dawn on Lio that this was obviously why he had been summoned by Poseidonios – this was presumably the subject of his concern for the future of humanity."

In the house next door to where Tom was telling his story, Alex sat in his bedroom, entertaining and generally keeping an eye on his sister. He waited as patiently as he could for the house valuer to finish his appraisal. It was a full hour later when he heard the door close. In due course, Penny came up the stairs and gave a gentle tap on his door before stepping in. Alex was disappointed – disappointed that she hadn't even mentioned the subject of selling the house to him. He didn't speak. Penny picked up Rachel as she broke the frosty silence. "Alex," she spoke sensitively, "I didn't want to say anything until I knew if any of this was possible – do-able."

He still didn't speak.

"You know, since your dad went missing, the bills have been mounting up steadily. If he had been on an expedition for work – the university – we'd still have his salary while everything's being sorted out – but he wasn't. Instead it was something to do with our neighbour."

As annoyed as he was, Alex began to realise that she had only kept all of this from him till now because she was trying to protect him. He looked at her again, wondering if this was why she had been so stand-offish with Tom.

She explained, "Look, there may not be any direct evidence, but they went away about the same time – your dad goes missing – and a year later this 'Tom' shows up all alone – no mention of my husband!" Alex listened on.

"I even went to talk to him in hospital on the afternoon after his accident – before you got there" – she finally admitted. "He knows something Alex, but he wouldn't tell *me*. All he would say was it was a 'big secret'. I just wish you didn't trust him so much."

"Herkoose odonton," Alex suggested.

"What?" she looked at him.

"Nothing."

"You know, moving away from here might be a good idea for all of us – away from all the memories – and him!"

"But I need those memories mam," Alex pleaded.

"Alex, we can't go on like this," she explained. "We're getting deeper into debt. If no *real* evidence shows up shortly we'll not even get the insurance money to pay off the mortgage," she hung her head.

"You mean dad's…" Alex began to realise.

She didn't answer. "All in all, it would be the best all round solution to put the house on the market and move on, wouldn't it?"

"But this is dad's house. And what about my friends – what about Conna and the girls – and everyone else?"

Just then, Boris ambled in through the door and lay down. "And what about him?" he asked.

"I'm sure we could find a good home for him…" she suggested. "Or… heck, we could see how much it would cost to take him along…" And we could come back every now and then to see Conna."

Alex sighed at the unrealistic idea. Suddenly, he began to get agitated. "I'm going to go and see Tom – find out what he really knows – maybe he can still help."

"Oh! I'm not sure that's such a good idea." She looked toward Tom's house.

"Why not," he shrugged. "Maybe if I just tell him how serious this all is getting… I'm sure he'll tell?"

Suddenly, she became agitated herself. "Alex, he's not to be trusted," she implored him. "He just won't talk about your dad. He wouldn't even talk to me about the time he picked you up to carry you away – except to say that he was going to sacrifice you!"

Alex shook his head. "It's not like that Mam, he already told me."

"Told you what?" she said, getting exasperated. "Alex, you were only a few days old. I'd only just brought you home from hospital a couple of evenings before," she explained at long last, reliving the traumatic event with him. "Your dad and I had been planning to take you down to York, to show you off to his old college friends," she wore a pained expression, remembering. "We wanted to catch the early train. So, we'd gotten up early, got you ready and placed you in the cot beside the opened car door. Then we went back in for the bags and other baby things. When I came back out of the house only a few moments later, you'd gone. At first, I thought that your dad had picked you up and taken you for a stroll while I sorted out the baby seat. But when he came back from the 'rest room' (whenever she was agitated she reverted to her native terms) that was when we realised what had happened.

Immediately, Stan – your dad – called out to our neighbour who was stood quite openly at the cliff edge." Penny pointed through the window at the exact spot. "Tom, as you call him, was stood there silhouetted against the rising sun in his nightgown, holding you up and over the edge, mumbling something about protecting you from Zeus. "I'm telling you Alex, he was going to throw you over – sacrifice you! And as for his excuse for it all – that that's what people did thousands of years ago!" Tears of anger welled up in her eyes.

"Hey, mam, I'm sorry, I didn't mean to disbelieve you." Alex reached out to calm her down. "It's just that it was all just a misunderstanding – Tom's explained all about it."

"What?" she accused. "What is there to be misunderstood? Your father had to grab you out of his hands before he dropped you onto the rocks below."

"No mam," Alex tried to calm her down, "look, for a start, it wasn't a nightgown…"

"What!" She almost shouted incredulously. "And what's *that* got to do with it?"

"Mam, calm down, I mean he wore an old robe of his – a jubbah, he always wears them at home – he wasn't about to 'sacrifice me' at all. Tom said all he wanted to do was hold me up – 'offer me' in dedication to the rising sun. As he says, acknowledge my birth into the natural world. He wouldn't have hurt me."

At that his mother lost her temper. "And how would *you* know?" She barged out of the room, taking the baby downstairs.

Alex looked sheepishly at Boris who sat bolt upright, woofed at him once then lay down flat again. Now he felt riddled with guilt. He sat down on his bed and thumbed the dent in his dad's watch, thinking the unthinkable – *just how much might the heirloom sell for?*

Back in Tom's house, his neighbour continued: "Lio sat in rags, tied bodily to the heavy wooden chair that in turn sat in the workshop, his bags thrown down beside him. By the look of it, they hadn't found what Miriam had stitched into the false bottom of the larger one, which was odd, given its weight. It was as though they had been looking for something more specific – larger – though unsuccessfully. There was no one but Lio there. No one of course except his 'old friend', the Time-Horse. He had sat staring at the machine for the past hour at least, trying to work out how this could possibly have happened. Gone, though, were any thoughts of happiness he might have associated with coming face to face with the object he had often wondered about – even sometimes dreamed of. Now, the sight of the bronze horse filled him only with a dark foreboding. It wasn't for nothing that he had found it, or more strictly, been led to it. He felt an ever growing feeling of something bordering on evil about this place: the villa, the workshops and the horse. Certainly, he was only too happy that he had not brought his computer – Kyrros' prototype time-key – with him, now fearing why he'd been asked to bring it.

Since he had sat in the chair, he'd looked the Hippo-Chronos up and down repeatedly, at first unsure if it was the very same machine and not some sort of copy. But everything about it seemed right. It definitely was the same machine, the same one that had been lost at the bottom of the sea. Though if anything, it seemed a lot more polished than when he'd last seen it properly – not tumbling through the ship's hatch – but before that, in the workshops, before it had been filled with modelling wax.

To begin with, now there was not a trace of wax on it. He could see quite clearly that the whole thing had been stripped and cleaned meticulously, probably even fully rebuilt. There was one tell-tale of its prolonged submersion in water though. Looking down at the hooves on its left side, Lio noticed the not properly cleaned off crud from both of them. White worm casts covered them – and pitting around the same area had begun to scar the delicately pierced skin. And, on the front hoof in particular, Lio noticed a deep crack that ran around the fetlock. He sat looking long and hard at the object, knowing that all the keys to its operation were destroyed or missing, or had at least been sent to the far end of the world. Now completely silent, Lio could only hope that the horse was dead.

Then, just as suddenly, his mind leapt back to his previous thought as he finally realised – this *was* the far end of the world. He concentrated now, taking his mind back years, to the workshop in Alexandria – that morning before the fire. He desperately tried to remember it. It was important. What had the librarian had said about his precious horse?

"That he had already taken the opportunity to despatch the first key to the furthest end of the world... an Arab trade vessel... heading out to what was likely to become the next extension to the Roman Empire... once known as the largest of the Cassiterides islands... the furthest settlement northwards along the eastern coast – just at the edge of the Scotos Lands... the river guarded by treacherous black rocks..." 'Arbeia!' Lio blurted the single word.

Now, for the first time in many, many years – the first time since he had grown into manhood – Lio became angry."

CHAPTER 21:

An Old Friend

"When the door opened behind Lio, and he heard the footsteps approach with a distinct, never to be forgotten, tapping all he could do was resign himself to whatever his fate may be, and attempt to fathom out how it had all happened. How it was that the figure that now stood behind him in the shadows, poking him in the bare shoulder with the thin walking stick, could possibly have made it here? Though in truth, he had probably always suspected he had since the day he'd rescued Ashur – and then, later, standing in the palace with Kyrros, in front of Caesar and Cleopatra – although, he had always sought to deny the frightening possibility of it to himself.

'Remember me boy?' The silky voice whispered in Greek as the Sicilian's head came close to his. 'Still got that ridiculous mop of red hair I see.'

Lio didn't answer, the anger building up inside.

'You know, I'm not worried that you cheated me out of the power I could have achieved – how long ago was it?'

'Eight years,' answered Lio flatly.

'Is it really? And I thought it was over five hundred. "Tempus fugit",' he smiled to himself." 'Time flies', translated Tom. "The figure walked out in front of him and pulled back the hood that had kept his face in shadow. The pock-marked face of the man Lio knew as Zeus looked down at him. Lio looked straight back – not afraid of him anymore.

'You're not surprised to see me then?'

'No,' said Lio calmly, 'just disappointed, you're so much smaller and more insignificant than I remembered, but there again I was almost half the age and height I am now, only ten years old. Ashur and Marduk were only children too.'

The short man blew out a thin stream of air, considering his past crimes and swishing his purple cloak around himself. 'Hmm' he said, his mind seeming to leave the room. 'But at least *she* still lives,' he smiled ironically... 'while I allow her to.'

Lio didn't react, unsure of what he knew of Ashur, and her whereabouts in particular.

Zeus stroked the back of his aged left hand. Switching the subject suddenly, he asked Lio, 'You do know how I got here, don't you?'

'I can guess,' said Lio, but clearly now clearly delighted with himself, Zeus was going to tell him the whole story anyway.

'That day, when you came back to the Temple of Helios for your... girl,' he decided to call her pointedly – 'I was right there. I watched you from the one place I knew no one would look for me – inside the inner sanctum itself. The noise and the flash from that thing,' he nodded towards the horse, 'was quite unmistakeable. Do you know,' he allowed himself a rare self-deprecating snort of a laugh, 'the night before, I almost believed in "the gods" myself when that man – Kyrros – arrived right in front of my eyes, his clothes billowing around him. But then, as you arrived only twenty four hours later, and I listened in to your touching conversation,' he smirked, 'I realised what that...' he put his hands up in submission "...genius" of a man had achieved – a way to move across time and distance. He really was, I have to admit, a very clever man. Perhaps almost as clever as myself,' he conceded. 'If only he'd had the sense to make the most of its benefits. Do you know how long I've waited to get my hands on this... ugly beast?' he sneered at its head.

'Still eight years,' Lio answered sarcastically.

Again the man snorted, 'Hmm, yes, indeed. But you kept on trying to outsmart me, or should I say, fate did. You know, from the moment I clung onto its underbelly and stumbled off outside the library to steal myself away – from the time I saw this machine being dragged away,' he tapped it with his cane, 'I was determined that it would one day be mine. All that wasted time,' he looked at the machine, 'but now *it is* mine.' He rubbed his withered hands together.

Lio looked from the horse, back to the wiry pock-marked face. Still he said nothing as Zeus continued to boast of how he'd finally 'won'.

'I knew where it was of course. The lock into the windowless room where it was kept behind the cupboard wasn't much of a deterrent. Both of the large hatches in the machine were open and it was obvious that parts of it were missing, something round and something long and box-like – it was clear from the empty spaces. So all I could do was assume that "the King's Engineer" had taken them with him, wherever that was. But try as I might to bribe one of these technicians,' he nodded behind him, indicating that they were now here, 'I never could find out where he had disappeared to.'

Yes, guessed Lio, he could imagine that, such was the bond between everyone in the Mouseion – except perhaps, the librarian, who had his own extraordinary priorities.

'It didn't take me long to get back on my feet, of course. I still had a small pouch of gold and a couple of nice emeralds,' he raised his eyebrows. 'I began trading with my motherland, Rome – marvellous to think of what a tiny town has achieved in such a short time, all through their absolute belief in themselves – that they were born to rule the world. We are superior in every way you know,' he said unnecessarily.

Lio snorted. 'Superior in ruthlessness and greed you mean.'

Zeus seemed to ignore him. 'Anyway I made quite a pile of money, what with the black market in grain: importing Egyptian grain to Sicily, to trade it on. For nearly two years I stored it away,' he smirked at Lio – until the king and queen decided to tear the country apart. No matter, even that worked in my favour. When Caesar arrived as anticipated, I tried to see him, but it was impossible. He was far too well guarded, and unlike some, I was not about to roll myself up in a mattress. Then I spotted one of his guards who was around the same size as myself.'

Lio was tempted to say something but didn't – now curious himself.

'You know, greed is fine! Greed is what makes the world go around, the constant grasping of half the world while the other half is content to be lazy.'

'While the other half are exploited,' corrected Lio.

'Perhaps,' he retorted, 'frankly I don't care. It's when the greed is tinged with stupidity that it doesn't work. The Praetorian Guard that accepted my bribe to accompany me to "collect a debt", walked right into my trap. The two thugs, Egyptian prison guards that I hired to take care of him didn't waste time, and I ended up with a very useful uniform,' he assured his prisoner. 'No one dares check the credentials of those wearing the black uniform. Unfortunately, however, this was all in the week of the fire. Time was running out.

Nevertheless, on the eve of the fire, I knew all I had to do was convince the librarian to hand over the 'keys' – as he called them. But I arrived too late – just as the Roman troops also arrived – though I did watch you and Kyrros being marched out. When I attempted to persuade the librarian to hand over the keys again, I nearly had him. I threatened I'd remove the fire watchers dousing the roof to protect his precious books. That was when he told me that he'd sent one of the missing keys to the far end of the world – the other was already out of the city. I even persuaded him to specify the exact location of the key sent here to this freezing place.' He tugged his precious cloak exaggeratedly tighter, 'with the north wind and the east wind constantly battling with each other,' he went on. 'Anyway, I could only ever get my hands on the machine itself for the time being, so I had it crated up and taken away.

'But the horse was on our corbita, I saw it.' Lio challenged the accuracy of his account.

'Ah yes, fate stepped in again, but not before I had one last try to find out the whereabouts of the other keys. Oh yes! I managed to squeeze that out of the librarian too before I...'

'Murdered him?' finished Lio.

'...Removed him.' He stopped, considering. 'I was about to try and get you out of jail, so that I could relieve Andronikos of the prototype keys, when, of all things, his own wife approached me for help! Me! Hah! It was an opportunity not to be missed. Collect the whole family onto a ship and carry them off together. That much I had previously managed to arrange with Caesar in order to get his haul of statues out of the city, destined for the Imperial Palace in Rome. Now all I had to do was let the great Andronikos bring his own keys with him, and once in Rhodos, follow him and have them "removed" from the man. I convinced Caesar that you should be put back in jail rather than let the Queen of the Nile have you killed prematurely, and then I would have you released.'

Lio was ahead of him. 'So it was you who bribed the guard when we managed to get free from the jail...'

'And thanks to my further considerable help, that you escaped the city.'

'But once aboard the galleys, your ship was struck by lightning, so you were delayed,' Lio had begun to figure it out for himself. 'Come on then,' he asked curiously, extracting as much information as the man was willing to give. 'How come the rest of your plan didn't work?'

Zeus was put out. 'Oh, but it did, didn't it? After all, we're all here now.'

'But it didn't exactly work did it? You don't have the keys do you?' he probed.

'If you mean, why was my plan *delayed*,' Zeus ignored the second prompt, 'it was because the commander of the galley fleet decided in my absence to ship out the statues from Rhodos before I had arrived. The master of the corbita,' the commander admitted to me later, 'had managed to squeeze the entire cargo onto it – including my own crated-up bronze horse. By the time I got off the beach at Lindos he had already left Rhodos for Rome.' Zeus paused, remembering his frustration. 'I followed him of course, commandeering both the Fleet Commander and his ship – it's surprising what this uniform does for a man. And I would have killed the thieving corbita master for stealing the extra bronze that was not on the manifest. But then, apparently not content with the most precious cargo that he had hauled in his entire life, he decided to detour and pick up one further lightweight cargo to take back with him to Rome. It was greed that killed him.'

This was rich, thought Lio. *Not only was the kettle calling the pot black – both clearly thieves – but now he was blaming someone else for his greed.* Lio couldn't resist. 'But I thought you just said greed was good,' he tested the Sicilian's patience, seeing how much he needed him alive.

Zeus gritted his teeth, he didn't like to be ridiculed – the red haired freak would pay for that – sometime at his leisure – after he'd finished extracting knowledge from him.

He continued: 'we must have passed him somewhere on the seas. In Rome I waited a whole month for him to arrive. The hire of that galley alone would have crippled me, except that the commander was so terrified of what Caesar would do to him if he realised he'd entrusted his precious cargo without my permission. That he'd let it all be taken on one boat instead of two – as were his instructions – thereby pocketing the difference in haulage costs. In the end, he was quite happy to go back to Rhodos without pay.' He sounded exasperated at telling the tale of his 'bad luck'. 'Of course, I had to tell Caesar about him eventually...' He smirked. 'The commander didn't live much longer after that.

No, the ship and the cargo had gone missing. At first, I thought, stolen. But then, who would dare steal from Caesar? I returned to Alexandria and explained to Caesar that the ship had probably been sunk. Thankfully he was magnanimous in his loss. He simply took back the monies I had charged him – and a little more in compensation' – he pursed his lips distastefully, remembering the enormous sum. 'And that, as they say, would have been that – until you gave the game away of course.'

Lio knew exactly what he meant, his shoulders dropped.

'The description of the red haired... "boy" on Aegilia,' Zeus stopped himself this time, '...that made star charts using a machine was unmistakable. It was I who sent the seafarer to your barren island to check on the tale. Then, when I told Caesar about the information I'd gathered, and assured him of how I could raise his precious statues for him' – Lio noticed that he did not mention whether he'd told the dictator about the horse – 'the Emperor authorised the whole operation, even part funding it – by returning the compensation that he had claimed previously from me.' He raised an eyebrow ironically. 'And, as he was passing toward Alexandria, he even took the opportunity to call in at the island and remove the pirate problem once and for all. Do you know,' said the Sicilian impressively, 'I really did admire that man's efficiency – killing three birds with one stone – calendar, pirates and you. The one thing I didn't expect was that he would allow you to live in freedom... strange?'

Lio remembered the ultimate pragmatist and his treatment of the Cretan pirates. Whilst it suited him to have Lio on hand and in freedom, possibly Caesar was also concerned that Lio might somehow lead a revolt of the Mouseion workers if he was put with them, that was all. But no doubt, he would have eventually been imprisoned with them if Caesar had not been assassinated. There would never be any admiration from Lio for one of the most ruthless killers in European history.

'Of course, you realise that it was I who funded your stay in Alexandria. Caesar refused. The plan was mine after all,' he grimaced again. 'Although, he did mention your rather silly disguise – that turbanos.'

Of course Poseidonios hadn't known about the headdress, Lio finally realised. *And neither was it a coincidence that he had been requested to wear it.* The young man felt suddenly humiliated at the late realisation.

'Then, of course, after Caesar's death, you went missing again. But I knew that if I was patient, you'd eventually return to your island... and her!'

Lio grew alarmed at the mention of Ashur again.

'Where was I?' he stroked his pock-marked face, 'oh yes.' He was enjoying telling Lio how clever he was and how naïve the young man had been. 'It was indeed your old friend Poseidonios who wrote to you initially from Syracuse; though he wrote it a *long* time ago. I discovered the letter of course, and he was "disciplined". However, it also suited me to let it be sent to you, even though I held onto it for years – until we were about to move on.' He smirked, 'the second short note was entirely mine though – untouched by the old man. Well, we had to get you here somehow, didn't we – and it was good of you to pay your own way!'

Zeus smirked again, watching the look of disappointment register on Lio's face.

Lio closed his eyes, guessing that he was too late to save Poseidonios. It was very clear to see who the hero of this story was – and it was not Caesar. And yet, knowing all of this did not make Lio wiser to the situation that he really wished to know – what about Ashur?

'I know what you are wondering now,' Zeus sneered. 'You're wondering about your girl. Yes, I know exactly where she lives, and Andronikos' wife… and his son. So this is the deal. It was I who rescued you all from Cleopatra and allowed you all to carry on your lives while I made my plans. So, even though you failed to bring the missing prototype key with you, you will show me how to work this thing behind me. It doesn't really matter now, it never did seem to work again since it was re-built – I'm sure it was that technician who was responsible. Anyway, if you do, I'll consider letting them all live.' He paused for emphasis. 'Show me what those dials are for – how to control the machine. You never know, I might even let you return to your island into the bargain, it would be no skin off my nose – not if I had the whole world at my own feet. I might fly to the past and live out my life as a king – or to the future. Who knows what riches and power might lay there for me. Anyway, I'll let you consider that – and what might befall your family if you don't – or should you decide to leave unannounced. Well, you're still a wanted man, aren't you! And I still have my contacts in that part of the world. Of course,' he emphasised, 'if my message was to arrive at its destination even one minute before you,' he made a sign that took Lio back to his childhood, drawing a single finger across his throat. Zeus turned to leave.

'One last thing,' asked Lio, taking advantage of the situation, 'why did you burn the Great Library of Alexandria down?'

The Sicilian stopped in his tracks, wondering. 'Really now,' he said, 'I was there, I saw everything, remember?'

'So?' Lio quizzed.

'So I saw you and Andronikos empty the shelves and pile up the scrolls to make the bonfire,' he accused. 'Are you trying to tell me that it wasn't you? Oh!… Oh, that's precious… so you're telling me that you got the blame for something you *really* didn't do, hah!'

With that, he strolled out of the door to leave Lio to think about the consequences. The Sicilian was clearly still convinced that it was Kyrros and his son that had started the fire. To Zeus it made no difference who had burned it down though. Once he knew he had the information he needed, he would take great pleasure in wiping out Lio and his family anyway. It was high time to use his stick again – to its fullest."

Maddie shifted uncomfortably in her seat. "So who was it who burned down the library?" she asked.

Tom scratched his head briefly. "Do you know, to this day no one ever found out. Some say it was the Romans who started it accidentally with the fire in the harbour. Some think that they might have started it deliberately, to deprive the Egyptians of getting their hands on even more sophisticated weapons. Some say it might have been Ptolemy – for the same reasons. And some even say Cleopatra herself – to stop her brother. It certainly would explain why she was so determined to pin the blame on two unlikely suspects like Kyrros and his son. I think almost certainly it was not the Head Librarian though. If Zeus had not denied it was he, Lio would have happily assumed that it was the Sicilian and no one else. But, in answer to your question," confirmed Tom, "I most certainly do not know."

Bex and Conna looked at their wristwatches simultaneously, wondering what had happened to Alex. Both had thought that it wouldn't be long before he came in – at least that's what Alex had told them. Maybe everything was not going according to plan.

In the meantime, Tom picked up from where he'd left off.

"Lio sat strapped in the chair, looking directly at the muzzle of the horse. Regardless of his personal situation, which he could now do nothing about, uppermost in his mind was preventing the machine from ever working again. With a working Hippo-Chronos in the Sicilian's hands he really would wreak havoc on the world.

Lio wondered whether or not he had managed to find the Chrono-key after all. If he had, it was only a matter of programming and installing it in the machine – if it still worked properly – and it would be able to take its rider both forward and back in time. Though without the other key – the Cosmos-key – obviously it would not be able to move across any distance – its geographical location would remain right here. At this present time though, even without either key, it was still capable of travelling in time – but only into the future. As Zeus had not mentioned this failsafe, Lio assumed that he did not know about it. Nevertheless, even if he, Lio, could get free from the chair and get his hands on the horse – assuming it still worked – and even though he would be able to re-programme it, without the key, he could not escape without endangering Ashur, Miriam and Andros. By going into the future, even by a few days, would be to lose that time. In the time it would take for Zeus to sail back to Aegilia, the high priest would have the advantage; it would effectively give Zeus more time to get to them! For now then, all Lio could do was play along with him. By playing along, the young man might perhaps get the opportunity to escape, even overpower him, destroy the machine and get back to Aegilia first.

He went through the last known whereabouts of the keys to make sure there wasn't the possibility of the Sicilian having them. The production Chrono-key – the computer – had been sent right here by the librarian. The damaged production Cosmos-key – the armillary – had been smashed by Kyrros. The prototype Cosmos-key was travelling somewhere inside the sarcophagus of Alexander. And the prototype Chrono-key would by now be consigned to Kyrros' sea grave. He absolutely trusted Ashur to have carried this out. The only key still remaining then, was the production Chrono-key that was hidden somewhere on this very promontory. If the Sicilian already had that, and Lio could get his hands on it and install it in the horse, he would be able to programme it and travel back in time, to undo the sequences that had brought this whole situation about. In other words, go back to Rhodos to rescue Ashur again, but this time make certain that the so called High Priest of Zeus did not hitch a ride."

"Oh… now I get it," said Conna at last. He had listened to the various descriptions of the various keys at various times and had always nodded his understanding of what each did – mainly to show 'certain people' that he wasn't 'thick' after all. But now he actually got why Lio couldn't have just climbed on the horse and put the world to rights. He looked back to each of the girls, happy that he was finally up to speed with the story, but still not knowing where it was leading to. Part of his mind drifted off for a moment. Even if he still didn't quite believe the story, he was far happier sitting here rather than be in his own house right now.

Maddie was happy to listen-on, especially since Tom's mood had picked up. She worried so much when he descended into those dark moods, as he had done on a couple of occasions. But now she was much happier that Tom seemed sharper, brighter and more determined to live out the tale.

Bex in turn, again analysed every word as Tom took another sip of water.

CHAPTER 22:

Another Old Friend

His mood now brightened, Tom continued:

"Lio sat upright all night, tied to the chair. He shivered from the lack of decent clothes. He had managed to doze off for only a short while, but that was, nevertheless, quite enough for him. In the morning, he sat in the gloom as the door opened and he heard the tap of a stick, but the expected figure did not appear. Instead, it was the man whom Lio had known as a boy in Alexandria.

Lio would never now have recognised him, he looked so ancient. His once best chequered robe, now threadbare, was pulled tightly around his emaciated frame. Standing with the spiral bull's pizzle in his hand, Poseidonios of Rhodos, the athlete and traveller, smiled weakly at the child he remembered from the museum workshops – now the splendid young man. He had recognised Lio instantly as he was being brought in through the yard, across the back of the mule. Lio looked up at him from his chair, now surprised to even see him alive. He couldn't help but smile. But *what was his full part in all this?* he wondered.

'Lio,' said the philosopher tiredly, 'how wonderful to see you – yet how sad under these circumstances. I've been sent to untie you…' he made his way unhurriedly around the back of the chair, 'no doubt, because this "athlete" is least likely to run away,' he made light of his infirmity. 'I see you still have my old pendant,' he smiled satisfactorily.

'What's happening, what are you all doing here?' Lio asked the philosopher.

'What are any of us doing here?' came the obscure reply. 'I'm quite certain that *I* should not be. Better that I had died years ago than be reduced to this. Do you know,' he started to undo the rope, 'many years ago, when I was only your age, I travelled to this country. Would you believe it, I made my way all the way to the far north of this island, well into the dark lands – right up as far as the sea itself begins to freeze! I kept an old record of it all – an atlas of my travels around the world. I carried it with me for years. In fact, I always meant to show it to you – until I lost it somewhere.'

Lio didn't wish to embarrass him by reminding him he'd once shown it to him as a boy, many years ago in Alexandria.

'Who knows where it's got to now?' the old man said wistfully. 'But, in all that time, I was never touched once by any of the strange tribes – perhaps because they were fascinated by my ways of dressing colourfully – perhaps because of my strange tongue… who knows? I never was good at languages. I just navigated by the stars, trying to reach Polaris – which I never did.'

Suddenly changing tack he said, 'you know that none of us can escape, don't you? He knows where all of our families live,' he nodded.

'Yes,' said Lio, 'I know.'

Switching tack once again, the very oldest man Lio ever knew, continued to reminisce. 'Do you know, on that occasion, on the way home to Alexandria from Arbeia, the Arab master refused to be delayed by a thick, rolling mist that appeared as we cast off from the mole. He swore that the black rocks were floating toward him, and tried to negotiate a way around. That was how he sank his boat. I was the only one of a handful to survive, simply by standing knee deep on top of the rocks until the mist lifted. Then I was picked up by the ferryman. I never did like to travel by boat since then, but it is a necessary evil.'

As interesting as the tale from his youth was, Lio was far more interested in finding out how and why he had found his way back. 'Poseidonios, why are you here now?' he asked, rubbing his wrists, no worse for wear.

'Oh, I was rounded-up from Rhodos after I returned from carrying out one last task for the Chronology Society. It was just after I had retired there – just after the Romans finally took Alexandria. They told everyone on Rhodos that I had died, and that they were taking my body back to be buried in Alexandria. Instead, we were all sent to Syracuse by boat. None of us had any choice in the matter. We were all rounded up – the museum workers, the teachers, the technicians – as I said, as soon as the Romans took Alexandria. We were all forced to build the various weapons that had been recorded in the library before its destruction. We were not about to argue with Caesar – he is quite ruthless, you know.'

Is? Clearly, Poseidonios was, even now, still unaware of Caesar's death.

'But at least when Caesar has people killed, it is swift, unlike him,' he nodded to indicate the position of the villa. 'Nobody argues with Caesar, the repeating ballistae were the first job, then the burning mirrors of course.'

Lio remembered the devastating effect. He suddenly thought of something. 'Was that what started the library fire – after the battle?'

'By the heavens no,' came the shocked reply. 'Besides, at that late time of the day the sun would have been too low, not hot enough by any means to burn anything substantial. In that winter sun, it only just worked on the oiled canvas sails. But also, by then, the whole invention had been packed up, and along with ourselves, shipped off to Syracuse. At that point, we were now simply his "special weapons people", led by Kyrros' own trusted technician.' He pointed at the Hippo-Chronos, 'it was even he who helped raise that from the sea bed. He made the divers' goggles, almost the same that he first made for Kyrros – for you – but this time using clear glass. And, he made the diving bell – which never came back. No one anticipated the "screaming death" though, although I'm sure the Sicilian would like to find out what caused it – if he could only find enough divers to experiment with.

Since then,' he continued, 'we were all held as prisoners, working on the machine. That was when I managed to persuade one of the guards to smuggle my letter to you,' he sighed. 'We were desperate. I thought you might influence things – bring some pressure to have us released – by using Caesar's name.' He revealed the heavily scarred palms of his hands. 'But then the guard handed the letter to Zeus!'

Obviously, Lio now knew, Poseidonios' part in the deception was entirely innocent.

'Finally, a few weeks ago, we were all brought here. No doubt we will continue to be held in captivity, presumably until we've run out of use to him. And then who knows what will happen to us in the workshop behind us.'

Lio ignored the reference to a workshop. Instead, he seized on the hope that the technician was there, an ally. 'So where is he – the technician?' he asked.

'Dead!' came the stark reply, 'only a week or so ago. He was accused of trying to repeatedly sabotage the Roman's work. So like that,' he clicked his fingers, 'he was whisked away to the villa, never to return. The screams could be heard for hours, before they finally stopped and his broken body was brought out.'

Lio's spirits dropped again. He looked once more at the bronze horse, now sharing the old man's pessimism.

'Lio, I'm sorry I involved you. I take it that he has now asked you to advise on the code,' said Poseidonios. 'I'm too old for this. Long ago I let it slip that you had once ridden the horse – and I foolishly boasted that you had programmed it all by yourself.'

Lio nodded, remembering the long since day that he'd taken the horse to rescue Ashur. 'Yes, he has asked me already,' he confirmed, 'though I don't know if he's managed to find the key.'

'Oh, I can answer that for you,' he said with a wry smile. 'Each day since we arrived here, there has been a small party of us searching, combing the entire rock for the Chrono-key that was left here. But,' he smiled conspiratorially, 'still no one has found it.' He placed his finger to his lips, making the old sign, then bent forward shakily to whisper: 'they're looking entirely in the wrong place. *I* left it "within a crevice in the rock –in the prom…"'

214

'What was that?' The slight figure of the Sicilian stood at the opened door. 'Have you been keeping something from me all this time? Have you?' the voice raised with his temper.

The old man's face turned ashen.

'I think... we'll have a word with you later.' Zeus tapped the cane in his hand. 'Be a good little old man, and hobble through to my workshop.'

It was only then that Lio finally understood. The anonymous travel writer who had advised on the secret hiding place had been he – Poseidonios himself. It was *he* who had been the courier of the key sent out from Alexandria. *That* had been his last job for the Chronology Society, before he had attempted to retire on Rhodos.

As Poseidonios shuffled out of the room, Zeus' cane was raised mockingly, forcing the old athlete to cower while he passed. 'So,' the Sicilian turned to Lio, 'have you made up your mind yet? What is it to be?' he made the imperial thumbs-up sign, 'or,' thumbs down.

'I'll help,' snapped Lio, 'on condition you don't beat him.'

Zeus sneered. 'Are you attempting to bargain with me?' he considered. 'Alright then, I won't "beat" him. A deal is a deal – after all I am a man of my word, am I not?'

Lio didn't answer. Without the keys, or the drawings of how to recreate them, without the technician left alive, he reasoned that it made little difference how the dials on the machine had once worked and whether or not he divulged how Kyrros' code was written. If Zeus attempted to use it, it would only transport him into the future, to be trapped there. Gambling that it might provide the ideal opportunity for him and the others to escape, Lio heard himself agree to the demands of the most dangerous man that time would ever know.

In almost complete capitulation, while he struggled to formulate a plan of escape, Lio began to explain the principle of Kyrros' constant digital code – the noughts and crosses – in detail. Even, at Zeus's insistence, writing the whole thing down. He started to freely explain how everything worked, including both of the missing keys.

But as the young man went through most of this information slowly and repeatedly, he was struck with the intensity of the bombardment of questions from the Sicilian. So, eventually, unless asked a direct question, he did not volunteer anything more. Now, he began to suspect that there may actually be another motive for all of these questions – although what that might be, he could not begin to imagine.

Lastly, at Zeus's seemingly random selection, a dozen rough locations around the world were translated 'theoretically' into Kyrros' digital format, including Rome, Athens, Rhodos, Alexandria, Londinium and lastly, along the coast of Asia minor to the city known long ago as Wilusha – but distinctly not, to Lio's relief, Aegilia. Without a large armillary to pinpoint the locations accurately enough though, the information, Lio knew, was useless.

When at last he had finished explaining repeatedly – all day long – Zeus finally let the young man take a break. He even offered to provide his prisoner with something to eat. Lio's mind now began to focus on getting away.

'Well,' said the Sicilian shortly, satisfied that at last he now understood everything, 'I'm so glad that you could take the time to sail from Aegilia and pay me a visit. 'But now,' he said succinctly, 'I think at last I should take some time for myself. With all the thanks in the world,' he sneered, 'I bid you goodbye – for now.' Without further ado Zeus got up and started to walk out of the room. Casually he said to the guard, 'Let him eat by all means, then let him go, he'll never again be able to escape me. If I ever do need him again, I'll know exactly where to find him. He'll always be right here and now!

Just as Lio began to think that Zeus had indeed found a way to use the horse again, he then heard him say: 'And after you've fed him, smash up the Hippo-Chronos permanently, it's served its purpose. In fact, make *him* smash it up,' he smirked. 'I'll be back before you know I've gone!'

The delivery of the Sicilian's bewildering instructions stunned Lio, throwing him into shock – just like that – let him go. Then, smash up the Hippo-Chronos'. He was astounded by both commands. They left his head reeling. The only good news was that he was glad to be out of his company. As the door closed, Lio stood alone with the illusion of freedom, unable to fathom out what was going on. He walked in a daze back to the Hippo-Chronos, where he looked at it in incredulity.

However, perhaps this was his chance after all. He looked it up and down in detail, studying it to see that it had been put back together properly. As far as he could tell, it had. Looking closely at the tightly coiled blue springs in its chest, he could even tell that it had been wound up ready for use. And yet, he couldn't for the life of him fathom out what all of the hugely wasted effort had been about. All of that subterfuge to control his life – almost to the point of destruction. All just so that Zeus could finally learn a secret code that didn't matter without possessing the keys. And then – 'make him smash up the Hippo-Chronos' the Sicilian's voice echoed in Lio's head, 'It's served its purpose!'

The guard found Lio again. Carrying a small bowl of unappetising grey food, he shoved it into his hands. Then he stood back by the door, watching him attempt to eat it. For the next ten minutes, Lio looked into the hollow eyes of the horse, contemplating how best to get out of this place and get home to Aegilia before Zeus could find out he'd gone. There was no point in writing again to try and forewarn his family. Any letter would have to travel on the same ship as himself anyway.

He wondered whether the Sicilian *would* come after him now that he'd given him everything that he wanted, but then realised that he was indeed more than likely to send somebody – from spite, if nothing else. *If only,* he thought, *he could use the Hippo-Chronos somehow. But did it still work after all?* Assuming it did still work, all Lio needed to do now, was find Poseidonios again and ask him for the precise location of where he'd the hidden Chrono-key.

But then the stone floor began to rumble massively beneath his feet and he was filled with a feeling of absolute dread at what secrets he had almost casually betrayed!"

CHAPTER 23:

The Mother of All Weapons!

"Outside on the crag, the local tribesmen felt the vibration growing steadily. It was something awful. No one had known this before. Earth tremors were not felt in this part of the world. Quickly, they realised that the accompanying noise must be coming from within the walls of the Roman's property. Within minutes, everyone around it, including the guards, started to flee. Simultaneously, as far away as the bear head rock, people felt the earth move. Already the tribal leaders decided it was time for another sacrifice.

Inside the walls, Lio stood up, feeling the rumble grow more and more, until it seemed the whole promontory shook. With sickening realisation, he began to guess what the noise might be. If the vibration of the Hippo-Chronos was loud, this was ten times louder, absolutely deafening. If the Hippo-Chronos caused something like a tremor, this was a much deeper, far more powerful rumbling, more akin to a full-blown earthquake.

As he stared at Lio, the guard's eyes opened wide with fear. Lio followed. Then he turned and ran through the door that Zeus had used earlier. The lobby behind the door led directly to another door, which, as he ran toward it, was flung wide open from the other side by a white uniformed worker. A blast of hot, acrid air and grey smoke billowed out behind him, catching Lio's breath. Rapidly, the lobby filled up with fleeing bodies. The white uniformed technicians streamed out one by one, hugging the centre, while guards stumbled and pushed past them in panic.

Lio picked his way carefully past them all, shoving his way in the opposite direction. A cloud of thick smoke carpeted the room's high ceiling as he struggled to see the cause of it all. Then, he stopped dead in his tracks.

The colossal monstrosity which occupied the centre of the cavernous room left him horrified. The grey iron and timber horse was at least five times higher than the Hippo-Chronos. The evil looking head, more naturalistic, though more angular than that of the Hippo-Chronos, stood glinting erect. Its decorative purple and white striped tuft of a mane ran from the top of its head and descended down its neck. It stood, huffing and puffing aggressively, nearly touching the peak of the vaulted roof. Steam and fire poured from its huge nostrils. Smoke and vapour poured from the furnace built into its belly which in turn heated its huge eolipile – the ancient rotating pressure vessel that was the world's first steam 'engine'. As it dripped with condensation, it whirred around and around, rubbing many bars of amber against a thick silk band – an electra wheel – which generated a ring of blue sparks. The metal surfaces of the machine reflected the red and orange glow that bounced around the workshop walls. The whole of its upper back was wooden, studded with four small hatches and one door hatch on each side. Its shape and form were clearly much different to the Hippo-Chronos, although the massive, perforated metal frame demonstrated its shared pedigree with Lio's own horse. Set inside its chassis, large cogs and other mechanisms whizzed around faster and faster, the enmeshing gears whirring and whining louder and louder. Steadily the whole of the machine's workings built up speed. And there, as if to confirm the obvious intentions of the beast, arranged on a rotating turret in the centre of its back, sat a repeating ballista, capable of firing many bolts per minute. The whole machine was exactly what Kyrros had feared his technology would be turned into if ever it fell into aggressive hands. The warlike stance of the horse, the lofty bearing of its head and neck, all told the story of what the machine was – the mother of all weapons!

Clinging to his stick, Zeus climbed up the rope ladder that hung from the opened wooden body hatch, his purple cloak hanging down his back, while two more ex-Praetorian guards kept the hatch open. Hitching his cloak to one side to climb into it, he caught sight of the young man and couldn't help but gloat. Over the noise he yelled out, 'Oh, did I forget to mention... before he died, the librarian told me that he had given the boy Ptolemy a third set of unfinished keys – and a master armillary – which he kept in his palace. Caesar willingly gave them to me as navigation devices to get his booty home. Given a little persuasion,' he tapped his cane against the hatch, 'it didn't take the technician long to finish them off exactly as Kyrros had originally designed them!'

In a sudden flashback, Lio finally realised that that was what he'd seen Ptolemy carrying with him on that long distant occasion of his first uncomfortable visit to his palace.

'How do you like my re-design of your Greek machine,' Zeus boasted, 'now that it is at least half-Roman, I call it the Hippo-Tempus!' He laughed outrageously as he closed the hatch behind him, and within moments, the noise grew deafening.

Now, seeing the old man lying on the floor beside the giant horse, Lio realised what was about to happen. He looked around for something to shield Poseidonios from the blast, at last noticing the large armillary in the corner. In the opposite corner glinted one of the old, concave burning mirrors, so Lio ran and grabbed it. Then, lying quickly down on the floor beside Poseidonios, he covered the pair of them. Within a split second, it seemed that the whole timber roof would crash down on them from above. With a searing blast of hot air and flames and a flash of orange light and black smoke, the Hippo-Tempus seemed to lift momentarily higher on its extending, sprung legs. Then, suddenly, it disappeared. The flash would have been enough to blind any man – with Lio's past weakened eyes especially so – if it were not for the fact that he and the old philosopher were completely shielded from it and the blast of flames. Still, Lio's ears rang with it all.

Immediately after the giant horse had gone, he threw the shield to one side. The old man lying on the floor had a large, familiar red flower growing across his chest. As he looked up at Lio, blood trickled from his mouth. 'I didn't tell him where the hidden key was,' the old man assured. 'Don't worry too much, he can't come back,' he smiled weakly. 'Before he was executed, the technician did indeed manage to change one or two details while he was copying the Hippo-Chronos.' As the boy looked down at him, Poseidonios' eyes crinkled. Reassuringly, he said, 'Just as Kyrros' original machine is destined to only move forward in time without the aid of the Chrono-key, the technician made certain that the Hippo-Tempus – with or without the keys – can only go back in time – forever. He has trapped himself.'

Before Lio had a chance to ask him to pinpoint where he had deposited the spare Chrono-key years earlier, the dying man slipped into unconsciousness. It was only a few moments later that Poseidonios stopped breathing. Lio gently laid down the white-haired figure that would be remembered forever for many things, but especially his world travels. Instantly, a wave of hopelessness crashed into Lio and took him to the depths of despair at the secret he had taken with him. But then, self-preservation forced him to his feet.

No time to think of where the Hippo-Tempus had gone – now he had to get out, make his way past the broken and burned equipment, and back through to what was left of the villa. Picking up Poseidonios' stick – the bull's pizzle – to defend himself with, he ran straight through the corridor. In the courtyard, the violent shaking had dropped most of the main building to the ground, reducing it to only a semblance of what it had been a few minutes earlier. It was all a shattered mess, especially the workshops. Yet, even now – even though one of the roof joists had fallen on it – the all surviving Hippo-Chronos stood virtually upright. Lio grabbed his bags – all he had left in the world. He turned to run toward it.

It was then that, through a gap in the crumbled villa walls, he saw movement from around the edge of the hill. A few of the more daring tribesmen had already donned their blue war-paint and were looking from afar at the solo figure of the strange, raggedly dressed young man. The leader decided that all strangers to their land had long overstayed their welcome. None of them looked friendly.

Slowly, the tribesmen began to encroach. It looked like he was going to be taken prisoner again – or worse. Lio turned toward the horse and cleared the roof-joist from its back, hoping for a miracle. Then, as he brushed away the debris, he heard it: the sound that he'd not heard the horse make since it had been on the corbita when he was twelve years old. The Hippo-Chronos seemed to breathe, beckoning to him! And yet, without the missing key, did he dare trust it?

Conscious that he was running out of time, he also knew that he had nothing in the world to look forward to unless he could get back to Aegilia. But he had no hope of getting there. He looked at the thumbwheels. From nowhere, a thought came to him. Now he didn't have to worry about Zeus going after Ashur and his family if he was locked in the past. *Perhaps*, the boy wondered, *if he carefully set the thumbwheels for a year ahead, although he would miss a year of Ashur's life, he would re-emerge in the same place a year hence and escape by boat to Aegilia. But then*, he thought immediately, *perhaps he should make it two years, just to be on the safe side.* During that time, anything could happen in that volatile world. Maybe Cleopatra herself would be dead or ousted from power again? Maybe the warrant for his arrest would have been rescinded, who knows? In two years, he might safely be able to make his way back to Aegilia forever. He would only be a year younger than Ashur again – their original age difference.

His desperate spirits temporarily raised, now Lio held the pizzle fast under his arm while he started to programme the machine. Someone shouted – something he could not make out. Warily he pressed on with the programming, conscious of the many eyes now watching him from around the walls. The digits in the barrel all clicked into place: a zero, another zero, now an X then another zero… he went on, and then the final zero. But, as it turned, the last thumbwheel jammed against the next and then the next in turn, until it all looked completely wrong. He would have to zero everything and start again. He repeated the same sequence. But, just as before, as he turned the last wheel, they all spun out of sequence again. He peered closely at it and what looked like brick dust or a tiny piece of roof tile poking out of the gap between the barrels. He looked back up at the blue faces, then back down to see if he could clear it with his thumbnail. In earnest, Lio prodded and bashed it repeatedly with his fist, but it wouldn't budge.

Another unintelligible cry went up, by its upward ending intonation, probably a question. Two warriors clambered over the rubble toward him, one palming a spear, another, a sword. He fumbled again but couldn't move the obstruction. Now they were getting too close, raising the spear toward him. He had no choice. Whatever the date had been set for, he had to get out of there – now! It was his only hope of survival.

A last thought came to him. At least if he survived, he might be able to find the key another time. After all, it would always be right here until the day it was eventually found. *Even if I am ten or more years out*, he thought, *I can always find it and then get back to my own time.* Lio climbed onto the horse's back and pushed the go lever forward, then he sat nervously, waiting for things to happen. He could almost see the whites of the approaching Britons' eyes.

Slowly, as the sound and vibration started to pick up, there came another shout – more of an accusation this time. Neither of the tribesmen liked the look of the strange horse. Lio grabbed the thin end of the pizzle and threatened those he could see over the remains of the walls. The whirring grew louder – then there was another shout. The black-haired one of the two raised his sword in the air while the horse started to vibrate. There was yet another clearly angry shout as the red-haired one started to run toward him, his arm holding the spear above his head, ready to throw it. Seeing the colour of Lio's hair, the thrower hesitated – but it was only for an instant.

Lio watched the spear leave the warrior's hand and travel directly at his face. In that instant, he knew that his life was over. Still he recognised only the same feeling from long ago, a deep, overwhelming disappointment that it had all ended like this. But then, the spear seemed to slow down as it flew through the air.

At the last moment, Lio managed to simultaneously duck and move his head to one side. Not enough for it to miss, but enough for the weapon to glance off his temple – albeit heavily. Lio's head began to swim and he began to lose consciousness. Now increasingly dizzy, he feared that he might fall off the machine himself. He clung on dearly to the control levers as he drooped forward.

Hearing the metallic scream of the Hippo-Chronos, the warriors stopped in slow motion. They looked at Lio in open-mouthed shock as the puff of wind blew them slowly backwards. And in a burst of light and a cloud of loose rubble and dirt, right in front of their own eyes, the stranger on the devil horse disappeared.

This time," Tom cautioned, "disastrously, well into the future!"

PART III:
THE COUNTDOWN

'KALO ASMI LOKA-KSAYA-KRIT PRAVARDHO,
LOKAN SAMARTUM IHA PRAVATTAH'

('NOW I AM BECOME DEATH,
THE DESTROYER OF WORLDS')

From the Hindu book of scripture, The Bhagavad Gita
30th century BC. Quoted by J Robert Oppenheimer after 'Trinity':
The first nuclear bomb test, 20th Cent AD

CHAPTER 24:

The First Arms Race

Wilusha, 1197 BC

Three days after the Hippo-Tempus had arrived out of the blue in Agamemnon's camp, the cursed weather finally broke.

To the still hopeful guards on the rain soaked walls of the great city, the Persian gods had at last heard their prayers. Now, it was time to thank Mithras, who crossed the skies towing the sun behind his four wheeled battle wagon. The rain-soaked walls glowed and the sun's warmth began to dry out the ground where the sprawling Greek camp had been. They had seemingly all gone home.

In fact, however, after striking a deal with the horse-machine's possessors and after much preparation, its controls had been re-set. The hands and dials of the compact bronze box were adjusted, and Ptolemy's time-key was replaced inside the beast. In the early hours of the morning, the Greek troops who had departed earlier by ship had secretly returned. In the dead of night, they began to amass behind the walls, where they waited for the terror beast to strike.

At precisely three hours after midnight, as arranged, the same thunderous roar and the crash came – supposedly without warning. The heavily barricaded wooden doors of the city were smashed to pieces and then incinerated as the machine-animal's weaponry prepared to wreak havoc amongst those of Priam's loyal guards who'd remained on duty. However, after Agamemnon's defecting Persian slave had warned of the approaching event, Priam and his royal family were long since gone, along with everyone else.

The repeating, turret-mounted ballista – the mechanically re-loading catapult on its back – mowed the guards down within minutes. Victory was swift and decisive, the city taken intact, much to the relief of not only the invading soldiers but also their generals and kings. Now that the fighting was over, Agamemnon himself would shortly be here to take charge. At last he could take over the running of the city, restart the hugely profitable tin trade and begin to regain the monies spent so far. However, it was not long after that the earth shook again.

Without warning, just as there was a single flash of lightning in the skies above, the secret horse-weapon seemed to be swallowed up entirely in a ball of fire and cloud. Winds picked up and fanned the flames which now engulfed the gatehouse. Within minutes, they spread out of control, leaping from rooftop to rooftop across the city. At the same time, as a result of frustration at not finding any form of reward, the Myrmidons – the crack Greek troops – went berserk. Despite Agamemnon's solemn warnings to them, everything in the city was put to the torch.

Hours later, the darkness began to recede. Now in the cold light of day, the full scope of the disaster began to dawn on the supreme commander. A dense pall of acrid grey smoke hung over the blackened ruin that had until yesterday been the glorious city of King Priam. Greek soldiers caroused drunkenly through what was left of the streets in final celebration of their hollow victory, kicking the enemy bodies roughly aside as they went. After ten futile years of the siege of Wilusha, the great prize itself was finally 'won'.

Whilst Agamemnon had not been there at its taking, nevertheless, he had dressed in celebration of the occasion. The 'conqueror' stood alone, his rich, multi-coloured gown hung loosely about him. He wore his plain but heavy gold crown and carried his short, ceremonial gold sword. After what was an age, he still glared open mouthed at the wide subterranean cavern that lay below the very spot where the Royal Palace had stood. As Priam's palace burned to the ground, below it, his vast treasure had doubtlessly been spirited away through the wide underground tunnel, as had the city's entire population. Agamemnon shook his head, mortified. *Perhaps*, he started to believe in his growing panic, *if he had offered Zeus the more expensive oil in sacrifice a few days ago when he'd had the opportunity?…*

He surveyed around him, his manic gaze scarce able to take in the scale of the devastation that had occurred in the early hours of the morning. He pondered again the giant machine-animal which had now brought him teetering to the edge of ruin. At the thought, he shook with rage at the sheer waste of it all. "Why?" he cursed aloud, "did I believe that *that* secret weapon could deliver?" He sighed through gritted teeth while he watched the famed Myrmidons poke around in the rubble, fruitlessly combing it for spoils. He cursed them too. No doubt, before long, the soldiers would turn to looting the scattered dead bodies of the remaining royal guard. Then they would look to someone else for more!

The outcome of Agamemnon's carefully laid financial plans could not have been a greater disaster. Everything had literally gone up in smoke. Only the heavy store of wine was rescued, although who knew what the retreating population of this 'City of Horses' might have laced it with. Certainly, it had a distinct whiff of ammonia about it. Not that his own completely drunken troops seemed to mind its taste. They all carried on with the celebration of their hollow victory. The king looked on as the brooding Menelaus kicked a clear path toward him. "She's gone," he growled.

Agamemnon looked across at him. "Really?" he said sarcastically, "my heart bleeds for you."

It was Menelaus' turn to glare. "Not Helen, *the city* has gone! What are we going to do?"

Coming back to shocked reality, Agamemnon looked warily at the growingly disgruntled Myrmidons. "Let's leave, quickly – before they all start looking to us for payment. If we go now, we'll at least have *some* money in the coffers – and I'd like to keep my head. I have no intention of chasing after Priam, we have no horses. And neither have I any intention, nor the funds, to rebuild an entirely burned out city."

The pair began to slope-off, hopefully unnoticed, toward the ruined city gateway. Agamemnon mumbled conspiratorially, "Once home, remember to talk the story up. We'll tell everyone that it was a great victory. That we slaughtered the entire population – no survivors – no one will ever find out the truth. In a few years it'll all be forgotten about anyway. You do realise though, he pointed out, we're never going to get back the vast fortunes that we've ploughed into this venture from the start. From this day forward, this city and its tin trade are dead!"

As they walked away, Menelaus once more pondered their bleak financial situation for a few moments. "I have another wife that the King of Cyprus's thirteen year old son might be keen on. And the place is awash with copper..." he floated the idea tentatively. Agamemnon gritted his teeth...

Only years later, as it was rebuilt gradually, a shadow of its former self and a fifth of its former size, did the enclosed citadel of the re-named city of Wilusha begin to recover. From that point however, the tin trade would be diverted to other cities and islands as the demand for bronze continued. Never again would there be a central port in Persia that would control the trade of the precious metal. For now, the arms race was halted. From now on, it would be easier even for it to be sourced from the other side of the world. It was rumoured that the Phoenicians knew of islands rich in tin, one of the islands in particular was covered with trees which could be used for fuel to extract it from the ore. The mythical Cassiterides floated not far from the edge of the earth – through the Pillars of Heracles and many sea-leagues to the north. In future, the metal would be brought from there.

Troy would be forever remembered simply as the city razed by fire. It would be the place where a great victory had been won by Greek genius and stealth and where a legendary 'horse' had been brought against the Persians. The mysterious 'Hippo-Tempus' had caused the place to be eclipsed from history and almost from memory. It would be a very long time indeed before the truth would finally begin to resurface...

CHAPTER 25:

Madness

Now calmed down after her outburst, Penny returned to Alex's room. "Alex," she began again placatingly, "who's to say that if we go back home – my home – it won't be the best thing all round?" She placed her hand on his shoulder.

Alex understood. She was probably right; no doubt they were running out of time and money. However, he still didn't want to quit, not without checking for himself. In silence, the boy got up to leave – to go and confront Tom, if that's what it took – alone. He would simply ask him for the truth this time – once and for all! He trusted that Tom wouldn't lie directly to him.

His mother guessed what he was about to do and, with his hand still on the door, he heard her say, "Alex, there's something else you should know before you go – his injuries – I checked with the hospital."

Alex closed his eyes, *more secrets!*

"I had a long and confidential talk with a nurse friend of mine when I was there – the one who was expecting you to visit him. Please, if you're going to talk to this Tom, you should know that you mustn't get him too excited – he's still struggling to recover from last year's surgery."

"Surgery… what surgery?" a deep furrow formed across Alex's brow.

"He had a major heart operation last year – I take it he didn't tell you."

Alex remembered the bandages. "I know about his cracked ribs," he volunteered.

"Alex, he's being a little 'economical with the truth'. Yes, his ribs are 'cracked' – his sternum was parted for the operation – it doesn't seem to want to heal though. It's been over a year and nothing seems to have healed very much at all."

"What kind of heart surgery?" he quizzed.

Penny inhaled. "Alex, Tom's heart is in very poor shape. He should have had a transplant, but he refused. He told my friend that he would rather die with the heart that had been given to him by nature, his mother and his father – the heart he claims that he once gave to a young girl – than live a moment longer with someone else's. Not that he disapproved of anyone else's choice in that matter – it just wasn't for him."

Alex frowned, "So what are you saying?"

"Alex," his mother continued softly, "unless the surgery starts to heal soon, Tom's not likely to be around for much longer."

Clearly upset, Alex decided not to confront Tom after all. Instead, the boy nodded his understanding and left the room quietly, heading for the kitchen and Boris. If this was all true and he *had* lost his dad after all, then he didn't want to lose his new friend along with him.

Next door, Tom cleared his throat, trying to bring his tale up to date:

"The year was now 1962 AD. As he began to awake, the first thought running through Lio's mind was that he might be back in Alexandria. He was warm and dry, and he again lay in a comfortable bed. But when he opened his eyes, it was immediately obvious that this time he was not in Egypt. The simple, modern room he now occupied was decorated in pastel shades. He could hear voices around him and echoing footsteps in a corridor outside. Though, for the second time in his life, he had absolutely no recollection of who he was!

It seemed that the young man had lain unconscious for many

days – since the night he'd been brought in. That had been the night when a small Alexandrian registered cargo vessel had run aground on the Black Midden rocks in the mouth of the Tyne – when a fire in its engine room had got out of control. All five of the skeleton crew died in the aftermath, along with a would be rescuer. Given the suspicious circumstances of Lio's own discovery on the nearby promontory, it was assumed that he had been on board. Before he died, the only other, though temporary survivor – the ship's engineer – had spoken of discovering a young Greek 'stowaway' on board. It was tacitly assumed, therefore, that although the name Lio had mumbled under his breath did not sound in the least Greek, and although he did not have the skin and hair colouring that would be immediately recognised as Mediterranean, they *must* be one and the same. In the absence of all other information, the survivor's name was duly recorded as Billy Woods. Despite the presence of cuts and bruises – some old, deep scars on his back, and one particularly nasty new gash in his hairline – no one could tell immediately what had caused him to drift into unconsciousness. Perhaps, they reasoned, it was mental trauma.

As Lio began to stir, he felt someone holding him by his plaster encased wrist while stroking his other hand. He looked over to his side, to see the strangely familiar face of a young woman looking steadily into his eyes. She spoke to him, but not in any of the languages he recognised from his youth. Instead, it was a pleasant, sing-song language that he immediately liked, even dimly recalled – although he did not understand a single word of it.

'There, there pet, you've been in an accident – an explosion – but you're safe now,' she comforted. 'Tell me, what's your proper name? Wait… don't go back to sleep…nurse!'

Lio smiled tiredly at her. Then he drifted off again.

It seemed only the blink of an eye when he next became conscious. But this time he did not open his eyes. Instead, he lay for days, listening to the intense conversation going on around him. Bizarrely, although it was conducted in the same foreign language, this time, he understood virtually every word. Two female voices and another male voice were worriedly discussing the latest in 'The Missile Crisis'. As Lio listened to the frightening tale unfold over the next week, he was quickly educated about life in the twentieth century.

Firstly, it seemed that the whole world had been at war – not once, but twice! Now the voices spoke of a 'Cold War', a war of threats rather than deeds – which at first seemed to Lio to be preferable to a 'Hot War'. Then however, it seemed that it was not.

Since the end of the Second World War, 'super-weapons' had now been developed – 'atom bombs'. They were described as harnessing the power of the atom to provide 'the destructive capability of the sun' – a term which Lio found particularly distasteful. As he listened on, the young man couldn't help but remember the ancient philosophers, Demokritos and Leukippos and their 'Atomos theory'. He wondered what they might make of it all. Now, new enemies that Lio had only just learned of were set on a path of 'Mutually Assured Destruction' – or MAD for short. Jupiter rockets were being pointed at a small island in a most beautiful part of the world, in retaliation for their leader accepting the help of their political allies to defend themselves from a second planned secret invasion and coup d'état. However, the full truth of this incident was a secret kept from the world's citizens for many years. Each side seemed equally happy to destroy each other and level the entire world into the bargain. The missiles of Zeus by his Roman name were about to wipe out two thousand years of history.

In conclusion, the male voice read out a quotation from someone called Albert Einstein:

'I know not with what weapons world war III will be fought,
But world war IV will be fought with sticks and stones'.

Then, one afternoon, the gloomy atmosphere in the small ward changed. Lio heard cheers from the female voices as a male voice read the latest news. The protagonists had stood down. The worst days of The Cuban Missile Crisis: what has now become *generally* regarded as the closest point to MADness – by which humanity would have come to full scale nuclear war – had already passed. Lio was for now, at least, thankful that self-preservation had stopped the lunacy. He guessed though, that decency and sanity had had nothing to do with it. The only reason why nuclear weapons had not been unleashed since the end of the Second World War was because each side knew that their rival could now match them, and that neither could win. It was a stand-off that would continue until such time as the custodians of the world could think of a better weapon. One with a strategic advantage that might in future bring victory through stealth!

Hearing the good news, Lio's eyes fluttered open. Yet, even now, to anyone who had previously known him, something had changed about them. Somehow, the green fire that had always burned bright in his eyes seemed extinguished – they had lost their sparkle. Within moments, a voice sounded urgently. 'Billy's awake again,' said one of the young women. She stepped toward him and stroked back his red hair as another, older woman shone a blinding light into his saddened eyes. 'Stay with us this time sunshine,' she said urgently. 'We don't want you drifting off for another three months, do we!' Lio smiled at her again, recognising her face. And with that, he was re-born into the modern world.

'What's your proper name?' she asked, trying to keep him there while the nurse went for the doctor.

He tried to hold up his hands in surrender but they were strapped down with strange tubes sticking out of them. 'Never mind,' soothed the young woman. 'You're alright pet, my name's Catherine. You're going to be fine now, okay?' This time, 'Billy' stayed awake.

The young woman who had been sitting with him throughout the whole period, had spent her time there since he was first discovered – the night her own husband had been killed in the same shipping accident. She taught the classics at the local school: including both Greek and Latin. Apparently, on hearing him babble-on outside the door of her house on the Spanish Battery, she had decided that she might be able to help him. Over his stay in hospital, she had at every spare moment of the evening and weekends, talked to him and read both the English and, when she could get them, Greek newspapers to him. He rarely gave a reaction, but somehow, he had assimilated all of this, including her mild Geordie accent, into his subconscious. Until now, whilst he could not yet speak the language, he could understand virtually everything.

Over the next few weeks, he learned to trust the young woman's kind smile and her voice. Tentatively, he began to find his own voice again and for another short while they got to know each other, before finally, he was declared fit enough to leave. In the absence of all other known friends, the young man who had become jocularly known to the hospital staff as 'Billy the Greek' was released into the temporary custody of the young woman who had stuck with him. She was the only person who could seemingly get through to him and at least raise a smile – even if it was somewhat saddened by both their experiences. However, Catherine never did tell him about the loss of her husband, and so, Billy remained completely oblivious to it.

Try for one moment to put yourself in Lio's shoes," continued Tom. "In the five hundred years that had elapsed from the time of his birth, to his resettlement in Alexandria, and to his varied life which spanned Aegilia and Alexandria once again, little had really changed. Fundamentally, the world had still been lit naturally by the sun – or by oil lamps. Transport was still by foot or animal cart, and they used essentially the same sea vessels that had been around for thousands of years. People dressed the same and the weather was essentially the same throughout the Mediterranean region – hot or at least warm.

Now, however, within a short period, he had become a wanted man again. He had lost the love of his life and had been duped into travelling to the end of the world, where it was cold. To Lio, it was freezing cold. And, he had ended up being transported into the future, to a land where everything around him was completely new: from light switches to clothes; from self-propelled metal boxes with wheels, to vast metal ships; from telephones to television. Lio was both quietened and bewildered by it all.

Catherine then, brought the troubled young man home with her, where he at least began to try to settle. She began to educate him properly about the things in this alien culture: the world, its history, its politics – and the many wars that had raged for the past two thousand years. All of it fascinated, but worried him greatly. Disillusioned, Lio now knew only one thing: in two thousand years, mankind, it seemed, had learned nothing more important than how to create more efficient ways of wiping each other off the planet. And nothing Lio or anyone else could ever say would stop the process.

Then, one day in particular, he noted a detail from the tale she'd told him of WWII. She showed him a photographic image of the man in uniform who had started it all. He wore a small moustache and an armband with a distinct sign on it. Even the good luck charm that had hung around Lio's neck as a youth disturbed him now. Without saying why, he went into the back garden and tore off the athlete pendant made from the sun wheel. In the hands of Caesar and Hitler, two thousand years apart, even that peace and good luck sign had been metamorphosed into something that now epitomised hatred and intolerance. Lio threw it away in disgust.

In the short time that Billy lodged in Catherine's house, he became company for her. She gradually encouraged him to speak a few more words at a time, cooked for him, and washed and ironed her husband's old clothes for him – a bizarre idea to him, having to have the strange looking things made flat before he was permitted to wear them. She even showed him how to wash with soap and shave with a safety razor, until she thought he had begun to settle. However, it was at this point that Catherine and other people began to worry about the quiet young man.

Each and every day, as soon as Catherine had left for work, Lio made his way over to the promontory of Pen Bal Crag and its priory, absolutely fascinated with it. He seemed to explore each and every part of the rock, peering into every crack and fissure. He began to climb its steep face – without ropes. Each day, he climbed higher and higher, until passersby began to fear first for his safety – then his sanity. Catherine was eventually informed of how dangerous it was all getting. She gently remonstrated with him, and he explained as best he could that he had lost something very precious. But by now the obsessive rock-climber was the talk of everyone in the vicinity.

Eventually, one stormy morning, the hospital was called, and the saturated Lio was picked up and 'interviewed' in their psychiatric unit. Once again he refused to talk, save to repeatedly utter the words 'herkoose odonton'. Unable to get anywhere with him, the staff asked him if he would at least consider Catherine's feelings – her husband had, after all, lost his life during his rescue. Shocked and saddened at this new revelation she'd been keeping from him, Billy was released the next day. Catherine came to pick him up in a taxi; she was the only one who seemed to care about him.

On the evening of his return to her house, he suddenly decided to go for a lone walk. Thunder and lightning raged over the town that evening, and Billy the Greek went missing without a trace!"

CHAPTER 26:

A Ball of Flame

"Tom," Maddie broke into the story, a little concerned, "don't you think Alex should be here to listen to all of this?"

"Don't worry," the old man soothed, "I'm sure he'll be along shortly, but I have already told this part of the story to him."

"Okay," said Maddie, "if you say so." Bex wasn't comfortable with his absence either, but didn't say, whilst Conna was raring to get on with it.

Tom carried on:

"Catherine became quite worried about the young man she had become attached to over the past months. For a short while, she searched high and low for him, but he was nowhere to be found. Many weeks passed by, and she began to think that she would never see him again.

Then, on New Year's Day 1963, as mysteriously as he had disappeared, 'Billy' stood once more knocking at her door, dressed in the same clothes, and otherwise looking almost exactly as he had on the day he left. Relieved at what Catherine saw as his homecoming, she immediately let him in, although he did not attempt to explain where he'd been – and Catherine didn't like to ask. But this time, he at least *began* to settle properly. And as he settled, so did he begin to recall his past. Also, just as when he was a boy, those memories returned to him in his dreams. This time however, the full dreams did not disturb him. This time, they were a comfort. They seemed to confirm that he was not the person the hospital and this modern world wanted him to be. One night, after staring alone at the stars, he got into his bed.

Lio vividly recalled crashing down painfully in the snow with a loud bang. As his horse touched the ice covered stone slabs, its already weakened right foreleg bent and skidded, once more sending the machine sideways. He, the bags and the pizzle he still carried with him were flung heavily in opposite directions, tearing clean-off the remains of his ripped and damaged clothing – scraping the entire left side of his body and, except for the pendant and goggles, leaving him completely naked in the moonlight. The shock of the cold broke him out of his daze. The remnants of what had been a snow storm howled around him as he looked in awe at the white covering he'd only ever seen before on the tips of mountains. The place was entirely blanketed in white. He didn't know where he was, nor what might be the year. Everything was completely changed – completely unrecognisable.

He stood-up dizzily, feeling the deep spear-wound on the side of his forehead which was now bleeding profusely. His hands and knees were also skinned. He was surrounded by the ruins of what looked to him had been a huge building of some sort, possibly a temple, now roofless and open to the elements. Shivering with the extreme cold, he looked around the industrial landscape, trying to work out what had happened to him. The snow gradually petered-out. Despite the freezing blast, he walked toward the sound of crashing waves. He looked out at the long piers and the tall, darkened towers that had been built way out to sea. Nothing seemed familiar until, there in the distance, all the way down the coast, he recognised the outline of the rock that had once had the bear's head on it – although erosion over the centuries now made it resemble an ape's head. He also recognised the rebuilt mole and the landfall of the town on the other side of the river – the port of Arbeia.

Lio knew, after all, that he was in the very same place he'd just left – on the high promontory of the Roman Acropolis – but now in an entirely different age. He was immediately filled with dread. He looked again at the towering skeletal remains of the temple building and at the heavy surrounding walls. Shivering almost uncontrollably now, he climbed through a low window portal to get out of the wind's direct blast, and then he retreated into a corner.

Silhouetted in the moonlight, the entire area was obviously covered with buildings of various sorts. Though, to Lio, the brick houses all looked far more like temples than the wattle and daub huts that were here, to him, only minutes ago. Nor were there any camp fires, and no yellow light from oil lamps. The whole world, it seemed to him, was changed beyond imagination. It was absolutely devastating to the young man.

Quickly, he forced himself to retrace his steps – to find the time-horse lying on its side. He tried to pick it up, heaving at it with his considerably fit body, but he could hardly budge it. Then he got his eye on a pile of slender tree trunks lying next to one of the walls. Going over to it, he went to pick one out, to use as a lever, but dropped the freezing cold metal as soon as he realised that it was not what it seemed. Tentatively, he tried again to pick up the rusty, steel scaffold pole, and with it, he crossed again back to where the machine lay. This time, using the long lever, he had it on its feet in next to no time. He then managed to drop three of the castors. The fourth, in the damaged right front hoof, refused to budge. A small wooden house of some sort stood on the opposite side of the temple square, so he heaved at its door until it broke open.

Inside, he moved what were obviously some sort of hand tools and a few large metal containers of paint. He jammed the pizzle into the ragged bag and threw it roughly inside, and then he dragged in the machine, to safely hide it in there. Exhausted and freezing, he climbed carefully into the now cramped space himself and was at last sheltered out of the biting wind and rain. Sitting hunched-up on the wooden floor, he began to realise that something had gone badly wrong. Clearly, a very long time had passed since the villa had stood there – he didn't like to guess. After all, these much larger buildings had been built and had fallen into decay since that time.

His head reeled as his blood loss continued. He stemmed the bleeding with his hand. Whenever he was, tens, even hundreds of years into the future – he did not begin to realise that he had travelled two *thousand* years into the future – only finding the Chrono-key would undo the damage. As soon as he could, he would have to go about searching the promontory until he found it.

Lio had never been so cold. He desperately needed to find dry clothing, but there was nowhere to look? An hour later, now frozen, shaking uncontrollably and drifting into physical shock, he was about to fall into the deep, final stages of hypothermia. Once asleep, he would never reawaken. It was then that the most ungodly blaring, whooshing noise hit him. The sound jolted him awake again. There was a long series of blasts that reminded him of the fog horn in the Pharos tower. But these were lower in pitch and far, far, louder. He got up and ran out toward the river again – the source of the noise. There, he part scrambled, part climbed, half-way up the priory walls to see exactly where the noise was coming from. Then, he jumped down from the portal and ran as fast as he could: down the hill and across the grassy saddle, then back up the other side to the lesser of the two promontories.

At its edge, still naked, Lio stood bolt upright in the snow. Dismayed, he looked down at the uncovered black rocks. There was a ship down there, though unlike any he'd seen before. It was not constructed from curved timber, and there were no sails. But instead, this square sided vessel had a cabin to its stern which had a red and black tube sticking up from its roof. Black smoke billowed from the ship. Waves lashed at the vessel locked onto the edge of the carpet of rocks. Bright lights shot into the sky, one after another, like Greek fire – but even brighter. There they hovered, until the whole snowy scene was illuminated in stark white. Other missiles, like flaming arrows, rocketed over the ship, trailing rescue ropes behind them. On the rocks, people clambered around in bright yellow clothes. They shouted as the ship tilted over further and further onto its side. One man, wearing a yellow jacket, clambered up the side of the vessel and secured a rope around the handrails. It was pulled taut by the rescuers below. Then, two people started to slide down to the shallows. But that was when tragedy struck. Suddenly, there came an enormous boom, and the hold of the ship exploded in a huge ball of black and orange flame!

The blast of hot, acrid air nearly knocked Lio off his feet. And as it did, the man in the yellow jacket was thrown high over the other side of the ship, landing in the river. Simultaneously, the two people who were now sliding down the ropes also plummeted into the shallows. Immediately, the other figures standing on the rock began to scramble to the water's edge. As Lio looked-on for minutes, in shock at the pall of black smoke, he was about to go down to see if he could help. But then he was startled by something else much nearer.

A thin tube of white light sprayed across his back as, for the very first time in his life, he heard that completely new language directed toward him. He stood and turned to greet another man in a yellow jacket and wearing a sou'wester hat. In turn, the rescue volunteer stood spraying his torch up and down the naked, scraped, bloodied and muddied youth. In broad Geordie, he said: 'Hey laddie! Wadd'ya think you're playin' at? You've got everybody lookin' for you!'

Not understanding a word, Lio smiled pitifully and held his palms upwards to show the pleasant face that he held no weapons. 'Elladdie,' he did his best to return the strange sounding greeting.

His rescuer continued. 'Ye'll catch ya death of cold goin' on like that man.' He saw that the boy had been injured, possibly by the blast; his forehead was still bleeding copiously. He was probably also traumatised and he was pale blue with hypothermia. 'What's ya name?' he asked. The young man did not reply. Taking off his own long jacket, the rescuer flicked-off the snow and then placed it gently around the lad's shoulders. 'Name?' he repeated, miming – 'me, Billy,'

'Bil-ly' The shivering Lio repeated the word as faithfully as he could.

'No matter,' the man shrugged and led him gently by the elbow,

243

over to the nearest of the two quirky houses on the top of Spanish Battery Hill. He knocked and waited for a reply.

Lio's head didn't stop moving. He looked curiously at the strange building and the small glass window pane in the tangerine painted door, while his rescuer tapped lightly at the round front window. Then, he wiped his eyes and looked in amazement past his rescuer, directly at the much larger glass window panes in the bay window. He nodded approvingly at the idea and said so in Latin, then Greek, but the man still did not respond. He was about to try Arabic when they eventually heard the click of the door bolt being withdrawn and the door was opened into the well lit interior. A young woman stood there in a long dressing gown, yawning. Her hair tied up in a towel. The rescuer stood there with his thin shirt sticking to him in the wet snow. He knew the house and immediately recognised the young schoolteacher: the wife of one of the other volunteer life guards. The woman's face looked blearily out at him. She yawned again. 'Billy, what's going on?' she asked. 'What's all the noise?' She looked beyond at the plume of smoke and flames coming from the river.

'I'm sorry to disturb you Catherine... but could I ask you a bit of a favour? Could you look after this lad for us? He's a foreigner – he looks like he's had a bit of a bad time,' he understated typically. As the man stepped aside, the woman looked at the sight of the bedraggled youth who looked blearily back at her.

'Good lord, where's he from? What's happening?' she repeated. 'I must have dozed off in the bath – what was that blast that woke me up?'

'There's been another bloody incident – just below Collin'wood's monument – the rocks again. All hell's broken loose, one of the lads is missin' – blown off the ship and into the river – they're still lookin'.'

'Woods' Lio again echoed the voice.

'Pardon?' the woman asked.

'Elladdie... Bil-ly... Woods,' Lio tried lamely to communicate, his speech slurred with the extreme cold. Blood streamed down his face.

She looked at his muddy bare legs and feet. 'I think he says he's Greek – he certainly sounds foreign enough. Anyway, I think you'd better fetch him in out of the cold,' she urged. Then she added, 'so who's gone missing?'

The rescuer shrugged, 'dunno pet, I just got here."

Suddenly concerned, the young woman asked 'Billy, is Stanley helping out down there? He should be in from the shipyard by now – his shift finished over an hour ago.'

'I'm not sure,' he shot her a worried glance, 'but if you look after this one while the ambulance arrives, I'll go and check.'

'Alright, I'll take care of him,' she agreed, 'he'll be fine with me. And if you see Stanley, tell him to hurry home – tell him I've got some important news for him – good news!'

'Righto then,' the rescuer agreed, 'I'll not be long. Oh, and another thing, you might want to find this lad some clothes, I'll need me jacket back.' He took hold of the shoulder epaulettes and reclaimed it.

'Oh my giddy aunt!' She covered her wide opened mouth.

'Efkaristo.' the stranger grinned tiredly at her, then collapsed into her arms.

With that, Lio awoke from his dream, once again in his bed at Catherine's house."

Maddie and Bex began to almost chuckle along with Conna at the amusing aside from the fairly intense story, picturing Lio standing naked in the hallway. Even Tom saw the funny side of what he'd just described, despite the tragedy of the whole event. But then it dawned on Maddie. "Tom," she asked seriously, "the woman's husband… did he ever get to hear Catherine's good news?

Tom shook his head, "alas not."

"So did they ever find his body?' asked Conna.

"Apparently they did," Tom confirmed, "along with two others, and the following week, his cremated ashes were scattered over the rocks. But by then, Lio was lying unconscious in hospital."

"And it all happened right here." Conna again mused in wonder.

The girls again said nothing. Bex especially looked quizzically at Tom.

Before long, they all settled down again.

"Of course, the moment that Lio remembered this event in his dream, and he realised that he was not Billy the Greek after all, he resolved to rescue the Hippo-Chronos. Next morning, just after Catherine had left for work, he took a blanket and ropes with him and made his way to the closed priory and the shed. Thankfully, even after months, it was still there – presumably because of the great effort it would have taken to move it – although it had obviously been found by others since he had left it. It had been shifted to the back, and covered with various cloths, tools and other paraphernalia. Also, some wag had daubed a crude smile on its face in the paint that was used to line the grass of the nearby cricket pitch.

It did not take too many hours to retrieve it. He began to haul the object down from the crag and up to the house on the lesser promontory. It was draped with a blanket, and although it aroused some passing curiosity on its short journey, Lio shortly explained: 'motorbike,' like the ones he'd seen in the street. Unknown to her, once more at her house, he stashed it safely at the back of the even more cavernous, but rickety old garden shed that held much of Catherine's husband's old hobby things. He stashed the now pitiful bag of his own personal belongings along with it."

Conna closed his eyes, remembering the *tiny* old shed in Alex's back garden, the one that Alex's dad had painted dark blue for fun. The one they used to play in as kids. *Obviously, then, in Tom's mind, it was one of those gadgets that was supposed to be small on the outside, but bigger on the inside.* He heaved a sigh, but kept it to himself just the same.

"Tom was disconcerted to see Conna's odd look; it put him off his stride. "Where was I? Oh yes…

Over time, Lio had many more memories return to him, but in all the period he lived in Catherine's house, he did not speak of any of his previous life. To do so, he knew, would be to jeopardise the secret of the horse's existence. He felt a slight pang of guilt at not admitting to Catherine that his true name was not the one she called him by, but the horse, he knew, must always remain herkoose odonton." Tom placed a finger to his lips. Then a troubled look fell across his face. His listeners wondered why.

"What I am about to tell you now may seem disloyal, perhaps even dishonest, or even immoral, but I would beg you to keep an open mind. After all, none of these events were the boy's fault, at least nothing he would have changed afterwards – even if he could. There is no simple way of saying this – so I will just tell you.

Within a short while of living as a lodger with the young woman who had looked after the stranger out of the goodness of her heart, she had taught him gradually how to speak and read English and how to dress and function in this modern world. More importantly, she taught him how to smile again. The fire in his eyes was even reignited briefly. Slowly they began to live in some semblance of peace and togetherness, if not strictly love. And as a result, that spring, Lio and Catherine agreed to be married."

Maddie looked slightly shocked, Bex told him so. "But what about Ashur – what about the secret marriage vow?"

Tom sighed deeply. "As much as it pained Lio to admit it, clearly there was no getting back to Ashur. After all, every day since the day he had returned, he had wandered the entire far rock promontory looking for the key, but had still found not a trace of it.

Eventually, even Lio had to concede defeat, although it broke his heart to do so. It seemed to him that Poseidonios had after all not delivered it to the place he'd said he would. Either that, or the philosopher, or perhaps someone else, had later removed it for safekeeping to some other place. As a result, it now seemed obvious to Lio that he was trapped in this modern world. From then on, all he could do was remember fondly, the girl he had loved and lost in his youth – the girl who had lived and died thousands of years ago. Therefore, in that respect, Lio never did break his solemn marriage vow to her. Instead, he was regretfully left only to store those memories away forever and try to make the most of his new life here."

"So he just decided to marry someone else instead?" asked Bex bluntly.

Tom considered. "Perhaps the healing partnership was good for them both." His pained expression pleaded. "Billy told her in his broken English of the ancient history of his own Mediterranean lands – though he still thought it best not to mention the Hippo-Chronos or his own past – and she told him of things he still didn't understand at all. Certainly, for many weeks, they were often seen wandering hand-in-hand around the monument overlooking the sea. And, of course, some local tongues began to wag at the now obvious swelling in her abdomen. But that was perhaps another reason why Billy agreed to marry her, to help bring up the child she was carrying – it was the least he could do.

Together they would go to talking picture shows, to see the uncomplicated old movies with the stars he preferred, like Stan Laurel and Oliver Hardy and Boris Karloff. And in the evenings they would together listen to his favourite 'modern' contraption: the by now old-fashioned wind-up gramophone that fascinated him. Then she would fail each time to teach the young man to dance her way, instead of the interpretive swaying he preferred. Once, he even played his rescued bagpipes to her, but she did not ask him to do so again.

Though, perhaps," Tom admitted, "it was indeed too soon for both of them. Perhaps they were both still grieving for the partners each of them had lost. Nevertheless, very soon, it was not long before their planned wedding day loomed, May 7th 1964."

CHAPTER 27:

The Truth Will Out

"It was a week before the wedding," continued Tom, "when out of the blue, Ashur returned to Lio in another dream. But this time it was a short, ill-timed dream. He dreamed that she was sat opposite him in, of all places, the darkened local bar room where he occasionally went with Catherine and the other Billy – the man who had rescued him – now his planned best man. There, the two 'Billys' each drank a small beer and discussed the wedding plans openly, but Lio could not bring himself to look at, nor speak to the woman he loved most in the world – in case by doing so, he would have to pull out of those same plans. Ashur looked disappointedly at him and he wanted only for the sad dream to stop. With a heavy heart he stood up and made toward the door.

As he awoke, the dream left him paralysed with regret and loss. It was as if quite by chance, she had appeared to him, to shatter the illusion that his marriage to someone other than Ashur could ever be a happy one. The dream had lasted no more than a moment, but when it had gone, although he knew that she was lost forever to him, still, it filled him with almost a feeling of disloyalty, and with a devastating loss for the girl he would never know or see again. That crushing feeling *never* left his soul again.

This same feeling of dishonesty also extended toward Catherine, in that he had not attempted to enlighten her about any of his past. This in turn prompted him to toss and turn all that night, wondering whether he should indeed try to tell her of his true past and not go on with the pretence of the identity he had conveniently assumed – the identity that everyone still wanted him to be – that of a young Greek stowaway. Then, the next day, another strange thing occurred.

On that morning, Lio had been poring through a newspaper, all the while learning the English Language for himself, when an archaeological story caught his attention. It was an article that discussed the story which all Greeks had been brought up on as children: the story of the Iliad – the Greek's capture of the city variously known at the time as Ilium or Troy – it did not mention Wilusha. The item suggested that the nineteenth century German archaeologist, Schliemann, who had long been suspected by academic minds of 'getting carried away with himself'', might have been right after all – about finding the legendary city of Troy. Lio read the article with interest, knowing its exact location. Everyone in his own time did: it was, in his own time in Alexandria, a Roman tourist destination. It was odd to think that the world could have simply forgotten about it or 'lost it'. How could a place so big, so famous and so wonderful just 'disappear?' He read on with curiosity as the article purported that one of the several city layers – it had been rebuilt successively at least seven times on the same spot – could, in all probability, now be named as Troy – because this particular layer looked as if it had been razed to the ground by fire!

It was this last detail that especially confused him. To Lio, the story of the Iliad was embedded. It was the story of the great city of Wilusha that grew rich by trading in tin at the height of the Bronze Age. It became known as Priam's city – after the famous King. Only much later did it became known as Troy. Priam was one of the richest men alive, his treasure enormous. Priam's son had rescued the Greek girl, Helen, from her tyrannical husband Menelaus. He had taken her back to the city. The Greeks had been presented with a perfect excuse to attack the city and attempt to take everything for themselves. After many years, the Greeks had successfully taken the city after a great siege engine – a fore-runner of the 'Scarab' used in Alexandria – had been used to slip past the city gates. The Greeks had then poured in behind it and had taken the city intact – had kept the city for themselves – to continue the trade in tin especially. Priam's treasure had then been used to rebuild the city into the place of wonder that it became. The Greeks' rule had lasted until Roman times. To burn the city down after all that effort would have been ridiculous and would have destroyed the vastly profitable trade. Obviously, whoever had written that article had got it completely wrong.

The story he read spoke of the great battles, the heroism of Achilles and Hector, Ajax and Patroclus and many more characters, without mentioning the real facts. This story had become a tale of revenge only and it ended – instead of the story he knew – with the destruction of the city by – 'a horse?' Whoever had written the article clearly did not know what he was talking about. It was such a silly twist to the end of the tale. So completely bizarre that he decided he would, at some time in future, check up on it.

It was no priority to Lio, in fact, fairly unimportant to him to begin with, but it did begin to rankle when, in later conversation, Catherine also began to question his own truthful version of events.

The next day, he called into the local library to which Catherine had introduced him – which in itself filled him with awe – but although he tried subsequently to verify his own version of the story, he found it completely impossible. It was staggering to him that the true version of events had been completely eradicated. Had all of the scholars and historians in the modern world got it wrong? Surely not.

It was then that it slowly began to dawn on Lio what had happened. From today's perspective there was nothing wrong at all. The story of Troy was the one which all people in the modern world knew, the story of the 'Wooden Horse', of the Greeks' victory and destruction of Priam's City. No one was aware that history had already been changed, but it obviously had been. And there was, of course, only one thing capable of causing that change – The Hippo-Tempus!

As this truth hit him, Lio subsequently realised three things. Firstly, that although *he* knew Troy had not been destroyed originally,

251

this was only because he had been born and lived before the Hippo-Tempus had been built and used. If so, how many other seemingly unconnected events even further back in history might have been influenced by the machine? What other damage had already been done?

Secondly, He realised that this and any other changes there might have been were the direct cause of his own actions. It was he, after all, who had taken Kyrros' Hippo-Chronos machine to rescue Ashur. He, who had inadvertently brought Zeus back with him.

Thirdly, it followed that he alone must therefore bear the responsibility for putting those events right. But then, he simultaneously realised that he could not. Anything he did now would be viewed as a *change* to history – would affect everything since the time of Troy. Everything in the modern world would be changed forever – possibly be even eradicated – eclipsed!

There was, after all, nothing he should or even could do now; it was too late. The past was firmly in the past. This was, however, all academic. Without finding the last Chrono-key, no one would ever be able to catch up to it or stop the Hippo-Tempus anyway.

And then, a last worrying thought occurred to Lio. Could there after all, ever be, even the remotest possibility of Zeus somehow managing to get his hands on one of the Chrono-keys – say at the Mouseion before its destruction – and then be able to move forward in time? If that could come about, everything in the world would surely be lost. That was when the young man made another promise, this time, to himself. He resolved that if he ever got the chance again – by finding the missing Chrono-key – he would remove even the most remote possibility from that ever happening. Lio promised himself that he would one day either destroy or disable the Hippo-Tempus so that it must remain forever in the past. However, the trick would be to intercept it not only in a *place* he knew it would turn up, but at the correct *time*. And Lio did not have a precise year, let alone a date for the destruction of Wilusha. Where else then – and when – might he find the weapon?

It was then, for all of those reasons that raced around his mind

– and perhaps because of some other nagging doubts – that on the very early morning of the eve of their marriage, sitting opposite each other at the breakfast table, Lio decided to tell Catherine that he was not who she thought he was. She, on the other hand, was only excited at the prospect of tomorrow's wedding day, and talked of selling the old house to move to something more modern – something with central heating. Hardly listening, Lio decided that it would be best to break his story to her gently. At first, just tell her a short version of where he had come from. But if he thought his honest approach would be to their benefit, he was mistaken. The truth would not save their relationship.

As usual, Catherine busied herself making a pot of tea from the ever present copper kettle that boiled over the old fashioned coal fire in the blackened iron range. Lio asked her to turn off the radio news so that he could speak to her – and so they sat down.

After an hour, when he had finished outlining a much more basic version of the unlikely story I have now told yourselves, Catherine, despite his strong protestations to the contrary, decided that the whole ridiculous tale was the most pathetic excuse she had ever heard for a man wanting to change his mind and get out of his promise of marriage. Feeling hurt after the way she had looked after him, after the loss of her husband, and now feeling jilted – that was when she got upset and told him she never wanted to see him again. Forget his lodgings – she just wanted him to pack his things and get out of the house before she came back.

Catherine picked herself up from the table and went silently back upstairs to get ready to go to school. She came back down the stairs and passed him still sitting there in a daze. Then, without a second glance, she picked up her best, shocking pink headscarf, walked out of the door and out of his life."

To all of Tom's guests, all of these details were actually the most believable things he had said for the past few days – always accepting that he had been accurate with the background of his ancient tale.

Bex looked at Tom, in her imagination, trying to re-interpret his tale. She wondered if this more up to date story of the sixties wasn't at last a more believable version of a past that the tale teller had buried.

Maddie simply looked pleased that Lio had considered his memory for Ashur and the feelings of the young woman he was about to marry. Tom had insisted on the total trustworthiness and loyalty of his character all through the story so far, and the idea of him slipping so quickly into another relationship without the best of reasons seemed so out of character with Lio. When Tom said that Lio had decided on that same evening to tell the truth about himself, she was almost relieved for all of the characters.

Conna began to wonder about *everything*.

Tom sensed their change in attitude. Despite his previously buoyant mood, he worried that once again, just like the other times, he might soon, after all, lose his audience. Despite everything, he felt so near and yet, so far.

"So what happened to Catherine?" asked Maddie.

The old man tilted back his head in resignation: s*o be it*. All he could do now was finish the tale and hope that everything would work out as he thought it somehow must:

"Lio hardly moved from the table all that day, knowing that once again, his insistence on honesty and integrity had hurt the woman who had brought him into the modern world from the one he had previously occupied. *What to do?* he thought. Should he show her the Hippo-Chronos, still hidden away in the garden shed? Or would that be too much of a shock? Should he show her the other physical evidence he had brought with him: the parting gift from his mother – the reserve – or would that be dismissed too? It could, after all, have been a copy, made anytime and anywhere. Perhaps though, it would be enough to convince her that they would not have to worry about money in future. He went into the shed and retrieved the solid gold object, but then stashed it safely away in the room, so that he could later produce it dramatically – the fire in the old fashioned range was dying down anyway.

All day long, he watched the ticking clock on the mantelpiece, distracted by the pendulum assisted escape movement. As it ticked to and fro, so it allowed the spring to wind down at a constant rate, keeping an accurate record of the time. He was so determined not to lose this woman to whom he owed so much. Sitting there alone, he decided that he must somehow undo the great hurt he had caused. And, if that's what it took, he would do something that he had never properly done before – he would lie!

All day he waited, working out his simple plan. He would tell her that he had, after all, been making the whole preposterous story up, although he still could not think of a reason why. He would then claim to be indeed a Greek sailor. Then, he would tell her that everyone had been right all along. He had been on the stricken cargo vessel, and that when the explosion had happened, the blast must have 'altered his mind'. It was not a good story, but it was the best that he could come up with. Since she had left for work that morning, he had now come back to his senses. It would not happen again – no more nonsense about the ancient world and Time-Horses. He would tell her what she wanted to hear. Then he would live out the rest of his natural life here in this village with Catherine. Here, as on Aegilia, where the people he had met were friendly to him, and were peaceful and honest and good.

He put just a few coals on the fire and waited in hope for her to return at her usual time – half past four – only just remembering at the last moment to go into the garden and cut a big bunch of flowers – the daffodils that grew in abundance there. Then, once back at the table, he sat with them in his hand and waited expectantly. Five o'clock came and passed, five thirty, then six, but still she did not return. The fire started to burn lower and he began to wonder. At seven, he became a little worried that she might have meant what she said about him moving out. At eight o'clock, as the fire died, he began to believe it. And at nine, with the light now fading, he realised at last, just how badly his insistence on the truth must have hurt the young woman. By ten o'clock, the cast iron range had long since cooled down and he sat once more alone in the cold and dark.

All that time, he had been sat at the table with the flowers wilting in his warm hand, not knowing what to do for the best.

Now he began to get agitated. Perhaps he *should* just go – do the decent thing. *After all*, he thought, *Catherine had made a simple, honest request – and he had no right to be in her house*. For a short while, after hearing what he mistakenly thought to be her footsteps, he was ready to throw himself at her feet and beg her forgiveness as she came in through the door. But, by twelve o'clock, he had finally resigned himself to the fact that she had, after all, meant him to leave. Uneasily, his thoughts turned again to the idea that he – the anachronism – should not in any case be here. He should have perished long ago. That was when the fire left Lio's eyes permanently. So it was, that in a daze and with a heavy heart – temporarily forgetting the reserve he had stashed away in the front room – Lio made his way into the garden shed.

In fact though, now calmed down after work, Catherine had caught the bus to visit one of her friends, an old confidante that she could talk to properly. Not knowing what to do with the still obviously unsettled young man, though still fearing a little for his sanity, after discussion, she had decided to go home and talk it out with him. This, despite the 'silly story' that she and her friend had each agreed was best forgotten. In time, the friends also decided, family life would also help the young man recover from the obvious shock of the blast. After taking a small nightcap with her friend, Catherine finally took a taxi home. As she looked out of the rain spattered window, the whole night sky over Tynemouth lit up with a crash of thunder and lightning.

By the time Catherine made it home in the early hours of the morning, her fiancé had gone. Only a bundle of withered flowers remained on the table where she had left him sitting. And this time, Billy the Greek disappeared for a very long time. Catherine was never the same."

Something about this whole part of the story rang especially true. This time Conna, Maddie and Bex started to consider really believing it. However, that drew the rest of the story dramatically into focus. Conna looked at his watch – twelve o'clock – and Alex still hadn't turned up. "Maybe we should do a bit more work on the machine parts?" he suggested.

"No, Conna." Tom realised he was pushing too hard again. "But perhaps you should go and see what's keeping Alex," he suggested. "Anyway, I think I need Alex here from this point forward."

"We'll come with you," Both Maddie and, more eagerly, Bex suggested, looking from one to the other.

"Yes, I'm feeling a little tired again anyway," Tom admitted. "Perhaps I could do with a short rest."

At that, Conna and the girls left. Making their way to Alex's house, they knocked on the door and were surprised not to be asked in as usual. Alex's mum explained that their friend was feeling a bit run down and wished to be left alone. If he wished to, it might be better if Conna rang him later. "Later then," she waved the girls off, and went back inside.

Conna still didn't want to contemplate what was going on inside Alex's house. "What we gonna do now, then?" he asked the girls distractedly.

Maddie shook her head. "I don't know, but we'd better tell Tom he's not coming."

"Yeah," agreed Bex, "but I don't want to go back without Alex. He needs to be here now – now that we've nearly reached the end of the tale."

"Okay," agreed Conna, so he went alone to tell Tom that they'd be sure to be back to help – whatever Tom had meant by that – in the morning. Tom thanked him for letting him know, and quietly closed the door.

Conna caught up with the girls, while rubbing the discoloured patch around his eye. "Fancy an ice-cream anyone?" he suggested.

"Why, are you paying for them?" teased Bex.

"Erm… can do," agreed the boy, hoping he had enough money with him.

"Triple choc banana boats?" asked Maddie.

Conna checked the change in his pocket; he frowned. "Yeah, if you want… I'm not really that hungry though. I think I'll just have a single scoop instead."

"Alright," Bex winked at Maddie, "come on then."

Alone in his laboratory, Tom walked toward his window disappointedly. He took off his sunglasses and looked at the white horses riding the tops of the distant waves. He knew he was losing them now; it was only Alex that had actually listened and given the story any real credence to date. Despite trying hard to believe him, the others, he guessed, were listening out of sympathy, trying to reinterpret his tale. As always, everyone else, it seemed to him, was bent on discrediting his every word – rather than simply accept it. It was outrageous to him that two thousand years into the future, mankind still seemed so conceited. That society only thought that the latest generation had invented the world – and no one else in its entire history could possibly have been cleverer than themselves. Yet, even now, they had still not learnt how to run their world properly – the manipulation, the wars and the killing had still not stopped.

At least this time though, he would be able to finally prove that he'd been telling the truth all along. Now, he was determined to reassemble the horse without waiting further – with or without help. With his good hand, he pulled back the dust cover once more and looked at the many complicated and heavy mechanisms that would somehow have to be refitted to the machine before he could use it. But first, Tom needed a short nap, to recharge his own battery.

CHAPTER 28:

The Killing Machine

The Pyramids of Giza 46 BC

Nearly a year since Ptolemy's sister, Queen Arsinoë's escaping barge had docked in Cyprus after the battle of the Nile, Alex's father Stan sat in the Arab camp in the shadow of The Great Sphinx. It had been a long and perilous journey back here, but now he was close to the final pick-up point at Drodos. As he sat there, he completed his story of the battle he had witnessed. This, although knowing full well that if he ever got home, he could never give his account to anyone. To do so, his professional standing as an archaeologist would be absolutely finished. He would be ridiculed mercilessly. Not to say that, like his neighbour, he would become a complete social pariah. And even though he loved his wife, Penny, he knew, would take great exception to the unbelievable tale. No, he decided, this account of his travels would be for Alex's eyes only. He would keep Tom's secret, as he'd promised.

As a young Arab boy waited patiently for him to finish writing his strange words, Stan pencilled in his pocket diary:

From the outset, Ptolemy's troops were doomed. Every advantage that they should have had was compromised. The few ships that remained of the onetime vast navy were useless through lack of the most basic equipment. Only half their oars remained serviceable due to poor maintenance and corruption; anything like ramming speed unachievable. They were then, reduced entirely to a supporting role.

His soldiers were physically weakened by the lack of proper rations; they had not seen bread for days. By contrast, the well fed Romans had only two vessels present themselves, but each was anchored at opposite ends of the river island.

In the first move toward naked aggression, the Egyptian archers loosed off volley after volley of arrows, but anticipating this obvious move, each century of Romans automatically formed themselves into their famed 'testudo', or tortoise shell. Each of the first rank held their barrel like shields together to form an almost impenetrable barrier, while those behind held their shields over their heads, masking themselves from above. The failed Egyptian attack did not last long.

Now, at Caesar's first given signal, a constant barrage of arrows was loosed from both the ships and the troops on the riverbank. The Egyptians could only cower under their small round shields, hoping that the missile attack would soon end. The mercenary army of Cretan archers that Caesar had brought with him were, however, well stocked. Only after a long and demoralising attack was the Roman barrage ended. Still, the shaken Egyptian troops began to rally with shouts and battle cries from their king.

Now Caesar's second command was given and three re-formed ranks of Roman troops began to march steadily into the river; their studded, leather soled boots giving them reasonable grip. As the Egyptians wielded their long pike hatchets, ready to slash into their adversaries as they waded ashore, the Romans stopped ten paces away from them and lined up to use their 'pila' – the short infamous javelins. At point-blank range, they loosed-off volley after volley into the hapless Egyptians, who were ordered by their own generals to stand. Each time one of the weapons made its mark, the metal tip snapped-off and the wooden shaft of each 'pilum' was retrieved on its long cord, to be reloaded. The punishment was merciless, but still the Egyptians stood their ground. Line after line of the hatchet-men fell, until the rear ranks of swordsmen were exposed. Now that the entire stretch of river was awash with dead and dying, each Roman simply pushed them all back.

The third command was shouted out, and, as one man, each Roman unsheathed his gladius – his short, thrusting sword – the weapon that had lent its name to the gladiators – sword bearers. Each held it at his right side, pointing forward. Now, the killing machine moved on. In response, the

Egyptians drew their curved scimitars, eager and ready to slash their way through their enemy. Ptolemy, distraught at the punishment his troops had already taken, began to raise his spirits. Perhaps he may have thought there was a chance after all. This was the last opportunity he would ever have to repel the invaders from Egyptian soil, the last chance to retain Egypt's independence. However it was not to be.

As the Romans continued to wade ashore, their long shields wrapped around their bodies, they again formed a solid wall. The curved, slashing Egyptian swords and remaining axes simply skidded off their targets while the soldiers were pushed back physically – their bare feet sliding easily on the soft, wet muddy and bloody ground. Another command was given, and the Romans' long shields were rotated slightly around to their left side. Now, each one was separated from the other by only a narrow gap. As each Egyptian attempted to attack the man directly in front of him, each Roman plunged his sword into the exposed ribs of the Egyptian ahead and to his right – not the man directly in front of him! It was a simple expedient that the Romans had used for many years and yet still, without fail, it always threw the enemy. Row after row dropped, and within minutes, panic set in – the Romans were unstoppable.

His troops now in complete disarray, Ptolemy stood transfixed on the spot while his generals fled. Here on this island there was no second chance to redeem the situation, nowhere left to withdraw and regroup. All they could attempt to do now was somehow save their own skins by making for the opposite side – and the deep, wide, river. The Egyptian army was routed. The king took off his blue and gold battle helmet and threw the royal headpiece into the Romans. Then, as commander of his troops, he turned to rescue his own skin.

In the first hour of battle, over a third of his soldiers had already fallen, but now, in the aftermath, 5,000 more would perish. Only the last 5,000 would escape the confusion that ensued – but then only to be delivered into the vengeful hands of Cleopatra.

Caesar gave his fourth signal. Realising the inevitable outcome, Arsinoë called out for her brother to join her on her barge. Hundreds of others had already clambered on board rather than run into the deep half of the river. The vessel's master had little choice than to move off before the vessel capsized. Now, *the generals who had themselves quickly made it on board, hacked away at any of their own troops who tried to do likewise. Reluctantly, Ptolemy followed his own men to the other side of the island, desperate to stop the panic, but knowing deep down that it was useless. He watched as his own troops swarmed into the river, abandoning their heavy weapons.*

The Romans did not follow – conscious of the last trick up the Emperor's sleeve! Unseen by Ptolemy, the nets upriver had been removed and now hundreds of crocodiles were following the scent of blood in the water. Just as at the fort of camels, hundreds of years earlier, the soldiers had fallen prey to the scourge of the Nile: some through crocodile attack but, seeing those around them drown screaming, by far the majority through panic.

Fighting and slashing through the backs of the Romans, Ptolemy and his loyal bodyguard backed slowly toward the barge. Only a few feet more and they would make it.

Arsinoë stood on the deck of the barge, calling out to her brother, the king. Then, as it started to pull away, the ornate gangplank fell into the river. She ignored the shouts from her own loyal bodyguard to take cover, instead imploring him to hurry. But just then, the Romans threw a lone grappling hook over the side and managed to stop the vessel. Instead of making for safety, Ptolemy threw his sword at the soldier who was trying to secure the rope around the makeshift tethering stake. At that, the Roman fell headlong into the river. But now there was a massive surge as more Romans began to physically push the Egyptians into the water. The king looked at the barge, thankful that his loyal sister looked to be making an escape. As he finally came to terms with his inevitable defeat, he was struck down from behind with the hilt of a sword. Without calling out, he sank briefly to his knees. He fell forward, and was immediately trampled underfoot. Finally, his limp body was kicked unceremoniously into the river. It was never retrieved.

Slowly, the barge moved off with the current, toward the sea. The last honest pharaoh had died in battle. Egypt, the fuel store of Rome and the last major independent country in the Mediterranean, now belonged to Rome in all but name. Roman troops had secured the fuel supply that would allow them to march anywhere they were ordered. At last, Caesar's army was truly able to take over the world.

Years later, much to the annoyance of Cleopatra, the fleeing Arsinoë was, after all, installed by Caesar as regent queen of the island-country of Cyprus. Nevertheless, she survived there for many years. That is, until after the assassination of Caesar, when the Emperor's old friend and ally Mark Antony would in turn be seduced by the charms of The Queen of the Nile. Then finally – at Cleopatra's pleading – he would have her remaining, younger sister executed. Arsinoë would be her last family victim – all other threats to her supremacy long since murdered. And of course, the name of Egypt's last puppet Pharaoh: Cleopatra would live on in infamy – though some would have it differently.

From now on, the 'Pax' Romana – the 'Peace' of Rome – would reign with impunity. The moral standards of the world would be decided only by each dubious successive Emperor. The Romans would systematically eradicate anyone or anything that did not comply with their own point of view – even history itself. For the next five hundred years, the 'civilised' world would live in the iron grip of fascism!

Sparing a last thought for Ptolemy, Stan's thoughts then drifted inevitably to his own son. Although he had been in the field many times, he had never stayed away more than six weeks. This time, he missed him and Penny terribly. Oblivious that Alex and his wife had been awaiting his return throughout the same year, he couldn't wait to get home for the birth of the new baby. Absent mindedly, he finished writing the account. Along with his pencil, he tucked the diary into the worn satchel. Again, he pondered whether his neighbour had actually got home safely on the defective Hippo-Chronos. He could only hope too, that if so, he would be able to persuade Alex to help him repair it so that he could get back to their planned rendezvous point. He looked up at his mixed Arab and African friends.

"Estam," the young boy standing next to him enquired eagerly. "May it be possible that for one last time you could tell us about the flying horse?"

"Of course," Stan grinned and put down his book. He got up to take his established place beside the leader of the salt caravan. He would miss the genuine people he had met and joined months ago.

He'd learned much from them during his slow trek through many ancient cultures. But, tonight would hopefully be his last night with them. Tomorrow was his allotted departure date – as long as his neighbour made it back through time to pick him up.

"One last time then…" He paused, looking at the dozens of mixed faces of adults and youths, staring back at him open-mouthed, waiting to hear the unbelievable tale.

"Are you all sitting comfortably?" he smiled wryly. "Then I'll begin!

The Hippo-Chronos, is without shadow of a doubt, the most amazing 'animal' that anyone in the whole world could ever imagine. And, it was made not long ago – right here in Egypt – in the Great City of Alexandria…"

CHAPTER 29:

Coming to Terms

Conna's reasons for detouring to the cafe were five-fold: Firstly, he loved ice-cream as much as any boy; secondly, he now felt hungry, not having had any proper breakfast (despite what he'd told Alex); thirdly, he wanted to cheer himself up; fourthly he wanted to continue the conversation with the girls (although he felt a bit disloyal about it without Alex being there to contribute to the conversation); and finally, because he didn't dare go home!

To Conna's protestations, the girls paid for their own when the waitress brought them to their table, but in truth, despite the teasing, they would never have had it any other way. "So, what do you think?" asked Conna as he dug in, perhaps a little more well-mannered than usual.

"Mine's good."

"And mine," Maddie echoed, smirking.

"Not the ice-creams. Tom and the story, do you believe it?"

Maddie pitched-in first, "Well, possibly… in a way" she reasoned, "even though it's all a bit far-fetched. I mean," she raised her eyebrows pointedly, "we're still not convinced about some things: 'X marks the spot'; the mechanical horse managing to make breathing sounds; and the crocodile song being so old. But I believe all the historical bits now that we've checked it…"

"Well actually," broke-in Conna, "Now that I come to think of it, I saw a documentary about old songs once. Did you know that 'London bridge is falling down' was about a Viking attack in six hundred and something – fourteen hundred years ago – so if that's anything to go by, it's only around another six hundred years that we're arguing about. Maybe it's not so daft after all?"

Bex still looked unconvinced.

"Anyway," Maddie continued, "I like Tom – and I don't think he's lying as such – but maybe he's changed the places and dates of the real story to mask it. He really started to get angry when he began talking about Hitler's Nazis, didn't he?"

The others nodded sagely.

"And there's something else I'd like to know." She continued. "How come he said that even though he was a natural at languages, Lio couldn't speak either the ancient or modern English language, and that he couldn't understand what Catherine had said – but then Tom translated it for us anyway?"

"Yep, and there's something *I'd* like to know too," said Bex. "You know he said he'd never seen or heard from Ashur again?"

"Yes." They agreed.

"Well, how come he knew that she was having his child?"

Conna considered the question. "Oh, yeah…" He wondered himself now.

They all thought for a few moments and then, leaving out the added problem of Alex's old shed for now, Conna said again. "Listen, *I* spotted something as well."

"Come on then," said Bex, "spit it out."

Conna frowned. "Well… look… it wasn't anything I could put my finger on properly until this morning, so I haven't checked it out yet. But when he told us about Lio waiting for Catherine sitting in the dining room – when he sat listening to the ticking of the clock – it reminded me of this other documentary I once saw about clock-making."

"Oh yeah? You certainly do watch a lot of TV." Bex commented.

"So what about it?" asked Maddie.

"It's just that, I think that I remember on this programme that they said that the thing that makes the ticking noise in all mechanical clocks and watches, the whatchamacallit."

"The... erm..." Bex tried to remember what Tom had called it, "...the escape movement."

"Yeah, that's it. Well, as he told us, that's the thing that keeps them all going at a constant rate – never faster, never slower – as long as the clock spring is wound or the counter-weight keeps it in tension – or whatever powers it."

"Anyway," concluded Conna, "it wasn't invented until, well... much later – I don't know when, but..."

Bex finished off the thought for him. "...but when I asked him what powered the clock in the Time-Horse he told us it was a spring!"

"...And a clock couldn't have worked without an escape movement," they all ended together.

It was at that precise moment that they all reached the same conclusion. However, Conna was the one who voiced it. "So, without a proper clock, the Time-Horse couldn't work then? So it couldn't be true... So there is no time-travel machine..." they agreed lamely – each of them, more than faintly disappointed.

"Wow," said Maddie, equally disappointedly, now that push had come to shove.

Bex didn't have to say it. The look of realisation on her face said it for her. As silly as it all sounded, there had always been a small part of her that had wanted to believe the whole thing. *Daft really*, she thought. She kept it to herself.

The three looked dejectedly at one another, heads in hands, just playing with the melting ice-creams; each of them now realising that all they'd really wanted all along was to be proven wrong. The dream that they'd all half-shared for the past few days was now deflated – or, rather, the bubble burst.

Conna perked up slightly, breaking the gloomy moment: "It would have been excellent if it had all been true though, wouldn't it? Not that Tom would have allowed us to use it to change anything in *our* lives."

"No, it would've been too dangerous," Maddie said distractedly, "I think we've learned that much."

Bex nodded in agreement.

"Still," finished Conna, "it was a brilliant story!"

Without finishing the ice-creams off, the three got up together, left the table and went outside. Conna wiped his mouth with a napkin this time, just in case.

"See you tomorrow then," said the girls, still subdued.

"Yeah," said Conna looking up and down the street. He watched the pair as they walked all the way down the street and then he turned and walked back toward the Priory, still avoiding going home.

As soon as Maddie and Bex walked in through the living room door, they realised things were not right. Their dad was sat on the sofa beside his pretty, but tired looking wife, her head clean shaven as it had been for weeks. The married couple held hands, obviously upset. Freddie scrunched up the printed letter in his other hand and tossed it toward the waste paper basket in the corner, but it bounced onto the floor instead. The twins' faces dropped. Exasperatedly, Freddy said: "We thought we might have had some good news for you. We thought things were going really well over the past few weeks. We thought it was isolated in your mum's knee and under control."

"Don't worry," their mother smiled bravely, continuing in her French patois: "it's not that bad. It's just that your father and I thought we might all get back home to the Caribbean early. Now we'll just have to get used to living here a little longer like we planned. It's fine, really… the treatment may take a little more time, that's all." She smiled. "Anyway, at least you've found some good friends to spend your time with."

As she sat back tiredly, Freddie got up silently and put his arms around his girls. Then they all wept together.

By mid-evening, tired of walking around aimlessly, Conna again knocked on Alex's door. He was unable to think of anything else to do with his time, but was determined not to go home and face things just yet. Boris jumped up and began barking noisily at the front window, drowning out the music that the boy could hear coming from Tom's opened French windows next door – some ancient gramophone record or other, one of the ones he'd seen there.

Opening the door wide, Alex's mum was pleasantly surprised to see him there again.

"Oh, hi Conna," she said, "what are you doing back here – at a loose end with yourself?"

"Yeah," he said, "something like that. Erm…"

"Yes Conna?"

"I don't suppose Alex is about, is he?"

"Well yes, kinda', but he's in the bathroom, just about ready for an early night in bed. Is it something important you wanted to see him about?"

"Well," shrugged Conna, "just wanted to see him, you know…"

"Okay, if you want to wait while he gets into his pyjamas."

"Righto," he volunteered quickly, before she could retract the offer. "I'll take Boris for a little walk while I'm waiting, shall I?" With that he clapped twice, the dog shot past him and Conna disappeared with his other close friend. Alex's mum shook her head to herself: "That boy really likes to be out *a lot*," she murmured under her breath.

Upstairs in Tom's house, for the first time since midday, the old man breathlessly put down his tools and mopped his brow. The exertion of lifting the heavy parts, with or without simple levers, had taken its toll. He crossed over to the bench and gazed at all the familiar objects that filled it and the room. Each one of them took him back in time. On a whim, he crossed to look at the records lying beside the old gramophone player. It was a while since he had heard them – too long. Too long since he had dared to revisit his past through playing them, the memories until now, best forgotten. Tonight though, he wished to hear them one last time.

Riffling through the pile of old fashioned records that he preferred, he spotted the one he was looking for – Bobby Darin. He plucked the EP out gently, blowing off the traces of dust before placing it on the turntable. Adjusting the speed down from 78rpm to 33rpm, he wound up the machine, released the brake lever and placed the heavy needle head on the disc. Returning to the window, he stood there gazing out at the distant horizon as the gramophone sounded out and he muttered, rather than sang along: 'Somewhere… beyond the sea, somewhere, watching for me… my lover stands on golden sands, watching the ships that go sailin'…'

As he listened, Tom's temperature began to soar. In an effort to cool himself, despite the growing force of the chill wind outside, he opened the windows to let it scour the room. Immediately, the blast lifted up the few bits of paper around him and carried them swirling high above his head before they died in the corner. When the record had finished, he heaved a deep sigh. He went into his kitchen and produced a bottle of wine and a short tumbler. Re-entering the room, he wound up the gramophone again. Then he replaced the record with another selected at random. Pouring a drink, he toasted the girl that still, after all those years, occupied his thoughts, deciding that enough was enough. Tonight, he would finally be on his way. Shortly, he would finally resolve the great paradox – all by himself! As Nat King Cole's smooth voice crooned out, "There may be trouble ahead…" Tom dragged the Hippo-Chronos around to face the window. He climbed uneasily astride it and looked down at the levers. All the while, the wild wind blew his hair around him. Then, he refilled his glass and held it high to the world outside. He downed it and took a sobbing breath: the stress of it all was getting to him again, where were those pills?

After twenty minutes, Conna and Boris came back to Alex's house. Now in his PJs and dressing gown, Alex answered the door. Boris shot in first and, within minutes, was lying flat out beneath the TV as if he'd never moved.

"Hi Alex, just wondered whether you were okay," said Conna, squeezing past him in the passage, "what with you not showing up earlier."

"Oh, I'm fine," said Alex, now beginning to come to terms with everything. "It was just a bit of a heavy day, that's all – a bit tiring." For now, he avoided the subject of moving away.

Conna didn't really wish to know either, although he'd wondered about it since well before that morning. Instead of asking, and not knowing how to tell his friend that he and both girls had decided that they couldn't believe Tom's story, he said: "So, what's been happening?" He wasn't very good at this.

Alex sensed his lack of comfort and decided to come clean after all. "Not sure about us moving – might be a good idea – maybe sometimes you could come over to America and stay with us if you like," he suggested half-heartedly.

"Mmm," Conna conceded doubtfully.

"Anyway, I've decided to help Tom a bit more," Alex advised. "I don't think I can believe his story though. It's probably that he's just a bit mixed up… you know?"

"Oh?" asked Conna, as if the subject of his sanity had never been mentioned before.

"Yeah," continued Alex. "I think I might have been getting a bit carried away with everything – what with dad and all that – wondering if Tom did know anything about him going missing. Clutching at straws really – I'm not sure now – about dad coming back, I mean." There – he'd finally said it – one short sentence.

Conna knew how important it had been for his friend to say it and was quite proud that Alex had chosen to tell him. "So what finally convinced you?" he asked, hoping not to rub salt into the wound.

"I'm not sure really," said Alex. "I think I knew all along: time-travel – it couldn't really work, could it? It was a good game to play when we were little, but we can't really turn back time – even if we want to."

Conna *was* going to mention Tom's description of the old shed in his garden, but then decided not to ridicule. "Nah," he agreed, "prob'ly not. Cracking story though, eh?"

Alex couldn't help but smile, knowing that his best friend had been concerned for him all along, despite the way that he had kept him at arm's length for the past few weeks. There was a short silence interrupted by Conna's stomach.

"Do you fancy a cuppa or anything?" Alex offered.

"Yeah, why not," Conna answered politely, "Cup of tea – maybe one of your dad's bacon sarnies?" he suggested.

Alex laughed to think that Conna also thought of them as his dad's bacon sarnies, so they strolled into the kitchen and Alex got out the frying pan, slinging a couple of rashers in for each of them.

"By the way," Conna asked, "where's your mum gone?"

"Oh, having an early night now. We had a bit of a row... well, not quite..." he let the thought peter out. "I'll tell you all about it tomorrow."

For a change, Conna decided not to probe further. Instead he asked, "So who do *you* think Tom really is?"

"I don't know," said Alex truthfully. "Nothing quite fits. He shrugged his shoulders, "perhaps we'll never find out."

"Or maybe we will, soon," Conna added.

"Yeah," said Alex, *soon or not at all*, he almost said.

Half an hour later, both proper friends again, Alex closed the door behind Conna after watching him walk past Tom's house. The short way was too dangerous tonight. Yet, despite the wind picking up more now, Tom's windows were still open and the wind-up gramophone still played out. On his way to the high street, Conna waved back at Alex while listening to the strains of an old record. He didn't recognise Nat King Cole's voice singing 'Let's face the music and dance...' but he smiled ironically to himself as the words hit him. *Well, that's what I'll do myself then – hang the consequences.* Conna hummed along with Nat as he disappeared into the dip: "Let's face the music... let's face the music... let's face the music, and dance!"

When Conna eventually reached his own door, he stood plucking up the courage to go in. *What could happen anyway?* he thought. He took a deep breath and rattled the key deliberately noisily in the back kitchen door. The room was exactly as he had left it. Frank Cooper's marmalade was still smeared across the granite work top. Yoghurt was strewn across the floor. And all over the exclusive hand-laid flooring was dribbled with reduced fat syllabubs. The real fruit smoothies had been squirted onto the front of the fridge. And more dried on, off-white yoghurt contrasted wonderfully with the polished black cupboard fronts, spelling out the point of his finger scrawled protest: 'I LIVE HERE TOO!' Including the exclamation mark! He stood, contemplating the scene of his crime in silence, knowing that it was only likely to be a hollow gesture. It wasn't even as though his mum was even remotely likely to clear up the mess. That would only end up being their poor maid, Sofia's job when she returned tomorrow. Frankly, looking back, he didn't know what had possessed him. He was only glad that he had finally plucked up the courage to do so.

Waiting for the inevitable blast, and deliberately ignoring the neatly stacked glasses in the eye-level glass cupboards in front of him, Conna opened the fridge door. He took out the plastic carton of skinny milk and took a swig directly from it. Hearing the fridge door close with a clunk, from within the TV room came the single worded scream of his mother: "CONSTANTINE!" Instantly jolted back to reality, he dropped the bottle on the floor where it glugged its white contents all over. Riveted to the spot, he wondered what his next move should be – but within moments he felt sickened as he listened to his father's pathetic attempt to pacify her.

"Listen, darling, why don't you calm down and speak to him in the morning, I'm sure he'll promise to behave."

It was at that moment that Conna finally realised in contempt that things were never likely to change. He grabbed his long, quilted puffer-coat from the cupboard, crossed hopelessly to the kitchen door, opened it and then slammed it shut as hard as he could. It smashed the stained-glass panel and almost took the door off its hinges. He discarded the handle that had come off in his hand into the neatly trimmed hedge. Leaving the drive, he headed back again for the last time that day towards Alex's house. The boy was determined that he would not suffer any more of his parents' sham marriage, the die had been cast.

The rain began to pour, and thunder and lightning crashed out as Conna made his way toward the shortcut to his friend's house in the gathering storm.

CHAPTER 30:

Gone!

Day Five: the Final Day of Tom's Story

At seven o'clock in the morning, just before dawn, the phone rang in Alex's mother's bedroom. It awakened Alex, next door. He turned to go back to sleep but heard the concerned tone in her voice, so he stayed awake, listening to the short, muffled conversation at the other side of the wall. "Oh!" Penny said. "No, I'm sorry… yes… sure… I certainly will." A moment later she knocked gently on his door. "Alex, may I come in please?"

Alex immediately sensed trouble. "Yeah…" he called out sleepily. "What is it?" he yawned, checking his dad's watch as his mother entered in her nightgown.

"Alex…" Penny sat at the foot of the bed, "Alex, it's your friend… he's gone."

"Gone?" said Alex, assuming the worst. "But he was okay when everybody spoke to him yesterday morning."

"Who… what?" replied his mum, a little confused.

"Tom," said Alex, now unsure of the situation. "That's who we're talking about, isn't it?"

"No! Not Tom – Conna. He didn't go home last night – that was his mother on the phone. She asked whether he was staying here, he's not answering his mobile."

"Whoa!" exclaimed Alex, "that's not like Conna." Although in hindsight he could probably have guessed that something had been going on.

"You don't know where he could be, do you?"

"I can think of a couple of places, have the police been called yet?"

"Actually, no, his mother said she didn't want them involved – doesn't want to embarrass Conna – give him time to see sense and come home first. I don't like it though."

Alex agreed. "Try ringing the girls," he suggested, "see if they've seen him. I think I'll take the dog for a walk."

Five minutes later he set off, well wrapped-up against the buffeting wind and rain that was driving in sideways. He walked in a wide loop towards Conna's house where he and Boris would attempt to retrace his steps. The wind was gusting strong today; it had continued all through the night. *Best not try Tom's house yet*, he thought, he didn't want to cause him any further stress.

Nearly two hours later, Alex returned home. He had taken both the long way through the town and then the short-cut along the steep, now slippery, muddy edge. He almost fell down it as a gust of wind caught him and blew him toward the sea and the beckoning Black Middens. In the distance, fifteen metre high waves lashed way over the top of the lighthouses, sweeping clean across the ends of the piers where Alex and his friend sometimes stood talking. Alex was getting worried, he checked again with his mother, but Conna still hadn't been there. *Okay*, he decided, *time to try Tom's house.*

Boris was saturated. Normally, he would have made a bolt for his own door, but instead, today the dog seemed agitated, keen to get into Tom's. Alex rapped smartly on the door but there was no reply. Again he tried, but to no avail. He ran back to his own house to get the spare key he still held, then, bracing himself against the wind, he came back. Opening the door, he shouted up the stairs for Tom but there was still no answer. Boris beat Alex into the laboratory, jumping over the scattered tools which lay all around. Alex was still calling out for his neighbour as he walked into the room. He almost tripped over the dust cover that had previously covered Tom's machine. And there, slumped over the Hippo-Chronos, lay the old man.

"Tom?" called out Alex warily. He crossed toward the horse. "Tom… are you okay?" Tom's arms and legs were stretched out like a rag-doll, dangling down onto the wooden rails that held the body of the legless machine upright. His head was slung down, the mop of hair unmoving. In his hand was a rolled-up piece of yellowed paper. The boy touched his shoulder, shaking him gently. "Tom?" again he shoved him, this time harder. "Tom!" he said louder but still he didn't move. Boris began to bark at the rag-doll. He jumped up on his back legs, pawing the air.

"Boris, get down, there's a good boy, I think we're too late," Alex said resignedly. He was about to go back to phone for an ambulance when the dog began to lick Tom's face. "Boris, no. Stop it!" called Alex, but the dog kept licking at him, trying to wake him up. When he still didn't move, as he'd done with Alex and his father before him, Boris nipped his ear.

"Aargh!" shouted Tom. He sat bolt upright: "What was that?"

The dog began to bark again as Tom rubbed at his eyes and face, trying to work out what had happened. He immediately put away the piece of paper. "Where am I?" he asked Alex "What time is this?"

Alex almost laughed at the same phrase he'd delivered when they'd fist met. He heaved a sigh of pure relief. "Tom, what are you doing there, are you alright?"

The old man sniffed, "I stayed up late last night – I had a glass of red wine."

Alex looked at the empty bottle lying beside the horse, "Just a glass?"

"Maybe a bit more," Tom admitted apologetically. "I never could handle alcohol. What time is it?"

"About nine o'clock now," answered the boy. Then, getting straight to why he had knocked in the first place, he asked, "Tom, you haven't seen anything of Conna, have you?"

"No," said Tom, still in a daze, "Why, what is wrong?"

"Tom, we're worried about him, he's gone."

"Gone, what do you mean, gone?" He screwed up his eyes in the early daylight.

"Conna's gone missing. He didn't stay at home last night – his mother was on the phone. She says he didn't even go home."

"Really?" said Tom, now himself concerned. "I saw him walk past here last night, and up out of the dip."

"What time?" asked Alex.

"I don't know – when he left your house."

"Are you sure he went toward the village?" Alex checked.

"Well, I think so. He went up the hill toward the priory." Tom narrowed his eyes as he wondered. "Actually, I think I might know where he could have gone – if it's still there," he smiled. He then told Alex precisely where to look, and Alex left hurriedly with the dog. Now that Tom had slept soundly for a change, he resolved to give them one last chance. He picked up his machine-polisher – this time ready to astound them all.

The tourist season was finished for the winter now, so Alex had no trouble climbing over the unguarded fence around the Priory and Castle. Boris squeezed under the notice that said 'Closed to the Public'. The gusting horizontal wind and rain pushed them both around as they ran down the steep grassy defence ditch and straight back up the other side. The castle entrance gate – the heavy portcullis – was down. Alex wandered around the side and started to climb the short wall below a large window portal. By now, Boris, left alone on the ground, looked like a drowned rat. He barked furiously and started to dig, in the vain hope of burrowing under the ten foot thick defences.

Disappearing through the window, Alex scrambled down and landed roughly in a heap at the bottom. There, in the opposite corner, even after all these years, was the now freshly painted and well kept old wooden tool shed. Alex ran over to it and rattled the metal thumb latch. He opened the door, and somehow Boris shot through first again. There, lying on the floor under several layers of gardeners' dungarees and jackets was Conna. As the dog barked excitedly at him and nipped his nose, the boy looked up at his friend, instantly awake, knowing exactly where he was and how he'd got there. "Conna," Alex asked gently, "what happened? We've been worried about you."

Conna, still on the floor, stretched out his hands and yawned. He smiled up sheepishly at his mate – "I'm starvin'. Any chance of another bacon sarnie and a cuppa?"

The job done, Boris launched himself across the grassy area outside and ran back through the gap under the portcullis. Minutes later, Tom waved cheerily, relieved as he saw the dog rush past his house, and the two friends linked shoulder to shoulder against the wind. Again they made their way towards Alex's, to share breakfast, and for Conna to freshen up after his freezing night in the shed. Everything that had brought Conna to the decision to run away from home was all explained by the boy to Alex and his mum as he munched his way through three bacon sarnies and several hot cups of tea. At ten o'clock they made ready to see Tom.

"Should I ring your mother yet?" asked Penny.

"Nah, not yet! Let her worry for a bit – take a day off work. It's only what she deserves for lying about me not coming home last night. I left enough evidence… Of all people, she should know that." They agreed with him, perhaps it would teach her and his dad a lesson, or at least force them to sort themselves out. "We'll go to Tom's first," said Conna. "Then, later, I'll decide what to do."

The wind and rain still slammed into the French windows as Tom, Alex and Conna waited for Maddie and Bex to arrive. In their absence, Tom had tidied his horse away again, the books once more holding down the dust sheet as it had done since the beginning of the week. Today would be the day – the unveiling!

The instant Alex answered the door, Bex stormed up the stairs, across the room and thumped Conna directly in the chest – hard. "That's for nothing," she said, sitting back down on the opposite end of the sofa, stone-faced.

Conna went red, but smiled inwardly.

Maddie and Alex had to look away, both shaking, trying to keep-in the nervous laugh.

"What's funny?" Bex challenged.

"Nothing," they said between resuming their week-long positions and settling down. No one wanted to further embarrass

Conna by discussing why he'd gone missing, so they all tactfully avoided the subject. All were happy that for now this particular scare was over. But then Maddie's mood seemed to change – worried.

"Are you okay Maddie?" Alex asked the girl.

"Mmm, just a little disappointed, mum got some bad news yesterday. It seems to have stopped spreading, but it isn't going away just yet." She shrugged.

"Oh," Alex felt her bitter disappointment. He instinctively took her hand in his and patted it. "So what happens next?"

"Another long course of treatment." She smiled bravely, "but mum'll pull through, just wait and see – won't she Bex?"

"Absolutely," Bex nodded steadfastly.

For no apparent reason, Boris gave a loud bark. The shock of it jolted them all out of their troubled thoughts, and the relief in the room now brightened everyone. Yesterday the story and other home events had been a bit of a downer for everyone. Thank goodness today would be different. *Finally*, thought Alex, *today will clear the air once and for all.*

"Alright," said Tom. "Before finishing off the story, and explaining why I need your help, are there any questions?"

"I have Tom," Maddie spoke up honestly. "Tom…" she asked, "Tom… I don't mean to be rude, but how come Lio knew how to translate what Catherine said to him in English, if you said that he'd never heard the language before?"

"Oh," said Tom, "Catherine repeated the tale to him much later. It was just that."

That was Maddie's simple problem solved.

Bex spoke up next, asking straight out the question they'd discussed in the coffee bar. "Okay then. How did Lio find out that Ashur was expecting, if he never saw or heard from her again?"

"Ah," corrected Tom, "I said only that Lio did not *see or hear* from her again. But much later he discovered a message – to let him know that she was safe. *That* – was when he finally learned of his child with Ashur."

Bex looked back at his flat smile, neither understanding nor convinced.

"Don't worry," said Tom, "if everything goes according to plan, all will be revealed. Now, are there any more questions?"

Reluctantly, Conna raised his hand as if in a classroom. "Er, Tom, I have."

"You too Conna, then let's have it."

Again Conna decided to skip over Tom's description of Alex's old shed. Instead, he began uncertainly. "Well... you know you said that the clock in the Hippo-Chronos was powered by a spring?"

"Yes?" Tom answered directly.

"Well then, I just wondered... about the escapement mechanism?"

Tom frowned. "Conna," he said, "I am impressed with such an expert question. Alright," he agreed, "I will try to explain as simply as I can, but this is technical stuff!

As you obviously know, at the heart of all modern clocks is some form of escapement mechanism which allows the spring to unwind constantly – bit by bit. This action gives the same effect as the constant water pressure of the klepsydra – or water clock – but has the advantage of being more portable. It would be difficult to imagine carrying a bucket of water around to power a clock or watch, would it not? There have been many variations on these systems, including the 'Verge' or 'Crown-wheeled' escapement mechanism and the 'Anchor escapement' – there are others. All of these devices share a common tell-tale ticking, and yet, the earliest of them only came about in mid-fourteenth century Italy."

Guessing, Bex chipped in, "So you're saying that this was yet another Greek idea that was rediscovered in the Renaissance?"

"Well... possibly," admitted Tom, "I do not know, but I personally doubt it. However, it is certainly a better and more reliable design solution. Kyrros' escape mechanism was somewhat prone to stopping, but it used none of these methods. I will show you his own version in a short while, I promise. It was the one, most delicate part of the machine which I removed before you all started to come here days ago. In fact, it was the one part which was never filled with wax – it was simply repaired from time to time."

Tom turned to Alex. "And you Alex, do you have any questions for me?"

Alex looked directly at the old man. He had dozens of questions that he could have asked, especially since yesterday. Nevertheless, he didn't want to humble the man in front of his new friends. *Besides, maybe*, he thought, *Tom might just pull one last trick out of the bag that will let everyone down gently, and finally prove the story he had already told – especially about his dad's involvement.* There was, after all, only one way to find out. The young boy smiled squarely back at his neighbour and said: "No Tom, I'm fine."

"Good," said Tom, "Then let us start to finish!"

CHAPTER 31:

A Relapse of Madness

The four settled down for one last time as Tom restarted: "Leaving Catherine and the early cold war years behind, Lio once more travelled forward in time on the back of his Hippo-Chronos. But, without the Cosmos-key, he did not leave its previous physical location – inside the big old shed in her garden. However, as the rickety shed was scrapped by her a couple of years after he had gone, he landed in the light of a beautiful spring morning, in the cleared back garden of the house next door to us – The garden which is presently yours Alex."

The others looked around to see Alex's reaction but the boy didn't give anything away.

It was only Conna that spoke up. "Hang on. What about the shed we used to play in then?" he frowned at Alex.

"The little blue one that dad made for me when I was six?" He smiled, remembering it vividly. "That fell to bits a couple of years ago."

"Oh… it was a different one." Conna decided not to explain.

Tom continued unabashed: "At first, Lio did not know which date it was, but he was immediately happy to still recognise the location. He wandered around to the front of the house, noticing that the damaged, vacant house next door was for sale – this house. He then made his way immediately to the riverside, where he had previously watched the stricken ship on the rocks. The Tyne had changed a great deal; there were far fewer ships, and the busy ship building industry was now all but gone. But he was at least pleased to see that there was only one warship down there. The rest were all cargo boats and, of course, there was the Scandinavian ferry heading into port. The previous one hundred dockside cranes that had lined the wide river were now reduced to a dozen or so – but the lie of the land was not fundamentally different.

A young man in a smart, plain grey suit, about the same age as himself, walked past him. They were not unlike the clothes that Catherine had given him in 1963, but not as tight in the leg. Also, his jacket had wider lapels, which seemed odd to Lio. The youth also carried a radio, a much larger and far less portable version than the small ivory and chrome one Lio had got used to in Catherine's house, very odd. It blasted a lot of music that sounded strange to his ears. *Whatever next?* thought Lio. The sound was not at all like the gramophone records that he'd got used to. The young man looked at Lio's mop of red hair and slim-line trousers. He smirked and kept on going.

Someone had dropped a folded newspaper at the top of the bank, so Lio picked it up and looked at the date. It read March 23, 1983. Then he looked at the headlines: 'Star Wars to go ahead'. Of course, this was not the popular movie, but something named after it. The article went on to describe the properly named 'US Strategic Defense Initiative'.

Tom sighed deeply and took a sip of water. He emphasised: "This scheme was *truly* the closest the world has so far come to madness! As the name suggests, it was supposedly a defence scheme designed to take out all incoming weapons which might be directed at the USA. However, in reality it was not a shield. It was, in fact, a first strike capability.

In extremely dubious theory, it would have included orbiting space platforms that could deliver thousands of nuclear warheads on the heads of the enemy before they had a chance to react. The rest of the world could only watch in fear and trepidation – powerless – as common sense went out of the window. Whilst, for the first time since its inception, generals on both sides of the iron curtain began to speculate on whether a nuclear war was winnable!

Thankfully, the system was never built. Surely, that project alone would have triggered the war that everyone in the world dreads. However, I suppose *that* particular threat finally got the sworn enemies around the negotiating table. At last a warm wind seemed to have blown the iron curtain open and finally began to take the chill off the Cold War. Hopefully, there will be no more grandiose claims to world supremacy – whatever the claimed cause!

Anyway, at least this time, Lio had moved not that many years forward from the sixties. In a way, he was glad. Catherine's house was still there, and he knew the area's geography well enough, although after twenty years, doubtlessly she would have now moved away. She had always claimed that the house was too big and cold for a single person. Lio could, he supposed, make his way back to Greece. Or, he could stay here and build a new, proper life, for himself – where at least he knew some of the modern English language.

He always had the option of going further forward in time, of course – in theory, until the very end of time – but what would be the use, he wondered? He was weary of it all. Not remotely curious as to what the future may have in store, all the young man wanted to do now was rest. The trauma of everything that had happened in the past and modern world was catching up with him. So, once again, he returned to his horse. But this time he dragged it, along with his bag, to where it could not be found: inside the back door of the house next door to him – right here!

That night, covered only by the clothes on his back, and insulated by the newspaper, Lio slept on the floor beside the machine. In the morning, his life would start to focus again on entirely different subjects.

At first light, after greeting the dawning sun, Lio re-read the headline story in full. On examination, it was no more than sheer co-incidence that the newspaper he had picked up held two other items that would at last afford him some stability, and separately might give him some hope. Both items were related to 'computers.'

Lio began to comb through the whole newspaper to see what he could find out about the times of the world he planned to live in – update his knowledge from the sixties. For the full morning, before he went outside – although by now he was very hungry – he read every inch of the paper before he eventually stumbled upon the first thing that caught his real attention. It was an advertisement in the 'situation's vacant' section – the job section – for a 'computer expert'; someone who was familiar with the newly emerging computer industry. Not that Lio knew what was meant by it. He imagined the machine that Kyrros had built. He knew, though, that if he was going to survive, he needed to find work this time. And so, he carefully tore out the advert and put it to one side.

The second short item was more obscure. It was tucked away at the bottom of a general interest column, and if Lio had not had anything better to do with his time – other than to comb every inch of the paper – he would never have found it. The tiny item had been reprinted from an American Magazine appropriately called 'Time'. It mentioned an earlier article by a physicist, who was also a historian of science. In his article – "Gears from the Greeks" – the writer, Professor de Solla Price had written of an ancient artefact that had lain undiscovered in a museum since the turn of the twentieth century, until not many years ago. The artefact, or rather fragments of it, he suggested, were a potential revelation to modern science. It appeared to him, and a few others, that it may have been some form of mechanical marvel – a calculator of sorts – the earliest known computer. It was named after the island where it had been found, 'The Antikythera device'. Price concluded his description of the device by pointing out disturbingly that, despite the Greeks' now apparently more sophisticated civilization, their scientific world had still come to an obscure end.

Few people believed de Solla Price's theory of course. It was easily dismissed as just another crackpot idea from a so-called British scientist who had moved to the USA: 'an atheist from a Jewish background who was out to grab publicity'. It would be many years before his work would be given the credit it deserved – although his version was unfortunately flawed. But Lio of course, knew the story of the computer to be perfectly true. It was, after all, built by his father – and it might yet be the key to getting him home!

After re-reading the article, he tore this out also and tucked it away. Elated that he might have been thrown another lifeline, he determined to contact the Antikythera device people and offer his assistance and expertise.

By mid afternoon of that same day, Lio needed to get something to eat, but having nothing that he could trade in proportion, he wondered long and hard about what to do. He had no intention of begging or making a nuisance of himself, so all he could do was see if the new owner of the house he had lived in until yesterday would let him inside. Maybe, he could retrieve the reserve that he had stashed there and had forgotten to collect in the daze he'd been in all those years ago. Although he had not shaved for days, Lio washed his face in the kitchen sink and tried to make himself as presentable as possible.

He went down the path and up to the front door before knocking politely. A young man of roughly the same age, build, and height answered the door to him and asked the stranger what he could do for him. Lio suggested that a friend of his had lived there some time ago. He asked if it would be possible to see the house for curiosity's sake – he might also have left something there. Taken temporarily aback – it was such an odd request – the affable young man decided to let him do so. Once inside though, Lio realised immediately that he was too late. The black iron cooking range, the oven and the ever present kettle had gone. They had all been replaced with a smaller, mock stone hearth – not nearly as useful. Obviously, along with the range – his hiding place – the object he had stashed there long ago must also be gone. He would now, absolutely, definitely, need a job if he was going to survive.

Realising the plight of Lio from his unshaven face and crumpled clothes, the young man at least let Lio stay for a while, even offering to make him a rudimentary meal if he wished – maybe a couple of bacon sarnies? Grateful for the offer, whatever a 'sarnie' was, Lio accepted gratefully. They chatted while he ate the meal, after which, Lio thanked him politely and went back next door for the night – along with a borrowed double sided safety razor and a blanket. The young man watched him slip in through the back door that he'd managed to prise open the day before, then he went back to sit and wait in front of the TV. His mother would be in from school shortly, as she always had been for the past ten years – at four-twenty. The car ride, she said, was much quicker than walking: it saved ten whole minutes every day and 'saved her legs'.

A few moments after she got in, Cath, as she was now known, put on her apron. She began to wash the few cups and plates that had been there only an hour, when her son forewarned her about the 'squatter' next door. She didn't like the idea at all. But then he told her not to worry, because he'd seemed a pleasant enough sort to him. He told her of the strange excuse he'd used to introduce himself as she was drying the plate he'd used. In reply, she cautiously asked if the young man had given his name. 'Billy…' he answered, 'Billy, the Greek.'

That was when the plate smashed on the floor."

CHAPTER 32:

The Great Unveiling

Each of Tom's audience watched in silence as he shifted his weight in his chair. After catching his breath, he continued unhurriedly. "For three consecutive days, Lio's neighbour, an archaeology student, invited him back in for a mid-day meal. Cath's son became fascinated at the squatter's knowledge of the ancient world, and they spoke of many things that captured the student's imagination, which drove forward his own study. Each time, although the young student insisted that it was not necessary, Lio assured him that he would eventually pay him back for his kindness. He had applied for an interview at the university, he told him, and was certain he had a good chance of getting a job. On the fourth day, Lio was given a small leather suitcase containing some good quality, if old fashioned, clothes that the boy believed had once belonged to his father. His mother had, only yesterday, finally decided to part with them, many years after her husband had lost his life in a sea rescue. Taking the case back to his 'squat', Lio opened it and immediately recognised the clothes that he himself had worn only last week. But try as he might to work out this coincidence, it was only later that evening that the mystery was solved for him.

The loud knock on the door found Lio sitting in the centre of the floor, reading another discarded newspaper which he quickly tossed into the corner. Cagily, he went to the letterbox and asked who it was, now wondering whether he was going to get into trouble for breaking into the house. Instead though, the woman's voice that answered put him at ease. Lio opened the door. Looking pointedly down at her feet, the rather frumpy woman that stood in a lime green headscarf seemed to tremble with controlled emotion. Then she began to shake uncontrollably and he wondered if she was ill. As she stepped forward into the house and removed the scarf, only now did Lio realise who she was. His eyes bulged. Catherine slowly looked up into his green eyes, and the phrase she delivered took him back to the day he'd first arrived. 'Oh my giddy aunt!' she exclaimed as she stared at him, trying to come to terms with what she saw. 'You're almost exactly the same as you were when I last saw you.' In sharp contrast though, Lio hardly recognised her at all.

Lio's onetime fiancé, now into her mid-forties, had put on considerable weight since a few days ago – especially around her bottom and legs. No longer like a potential partner, she now looked ages with – although was considerably less fit than – Miriam, Lio's mother.

'Catherine?' His response was written all over his face: surprise at her being there, relief at finding her again, but something akin to shock at how she now appeared. He had suddenly been confronted by the memory of the girl he had known in her early twenties, and now the change was somewhat 'dramatic'. Not unattractive, but completely different to the mental picture he carried in his head – and now, twice his age. He staggered back, trying unsuccessfully not to show his mixed emotions.

'Please… come in,' he stammered.

'Yes,' she said, 'I think I'd better had.'

Starting from the beginning, Catherine told him she had been returning home on the day they'd had the row about his ancient past. She saw the thunder and lightning, just as he had described always happened when the Hippo-Chronos was used, and urged the taxi driver to hurry. But by the time she got home, he was gone. Not knowing what to believe herself, whether he had simply run away, or whether he had after all been whisked away in time as he had said he could achieve, she never again mentioned the whole affair.

'Oh, Billy,' she said in conclusion, leaning forward to stroke his hair, now remembering her own youth. 'We could have been so happy together, if only I'd believed you. But just look at me now,' She backed away from him, realising the toll that time had had on her. Cath smiled at the young man, 'Don't worry,' she joked, 'I won't hold you to your offer of marriage.' Then, she looked at him imploringly, 'But I'd rather not let anyone know about us now. Please don't spoil it for me.'

'I won't,' promised Lio. 'But,' he asked, 'if you don't mind… would it be possible for me to settle down here now. There is something about this place that reminds me of Alexandria – perhaps the high and low beacons or the tall dock cranes along the riverside – and I have nowhere else to go?'

She looked into his shining eyes, realising this much was true. 'Yes,' she considered, 'I'd like that. But Lio,' she at last accepted his identity, 'please don't bother my son any more. How could I begin to explain my relationship with a young man half my age – his age? It just wouldn't be right, would it?'

She turned to leave and, almost as an afterthought, reached into her handbag and pulled out a small newspaper wrapped parcel. 'Here,' she said, shoving the heavy object into his hand, 'I found this years ago when we had the old fire range changed. I kept it safe for you ever since – just in case you ever came back.' She looked at him regretfully again. 'I suppose deep down I always did wish your story was true – though I'm sorry for you that it really was.'

Lio accepted the gold torc back into his custody and thanked her. In a parting gesture of his own, he ran back to reach into his satchel of small things. He fetched out a small cloth wrapped parcel. 'Perhaps,' he suggested, 'your son would like this? I have no use for it.' Catherine looked at the almost brand-new and clearly expensive watch, unsure. 'Where on earth did you get this?' she asked.

Lio shrugged, 'I'm afraid that's another story', he offered.

'Alright Billy pet, I'll keep it for him till he's twenty-one. If he asks, I'll just tell him that it was his dad's.' She kissed his cheek appropriately and then walked back to her own house."

Alex said nothing. Maddie and Bex listened in silence. Conna was the only one who spoke. "And that was Alex's gran?" He checked to make sure.

"Yes, Conna," said Tom, looking to see what Alex's reaction was. Alex avoided looking back at him.

"So… how long did they go on living next door to each other?"

"Oh," said Tom, "till the day she decided to move out of the big house – when her son was married."

"And did they never speak to each other again?" asked Maddie, the idea seemed strange.

"Oh, certainly!" Tom sounded surprised, "They became good friends. He often sent her bunches of daffodils each springtime. Also, they often wrote to each other until the day she passed away."

One by one, the four faces looked around at each other. Tom again began to detect an air of uncertainty in the room, though about what exactly, he was unsure. There was an uncomfortable silence, broken only by the whistling of the wind outside. He wondered for the last time whether he had really lost them all now – including Alex. *So be it,* he thought – *crunch time.* Now he would prove it all to be true.

"Please Alex," he asked without further thought, would you once again help me to take off the dust sheet?"

The four stood warily, wondering how many hours he would have them cleaning and polishing now.

But this time, when he and the boy peeled back the cover, each in turn took a sharp intake of breath. Instead of the untidy heap they'd previously been used to, now, the whole machine gleamed from top to bottom. Clearly, although Alex had missed the fact earlier this morning, all of the animal's 'innards' had already been reassembled inside it. Gone also was the silly painted smile. The finished Hippo-Chronos looked resplendent – ready to go – even bursting with new life!

The bronze body gleamed; the leather seat restored to its original state with saddle soap. The dark eyes of the machine seemed to bore into each of them, forcing them to seriously reconsider the possibility of its truth. A bright new topknot of red bristle had been added along with a matching plaited tail. "Come closer," Tom invited, at long last taking off his dark sunglasses to reveal the most devastatingly bright green eyes that before now only Alex had ever seen. Each of them was astounded, not appreciating till now what it was like to come into direct contact with Tom's burning gaze.

"Please," asked Tom, "witness it properly for yourselves."

No one said a word. Boris hopped down to let Maddie stand, and, one by one, each of them came forward to look at it closer. It really was most splendid.

"Conna," Tom spoke softly, "you asked me about the clock escapement. Last night before I… 'fell asleep'… I wound up everything fully."

"I thought you couldn't manage?" asked Alex.

"Physically, no, but this time I wound it up with that," he pointed down to the corner behind them, to an enormous electric drill with a double pinned drive on the end. "I adapted it." Tom smiled triumphantly, raising his eyebrows.

Alex looked quizzically back at him. Strangely, for all he had indeed begun to dismiss all of Tom's story, once more, he began to smile as he allowed his imagination to reign and his hopes to be raised.

"Conna," Tom continued, "here, look into its heart." He bent down to open an inspection hatch at its sternum. Conna and the others stooped to look inside at a small hooped orb, no bigger than the size of an apple. This was the one and only part of the horse that had never been encapsulated in wax – the various precious metals it was made from being entirely impervious to corrosion. The device rotated slowly clockwise on a vertical axis. Instantly they were all reminded of the gyrotourbillon – the tiny rotating mechanism in Alex's dad's watch. Inside the orb, there was a ruby-tipped rod mounted horizontally – a small, steel-blue spring wound around it. The rod was connected via a pair of bevelled gears to a second ruby-tipped rod, which ran vertically – top to bottom. To this second, vertical rod, fixed at a right angle was a tiny sculpted arm and a clenched fist. It was from that fist, that a gold weight, no bigger than the size of a pea, was suspended on the thinnest gold thread. As they all watched together, the arm spun around on its axis, flinging the ball out on its thread. This caught against a stubby vertical pin, wrapping itself around and finishing with a 'tink' – rather than a 'tick' – as the ball stopped against the pin. Then the ball and thread slowly unwrapped itself, allowing the spring powered axle, the arm and the hand to continue its clockwise journey through another one hundred and eighty degrees. Now the ball and thread re-wrapped itself around a second stubby pin on the opposite side.

Each *half* revolution took ten seconds precisely, so that, constantly, every three *full* revolutions marked one minute. Thirty revolutions became ten minutes; one hundred and eighty revolutions, one hour; and so on, and so forth. It was all punctuated by the slow 'tink… tink… tink', as opposed to a rapid tick-tock, tick-tock, of any other clock they had seen. And, in order to keep the bar upright at all times, so that the arm wouldn't stop rotating, the spherical cage allowed it to roll around and was itself counterbalanced by a lead plumbum at the bottom. Even if the horse fell over onto its side, which it had been prone to do, Kyrros' slow escapement mechanism was designed to rotate and remain 'tinking' away.

Additionally, every ten seconds, if listened to closely, the tiny blue spring inside it shiveringly released a little more energy with a noise akin to a hiss – not unlike a breathless sigh. The horse really did seem to everyone, to be alive.

"Kyrros really was clever", said Conna, finally beginning to accept that this was his ancient machine after all. Alex stared at it non-committally, waiting for his friends to speak first. Maddie continued to scan the rest of the machine. Only Bex seemed unconvinced. But, there again, hers was the only question that Tom hadn't answered – yet.

"To continue *Lio's* story then…" Tom took a deep breath as he sat back down, waiting for the other's to follow suit before he announced:

"*I*… have lived here ever since!"

It took a while for the impact of the simple confirmation to sink in. It was of course the belief which everyone had nursed all along for at least a few days, despite the twists and turns and the red herrings. A few times they'd wondered, but having Tom finally spell it out was somehow reassuring to everyone. He no longer held the suspicion that anyone might betray him to the various authorities. Now he *knew* that he was in safe hands.

"So Tom… Lio," Conna accepted faithfully, "what did *he… you*, do in all those years since then?"

"Since then," the old man said wistfully, "I have waited here patiently, sustained by the knowledge that once, in my youth, I was loved by my admittedly disparate family – until war tore us apart. And, that for a short, precious time, I also knew what it was like to love and be loved by the most beautiful girl in the world – a girl who I will *never* forget – even until the end of time!" Tom gazed toward the window. "Better to have loved and lost…" He took a deep breath and smiled proudly.

A moment later, he gave a short cough and looked back, fixing each in turn. "In the meantime I have patiently watched the world go by, wondering how I might keep the various promises I made. Of course, in that time, I have seen many horrific wars come and go. And, I have watched many stealth weapons being successively developed, bringing the world closer to the edge of destruction."

He mused toward the ceiling. "Let us not forget the many *smaller*, conflicts – many smouldering embers which threaten at any moment to burst into flame – in the name of defence and race and religious belief – but never, of course, about domination, greed, or mineral wealth! As we speak, new and innovative weapons kill and maim hundreds of thousands of people. Let us hope that these burning disputes are salved before they once more rage into a worldwide firestorm."

Everyone understood.

"Otherwise, personally, to begin with – the torc was immediately valued at an extraordinary price, more than the value of this house at that time. So it was used as collateral to buy and repair my home, until the mortgage was eventually paid off in full. Additionally, I now sell some of my 'ancient technopunk' sculptures, as I have learned from Alex to call them – though only to discerning private collectors. Since my 'retirement', I have become 'a man of independent means' – quite wealthy I suppose. But I would gladly exchange it all…"

"So what happened next – in the story?" asked Maddie eagerly.

"Well," said Tom, slipping back into the third person rather oddly now, speaking about his past self as Lio from an historical perspective. "Lio lived on into his last age – if you like – his fourth life:

He had been born Helio, and lived out his early childhood with his grandfather on Rhodos. As Lio – he lived his youth in Alexandria and Aegilia. During the Cold War, he continued his life here as Billy. And now, he had no choice other than begin again. From the time he started his job at the university in 1983, until the time he accepted 'early retirement' much later, he was known as the professor. And now, of course, I am simply Tom…"

"Tom, what *were* you a professor of?" quizzed Bex, wishing to sort out the confusion once and for all. "Was it computer studies, or history?"

Tom looked shocked. "Oh no," he looked at her askance, then to the others. "Perhaps I should have explained. Lio went for the interview in the computer department but he had no formal education or qualifications – pieces of paper – and that was frowned upon. Also, while he impressed the interviewers with his depth of understanding of binary computer codes and his general understanding of gearing, and how mechanical computers worked, faced with the electronic marvels that they had at that time become – each one occupying a large, specially constructed room – Lio had to admit that he knew nothing of them. Instead, as he claimed expert knowledge of the ancient world, the history department also granted him an interview, but they were immediately scathing in his fantastical view of the ancient Greeks' supposed knowledge of scientific understanding and technology. Obviously, to those more well-educated experts, Lio suffered from an overactive imagination. Finally, he tried the languages department, but his English was not at that time considered good enough. Also, his ancient island accent was deemed uneducated – unacceptable – even ignorant!

Perhaps it is not given to us all to achieve the lofty ambitions we would desire for ourselves. Perhaps that is simply not the way of the world. But, no, Lio was offered a quite different job, for which, as an extremely practical youth and a onetime odd job boy, he was ideally qualified. It was a job which he accepted gratefully. He was always very popular with the students and often helped them understand problems that their mentors could not, hence his well-meant nickname, 'the professor'. But all the time in the university, Lio worked quite happily as a caretaker – a janitor!"

The four mouths suddenly dropped open incredulously.

"It is, after all, a very worthwhile job – even essential – which someone has to do. However, the main reason for him keeping the job all that time was for one particular purpose. It gave him free access to the many sculpture and mechanical workshops. Long after everyone else had gone home, it allowed him to make or recreate the many models he remembered from his youth, sometimes just for fun. And it allowed him to continue to try and recreate the one mechanism that could get him out of there – the Chrono-key. In fact, Lio virtually lived there – rarely coming home even to sleep."

"You were trying to build an Antikythera key!" Alex exclaimed.

"Yes, one and the same," confirmed Tom.

"All through the years, Lio kept in touch with the various experts who tried to reconstruct the complicated machine for themselves, but they could never agree on its exact design. He made several attempts to solve its design problems on his own, but failed each time. Each passing failure of course, allowing him to grow older and more resigned to having no choice but to make the best of his life here and now – which he has done." He smiled at the four faces. "And in studying – completing the education he longed for as a boy. The Open University is a wonderful thing," said Tom proudly.

"Until finally, two years ago, he gave up on the task of trying to rebuild the key altogether.

By now he was too old, he realised. And too unwell to confront the younger, fitter Zeus – or even go back to where he really wanted anyway. It was too late to live the life he'd wished for in his youth. Even if he could have just returned to Ashur, he was now a much older man – and the girl was still seventeen! He was not about to follow the example of Caesar's relationship with Cleopatra. And just as he had been taken aback at meeting Catherine under similar, but reversed circumstances, he now had no intention of inflicting himself on his beautiful wife. Even to return incognito – just to gaze at Ashur from afar – the prospect of again seeing her without being able to hold her in his arms was even more cruel than the thought of staying here alone.

No, since that time, Lio studied, sat and read books, played music and made strange mechanical sculptures. And, of course, he continued to look eastwards out of the window – especially to meditate upon the wonders of this whole scientific universe – and the majesty of the dawning sun in particular. The long past day that Lio lost his job was the day that he began to live properly in this world."

Alex looked sheepishly at him, "I'm sorry about mam," he offered.

Tom frowned, "Oh, please don't blame your mother – it was nothing to do with her. It was Lio who did it to himself. Anyway, as I said, it was probably the best thing for it. I am afraid that Lio overstepped the mark one time in the college refectory – the canteen. He was talking to a few young students one day, discussing the so called Antikythera device. One of the girls – a foreign exchange student, an archaeologist – shared his unpopular academic view that it might soon prove to be the tip of an undiscovered iceberg. She expostulated that the device might represent a whole new, that is, hitherto unknown dimension to ancient society. A male history lecturer on the next table overheard them and rudely interrupted her. He was showing off. He was immediately sarcastic and overbearing with her and her quite correct view.

Lio took great exception to the way he spoke down to her and he told him so. As an expert member of the academic staff, the lecturer demanded to know what a mere cleaner and odd job man could possibly know about the subject. He told him to go back to his mop and bucket. That was when Lio finally snapped and told him that he had seen it with his own eyes, had lived on the island himself as a boy and had been working on its reconstruction right there in the workshops each evening for years. He told him in exact detail what the device was, what it did and how and when it had been made. Humiliated, the lecturer later reported him for inappropriate use of university resources – keeping the lights on in the workshop after closing time and using university tools and equipment for personal work. Regrettably, Lio was suspended, pending investigation. Temporarily though, perhaps due to the stress of his situation at work, he got a little carried away with himself one morning. At home, seeing a newborn baby lying there all alone outside of his neighbour's house, he picked the infant boy up and offered him to the early morning sun, to be baptised in its natural light." Tom shrugged apologetically. "I am sorry Alex," he offered.

Alex smiled warmly. "That's okay Tom," he already understood.

"Of course, after those incidents, and possibly quite rightly so, Lio was eventually sacked from his post." Tom sighed. "But… as I said, it was a blessing in disguise. It forced him to abandon his obsession and concentrate on other things instead – his sculptures, and his life here and now.

Finally, after failing for years, he was even awarded a degree in ancient history – after someone took pity on him and allowed him an unclassified pass for his 'fanciful but stimulating interpretations' of ancient Greek life." Tom smiled and looked around the room again.

"That is, of course, until around eighteen months ago. But perhaps," Tom suggested, "it might be more appropriate for Alex to pick up the story as I first told it to him in hospital. Then you may all begin to appreciate why I need your help. After all, Alex *is* my grandson."

CHAPTER 33:

Boris and the Rabbits

Grandson! Of course, each of them had easily recognised Alex's dad's description, even down to the 'bacon sarnies', but they had all along missed the possibility of Catherine's son being fathered by anyone other than his namesake, Stanley. Maddie, Bex and Conna all gaped at Alex, who looked innocently back at them. Even when Cath had asked him to stay away from her son, they'd thought it was only to save her from having to try and explain the unexplainable.

It was Tom who broke the embarrassing silence. "As I said, Stan's mother Catherine and I were both young, and the early sixties were a time when no one knew if they would live or die – or whether the world was about to come to an abrupt and horrific end!"

"Hang on though," Maddie shook her head, "What about the good news that Catherine had wanted to tell her husband Stanley – on the night of the accident?"

"Oh!" said Tom, "that important news was that she had just been promoted at school – to head of the classical studies department – she was very excited about it."

Now Bex Conna and Maddie looked pointedly at Alex. Quite obviously, he had known all along, but nevertheless, they couldn't help but smile.

Only Alex looked entirely comfortable with the situation. "Well…" he began confidently, "my grandmother, told my dad, Stan, that her husband, Stanley, had been killed in a sea rescue – months before dad was born. And Stanley *had* died in the rescue – but that was much earlier than dad was conceived. She also let him go on thinking that the same man was his father – a bit of a white lie, but one that hurt nobody."

Tom backed up the tale: "To admit anything else was at that time still a bit of a social taboo!"

All three understood immediately. "Anyway," Alex re-started. "It's just that Tom's told me this bit, so I can't really say whether it's true or not. But – for what it's worth – I believe him!" There, he'd said it out loud, and he felt instantly better for committing himself.

"Well…" Alex continued "…about eighteen months ago, Tom here, was standing at the windows, first thing in the morning – watching the sun come up. He spotted dad taking Boris for a walk – dad often did that – he was always a bit of an early riser. Anyway, he watched for a while as Boris chased a couple of the rabbits around on the green outside. Then, the dog darted over the edge of the bank overlooking the river, but he didn't come back. Dad kept clapping his hands at him but, well… you know what he's like – he still didn't come back." Alex smirked down at the dog. "So after a while, dad decided to go down and see where he had gone to. But then he slipped on the dewy grass, sliding over the edge before managing to grasp a few tufts to stop himself going right down onto the rocks. Tom here saw him and ran outside with an old rope to pull him back up, that's right isn't it Tom?" Alex checked.

Tom nodded.

"Anyway, dad wouldn't come back up without Boris. He said he could just see the dog's tail poking out of a rabbit burrow which disappeared toward a solitary massive piece of rock below him: a rock that jutted out of the surrounding embankment. But Boris wouldn't let go, obviously he had got hold of something and wasn't about to drop it – that's the terrier in him. He just kept growling at whatever he had hold of, pulling at it, digging and scratching around it a bit more. Dad got quite cross with Boris at the finish and tried to grab him by the tail and drag him out, but each time he did, the dog disappeared back in, until eventually, dad had to give in and come back up without him to get some of his work equipment. After another hour, with lots of rope to lower himself down, and with a couple of climbing picks and a headlight torch, he finally pulled Boris out.

Now I can personally vouch for that – I remember that bit," assured Alex: "because I was just going off to school and I was a bit worried about dad and the dog. But dad said they weren't any danger. Then, while Tom anchored dad's climbing rope – pinned and tied down at the top – he went back down to see what had got Boris so agitated. Look…" Alex explained again for the sake of clarity "…although dad never told me about *all* of this, this sounds really typical of him, and he had all of that gear in the Land Rover for his archaeology field trips. Anyway, after a while, he said he could see something glinting deep inside the burrow – something deep within a natural fissure in the rock. Boris must have scratched it to the surface but couldn't manage to get it out. But after a few attempts, and after clearing loads of other debris, surely enough, dad managed to drag this out." Alex shoved his hand into his trouser pocket and pulled out the gold coin that Tom had given him days earlier.

"Wow," Conna almost shouted, "is that for real?"

"I guess so," said Alex, "I've checked it against dad's books. And I've seen plenty of them that dad's been handed from the Roman ruins around here. Here, take a look – it's an old Roman coin. It's treasure trove though, so it has to be handed to the coroner's office eventually – it could be important." He flipped it across to Conna and the girls. "But that wasn't the thing that caused the real stir. Deep inside the burrow, I mean, buried *way* inside, lying behind what would have been the cleared debris was a lead container. It took ages to get to it. Dad hung onto a climbing axe while he used a trowel to dig away bit by bit with his other hand. Well, eventually, he managed to get it free and pulled it half out of the fissure in the rock. Tom threw down the end of another rope for him, to tie it securely. Then, he and dad pulled the heavy box up onto the top and laid it on the grass. It was over half a metre long, about twenty centimetres wide and about a hundred and fifty deep. Tom recognised it at once.

To cut a long story short, Boris here, had found the missing Chrono-key that everyone had ever given up hope of seeing again." The dog cocked his head to one side on hearing his name. "It was right here, exactly as described – 'within a crevice in the rock – in the promontory overlooking the river'! Not the higher, rock promontory: Pen-bal-Crag, as everyone had always assumed, but a single black outcrop on the smaller Spanish Battery promontory, '*directly* overlooking the river'. Obviously it was formed from the same rock as the black middens, and frankly, it sticks out like a sore thumb once you know it's there.

Obviously, everyone who had heard the description had made the same mistake. Even though the whole place must have changed over two thousand years, and it would have naturally been covered by tons and tons of soil, the face of the smooth, hard boulder hadn't been – and the box had never really moved that far from reach. No one but the rabbits must have seen it for over two thousand years."

Maddie thumbed the coin before handing it to Bex, who in turn rubbed it, wondering if this was possibly at last, a piece of tangible evidence. But then she quickly decided that it could have come from anywhere – real or not.

"You do realise what this meant to Tom, don't you?" continued Alex. "If the key was still in good order, it could be used to take Tom *back* in time – for the first time since the young Lio had been able to rescue Ashur."

"And was it…" asked Conna – "intact, I mean?"

"Oh yes," confirmed Tom. "As soon as the lead had been carefully stripped from the wooden box inside it, which itself only showed minor damage, there indeed was the wax covered computer, just as the day it was made – in absolutely perfect condition. Stan struggled at first to believe the story of how it had come to be here of course, but the deciding factor had been the bizarre circumstances surrounding our identical watches, which neither of us could work out."

"You mean about the watch only being made not so long ago?" Conna checked.

Now, in particular, Maddie and Bex shot Alex another disappointed glance.

"Tom told me not to tell anyone – it just slipped out to Conna," he shrugged again in apology.

"Quite right!" Tom confirmed.

The girls both pursed their lips.

Tom begged. "I thought that *that* particular truth might make you worry about what I might be dragging you into – before you had a chance to listen to the tale fully."

"Okay, If you say so," Maddie rolled her eyes, as Bex just shook her head.

"But the watch," continued Tom, "the heirloom that was handed to Alex from his father, could have only been made a few years ago. Is that not so Alex?"

Alex nodded. "Well, that much is true; I checked it with the manufacturers."

"What is more," continued Tom, "I only purchased it about six – or is that eighteen – months ago," he frowned again. "Regardless, I found the receipt. Here." he handed the thin paper slip over.

Conna, Maddie and Bex examined the paper and its date, but it was the purchase price that especially made their jaws drop! No wonder there were so few of them! Nevertheless, they still looked confused. They looked from Alex's wrist, back to Tom for further explanation.

Tom continued, "It was on seeing both Stan's watch and mine together, that we compared the serial numbers. And, although mine was brand new, they were patently one and the same. Moreover, when I told Stan that they had only been made for a few short years, and he later checked this with the manufacturer, Stan was persuaded to believe my story – if not in full, then at least a little more?" He paused, "But then, there was also another odd effect… look," Tom conveniently produced his own missing watch from the folds of his jubbah. "I found this yesterday when you'd gone. I must have picked it up and put it in my bedside drawer – somewhere safe!"

Taken aback, Alex shook his head and grinned. As Tom

beckoned to him, he took off the one he was wearing, and together he and Tom passed them to Maddie, Bex and Conna to examine them. The coincidence really was strange, though they were not *identical* at all. Alex's was obviously far older, far more worn than Tom's almost brand new watch, but otherwise, everything, including the few scratches and dents that were on the new one, were exactly repeated on the older one. Eventually, they passed the watches back to Tom. As the four looked-on, Tom touched the two watches together. Immediately, there was a bright, silent and slow flash from his hands. Then, a single blue spark of static electricity bridged the gap from one to the other. From there, as everyone watched, the sparks divided themselves over and over. They seemed to wiggle up both of his arms, only to fizzle out into the air by the time they'd reached his shoulders.

"What happened – how did you do that?" Bex almost accused.

"I don't know," said Tom. "It seems that the timepieces only have to touch against each other for a split second for it to happen."

All five looked at each other, equally taken aback – confused. It was such an odd effect. Maddie in particular remembered back to the now distant day of Tom's accident, and the similar sparks playing around the window frame. Bex continued to look suspiciously at Tom and over at the equipment on the bench – and the Elektra wheel in particular. Tom handed Alex's watch back to him. There was a further moment of silence while everyone wondered what had just happened. The old man stared into space for a long while, evidently still none the wiser himself, and then he prompted Alex to continue with the story of the discovery of the key. So, a little reluctantly, the boy did.

Alex began again. "Well, after a few days of carefully stripping it down, dad, being an expert on ancient gadgets, knew straight away that it was an original – something to do with the way the gears were cut and filed, so he gave Tom a hand to clean and rebuild it."

Bex felt that she had to ask the question that nobody else had. "So, Alex, what did your dad think it was then, another Antikythera device?" She narrowed her eyes.

"Well possibly, I guess that dad recognised it, but he also knew that it was the missing Chrono-key – the one that was built for the Time-Horse."

"What!" Bex almost shouted incredulously.

"Dad already knew," repeated Alex. "It was one of those things that only our family knew about. "Just before grandma passed away she'd been lying in hospital talking to dad for days. Dad told me part of the story, but never all of it. I suppose he only told me because he thought it was such an odd story for her to be telling. As an ex-headmistress she was always so sensible – and dad swore that she wasn't going senile. Anyway, according to him, the tale was 'as daft as it gets'. Grandma had told him that maybe, just maybe, his own dad: Stanley – her husband – who'd died before dad was born, hadn't been his real father anyway. Instead, his real father might have been Greek by birth, and born a long time before anyone would believe. Maybe, she suggested, he might even have travelled through time – on a Time-Machine of sorts – a 'Time-Horse', she called it. Then, of course, the tale unravelled bit by bit. But while dad was flabbergasted at what he called her silly excuse for the cold war fling, it never really bothered him at all who his real father was. He was quite happy just to be her son.

The thing is, dad obviously believed not a word of the ancient tale of this or that, but he did see it as another version of how he got here – his own birth. It might have been a bit disappointing to learn that it was likely that his own dad wasn't who he had been brought up to believe he was, but it was at least interesting. The day before grandma finally passed away, she finally decided to tell dad that his father was, after all, their mysterious neighbour, and her long time pen friend. As dad said, 'patently silly', given that they both looked roughly the same age – but not worth objecting to at this stage in his mother's life. This last part, by the way," pointed out Alex, "wasn't told to me until the Friday before dad left home – and then it was only in the most roundabout way.

That evening, my mam had gone out to see a friend of hers, leaving me, dad and Boris sat alone in front of the fire. So we had this long conversation about the sophistication of ancient civilisations, of amazing machines and computers, of archaeology and how it would be fantastic to be able to travel to the past or turn back the clock and go there. Then, in the middle of it all, dad started to talk about the story that he had been told by his mother. It was about one such mysterious machine, and how, by the strangest set of circumstances, it had ended up not a million miles away from this exact spot.

Later, when mam came home, I went off to bed but couldn't get to sleep for thinking about it. I lay awake for a while listening to them talking softly to each other downstairs. And then, on the following morning, dad told me that he would be leaving on this private journey of exploration.

Well, within a couple of days, on the Sunday, the two-seater Land Rover was packed up with all of his expedition equipment and most of his other portable belongings – under the canvas cover in the rear cargo bed. It certainly looked to me that he would be away a long time. After hugging me and telling me to be brave and to look after mam, dad left home."

As Alex continued the tale, Conna was able to confirm that he remembered standing on the Spanish Battery with Alex. As the Scandinavian ferry passed close by, the two waved Stan off while he stood on its rear deck as it headed for Amsterdam. And with that, he was gone.

"Then, a couple of weeks later – a year ago – when we found out at my birthday party that the Land Rover had been found abandoned in the desert, everyone began to panic. No one told me at the time, but machine-pistol shells littered the area and there had been no trace of my dad and the travel partner they remembered him with. But no one even knew who the second traveller was – maybe a hitchhiker. It looked like dad had been taken hostage by terrorists, but when no ransom demands had been made, well... mostly everyone assumed the worst.

After Tom's accident, and after what he told me in the hospital, loads of his short version of the tale sounded so familiar. And as daft as it all was, I decided I wasn't going to give up hope after all." Alex wondered about what he'd last night almost finally accepted; he avoided looking at Conna.

Not even Conna had known Alex to speak like this before, and that he had kept to himself all of what he had just now told them. It was heartening to see Alex share all of this now, although he wondered where it was all headed: that is until Alex blurted it all out.

"Look, After stripping down and rebuilding the 'replica device', as dad had insisted on calling it for the sake of appearances, as an archaeologist Tom had allowed him to see and examine the Hippo-Chronos itself. Straight away Dad was impressed at what it appeared to be – some kind of ancient power generating machine. Just like us, he'd also been curious as to what its *real* purpose was – not just the purpose given by Tom. But try as he might, while he even accepted that the technology *was* from the same era as the Antikythera device, there was no absolute reason why he couldn't at least believe that it *was* as old as Tom said. Although it certainly didn't appear to be that old, frankly, well, look for yourselves, it looks about forty or fifty years old at the most. The springs alone would have been heavily rusted had it been anything older than an antique clock. But that was why, taking a chance, Tom had enrolled dad in the scheme to help him test the machine after all this time. And, as far as dad was concerned, it was also because of his mother's last wish for her son to help 'Billy' if he ever asked him. That's right Tom, isn't it?"

Tom again nodded and went on to confirm that after an exhaustive week of questioning, much as this week had been, (although Alex's dad was far more direct with his questions), Stan, had reluctantly gone along with what he was still sceptical about, but didn't question any longer. Besides, it suited him to get away for a while: he had never been to Giza and it was agreed that it would be Tom who would foot the bill for the entire expedition. He had also offered to pay him into the bargain, which Stan had refused. The only idea Stan absolutely, steadfastly, refused to entertain was

that the two could be anything but brothers or half-brothers –
anything other than believe that they might be father and son.

Maddie held up her hand. "Tom... or whoever? Why couldn't
the machine be tested right here?"

"Oh," said Tom, "I can answer that quite simply. Some of you
have already witnessed what a commotion the machine makes each
time it is used. And each time it is used, trouble almost always
follows. If it had been deliberately tested on the spot, who knows
what might have come about. No, far better that it be tested
somewhere more remote. We took it to Alexandria, so that if it was
to break down, the rider – I myself – would at least end up stranded
both in the time and place I was comfortable with."

"So anyway," continued Alex, "that was why Tom and dad left
to drive all the way to Alexandria with both the Hippo-Chronos and
the Chrono-key in the back."

"But not the Cosmos-key?" Conna checked.

"No Conna," Alex explained patiently, "that was why they were
going back to Giza, to find the only remaining Cosmos-key – stored
inside the sarcophagus of Alexander."

"Oh, right!" The penny dropped again – "and that was in Giza?"

"Not necessarily Conna," cautioned Tom again, "we had to
search for it." Now taking responsibility for the storytelling back
from Alex, Tom at long last began to talk in the first person, about
himself – Tom – not Helio, Lio or Billy. It was time to 'get real'!

CHAPTER 34:

A Trip to the Farm

"All that was known of the last whereabouts of the sarcophagus of Alexander," continued Tom "was that Ptolemy planned to remove the relic from the city of Alexandria shortly after the sea battle for the city.

However, whether the sarcophagus had even made it out of the Mouseion before the fire was not known. There was only one way to find out – go look for it! Nevertheless, given that Ptolemy's troops were about to retreat for the Nile in order to regroup around Giza, and given also that the distant Kings of Egypt were also buried around that place, it seemed a sensible place to begin looking. Although, rather than risk causing a commotion at the Pyramids themselves, Alex's father Stan decided to return to an area which was a little more remote: a place which could also be more assured to be friendlier to receive us – Kyrros' farm at the hill of Drodos.

Firstly though, Alex's father and I had to get there, and that was not without some more mundane complications. For the first time in my life, I had to apply for a passport: in the only name I knew would be acceptable to the authorities – Billy Woods, granted national citizenship in 1963. Although," Tom smiled to himself cheekily, "when I posed for the photograph, Alex's father insisted that I apply theatrical make-up to my face to age me by twenty years! However, the main problem was far more delicate. You may or may not know that six months ago I was due to have a quite serious operation – I needed a heart bypass."

Alex raised his eyebrows: Tom hadn't spoken of this to anyone before – including him.

"It had been scheduled for the past year, and I was not able to change my place in the queue. Therefore, I decided to go through with it and then wait until I was at least properly mobile before taking the risk of travel – which was, in any case, strictly against doctors' orders – and air travel especially. However, after a further few months, I decided that I felt well enough.

For the sake of confidentiality, Alex's father did not tell anyone about the true nature of his expedition and he certainly didn't want anyone to know that I was accompanying him – for many reasons. Nevertheless, we left on the shortest 'overland' route through continental Europe. Taking the overnight ferry from Tynemouth to Amsterdam, we then drove from Holland, through Germany and Switzerland and into Italy to take another vessel from Ancona to Alexandria. The first part of the trip took only three days and the ferry to Alexandria another four. Within the week then, we had arrived at our destination. Unfortunately, however, in the vast congested port of Africa that the city had become, we immediately, but unknowingly picked up attention that would later cause us some trouble.

It really was quite amazing to see what the place had turned into – absolutely unrecognisable for anyone who might have been there to witness its glorious ancient past. The noise and smog of the crowded streets, the skyline crammed with the many skyscrapers and minarets and the sheer volume of vehicular and pedestrian traffic was quite exhilarating. But sadly, it seemed to Alex's father especially, quite disrespectful to the ancient sites within this once splendid city. There were few ancient remains. Gone was the Pharos Tower – the lighthouse – and gone was the palace, along with all traces of where the Mouseion buildings had once stood.

We passed the only sad remains recognisable, those of the Serapeion: one column and a few small, quite ugly, carved sphinxes that had always stood around the square in front of it. We did not stay for long, stopping only to check its precise geographical location by GPS. We did not leave the Land Rover unattended or otherwise risk anyone trying to take our precious cargo. And so, we drove straight out of the city, knowing only that the landscape and the shape of the harbour had changed so much that most of it was now submerged beneath the sea.

Regardless, a full day's drive later along the reasonably well developed highways, we arrived at the area of the Pyramids of Giza and began to try to locate, at least approximately, the site of the farm there. The area was now entirely built up within the sprawling city of Giza, now the third largest city in Egypt. Unsurprisingly, there were no immediately obvious remains of the farm buildings. However, it was known to us that the farm had been perched on the only small hill in the otherwise flat landscape that would still be visible from the pyramids in the distance. As we made for the highest of the undulations directly, I must say that throughout the whole journey, Alex's father was excellent company. It was he who did all of the driving. Sadly, I never did learn how to myself. Although he was perhaps still sceptical of the whole affair, he never did voice this opinion – he stayed diligent throughout – never being less than one hundred per cent true to our joint goal. It was though, as I said earlier, unfortunate that seeing our foreign number plates, we were followed. Obviously it was assumed that as we had driven the Land Rover all the way from England, we must have had something of value to transport with us in the back. In fact, this much was true. Apart from the horse, in order to be able to tell the time with pinpoint accuracy wherever we were, I took my own brand new and most valuable watch." Tom flashed it again, smiling. "Accordingly, as we made our way to the small hill on the edge of the desert, we were unaware of being spied upon.

Driving slowly over the sand and directly onto the top of the barren hill, we stopped – although nothing was left of the farm at the hill of Drodos. Only the water-well remained at the foot of it – Kyrros' secret bank – rebuilt countless times over the years – from which I was happy to draw enough water to fill our kettle. Within a few minutes, ever the professional archaeologist, Alex's father had erected a canvas windbreak, and he had the camping stove primed, lit and ready to boil the kettle for tea. It was only now that both of us realised: neither of us had thought the plan through any further than that point. We sat and drank the black tea while we pondered what to do next.

I repeated my intention to simply change my clothing into the long white jubbah that I had brought with me for the purpose, I loaded the pre-set Chrono-key, installed it into the already wound-up horse and then simply hoped that it would transport me into the past as I had planned. Remember, it had not been used since I travelled here from the sixties to the eighties. Alex's father, on the other hand, had no need to change his way of dress from the shorts and collarless granddad-shirt he wore. It was his duty to stay in the Land Rover and wait for me to return. Once in the past – no matter whether I was away hours, days, weeks or months, I would return to that same spot at exactly one hour after I had left. Duly, we, that is to say, your father Alex, rolled the machine down the ramp from the back of the Land Rover where it got stuck immediately in the soft, sandy ground. I was unable to help" – Tom patted his chest as a reminder of his operation.

"So what did you plan to do?" Maddie asked. "Once in the past, that is."

"In truth, I don't know: get back to the farm, borrow a donkey or a camel from the servants and somehow locate Ptolemy's forces and make my way to meet him perhaps. Though I knew I would not dare to explain who I was. If I did, I thought, the boy king would understandably, almost certainly, seize the machine and use it to change history. He might perhaps eventually turn back the Battle of the Nile and all of subsequent events – everything we know! All I really knew was that I had one chance to find the Cosmos-key, otherwise I would only be able to go on moving through time, 'on the spot', so to speak. And to achieve all I wanted to do, or more correctly undo, especially to lessen the chances of failure, I desperately needed the missing Cosmos-key. However, as I have already said, the only way to achieve that goal was to go and look for it.

It was starting to grow dark as Alex's father began to clear away and briefly wipe our two cups, while I myself checked the Hippo-Chronos to see that everything was set properly. Bear in mind that it was some time since I had last used it. I wasn't entirely sure that I had programmed it properly, but at last I satisfied myself that everything was ready to go. With the stars starting to appear above, and the sound of a very early owl hooting somewhere nearby, I checked my watch. Next, I picked up the small leather pouch that held my medicines and a few other things. I took my place on the machine and for the first time in many years, gently pushed forward the lever. As I did, another owl, much nearer again, hooted its reply in a slightly higher pitch, and my companion wished me luck.

Stan folded his arms, waiting, I guessed, to see if anything would happen. Anything that is, apart from me proving myself wrong and making a complete fool of myself. But then, as I held up my hand in salute to him, I saw him slowly put up both of his hands in return. I looked at him curiously, not knowing what he meant by the gesture. That is, until I heard the metallic click of a machine-pistol being cocked behind me. The little Arabic language that I have was too archaic, the gunman's pronunciation too different to understand what the experienced field archaeologist obviously had. Calmly, Stan told me not to move or turn around. There were two men approaching – pointing guns. Two voices called out, and Alex's father told me not to get off the horse. Do you know though, for all I was unsure of the situation, I decided not to be scared or frightened. Instead, that familiar old feeling of earth-shattering disappointment kicked in: that after all this time, all of this waiting, I would not have the chance to find out whether the Hippo-Chronos would still take me to the past after all.

Whether it was out of frustration, anger or stupidity, I refused to pull back the lever. Instead, I sat tight as the machine began to make the noise that I had not heard since my youth. I looked slowly behind me at the men in camouflage jackets, and wearing black and white headdresses and sunglasses. They began to shout directly at me, but all I did was hold up my hands. I could see out of the corner of my eye that my companion had stood up and was walking to meet the others, and myself in the middle. He was talking all the while, trying to calm them down as the noise of the machine grew.

The two robbers were getting angry, starting to shout what were clearly commands to stop the machine, but I was not about to risk damaging it, it was already picking up speed. The first gunman cocked his own hand-pistol and fired a single shot directly over my head. Then, the second let off a short, noisy burst into the air before shouting at us again. Stan was beside me now, standing slightly behind me as I recognised the imminent signs of the machine's departure. So I shuffled forward, turned to him and shouted above the noise, "Stan, get on!" Thank goodness I did not have to tell him twice. For all he was not convinced of what I had previously described would happen, he had, in that instant, finally trusted me completely. As his backside hit the saddle and the gunmen began to point their weapons directly at us, a storm of dry sand erupted around us and into their astonished faces. Then the horse leapt – for the first time in over two thousand years, *back* through time!

As the Hippo-Chronos landed, within an instant and bearing the weight of two adults this time, the front, damaged hoof almost snapped off. This pitched us forward and to the side. The extra stress in turn buckled the rear leg on the same side and, once again, it threw both of its riders unceremoniously to the ground. Thankfully though, it was not too violent a landing in the centre of the deserted farmyard. By his reaction, Alex's father thought our night-time jaunt hysterically funny. He immediately clambered to his feet and patted off the dust and sand. Whatever had just happened was not only miraculous, but, as Stan had realised, quite unbelievable. Not that he was as yet convinced that he had been transported through time. Only, as far as he was concerned, somewhere else in the near dark – and out of immediate danger. And that, for now, was more than enough for him.

Ordinarily, I might have done the same and burst out laughing with sheer relief. But unfortunately, as I landed, not only did my left elbow crash into the ground, the shock of the fall heaved my ribcage, almost tearing the stitches to my sternum. The pain almost knocked me unconscious and caused me to shout out uncontrollably. Trying to contain my discomfort, and looking around us at the state of the buildings, I realised that the farm had been all but destroyed – though at least, not the bare walls. The roofs of the farm buildings had been stripped along with the upper floors. Everything made of timber had been removed – even the wooden block that was the sundial had been taken – along with the wind paddle I had made as a boy. I was also slightly disappointed in not seeing my childhood friends there – especially the Macedonian bagpipe player. Evidently, in their flight from Alexandria the refugees had centred on this area by invitation. But on their eventual return only a few weeks later, they had, like locusts, stripped everything they could carry – to try and rebuild their own homes in the city. I could only shake my head, wondering what Kyrros and Miriam would have thought of this returned favour. But then I realised that they would probably have been perfectly accepting. The refugees would, in all honesty, have very little left – while to Kyrros this was just a second home. I only hoped his workers, my friends, had found somewhere new and safe to live out their lives. As soon as I could begin to sit, Stan helped pick me up gingerly and patted my satchel to find the painkillers. Then he ran to the well, so that he could fetch a drink of water for me.

Twenty minutes later, still unable to fully accept what had happened, Stan had by then manhandled and hidden the machine in the empty shell of the house. He came back to check that I was at least able to walk. Thankfully I was. I would have gone on alone, but he saw that I was in no fit state. Therefore, he said he would accompany me. So, to our amusement, ever the improviser, he removed his jacket and short trousers. Thank goodness he was wearing that long grandfather shirt! He tied the centre of it around with his belt. Not the most convincing costume – it looked like a very short chiton – but at least it did make him look vaguely like he belonged – like a foreigner perhaps, or a slave. And so it was that we made our way into the house ourselves and lay quietly all night beside the machine."

CHAPTER 35:

A Final Audience

Tom carried straight on: "I was most surprised to be awoken at dawn by the crowing of a lone cockerel. Though how the scrawny bird had managed to survive out there was quite beyond me. With another painkiller inside me it was not long before we began to make our way. Although, in the absence of all other animals, we had no choice other than to set off on foot, toward the distant pyramids and the Nile, to attempt to track down Ptolemy.

By mid-day, as the sun scorched overhead, my eyes started to burn and water. Silly of me, after all those years of planning, I forgot to take my eye-protectors. Seeing the discomfort I was in, Stan reached into his pocket and lent me these," Tom pointed to the arm of the chair and at the Ray-Bans. "But it was then that we were spotted by two of Ptolemy's lookouts. Within a short while, they rode out in chariots to challenge us. Just in time, Stan reminded me to place the glasses and my watch into the satchel. As they approached, they began to shout. And then, almost upon us, I told my incredulous partner: 'Leave this to me.'

In a passable imitation of Kyrros, although clearly I do not have his deep voice, I called out, 'My name is Helio of Aegilia. I am the assistant to the engineer of His Majesty King Ptolemy – take me to him at once!' Now, quite unsure of themselves, both charioteers wondered. Then, they decided that they would be best served by doing exactly as we said, just in case I was telling the truth. At that, we were carried off toward the pyramids.

There were no more than perhaps five thousand of the king's elite troops there, beginning to collect together for the one last battle of Ptolemy XIII's choosing. Alexandria had already completely fallen to Julius Caesar. Though, at least, in magnanimity, he did allow all former citizens to return to the city forthwith – to rebuild it and to try to rebuild their own shattered homes and lives. By now, however, Ptolemy was all but defeated in advance. There was little left of his once great navy, now so badly in need of repair. His own troops struggled not to be demoralised in front of the battle hardened Romans, and his many alliances with other countries were breaking down as Caesar made it known that those who took up arms against him would be 'persona non grata' – unwelcome persons – effectively his enemy for life. Gradually, those troops who were either hired or pledged to Ptolemy began to wander back to where they came from, leaving the Egyptian King largely on his own. Many other troops would eventually rally to him though, including those of his sister Arsinoë, already beginning to see that the Romans were bent on complete domination and looting of the country. They were plainly not, as they had announced, only there to bolster up Cleopatra's troops. News had spread that the many treasures of the city had already been stripped and removed to Rome. Even both of the supposed bodies of Alexander on public show in the Sema and the Serapeion had gone missing. They had also heard of the horrors that awaited Cleopatra's enemies in the subterranean dungeon. All were determined that they would not suffer that fate without a fight to the death.

As the chariots approached along the flanks of the great Sphinx, Alex's father and I guessed correctly that the largest of the tents, directly beneath the gaze of the monument, was indeed that of Ptolemy. With a little educated guesswork and deduction – and a pinch of luck – we had pinpointed the location of the camp of the last true Pharaoh. Whilst I was relieved to have found him, Stan was simply flabbergasted that here, at last, all around him, was the solid proof that I had indeed been telling the truth all along. There he was, surrounded by the white uniformed Egyptian army. Not only that, but there in front of him was the Sphinx – already ancient of

317

course, but fully intact. The monument's face had been re-carved a few times, but it was more or less just as it appears now, though less worn by the desert sands.

Now, with the undeniable realisation that they had been somehow transported to the past, Alex's father had no other choice than to capitulate. The Hippo-Chronos machine, exactly as described by his strange neighbour, Billy Woods, had in fact been real all along! Undoubtedly, this was then followed by the dawning realisation that, if that was true, and time-travel was a reality, then perhaps his mother had also been right all along. Perhaps his neighbour – Billy, or Lio – myself could even be his own... It was, he said, too bizarre for him to actually say the word. However, he began to look at me anew. Certainly, we were the same size and build. We had always been alike, could even be taken as brothers – but father and son? Even as the chariot stopped abruptly at the entrance to the tent, he still looked across at me – clearly wondering.

Exchanges were made between the charioteers and the guards. They disappeared inside the tent, leaving the two of us to wait outside. After only a few moments, Ptolemy himself emerged hurriedly, flanked by two bodyguards. Shorter now, without the platforms on his shoes, and now somewhat dishevelled without the Nemes on his head, still, he now looked curiously more like a real man and a king. I was surprised at the look of him, at how he had seemed to grow in true confidence.

Ptolemy looked quickly, almost excitedly at the faces of the two figures stood beside the chariots. But then, just as quickly, the hopeful smile on his face subsided as he realised that it was not the young boy he'd expected it to be. Instead, goodness knows what he thought of us, especially Stan in his strange garb.

'Yes,' said the king disappointedly, 'what is it? Why do you wish to see me?'

'Your majesty,' I addressed him, 'I have come to ask a personal favour – from the boy you know as your friend Helio.'

'Yes,' the king smiled and rallied his spirits a little. 'What can I do for the boy?'

'Your majesty, Helio asks that myself and my assistant be taken to the place where the greatest of all heroes – the memory of the Greek ruler of the world is kept alive.' Of course, few people knew of Alexander's body – assuming it was here – it had so far travelled shrouded in complete secrecy.

'Yes?' said the king suspiciously, attempting to reassess the stranger.

'Your majesty,' I continued, 'your chief engineer and the librarian both placed an object for safekeeping at the foot of the body itself – something of great importance.'

Ptolemy knew exactly what it was. To ensure due reverence, he had personally supervised the transferral of Alexander's body into the portable sarcophagus. He had watched Alexander sealed-into it with the world at his feet. I tried to let the young king know just how important the object was. 'My king,' I said, 'This object has the power to help me change the whole history of the world. In the future, it can stop the Romans' attempted domination of the earth for all time – but only if it is retrieved now.'

Ptolemy stroked his chin. 'Can it save me?' he asked.

I shook my head regretfully.

'Then, can it save Egypt?' he asked wistfully.

'No, my king,' I answered truthfully. 'I'm afraid nothing can.'

Ptolemy contemplated his fate stoically, he looked back into my eyes – as if he was looking at the boy he had seemingly once met before. 'Then tell me,' he asked, 'why should I hand it over to you?'

All I could do was look directly back into the eyes of the king. 'Because, your majesty,' I answered earnestly, 'if you do not, the Roman way of life, this fascism, their morals, their eternal lust for war and their lack of *real* honour will dominate the world for the rest of time. The world will be forever enslaved by them.'

Ptolemy thought the scenario through, seeming to see where it might all end; their ruthless approach and intolerance on a far greater scale than even the admittedly oppressive Egyptian way. Perhaps it was also the way he had been personally treated by Caesar that made him decide. The king looked back at me. 'And if I open the sarcophagus one last time and allow you to take the object – you can one day stop this?'

I looked at the determined face already resigned to personal defeat. 'Your majesty, rest assured,' I vouched solemnly, 'I will try my very best to do so'.

Ptolemy rubbed his bristled, no longer daily shaven scalp. He looked across at Alex's father, and at something which I only just noticed myself – a silvered pendant which poked out of Stan's shirt – my old athlete pendant. 'Then perhaps the future is already written!' The king turned to walk back into his tent.

Stan looked at me, wondering what to do, having been able to only half-follow the archaic pronunciation of our words.

Shortly afterwards, having had only the briefest time to contemplate his likely fate, Ptolemy reappeared with his headdress in place. He stood proudly with his shoulders back, carrying an old ceremonial crook in his hand. Resignedly, he admitted, 'In my whole life I met only one person that I actually managed to trust. He was a young boy with the same name you spoke of, Helio… just an ordinary youth. In the past weeks, I have often wondered whether he managed to escape Alexandria with his family as they deserved. Though now, it seems that I myself will not. Perhaps, this is the way it should be. That the kings and rulers of this earth should only be allowed to live in luxury, knowing that at all times they are responsible to their people. That if they do not act responsibly, at any time their own life might be held forfeit.'

As a boy, I had at first pitied him. Later, I began to like – even trust him. But now, from the perspective of my much greater age and experience, I had nothing but the greatest admiration and respect for the young man standing in front of me. Without me saying as much, he had gathered that his time was limited. He was destined neither to be a great king, nor even pass on the throne of Egypt to his own offspring. And yet, even as his own inept generals plotted to take over command from him, he bore the headdress as a true king. 'Yes,' he decided, 'come with me – luckily, you are just in time!'

Ptolemy dismissed the two guards and led the two strangers directly toward the head of the Sphinx. Below the huge stone head of the animal was a narrow slot in the monument; rubble lay all around it. Beside it was a small party of stonemasons who chipped expertly at a large replacement stone. It was obviously destined to replace the one that had been previously hacked out of the beast's recently opened chest. There, Ptolemy stopped and turned. 'As long as you both shall live, and as long as your ancestors shall live, you will never reveal the riddle of the Sphinx.' It was not a request. We both nodded solemnly in absolute agreement. 'Take warning,' The king said, 'any attempt to break in forcibly will send out a sheet of liquid flame to devour anyone who would dare to disturb the peace of my forebears.' He pointed at a narrow slit in the neck above him. At that, he began to squeeze through the narrow gap that was the entrance to a small chamber. He beckoned to us to follow. Gradually, in the dim light, we saw a heavy bronze door.

Now, he opened it, revealing a long descending staircase. Stan and I followed Ptolemy down almost blindly. As he reached the bottom of the long flight, we realised that we were now inside a complex of tunnels that extended way below the sculpture above. The tunnels were already dimly and mysteriously lit by oil lamps placed at regular intervals, but the steep descent left us wondering how deep we were going. The king led us on into a long, subterranean hall which was full of variously sized and shaped solid stone sarcophagi: more than thirty in all. Stan tugged at my sleeve, 'You know that in our time no one knows that this is here, don't you?'

'And neither should they.' I reminded him.

'Of course not,' agreed my companion readily before plodding on. Stan's eyes were wide open as if lost in a marvellous dream, knowing that what he had been shown could never be revealed.

At the end was another ramp, and there we entered another larger chamber with perhaps fifty or more sarcophagi. Then the chamber dropped again to a small landing which led three ways, left, right and straight ahead. The whole place was vast. Ptolemy stopped:

'May your soul never rest in peace if you betray this final secret,' he said meaningfully. 'And may you eternally forfeit the respect of your forebears if you ever in future reveal this final resting place – unless it is to someone you would trust with your own life.'

The solemn oath was not lost on either of us. Neither of us would ever betray the secret location of the tomb that lay directly ahead. 'Look away,' said Ptolemy, before again using the key to open the stone door. It moved automatically, and all three of us walked steadily inside.

As that last stone door opened into the tomb, Ptolemy stood until it was fully hinged back against the walls and his eyes were adjusted to the reflected golden light inside. The room was a perfect replica of the one below the Serapeion, but instead of the heavy open sarcophagus, two bronze trestles held up the electrum sarcophagus. The foot wide oil channel that ran around the perimeter of this chamber was bridged at the door by a wide wooden floor panel. Excitedly, Stan, the archaeologist, made to step forward past the king, before Ptolemy silently held out his arm to bar his way. He looked sternly at the visitor with admonishment, pointedly fixing him to the spot. Then, he exaggeratedly stepped across the wooden panel. 'To stand on it will cause it to rotate and seal the whole tomb forever,' warned the king. Now, Ptolemy let his visitors past to gaze through the glass panel and upon the face of Alexander. After a moment, I removed the carrying poles that locked the upper and lower halves of the sarcophagus together, and as Ptolemy looked on, we carefully removed the upper half of the case and laid it aside.

Stan looked in wonder at the sight of the fully clothed golden body laid-out as if in sleep, while I gently grasped the orb at Alexander's feet and removed it from its safekeeping. 'Come along,' I said to Alex's father, as he stood transfixed, trying to record every detail in his mind so that he could at least describe the face to his son. The task complete, the sarcophagus was again sealed. Ptolemy and I stepped out of the chamber, leaving Alex's father to stand and stare alone in contemplation for a further few moments.

Ptolemy looked directly at me, 'I must now lock this place

forever,' he decided. 'I will not risk the betrayal of this tomb to my sister, or the Romans – who knows what would become of the royal remains.' I nodded in agreement, and with that, after waiting for Stan to exit, the king stepped deliberately onto the wooden bridge. As we all walked swiftly back up the ramp, we heard the heavy, echoing rasp of stone blocks moving. And as we reached the surface, we heard the repeated, solid clonks of various locking mechanisms dropping into place one last time. The bronze door was closed, and we squeezed out into the blinding sunlight again. There, Ptolemy signalled to the expert masons to complete their task. 'Be sure not to leave any trace whatsoever,' he warned them.

Once again standing outside of Ptolemy's tent, enormously grateful for his understanding – and knowing his eventual fate – for the first and only time in my entire life I was tempted to offer the king a way to change history and defeat the Romans. However, of course, I realised I could not. Given the chain of events that had already been caused by the lax adherence to the Chronology Society's code of conduct, who knows what further disastrous events may occur if I did. Perhaps the modern world would not have existed."

Tom turned to them all. "You, my friends, may not have been born. Perhaps the opportunity would never have arisen for me to meet Stan and make it back to find the King. All might have become the most cataclysmic paradox imaginable.

So, instead, we climbed back onto the chariots in order to head toward the farm, and as we did, each gave our thanks again – Stan in his strange, modern Greek accent. Then, he took hold of the handrail to steady himself.

Unexpectedly, just before we rode off, Ptolemy called out, 'Helio, remember me to the future my friend!' It was then that I realised he had guessed my real identity all along – and that he had indeed heard the rumour of the Time-Horse. Furthermore, he now knew it to be entirely true. And yet, he had accepted my word that no good would become of seizing it for himself. The only way to eventually stop the Romans was my way: to let history run its painful course. It was with great respect for the bravery of that young man that I called back from the moving chariot, 'I will, my king – my friend!'

The pains in my chest suddenly grew as the tent receded in the distance.

The charioteers left us as commanded, at the walls of the farm. Once inside, we immediately set about fitting the Cosmos-key into its rightful place in the Hippo-Chronos. Thankfully, neither part had been damaged. Even after their long time apart, everything still fitted perfectly, slipping into place with engineering precision. Still inside the ruined farmhouse, we began to stack some of the clay bricks which lay around us from where the roof timbers had been wrenched free. It was the only way to support the machine upright – the two twisted legs being far too weak to take even the horse's own weight. We propped it upright and, I have to confess, that time the effort nearly killed me. But then, finally, the horse was ready to go. Already programmed, it would bring us directly here, on the day we had left on the ferry – and in time for Alex's birthday.

Then, something went wrong! Don't ask me what, I do not know. Sometimes, it seems, the horse almost has a mind and a will of its own. This time, it was certainly not the programming, which both of us checked.

After the exertion of hauling the machine upright, and several more painkillers to get back my composure, eventually, I sat clutching my chest atop the horse's back while Stan checked the steadiness of the brick stacks. Patently though, they were not steady enough to take the added weight of another passenger. I decided that we should change places so that he wouldn't be left behind. After all, this was my own time, and a problem of my own doing. However, Stan insisted that rather than abandon my whole plan, I should get back home and make for the hospital before the pains got worse. And besides, he reasoned, I would then be able to make the machine more stable and return for him later. That was when he advised me that if anything went wrong, and I needed help, I would be able to trust Alex here. It did seem to make some sense at the time, so we both agreed that this should happen.

Then, after a further thought, he made a request. That as he was already in ancient Roman Egypt, he would be allowed to spend a full year in that world before being collected – the opportunity of a lifetime for an archaeologist. It was, we both knew, fraught with dangers for him, but, if anything went wrong, I could always return to the farm one year earlier in order to rescue him a few seconds after I had left. As I said, it all seemed to make perfect sense, so I agreed. The only material change it would make to Stan's life would be that even though he would eventually return home on the same day we'd left for the ferry, he would be a year older. No one else would be any the wiser. Without further ado, I put on Stan's glasses and started to fasten my watch. Meanwhile, Stan took the satchel in case he should need it. Finally I wished him well and sat up on the horse. Then I pushed forward the return lever, still trying to adjust my watch strap.

At first, everything seemed alright, the familiar whine building steadily as the moving parts picked up speed. But then the brick pillars started to shift with the vibration and Stan ran towards me to grasp them and stop the stack from collapsing. Now, the horse began to jump and buck wildly, something it had never done before.

'I can't hold it,' shouted Stan, 'you'll have to stop the machine!'

But if I do, I thought, *then what will happen? How much damage might be caused? And will either of us ever get back?* The horse continued to buck dangerously. Something had obviously gone wrong with it. *Perhaps,* I thought, *sand had got into the machine.* I looked at Stan's face as I realised that the machine was about to reach its full power-burst-initiation sequence, and this time I decided I must abort. But as I pulled the lever back, the burst of warm wind knocked Stan backwards, the brick support fell apart and the ball of light enveloped me, almost blinding me this time – despite the Ray-Bans. As it did, the machine started to tumble, both sideways and head over heels. I cascaded through the air, almost falling off. My watch hand struck something hard and I damaged both my hand and the timepiece. But all the while, I managed to cling to its neck for dear life.

The noise was far greater than usual, my ears felt like they would burst. I did not know whether I was going to make it back. This time, the journey seemed endless, but the next thing I felt was a great deal of pain as I landed heavily in the attic room above here and the floor gave way. It sent me crashing through the ceiling to land right here. Unfortunately, this time, it further tore at the stitches in my chest, reopening the wound again. Furthermore, the fall broke my arm into the bargain."

Tom sat back. "And that, as they say, is where you came to my rescue, disappointingly, exactly one year later than planned!"

PART IV:
ZERO HOUR

IT IS EASY TO SIT UP AND TAKE NOTICE,

WHAT IS DIFFICULT IS GETTING UP AND TAKING
ACTION

Honore De Balzac 19th Cent AD

CHAPTER 36:

Trouble

At long last, Tom had closed the loop. Now everyone could breathe a sigh of relief. Alex even began to chuckle to himself at Tom's storytelling prowess. He looked at Conna, who began to smile and chuckle too. The girls looked at each other in amazement, and then they too caught the contagious humour. Now, even Tom smiled broadly – his eyes sparkling like a child's – willing everyone to believe.

"I don't know why Tom," choked Alex, "but now I believe every word of it, don't you Conna?"

"Yeah Alex," Conna agreed. "Yes Tom – of course I do."

"And so do I" Maddie stood up abruptly and crossed over to give Tom a hug. Only Bex didn't come right out and say it, but she was sorely tempted. All she wanted was that one piece of proper – that is, real – tangible evidence.

"So what do you want now Tom?" offered Maddie. "What do you actually need us for?"

Tom dissolved into tears of relief. At last, he had finally managed to convince them that he had not been making the whole story up. "Well…" he said falteringly "…I suppose we should plan out between us what has to happen next. It will take us several trips to repair the damage that has already been done. And as a safety precaution, to minimise the risk of something else going wrong in-between those trips, we should carry out everything in quick succession – even though we will have to completely abandon all of the strict ethical rules of the Chronology Society of Alexandria. Sadly, although I have been sorely tempted, I could never really have dared risk doing all of these things myself – the risk of bumping into myself and causing another major time-paradox was always too great. But preventing the stealth weapon, the Hippo-Tempus from being used effectively again is the major priority, and for that I must risk personally returning to Alexandria myself, although I would like one of you to accompany me as a backup – Alex, would you?

"Yes, Tom," he said unequivocally.

"However, first," Tom continued, "Alex's father must be rescued from the farm. We must get him out of danger. For that task, we need someone light so that we do not overtax the machine this time."

Maddie suddenly heard herself saying, "I'll do it Tom."

"Really?" asked Tom. "It is dangerous work, especially as you must go alone."

"I know," she assured him, "but I weigh the least, and I'd like to go." She looked at Alex, "Please Tom, let me help, for Alex's sake. I want him to get his father back – if it's really possible. No-one should lose a parent while they're young."

"Alright," he said, "you go."

Alex looked into her eyes and smiled, guessing why she'd spoken up. He thanked his new friend for her unselfish offer.

"The next task is to keep a promise made many, many years ago. For that, we need an excellent swimmer – someone physically strong."

"I can do that Tom," Conna almost yelled, putting up his hand. "Except…" he admitted, "I'm not all that good a swimmer…" he trailed off. He didn't look around, but he wondered whether she might speak up.

Finally, sheepishly, Bex committed herself, perhaps a little less than enthusiastically. "Okay, then," she offered. "I'll go too – I'll go with Conna."

Conna smiled triumphantly. "Great," he said, trying not to get too carried away.

"So, how do we start?" asked Alex.

"I should think, by clearing the room," answered Tom. "If everything goes according to plan, there will be much commotion here, I am certain."

Alex and his friends hadn't much thought of the practicalities. "Okay," they each agreed. They began to move the piles of books into the empty bedroom next door. After that, Tom asked the girls to tape up the windows with masking tape, marking each glass pane with a large X. While they did, the boys busied themselves moving out the models and the collapsible benches. The sofa and chair, Tom advised, would be too heavy to be blown around, but it would perhaps be best placed around the walls of the room. The only remaining large object – the armillary – was moved into the far corner.

"What's next then Tom," asked Conna.

"Well", he suggested, "we need to gather all of the equipment together. And for that, I think we should split up for now. Girls," he turned to face them, "I think it would be best for you to return home. Bring some appropriate clothes – at least a bathing suit and some warm clothes for Bex. The boys can borrow some of my own – they will be good enough for what I have in mind. And while the girls are gone, he turned back to Alex and Conna, if you follow me to the workshop outside – the rocket house – I will point out the other things that will be required."

Boris began to bark excitedly at the feeling of positive energy in the room.

"And what about you?" Tom asked the dog. "Surely you've already played your part, it was you who found the missing key. The dog stood up and began to paw the air. For the first time ever, Tom was now confident that everything might turn out as he planned.

By three o'clock in Conna's family household, the atmosphere was electric. The unhappily married couple once more looked at the clock before Conna's dad wondered whether to suggest again that they call the police to report him missing. It had been a long day.

From the early hours of the morning, both of them had sat and discussed the problem of their wayward son – although in truth, it was a pretty one-sided conversation. She had always given everything to him, she insisted: games, clothes, gadgets. And yet, she complained bitterly, this was the way he repaid her. Her husband listened again as she repeated the causes of everything that had gone wrong with her life. From the time they could have bought the house opposite for a snip, to the 'pill' incident – and now to being passed over once again last month for the position of Queen's Councillor.

She went on to the subject of the holiday home in the Maldives that had stood empty since they'd bought it – because she was far too busy to take more than a week's holiday (and that had been their cruise, the year before). And now she'd descended back into 'the marmalade incident'. Though never once did she express concern for the safety of her missing son. First thing that morning, when Sofia the housekeeper had arrived back, she had immediately thrown in the tea-towel in protest and support for what Conna had finally plucked up the courage to do. It was his father that had then cleared up most of the mess himself. Not to his wife's required standard of course, although she was not about to get her own hands dirty. Then they had sat watching the clock.

"Look dear, I think we should at least start ringing around again," he suggested.

"Oh, yes, very clever!" she retaliated. "And when the police start asking about the circumstances of what happened, we're supposed to tell them of the 'domestic tiff', and that I lied to them about him not coming home – so that they can repeat the 'cover-up' all around the town and in the courthouse. And I'm supposed to carry my head high am I? Just ignore the tittle-tattle. That boy's brought nothing but trouble with him since the day he was born."

"I'm just saying, the longer we leave it, the worse it's going to get and the more harm Conna could come to."

"And I'm just saying – that hell will freeze over before I let that spoiled brat ruin my reputation. I've lost a full day's work through this episode – and that's enough. Do you know how much my time is worth… do you?" It was the same boast as always. "My clients pay me far more for my services yours."

It was genuinely nothing to do with the difference in their professional charges, nor their actual earnings. Neither was it much to do with the way she constantly taunted him about it. She did it, he knew, to show who wore the trousers in the household. That was what finally tipped him over the edge:

"OH, SHUT UP!" came the shout.

"What?" was the gobsmacked reply.

"I said, SHUT UP!"

"Who the HELL do you think you're talking to" she reeled.

"YOU! You ridiculous, vicious tongued woman. Our son's so distraught with his life here that he almost cracks up – and *you* still haven't either the sense or the decency to see it."

"I'm not listening to this…"

"Yes you are," he retaliated calmly, "or else I'll ring the police myself! What's happened to us? We were never like this when we met, we were fun, and now look at us: obsessed with ambition, money and status – this is madness. Whoever said money couldn't buy happiness was absolutely bang on the nail."

"I don't hear you complain. What about all of those bloody sports cars?"

"Absolutely, I admit it. All I do is clean and polish them, take them for a lone spin around the block and put them away again. Not even Conna will come with me – he's not remotely interested. And do you know something? That boy's just opened my eyes. Half my life's shot past me and all I have to show is a few trinkets… no happy memories any more… they're all gone. We're here, sitting in the corner of a TV room bigger than most people's houses, bemoaning our plight, while the one positive thing I have to show in my life, my son, the boy that I've constantly ignored or failed to protect against you, has gone missing. And even now, all you can think of is your reputation." He stood up to leave the room.

"And where the hell do you think you're going?" came the indignant voice.

"I'm going to find Conna and then I'm going to get my life back. I've had enough! I quit! I don't want anything more to do with you!"

"You leave this bloody house and you'll not be coming back…" she retaliated. "I'll see you in court first."

"Oh, I'll be back alright," he countered. "I'll be back for Conna's and my own things. And by the way, if you so much as touch any of our belongings I'll be letting your police friends know where Conna's bruises have really come from." The look of open-mouthed shock on her face let him know that he'd been right about what he'd dared not let himself believe previously. He shook his head pitifully at her and walked out of the room.

The front door slammed shut in the wind as the woman got what she'd always dreamed of, the whole house to herself. Then it gradually dawned on her that half the house was legally her husband's: it was time to hit the bottle.

By six thirty, the Hippo-Chronos sat in the middle of the room. A varying collection of odd equipment was arranged around it. It was grouped into two distinct piles. The first pile consisted of a pair of heavy, perfectly round stones with the looped handles on top: 'kettle-weights' like the ones Alex and Conna trained with in the school gym. Both were tied together with a short rope. A self-inflating lifejacket lay beside them. Then there was a large coil of thin hessian rope, together with a small deflated buoy of sorts – like a beach ball. Next to that was a pair of swimming fins that Bex had brought from home. There was a small day-glo yellow diving torch, a small diving knife and leg-sheath, and a lightweight satchel to hold the small items. And lastly was a pair of heavy, long handled bolt-crops: substantial enough, Tom assured Conna, to cut through a very heavy bolt.

The second pile consisted of two rolled up sleeping bags and a few much smaller things beside a smaller cotton side-satchel. Included amongst these things were high energy drinks and snacks for everyone to take with them.

Two other items lay nearby: the first was the electric drill with

334

the wind-up drive pins; the second was a rather nifty vacuum cleaner. Lastly, there was a spiral walking stick – the bull's pizzle! "When I was looking around for the watch, I also found this in the back of one of my bedroom cupboards," Tom beamed to no one in particular.

Everyone was now dressed as Tom had advised. Maddie and Conna looked quite at ease in their straightforward clothes: Maddie in a pair of comfortable jeans and a lightweight cotton blouse. Conna still in his usual heavy track suits and the heavily insulated puffer-coat, along with the pair of slightly oversized worn black leather boots that he'd borrowed from Tom. Alex looked slightly less comfortable now, dressed in one of Tom's jubbahs, cut off just above the knee and tied with a cord. Lastly, feeling distinctly uncomfortable – not to say ridiculous – and now having second thoughts about volunteering, Bex wore her heavy dressing gown over her single piece bathing suit. On her head, she wore a bathing cap. Swimming goggles were draped around her neck, and she wore lightweight beach shoes on her feet.

"Alright," began Tom, "next, we need the precise locations."

"You mean as far as the scale of the armillary will allow?" stated Alex.

"Oh no," smiled Tom, "since my trip with your father, I already have a recorded location for two of our destinations. All we need now is a precise location for Antikythera – preferably at the foot of the high rock escarpment – as close to the wreck site as possible without getting too close to the sea."

"But I thought you said without going there first and taking precise measurements, the settings wouldn't be accurate enough."

"Yes, in the past that would have been true," advised Tom: "But now there is a much simpler way." Tom bent down to pick-up and open a vast, thick, World Atlas. Turning to the pre-marked page, he read-off the precise latitude and longitude of the wreck site, noting it down carefully. He then adjusted the value of longitude from Greenwich to Ancient Rhodos – the ancient system on which the Hippo-Chronos was based – by 25.91 degrees and some more decimal places. The lines of latitude remained the same. That location was then translated into Kyrros' digital system. Finally the row of noughts and crosses were written down and checked again before being added to Tom's notebook.

Tom sat down and explained once more what each of them must do, rehearsing everything in detail and going over why they needed to take the various pieces of equipment with them when it came time for their own return journey. He had calculated fifteen minute intervals precisely between each of their trips, which would be adequate time in which to prepare the machine. Each part of the outbound and inbound journey however, would be separated by only two seconds. But it was hopefully long enough to prevent the risk of overlapping across each other and causing a time-paradox. Once in the past, each would have as much time as they wished to perform their task before having to return. The only proviso was to get back to the machine as quickly as possible – to lessen the chance of it being discovered. Tom himself would each time programme the thumbwheels, therefore only the forward and reverse levers should ever be touched. Once set, under no circumstances should the thumbwheels ever be moved. Finally, if for any reason the horse needed to be rewound, he showed them how to engage the retractable pedals before stowing them again.

Alex still wore his father's wristwatch – to time everything precisely. He looked at it. Suddenly the potential danger of all this seemed very real. Only Bex looked not especially worried. In fact she now felt only embarrassment at what she thought was a thoroughly silly charade.

"Is everyone still agreeable?" Tom asked.

"I am," confirmed Alex.

"So am I," said Maddie.

"And me," said Conna.

"Alright… me too," said Bex reluctantly, starting to cringe.

"Remember, as each arrives back here, we have only fifteen minutes to clean off any sand or dust with the vacuum cleaner, wind up both motors with the electric drill, load up the equipment and go again. Any longer and we risk muddling things and a paradox occurring; no one would want to meet themselves, would they? And goodness knows what would be the negative effect."

The four laughed nervously at the bizarre thought.

"Very well, Maddie my girl," said Tom endearingly: "You're first, still alright?"

"Yes," she said nervously.

"Then climb aboard."

"Shouldn't we go first Tom?" asked Alex.

"No, no my boy, this is the only way to be certain that everything is going according to plan and that I am on hand here, in case of any mistakes. Besides, once back here, your father can join in and help us."

Alex's eyes brightened at the thought; he stood back expectantly.

Maddie took a breath. She steadied her nerves and climbed comfortably onto the horse's back. "Come on then," she said as cheerfully as she could manage, "this had better be good."

"Push the lever forward Maddie," coaxed Tom, looking at her. "You'll be fine – you'll see."

As she did so, she looked at the surrounding faces. "Wish me luck," she shouted as the machine noise picked up.

"Good luck." They echoed each other nervously.

"And remember not to leave the machine unattended," called out Tom. The vibration started, then the wind picked up. "Open the window…" he shouted "to relieve the air pressure on the glass."

As Conna did, the howling north wind blew the rain horizontally into the room, soaking both he and Boris. The dog shot away from the window. From outside, a flash of lightning briefly lit up the room. A second later, a massive crash of thunder sounded directly overhead, further spooking the dog. Just at the precise moment that a warm puff of wind began to push everyone else away from it, Boris leapt onto the machine. He skidded to a stop directly in front of Maddie. And as he did, the ball of bright light appeared – just as Tom had described. Everyone shielded their eyes. After a moment, there was a second, almost instantaneous flash, and

Maddie returned exactly two seconds after she'd gone. As everyone returned their gaze, they saw Maddie in exactly the same place – with Boris only – no sign of Alex's dad.

Alex's hopeful expression evaporated instantly.

Bex let out a distinct "humph." Looking suspiciously at everything, including her sister and the dog, she wondered if she was the only one who was unimpressed. She was just about to finally lose patience at what she'd half expected to be a complete failure to demonstrate anything but a noisy wind machine with lights, but then Boris jumped down and shook himself, now absolutely bone dry and showering sand all over the floor.

Tom looked concerned, something had gone wrong. Maddie looked in shock at her sister.

"Maddie?" asked Bex, "Are you okay, what's happened?"

Maddie climbed down looking shattered, bags under her eyes, as if she hadn't slept for ages.

"Sandstorm," she explained. "I didn't know where I was."

"What?" asked Bex, still struggling to believe – "It worked?"

"Yes," confirmed Maddie, "I settled on a hill, on the edge of the desert, but it wasn't the farm at Drodos as Tom described. There, it was all green and there were flowers growing – like a meadow. It was obviously a failure. There was no sign of anyone. I'm really sorry Alex – Tom. I don't know what happened."

The boys came over to comfort her as Boris spread himself out on the floor.

"It all happened so quickly," she garbled, "one minute I was here, the next there – with the dog – and we waited for ages but no one showed up."

Tom scratched his head, wondering what had gone wrong. "The house wasn't as I described?"

"No," assured Maddie, "nothing like. There was a ruin of sorts, but for a start it was round, without a roof – more like a mini Stonehenge if you ask me – a circle of stones around a tree. But I didn't know where I was. Oh, and I brought this, in case you were curious." She opened her hand to reveal a crinkly edged leaf.

Tom took it from her. "More?" He asked urgently. "What else could you see?"

"Well," she spoke on while everyone made their way to the sofa and Maddie sat down, shaking a little. "I could see the pyramids in the distance, beside a wide river, and there was no one else around. So Boris and I walked toward them – into where the desert started – there was nothing else I could try. But as I got toward them I realised there was still something wrong. The first pyramid was completed well enough and its electrum cap glinted in the baking sun, but the second looked quite strange. There was a flat spot on its top and there was a shallow ramp which ran all the way around it. But the strange thing was that the place was entirely deserted. Well, I must have walked about a mile or so and got quite near it. But there was no third, smaller pyramid. And as for the Sphinx, it wasn't there at all!"

Tom looked at her and the machine, wondering what could have happened. But then Maddie worked it out for him.

"I could only think that I had gone too far back in time…"

"…Before the Sphinx had been built," completed Tom, sounding relieved that he knew the answer but still concerned at how the mistake could have happened.

"Anyway, a long line of people appeared, walking from the river toward the unfinished pyramid; a procession of some sort. So I dug myself into a shallow depression in the sand and waited for hours for it to pass. It was quite scary really – being on my own."

Alex patted her arm. "So, what did you do then?" he asked.

"Well, I would have made my way straight back, but that's when I noticed that the dog had gone. I tried yelling out a couple of times, and clapping for him, but there was still no sign of him. So I just waited and waited – but he didn't come back. Alex, I'm sorry about your dad, but I was more upset about the dog going missing – and about me getting lost. I just ran back to the horse as fast as I could and climbed straight on, glad it was still there. Then, as I looked at the thumbwheels, I noticed that the last digit in the first row was an X, and I thought I remembered it was supposed to be a zero. Well," she breathed a sigh of relief; "it must have been hours and hours before this silly dog," she laughed at the way he sat up at the mention of him, "trotted up to me as if nothing was wrong. Goodness knows where he'd got to." The dog jumped up onto her lap again and began to lick Maddie's hand.

"Well, we still waited for hours after that, and I was convinced by then that I was definitely in the wrong time. But I was so worried that something had gone wrong with the machine, I thought it best to abandon the backup plan and come straight back here. Anyway, by then I could see a sandstorm approaching from the direction of the unfinished pyramids – fast. That was when I began to worry that the sand might clog the machine, so I pushed forward the lever and got straight back, just as the cloud of sand hit us. I'm sorry Alex," she turned to the boy beside her. "That's why I didn't bring your dad back."

"Don't worry," assured Alex, "you did the right thing. I wouldn't want you to get hurt or lost, and neither would dad." He patted her arm again reassuringly, if not more than a little disappointed.

Tom sat back heavily in his chair, his face covered with his good hand. "I could have got you lost forever," he mumbled. Then he looked directly at her. "It is I who should be sorry – I made a mistake – a serious mistake." He sat staring into space. "I should never have attempted any of this."

"Well actually," suggested Alex, "I think it might be Boris to blame, jumping onto the horse suddenly like that, he probably caught one of the wheels with his long nails and changed the digit."

"Quite possibly," said Tom, "but the problem is that I should have guessed the plan was flawed."

"Alex could still go back and rescue his dad though, couldn't he?" suggested Conna.

"Yes… yes, he can." Tom pondered, "But I think that that is all that should happen, this is all far too dangerous now – too dangerous to go on." A look of sudden realisation dawned on his face, looking at the young faces around him. "I think I've wanted this for so long that I've become blind to its dangers." Reluctantly, he admitted, "You're all so young – too young!"

"I don't agree – we're not," said Alex, "we're old enough, aren't we! I think we've got to go through with the plan – don't you Conna?"

"Of course we have," Conna nodded enthusiastically, not wishing to miss his own opportunity to ride the horse. "Anyway, we're nearly as old as Ptolemy aren't we?"

"I agree," said Maddie.

Now Bex added separately, "we've all come far too far to abandon things now."

"Well… if you still think so?" Tom looked at them all worriedly.

"Absolutely," they all agreed.

"Well then," Tom suggested tentatively, "if we don't want to have to re-calculate everything, we'd better get a move on. We've only a few minutes left before we have to go again, we'll leave your father till last. Let's get straight on with the next part of the plan – get ready everyone."

CHAPTER 37:

A Last Goodbye?

Conna's father was soaked through and frantic with worry now, having searched for him all the rest of the morning. His imagination ran riot when, buffeted by the winds, he'd taken the shortcut past the Middens and had almost slipped down the muddy bank. Now, he knocked at Alex's house. Alex's mother held the door ajar.

"Yes?" she yelled out over the noise of the wind and rain.

"Look, I'm sorry to disturb you," he called back, "I know we've never met, but I'm Conna's dad."

"You mean his father." she called back pointedly, trying to keep out of the rain. "Any man can be a father – a *dad* is someone special."

"Yes," he accepted the criticism fully. "Look, I know I haven't been very good with Conna, but that's all going to change now – honestly!"

"Really?" said Penny, "then you'd best come in." She opened the door fully. *It's about time too*, she thought privately, *but better late than never*. There was another crash of thunder as she shut the door behind him.

While they sat in the empty lounge, Alex's mother listened to him confess to not looking out for the boy as he'd ought to. "I'm not making excuses," he said, "I've got one of those careers that keeps me out of the house all the time. His mother and I have had a difficult marriage. I suppose I just turned a blind eye to it all."

"You mean two blind eyes, don't you?"

"Yes," he bowed his head shamefully, "but his mother can be so demanding… it was always just easier to go along with it all."

"Even to the point of black eyes?" she asked, stern faced.

"Look," he said, "I see that now, but even Conna covered those things up from me. He used to tell me that they were rugby knocks and scars, but I did begin to guess a few weeks ago – since she was passed over in her career again – they thought she was too unstable – too ambitious. I just didn't realise that she would keep going on like this, I thought it would all blow over."

"So now what?" she asked, remembering the always aloof expression of the woman way back in the nursery days. "How's it all going to change? Have you strangled her?" Penny enquired sarcastically.

"Maybe I should," he shook his head, "but no, this time I've left her – for good. I'm going to find Conna and then we'll find somewhere to stay tonight. Tomorrow, I'll go back and get our things… I'll work out the details later. For now, I just want to bring him back, make sure he's safe. Have you any ideas where he might be?"

Penny relented. "I may just know," she admitted, "but promise me something: you'll find somewhere to stay around the town. Alex and Conna are great friends – I wouldn't like them to lose touch with one another."

"Oh?" he looked quizzically, "Conna wondered weeks ago if you might have plans to move away."

"Thought about it," she said honestly. "Baaad idea – wouldn't work. Even if I have to remortgage the house, we're staying. Now, before I tell you where he is, let's talk!"

Next door, as Bex readied herself, she handed Alex a sheet of paper – "Here," she said urgently, "Alex, you're the best at Greek. Translate this for me."

Alex took the note and read it.

"Hurry," said Bex, "but don't tell anyone."

Conna climbed onto the horse, now decked out with the various pieces of equipment hanging on it. Kettle-weights suspended across its back, the life-jacket over his head, the rope and satchel across his shoulder and the swimming fins pinned beneath his left arm. Bex had strapped the diving knife to her leg and already wore the satchel over her shoulder. Now she stooped to pick up the heavy bolt-crops by their improvised rope carrying cord.

"Quickly!" urged Tom, placing the last, heavy item into the satchel. Now he re-checked the thumbwheels for the fourth time as Maddie finished off winding the second spring motor with the drill. Just in time, Tom picked up the vacuum cleaner to blast off any possible loose particles of sand.

"Here, Tom called out to Conna – take my watch while I finish this."

Conna took over: "Five... four... three..."

"Alex quickly," repeated Bex, *"please!"*

"Two... one."

Conna pushed the control forward as Alex rushed over with the note, now translated on the same sheet as Bex's handwriting. He handed it to Tom, who fumbled it, then quickly retrieved it from the floor before giving it to Conna. Tom quickly retreated. In the confusion, Conna held out Tom's watch for Alex to take back. However, as he did, Alex ran to open the window again – his turn to get drenched. "We'll get it back later," Tom called out, just don't lose it. And don't forget – don't leave any evidence behind that you've been there."

"Okay, we won't. Hang on Bex," yelled Conna, as she grasped him around the waist, "here we go."

The machine held steady, this time Boris keeping well away from it. Then there was the puff of noise and light as Conna shouted out cheerily, "Tally-ho!" Then came the double flash.

Within two seconds the pair reappeared, but without any of the equipment other than the bag.

Bex was first off, shivering with cold, her bare arms bristling with goose pimples as Maddie rubbed her sister dry with a towel. Conna was also soaked to the skin, slightly out of breath, wearing one boot only. His bare right foot was cut and bleeding, but otherwise he was none the worse for wear. "Are you alright Bex?" he checked.

"Yes." She answered sheepishly.

Tom looked open-mouthed from Conna's bare foot, to Bex, wearing Conna's coat and her swimming goggles. He gave a short laugh. Snapping out of his trance, he asked: "Did everything go according to plan?"

"Yeah, perfectly… like a dream… sort of," puffed Conna. "I can't believe it, it all worked out just like you said… it did, didn't it Bex?" He finally pulled off the boot and, ignoring his still damp trousers, got his own shoes back on.

Bex raised her eyebrows and nodded in reply: "hmm," she said simply, "as Conna says, sort of."

"Good, then get the horse ready again, you can tell us all about it later."

Aside, Maddie asked, "Bex, what happened, why are you smiling to yourself?"

"I'm not," she denied at first.

"You're fib…bing," Maddie teased. Something else happened, didn't it?"

"Well, maybe," she admitted, "I'll tell you later."

Alex closed the windows and began to wind up the motors with the drill. Beside him, Tom clicked the thumbwheels around, then busied himself checking that he had everything in his own side-satchel before picking up the pizzle and climbing onto the horse. Ready once more, Alex stooped to pick up the two new sleeping bags that Tom had provided. He crisscrossed both of their carrying straps around his chest, and made to get on behind him. It was only then that Tom stopped the boy. "No Alex," he announced.

Alex looked shocked. "But… Tom, what's wrong? I'm supposed to be coming with you aren't I?"

"Of course you are Alex, but this time it is I who must sit at the back – this time I'm the passenger. It is you who must take the controls." Tom looked again at the faces of his young friends. Reaching into his satchel, he retrieved an odd pair of cracked, green glass goggles and handed them to Alex. Alex immediately recognised them from Tom's description. He tied the thongs around the back of his head.

"Alex," Tom cautioned, "if anything happens to me, get back here as quickly as you can. Re-programme the machine to rescue your father and never come to search for me, promise!"

Alex looked into his burning green eyes, not knowing what to say.

"Promise me Alex." Tom repeated. "Promise me, otherwise I must go alone. What I am about to do now has a very real danger of causing a devastating time paradox – I dare not meet myself as a boy. But, as nothing like this has ever happened before, no-one knows what the trigger mechanism might be, or what might be the result! You have to promise me that you will come straight back."

The others began to sense something new: something Tom hadn't told them about. They too began to stare at him.

"Tom," asked Maddie, "you are coming back, aren't you?"

"I will try," he said, "but I can't promise anything… there are far more important things at stake here than whether or not I return. But please know that you have all helped me at least try to prevent a great cataclysm happening – and I for one will be eternally grateful wherever and whenever I end up. Come Alex, sit here in front of me and take control."

"Tom," said Conna earnestly, "I'm sorry if I didn't believe you at first and everything… it's just that…"

"No need to explain," said Tom, "I know. Now, Alex… the time please?"

The boy looked at his wrist. "That reminds me, where's Tom's watch Conna?"

Conna patted his pockets, "I dunno, I had it a minute ago," he went on searching as his face started to redden. Alex tried to calm Conna down as he started to panic.

"Don't worry," assured Tom, "I'm sure I'll get it back."

Maddie threw her hands around Tom's neck and gently hugged him, tears in her eyes, suddenly worried over whether she would

346

ever see him again. "Bye Tom," she said, "and good luck."

Bex, now a little warmer, stood beside him. "Bye Tom," she said, throwing an arm around his back. "I'm sorry I doubted you, but just in case we don't see you again, I just want to tell you that... I met her!"

"Yes," acknowledged Tom, "I know."

Bex screwed up her face quizzically.

"We're picking up speed," called out Alex.

"She really was very beautiful," complimented Bex.

Tom smiled. "*Is*," he corrected. "Somewhere in time – she still is!"

"Three... two... one..." Alex sat tight as Maddie opened the window and there was the flash of light and noise. But this time, worryingly, there was no second bang.

CHAPTER 38:

A Trip to the Seaside

Sitting there in Tom's laboratory, waiting for Alex and Tom, Conna and Bex both mulled over their now completed journey, still pinching themselves to make sure it was all true:

Tom's best guess had been that the Roman corbita carrying Kyrros, Miriam, Ashur and Lio had run aground at some time in the hours of the early morning. Unlike the tourist maps, which were incorrect, he also knew where the exact site of the shipwreck was. Although the sea-level had dropped a little, The exact jagged outcrop that the ship had struck was still clearly visible; he'd previously seen it for himself. Armed with this information, and once again the accurate location taken from the map book, Tom was able to place the Hippo-Chronos with pinpoint accuracy in the right time and the right place. That part of the island was completely uninhabited, so when Tom and Bex touched down in the dark, no one witnessed the event.

"Whoaah, bloody… heck!" Conna partly relapsed. "Sorry Bex," he quickly jumped off and laid Tom's watch carefully over the back of the horse.

Bex sat incredulously, open-mouthed and stock-still. She stared out around her, surveying the craggy, alien landscape, unable to take in what had happened. Until now, even though Maddie had assured her that she'd not made up the tale about losing the dog in the desert, did it all sink in. The machine had, in fact, actually managed to transport her, Bex, somewhere else. Though like Alex's dad, exactly where and when had still to be proven to her. By contrast, Conna, with the high escarpment at his back, elatedly crunched up and down on the rocky soil, whilst looking out to sea.

"Unbelievable," he said, believing everything. "It looks like the surface of the moon." He turned to Bex, grinning like the Cheshire cat. "The eagle has landed… grk-cheet," he mimicked the famous delivery of the American moon landing – complete with static. Then he ran up to Bex, still sat on the horse. He placed a hand on each side of her face and kissed her loudly on the forehead before he realised how carried away he was getting with himself. "Sorry," he said, suddenly looking sheepish before feeling himself turn red again.

Bex didn't say a word, still in shock. She just stared around her.

"Come on then," Conna suggested eventually, "we'd better get ready, hadn't we?"

"Yeah," said Bex breathlessly. Still in a daze, she looked up in amazement at the sky full of stars, visible through the thinnest of cloud cover. Slowly, she got down with the bolt-cutters now gripped tightly in her hands. She started to make her way after Conna toward the sea. Conna carried the makeshift skandalopetra, and as he crossed from the soil onto the rock, now realised why Tom had insisted on him wearing the heavy soled boots. The whole surface of the rock looked as sharp as razor blades. The heavy kettle-weights pulling him down would have destroyed a lighter pair of shoes – making it impossible to walk across without cutting his feet to ribbons. Bex stopped where the rocks started, gauging the direction of the wind and trying to imagine where the vessel might head-in.

"Where do you reckon we should put these then?" asked Conna.

"Over there," said Bex, now suddenly decisive, "but not too near the outcrop – we don't want anything to get hit."

"Alright," he nodded, and clambered to the water's edge to place them almost in the water. He came back, took the bolt-crops from Bex and snapped them shut a couple of times. "Bex, are you sure you'll be able to manage with these? They are a bit heavy to work."

Bex pursed her lips in reply.

"Okay," he said placatingly, "just asking."

Conna was loving every moment. He clambered back to the water's edge then made his way back to the horse to collect the rest of the equipment. The wind started to pick up again, now changing direction and reaching Bex. He saw her shiver. "Wait a minute," he said, "take this." He took off the long insulated coat, "I don't need it – honest."

For once, Bex didn't argue. "Thanks," she said, as he placed it around her shoulders. "I can't believe we're doing this," she confessed, "it's all too weird."

"You're still okay about it though?" he checked – "Haven't bottled out or anything?"

She narrowed her eyes fiercely at him. "Of course I'm okay," she said, "I still can't believe it, that's all."

"Okay, come on then," Conna urged, "we'd better get into position."

"Ow!" Bex let out a yelp and almost tripped, her own lightweight shoes affording little protection from the rocks.

"Hang on," suggested Conna, turning his back toward her and crouching down, "jump on."

"What!"

"Jump on, come on I'll give you a piggy-back."

"Certainly not Conna," she said indignantly, nearly stumbling again, so instead, Conna held out his hand again for her to take it. "At least let's help you get to the water in one piece," he suggested. "No good you getting injured now."

Reluctantly, she took his hand. Slowly, they hobbled toward the water before Conna asked, "So, does this count as a first date then?"

"Clown," She muttered at him.

"Oh, good, I've never been on a date before... actually... pretty flash really. Our first date... together... alone on a Greek island."

Tiptoeing or not, Bex still managed to land him a hefty punch in the shoulder.

After tying one end of the rope securely around the rocks and

350

the other end to the balloon sized buoy which Conna had inflated with a two breaths of air, they crouched down together and waited.

"Are you sure you're not cold?" asked Bex, hopeful that he wouldn't take the coat back.

"No, I'm fine" Conna lied.

"We can share the jacket if you like," she offered.

"Nah, don't worry." He could have punched himself as soon as the words left his mouth. "You'd best keep wrapped up properly – that water looks freezing. And you'll need all the body warmth you can get soon."

"Yeah," Bex said disappointedly. "I will,"

For the next hour they went over the plan a couple of times, such as it was. The moment that the ship began to sink, from the outcrop, Bex would swing the kettle weights and herself as far out from the rocks and toward the boat as possible. Then she would quickly grasp the sinking vessel and swim inside. Using the bolt crops strapped around her, she would then affect Kyrros' rescue. She would inflate the life vest around her neck – or if at any time things went wrong – and finally, using the rope and buoy, Conna would haul both Kyrros and herself back to the shore. It would not be an easy task by any means. Actually, ridiculously dangerous, now that she actually had to contemplate doing it for real – not just talk about doing it. Fully rehearsed, they then chatted about 'other stuff' to take their minds off the danger: like parents and money, and health and happiness.

Huddled there together under the stars, they started to talk properly to each other for the first time, and Bex confessed her true fears for her mother's health, while Conna listened in silence. Until at last, in the distance, under the pale moonlight, Conna spotted the rolling corbita. The sight of it shocked them back to their task. Not long after, came the swiftly pursuing galley. Together, they both swallowed, now absolutely realising the danger of what they were going to attempt to do.

At first, as they watched the corbita staying well offshore, it seemed to be about to head straight past them, moving toward the bulge of the headland. "What's he doing?" asked Bex.

"I don't know," said Conna, "there's no way he's ever going to get away from the galley." It was gaining rapidly now, when suddenly, the rolling vessel changed tack and headed straight towards them, the galley starting to follow. As they got closer, Conna and Bex watched as the second volley of arrows drifted high into the sky from galley to corbita. Then the galley seemed to stop abruptly as the heavier vessel came onward. This was it – exactly as Tom said – it was coming straight toward them.

"Erm, Bex, I think we'd better move," said Conna, now grabbing the bolt-crops to get them out of the way. "We're sitting on the wrong side of the outcrop. Come on!"

They clambered rapidly out of the way for safety's sake. Then all they could do was wait for the sickening, splintering crash as the ship hit the rocks full-pelt, its bow rising up onto the rocks and jerking back down. The crew standing at the stern were instantly and almost silently catapulted into the sea.

In turn, this instantly triggered Conna and Bex's reactions. Bex dropped both the jacket and the dressing gown and clambered back to the water's edge, slipping the deflated life-jacket over her head and pulling the goggles over her face. The ship had lodged directly where they'd been sitting. It scattered all of the rest of the equipment – the kettle-weights and the fins – into the sea, ruining their plan. Bex looked around to see Conna peeling off his tee shirt and trying to take off the boots, but he couldn't untie the knotted laces. He heaved at one, which shot off into the sea. "Shhh…ugar," he called out, giving up on the second. "Come on, quickly, I've got a better idea." Grabbing the bolt-crops and throwing the rope and the float into the water, he half-tiptoed, half-hobbled toward the ship, leaving no choice for Bex other than to follow. Spotting the fluorescent yellow torch, she slipped its securing hoop over her wrist and skipped lightly after him.

From the back of the ship, a few of the remaining crew jumped either into the water or onto the surrounding sharp rocks, only to scream loudly and fall back into the sea. A few others clung desperately to the back of the vessel as Conna grabbed at one of the lead anchors and hauled himself up and onto the deck. He waited for Bex to follow. As soon as she arrived, he bent down and pulled her up on board. "Now what?" Bex asked.

On the larboard side, both watched as a woman emerged at the top of the staircase and stood on deck. She looked over the side at the rocks before returning half-way down into the hold again to reach her hand out. Then, just ahead of her, they saw the Roman master snap-off two arrows that pierced his chest. He made his way toward the hatch. A moment later, at the top of the stairs, a little girl much smaller than Bex emerged at the end of the woman's arm. Bex stood and watched the woman leap across to the rocks, but as she did, the boat moved, slipping back down into the sea. The little girl crossed to the other side of the bow as the woman coaxed her to come back toward her, but instead, she kept on staring down into the water.

"Come on," yelled Conna into the wind, and he and Bex made their way toward the stairs. As Bex made her way along the deck, the ship gave another, much heavier jolt that sent the cargo crashing below. The pair peered through the hatch to see the Hippo-Chronos shoot past and collide with the arm and trident of Poseidon. Both winced, turning away instantly, knowing what was about to happen to the master – villain or not.

The ship was starting to move constantly now. Even though it was slowly beginning to pitch onto its side, Conna and Bex waded down the submerging steps and into the freezing water. The weight of the bolt-crops kept Conna on the deck as he fought his way into the cabin. Bex switched on the torch and followed into the almost submerged space. There, they both clearly saw a red haired boy half swim, half clamber toward them. Then, in the torchlight, for a full second – a long time in those perilous circumstances – the three came face to face. The boy gave a smile and a look of instant relief before the ship lurched violently on its side and they were separated. Each took a breath from the small air-pocket on the roof, then Conna plunged through the water toward the stern.

The old man, Kyrros, was well submerged, struggling to hold onto his breath and about to let it go when he saw the white tube of light spray across him. Instantly guessing what was happening – in all its outrageous improbability – he sat and watched in wonder as the boy from the future clambered around his feet, and the girl slipped the bright orange vest from her neck and over his head. Somehow, little Lio had kept his promise!

Conna struggled with the chain, the rotating vessel pitching him around so that he couldn't get it between the jaws of the cutter. The old man struggled to keep his breath, letting it begin to seep from his lips, unable to hold on for the vital seconds it would take Conna to realign the chain. Then, the girl who had been looking directly into his eyes, disappeared for a few moments while he finally breathed out. Instantly, there she was again, her face now against his. Placing her mouth over his and pinching his nose with her thumb and forefinger, she breathed a lungful of air into him and went back toward the air pocket. In his turn, as he began to breath out, Conna had no idea why Bex had chosen that particular moment to snog him, until she blew directly and powerfully, re-inflating his lungs. Diving below the surface, she held the chain with one hand and pointed the torch at it while placing it directly into the jaws of the bolt-crops. With Conna's single, powerful crank of the handles, the chain snapped and he let the crops go. As the vessel rolled and sank, stern down, the two each grabbed Kyrros by his upper-arms and began to kick furiously upward and out of the cabin.

The patch of moonlight beckoned the way through the hold. It was a completely startled Bex that almost let out her breath in a scream as the dead, staring face of the master appeared directly above her. Conna reached up and pushed the body out of the way. As he did, they all passed from the hull and into the open water, and Bex pulled the jacket's inflation cord once. Now, they kicked steadily, starting to ascend. Reaching the surface just before they ran out of breath, Conna spotted the float. The pair kicked their way toward it so that they could pull themselves along the rope and get back onto the rocks. Within a couple of minutes, making firstly sure that the rescued man had managed to grab hold securely onto the rocks, each waited to get their breath back. Kyrros looked at each face in turn – completely out of breath and unable to say anything.

"Come on," said Conna, "let's get him out – before we all freeze."

The youths climbed up carefully, trying not to get cut. Then each took one of Kyrros' hands and helped haul him out to sit on the rocks. Finally, they heard the garbled tongue – similar to that of Tom's when they'd first met him in the wreckage of his home – but still the only word each was able to make out was the one that hadn't changed for thousands of years. Breathlessly, Kyrros mumbled, "Efkaristo."

Now out of danger, Bex asked, "May I?" and beckoned to take the inflated life vest. Then she reached down just as Tom had instructed her, took the knife out of the ankle sheath and stabbed the jacket twice before throwing it out to sea. Next, she dutifully pulled on the rope and stabbed the float too, before letting it sink. "Come on," Conna urged, "let's get on with it." Between them, they helped Kyrros to his feet. Conna held a finger to his lips, signalling to the old man that this was obviously some sort of secret mission. Kyrros recognised the sign; he nodded his acceptance. Walking away from the opposite side of the outcrop, unseen by Miriam, he looked wistfully behind him at his wife, trusting the two strangers implicitly. Together, the three treaded carefully away, Conna limping, still with only one boot. If there had been any doubt in the philosopher's mind over who they were or where they came from, as soon as he saw the Hippo-Chronos, he was instantly relieved that somehow it had not only survived, but was in good hands. During the next hour, Conna and Bex then continued with the second part of Tom's plan, but added their own impromptu part to it.

While Conna and Bex busied themselves, Kyrros sat patiently, starting to fathom out that he could not just simply reappear from what had supposedly been his own drowning. Still trusting them, he watched the two youths work intently.

Unknown to Bex, Conna's foot was bleeding. Had she known, she would not have let him persevere for so long in trying to wind up the machine. As soon as she did realise though, she took over. Now, after half an hour of combined effort, it was ready again. "Wait here with Kyrros," she said, "I'll be back in an hour."

Conna finished off the high energy drink and held onto the empty bottle. "No way!" he replied.

"Why," she baited him, "are you scared of the dark?"

Conna pulled a face: "I'm not letting you go alone," he said stubbornly, "I don't know how far it is, but you're not going by yourself."

"Oh, alright then," she conceded, "follow if you must, Sir Galahad."

Conna asked, or rather mimed for the old man to stay there, and Kyrros again nodded his understanding. To make sure it didn't go missing, Conna picked up Tom's watch. "Uno houro, okay-o!" he improvised his own Geordie form of Esperanto. He handed it to the philosopher, pointing out the hour hand. Kyrros was instantly fascinated with it. "Ahh… alpha hora," he nodded.

Then the boy started out with Bex.

After walking all the way up the hill to Xiropotamos, discussing every impromptu step of their plan, eventually, Conna handed over the glass bottle and the letter that he'd inserted into it. Bex immediately squeezed inside the small-ish natural entrance to the cave that was the well of Andronicus, and with the torch, she quickly found Miriam's future hiding place. She deposited the bottle, then came straight back out to see Conna standing with his back to her. Absent mindedly, he looked from the ruined old farmhouse and out over the dawn view, right across the other side of the island. It was now that his own situation at home hit him – hard.

"Penny for them," Bex cajoled.

Conna took a sobbing breath. Uncharacteristically, he spoke up about his own most private matter. "I was just thinking – I know what Tom means about being a paradox – about not being meant to exist. That's why I listened to him, I suppose. I wanted to believe him. It's not very nice to know that you were unplanned you know – unwanted." He glanced at the girl. "I was just wondering about how nice it would be to stay here – forget home and everything."

It was now that Bex finally realised how desperate he felt. By all accounts, her own home life was idyllic, especially compared to his. Even through her mother's health problems, her family were all still perfectly happy to pull together. "But Conna," she said genuinely, trying to rescue him from the mood he now found himself in, "what would we all do without you – we'd have to find someone else to tease!"

Conna half-turned toward her. Smiling, wondering what she did think of him – lardy-boy – before he broke out of the silly moment. "Come on then, he said, we'd better go."

On the way back to the machine, this time Bex supported Conna's shoulder while he took her waist – only to take the weight off his foot, of course. But this time neither said a word, accurately pacing out the distance instead.

Once they got back to the horse, the waiting Kyrros stood up, now back to his old self. He dutifully handed Conna back the watch. Then Conna and Bex set about carrying out the next part of their mission. The three squeezed onto the Hippo-Chronos, hoping that the load wouldn't overtax the machine on its short journey. And this time, the horse leapt the small distance back to the top of the hill and Lio's now rebuilt farmhouse.

Seven years later, in the moonless late midsummer's evening, the Hippo-Chronos touched down again – this time, right beside Lio's apple tree. Bex was first off. She took Kyrros by the arm and pointed to the house where Miriam and Ashur lived, beckoning him to go. Unsure, he walked toward it in trepidation as Conna laid the watch on the horse's saddle and then shooed him on theatrically. Together, they watched Kyrros bow in capitulation and thanks, then he walked away.

Now, as the entrance to the underground spring had been improved, walled in and with a door hatch fitted, it was Conna's turn – he insisted – on going inside the cave. At first, disappointed at finding the bottle still there, he checked the letter to see if their message had got through. He took it from the bottle, unrolled it and attempted to read the note, but at first couldn't tell if it had been read or not. Then he turned it over. And there, at the bottom of the sheet, a curious set of figures had been drawn on it. It *had* been found and replaced after all. Conna was, of course, hopeless at Greek. He wasn't particularly good at Latin either, but he now squeezed-in a personal note all the same – as best he could. Next, he took the torc out of the satchel he was carrying and placed it in the same hiding place before spraying the torch around the interior of the cave and the deep natural water reserve.

Satisfied that the task was complete, he came back out and then walked over to where he had just stood seven years earlier. He looked out at where the sun had not long since set, breathing-in the feeling of peace and contentment. Now standing a few paces away, Bex couldn't help it, but something drove her to wander up behind him and take his hand, just to let him know that his friends cared about him. And perhaps herself especially – just a little. For a few minutes more, they just stood and watched the darkening wine red sea. Eventually, tentatively, the two turned to face each other. Conna stepped toward the girl, and now Bex didn't back away. But as they grew closer, there came a growing, gleeful clamour in the background, startling them both.

There, walking hurriedly toward them was the whole excited family, Miriam delighted to have her husband back – and just the same age as she had lost him. His own confidence in the two absolutely confirmed, Kyrros and his wife walked straight over and hugged and kissed the two repeatedly. And to Conna's surprise, this time, he wasn't embarrassed at all. Behind the couple stood their now six year old son, Andros, and lastly, their clearly delighted eighteen year old daughter. She held a tiny bundle in her arms. Seeing her, Bex walked toward her, smiling. "May I see?" she asked.

Intuitively, Ashur understood. She nodded and uncovered the baby's face and head.

Taking care not to startle anyone, Conna stepped forward and handed back the torch to Bex. In order to let them see that it was safe, the girl flicked the now fading beam onto the ground. Kyrros laughed and nodded approvingly at this particular delight, while Andros now stood behind his mother's back, a little nervously. Ashur beckoned Bex forward with her hand, so the younger girl held the torch up, illuminating the baby's face and hair. Both Conna and Bex smiled; the baby girl was as dark skinned and as dark-haired as Ashur herself. For the briefest moment though, her dreaming eyes flashed open – the palest green.

Bex made to give away the torch to Miriam, but she shied away. Then Kyrros reminded them, "Anachronismos," he said, fending it off with the palms of his hands stretched outwards. At that, Miriam stepped forward again and reached into the pocket of her apron. Then, in a heartfelt token of thanks, she presented the two children from the future with a ripened apple each, and everyone nodded their understanding – time and gifts could only be allowed to travel one way. Without further ado, the family bowed respectfully. Then they turned to leave, returning to their shuttered house before the clamour of Kyrros' machine could frighten the young ones. Only Andros turned to take a last look. He waved as they disappeared inside.

Once more alone, Conna darted in toward Bex and gave her a short smacker on the lips. She jumped back, literally gobsmacked. He squeezed his eyes shut, bracing himself for the punch. The girl stared. Then, as the boy open one eye, she leaned in and kissed him – just a tiny bit longer. No-one spoke. Instead they smirked at each other as they walked, or at least limped, hand in hand, back to the Hippo-Chronos and back to their own time. Each happy, and safe in the knowledge that both could never have had the same dream.

Unfortunately however, being distracted, neither noticed that Tom's watch had slipped off the back of the horse where the boy had left it perched. It now lay plainly on the ground beneath Lio's apple tree.

CHAPTER 39:

A Trip to the Library

Alex held on tightly to the levers for the short moment that the machine shifted through time. Tom tucked in behind him. It was anyone's guess as to where the Royal Palace or the library was, let alone try to pinpoint the location of the Hippo-Chronos room within it. It was for that reason that Tom had used the co-ordinates of the Serapeion as the location for their own journey back to the past. At midnight on the night that Lio and his family were to cross beneath the Roman siege lines then, the Hippo-Chronos arrived back in Alexandria. Alex and Tom touched down in the centre of the stripped-out inner sanctum of the temple, directly above Alexander's secret tomb.

The boy's relief that he had been right to trust Tom was overwhelming. He had watched with bewilderment as Maddie had seemingly returned empty handed. He had also seen Conna and Bex as they had returned themselves, exhilarated at their own victorious jaunt – although, once more at home, Bex had still been reluctant to show it. But it was only now – physically transported inside a vast ancient temple – that the scale of the truth hit Alex. Tom climbed carefully off, holding his chest.

"Are you okay Tom?" Alex checked.

"Yes, thank you," Tom breathed a sigh of relief at the perfect landing.

He looked around, expecting to find the huge statue of Serapis behind him, but it wasn't there. Like everything else in this part of the city, it had already been cleared out by the Romans. He looked casually at the empty, but grandly decorated, sarcophagus that was one of the places supposed to have contained the remains of Alexander the Great. Then he was shaken out of his thoughts by Tom. "Alex, push the horse into the corner, just in case anyone enters and sees it," he prompted. Remember, one of the priests will be still in the attached sleeping quarters – the temple is never left unattended.

After he'd done so, creeping toward the front of the temple, Alex saw the offering bowl built into the niche in the side wall. He remembered the trick of the prayer-powered doors, and watched as Tom carefully tore a strip of cloth from the hem of his robe. Tom then carefully curled it loosely into the bowl, after which he produced, as if by magic, a disposable cigarette lighter. Then, with it, he lit the strip. Alex stood and watched the performance as Tom further placed on top of the small flames, a few of the twigs and sticks of wood that remained in the basket below. Together, as they waited for the fire to take hold, each prayed – that the mechanical device would work. Slowly, as the heat built up in the container, a vacuum was caused in the hidden tube below the floor. There was a faint click and the doors began to open silently. *Tom really has got everything prepared,* thought Alex. *He's thought out every detail in advance.* The boy said as much as he watched the old man return the lighter back to his satchel. Tom knocked out the fire, urging Alex to go through the gap before they both heaved the doors shut behind them again. Then, they crossed through the temple and out of the main, automatically locked doors.

Once outside, Alex's mouth dropped wide open in awe and wonderment. From the elevated steps of the temple square, his eyes scanned the midnight skyline of the ancient city of Alexandria. As huge as everything seemed, it all felt so crowded with buildings, so compact. It was this that gave the city an altogether quaint feel. It felt to Alex himself that he had somehow come home. Of course, the first thing he noticed about the place was that it looked entirely deserted. Everyone who now remained was staying inside their own houses for fear of getting caught up in Roman trouble. The fear was almost palpable – Alex felt it immediately. Apart from the occasional bark of a dog, there was complete silence. Then there was the smoke coming from the campfires burning throughout the area, it really was quite choking – enough to make him hold his hand in front of his mouth in a futile attempt to breathe through his fingers. He was unused to this level of pollution in his own, modern world. All in all, Alex smelled the doom.

"Alright," whispered Tom, "just to make sure we don't bump into them, we'll wait here until everyone emerges from the crypt and then we'll follow them, alright? And remember, it may be fine for you, but I cannot get too close to my younger self. The results might be cataclysmic – at least for me!"

Nodding, Alex said, "alright." Then, together, they each crouched behind the pillar, perched on the rolled up sleeping bags, waiting for the secret door into the street to be opened from inside.

The deathly quiet of the city was broken an hour later by the sound of stone scraping on stone. Then they heard the cautious whispering as the soaking wet figures of Kyrros, Lio, Miriam and Ashur slipped into the street and heaved the door shut behind them. Tom couldn't help but sigh wistfully at the sight of them all, but especially the young Ashur. Alex noticed. "Come on Tom," he pressed. They left a discrete interval before they picked up the sleeping bags again and followed the ancient family on their mile long journey. Thankfully, the wet trail was easily picked up through the narrow, winding streets of houses crammed one against the other. In only a short while – though breathlessly for Tom – Alex walked into the square of the Great Library and stopped dead in front of it. Tom kept tapping his way forward with his stick before he turned around and looked at the boy.

"It really is amazing, isn't it?" Alex gawped.

Tom smiled, until that instant, not appreciating the profound effect that the experience was having on him. Here was a boy from the twenty-first century, standing in front of one of the truly greatest wonders of the ancient world. Alex stared at the sight. It was exactly as he had imagined, but bigger and bolder – the only thing that disappointed him was the lack of statues that Tom had earlier described. "Romans", the old man reminded him succinctly. They kept on towards their goal.

"We need to get inside, out of the way before we're seen," said Tom. Hurriedly, as Kyrros' family slept soundly in the house just across the way, the pair scurried across the open square in the moonlight to bed down in the sleeping bags for the night, right there on the floor of the Great Library itself.

The two awoke early, before the sea battle had begun to get underway in the harbour. Taking a chance, before Tom knew he could bump into himself, the pair ran briefly to the dock gates – not to watch the battle, but to see the other wonder: the Pharos tower. Alex's eyes lit up at the sight of the huge structure now being passed by some of the biggest sailing ships he had ever seen. The sight that met him reminded the boy of home, especially the tower. It was indeed not unlike the square High and Low Lights of Tynemouth, seeming to stand atop each other. To Alex, the sight was truly magnificent – unforgettable.

Just before the battle commenced, the two hurriedly returned to the library. There, they made a small meal of the things they had brought with them in the satchel: the high energy drinks and the breakfast bars. Afterwards, for the rest of the morning, Tom guided Alex around the closed building, touring the library and workshops before anyone else arrived. He carefully removed selected works for Alex to muse over. There were only a couple of times that they were required to hide. Both times were when they heard the voices of Kyrros and others making their way through the library on their way to and from the workshops. Each time, after they'd gone by, Tom held the bottom of the ladder while Alex climbed up to browse the names of the published list of writers who adorned each of the pigeon holes – from Archimedes to Aristotle and from Plato to Poseidonios.

Deliberately ignoring the battle which now raged outside in the harbour, Tom handed Alex account after account of the many distant places which the Greek culture had claimed to visit, or know about. "What's this?" asked Alex, "*Timaeus.*"

"I believe it is an early, rather exaggerated tale by Plato," Tom described the work. "It is, I also believe, the only *full* account to survive the ravages of time. It does, however, include a rather unbelievable account of sophisticated life many years ago – a distant continent in the sea of Atlas," he said grudgingly, "a place called Atlantis!"

Alex shook his head in wonderment.

"Here," said Tom, "put it in the satchel we brought with us. In fact, take as many as you like. After all, the library will not be here tomorrow." He started to throw down more fantastical accounts, from across the wider globe: of past civilizations in Africa; of Spice Islands in a great sea to the Far East; and a full account of the successful siege of Wilusha, just as Tom had spoken of – including the date of its downfall. Tom especially pointed out the whereabouts of the travel accounts of Poseidonios. There, Alex read about the writer's many journeys – across North Africa and Spain, the Gauls and Britannia – where he had described the Keltes as a most peaceful culture of traders who are accepting of strangers and who love to hear tales of foreign cultures and customs. The people in the Scotos lands seemed particularly taken with the Greek's brightly chequered way of dress. It even mentioned the Roman guide's golden coin that had been placed 'in the crack in the rock overlooking the black rocks that lurked just below the water'.

Then, just before he returned the scroll, Alex stumbled upon a very well worn piece of Papyrus. Opening it carefully, he realised at once that it was a most extraordinary map. It was almost in pieces but he still recognised it – the mislaid working record of the travels of Poseidonios – the world as the philosopher and athlete saw it. Alex was immediately captured by it, and by the many animals depicted on it. They were all real, although, to be honest, not particularly well observed – even a bit naïve. Nevertheless, it kept the boy occupied for ages, before he returned it to Tom. Similarly, Tom smiled at the map he'd not seen since he was a boy.

Alex never felt more privileged than at that point – to have the accounts of the ancient world at his fingertips. Completely oblivious to the raging battles outside – both on land and at sea, dutifully, he helped Tom fill the satchel with the various accounts. He knew now what the librarian must have felt like to be faced with the threat of losing all this in a single fire, and why he might have begun to think that both Kyrros and Lio might be expendable to save it all. He drank in the whole experience in silence.

As the late afternoon light gradually faded and it became difficult to see any more, Tom and Alex sat on the floor. "Tom," he said, "I think I get it. I think I understand why you had to come back and try to save all of this for future generations: it's so that the world won't be plunged into the darkness that existed since the library's destruction, isn't it. It would be amazing to think of what would happen if we manage to save it – for the future of mankind. Just think of how advanced the world would be, back in our own time. The advances in medicine, in technology – in everything," he gushed.

Throughout the boy's enthusiastic speech Tom sat quietly with his back against the bookshelves, his shoulders hunched forward, not looking at him. To Alex he looked unwell. Again the boy encouraged him to take a sip of water and one of his pills, if he must. But while Tom patiently thanked him for his concern, he told Alex that this time, *that* was not what was wrong. It was something entirely different that troubled him.

"Then, what's that?" Alex frowned.

Tom put down the pizzle he'd carried since their arrival and looked into the eyes of the innocent youth who knew and appreciated the value of all this knowledge. He wondered how to break it to him.

"Al-lex," Tom began patiently, "the achievements of mankind are many and various. Think of all those things which are in your time almost taken for granted: motor cars; aeroplanes; space travel – men on the moon! Think of the machines which keep people alive in hospitals: heart pumps; blood filters; baby incubators. They are all truly wondrous. Or think of the many gadgets which you say increase the *quality* of your lives: televisions and radios; CD's and games; and, of course, the lifeline of the whole modern world – computers!"

"Yes?" Alex frowned, wondering what troubled Tom about them.

"Alex, think also, however, of what has driven many of these inventions forward at such a pace. Sadly, it has not always been the desire to do wondrous things, but instead, man's desire to dominate his neighbours on this small planet. These disputes are rarely about the higher moral reasons they are purported to be – for truth and justice, or love and real honour. Almost always, there is at least one underlying reason – for personal gain. Ask yourself, in your own time, why is it that moral outrage and rebellion are supported only in the case of wayward oil-rich states, while poorer or 'unimportant' countries are left alone to be ruled over by terror?

Then ask yourself about other things. Think, for instance, of the power of the sun – nuclear energy. Surely this is the greatest gift to the planet. It has powered everything in our world since its birth, four and a half *billion* years ago. Nothing would have existed here if it were not for the sun and other stars. Everything that grows on Earth – including ourselves – is made from the very same atomic particles that once came from an exploding star on the other side of the universe – an estimated *fourteen* billion years ago – 'the Big Bang', as it is called. It is both a sobering and wonderful thought is it not? that every single particle in our bodies was once a part of the stars – and will be again someday. That all we might achieve in our own short, precious lifetimes will eventually be lost in the vastness of time and space; and, as my grandfather once said, for that reason alone, we should respect each and every person living on this planet."

Alex listened on, wondering where Tom was headed.

"Man's harnessing of this almost limitless energy – atomic power – should have been a marvellous boon for the population of the whole world – could have helped to spell the end of poverty.

And yet, from the very first idea that Albert Einstein had – to unlock the potential power of the sun right here on earth and solve the energy problems of the planet forever – his idea was fatally flawed. The great physicist of the twentieth century had failed to take into account man's one true and overriding genius – 'the art of war and destruction'. Alex", Tom continued sadly, "perhaps it was with all the best intentions, for all the right reasons – not least in the face of Hitler's advancing world fascism and evil – that the physicist Oppenheimer himself manipulated this technology to create one of the world's most deadly weapons. But as he was to later discover, to his personal cost, not even he – 'the father of the atom bomb' – could persuade the world to 'un-invent', or even share its 'protection'.

From sticks and stones, to arrows, spears and much deadlier missiles which they have named after the gods, their weapons and even my grandfather's star – Jupiter, Trident and Polaris – man has excelled at the art of warfare. In the twenty-first century AD, the destructive capability of this weaponry is on an unprecedented scale. The clamour to wipe away anyone of a different culture, a different race, a different belief abounds. Reason and tolerance have gone out of the window – only hatred now threatens to rule. Where will it all end?"

The boy shifted uncomfortably.

"Al-lex, within these walls are many wonderful things, as you have now seen for yourself. The Greeks had mused over many subjects – how to govern their society, how to most fairly deal with their neighbours honourably – not that they always got it right by any means. But the desire of their society, Alex, their ideals: to take only sufficient for their needs; to accept and adapt foreign culture rather than smash it; to explore everything in the world scientifically; and to use this knowledge for the benefit of mankind – all of this made them prey to the greedier ambitions of man. Their ideas were jealously seized upon and either destroyed or adapted into the most sophisticated weaponry. Outside this very library as we speak, the secret designs of weapons that were devised and deposited right here in this building over hundreds of years – the burning mirrors of Archimedes – have now been turned against our culture.

The proper use of technology should be in *saving* life, not *taking* it," Tom emphasised. "But these weapons will go on being revised and developed further. Who knows what other seeds of destruction lurk in this place? What about the seeds of medicine and biology? seeds which could be nurtured into weapons of horror and developed at break-neck speed. Who knows how long it might be from this day, before some, as yet unknown genius seizes upon the idea of bacteriological or biological warfare? How long might it take before someone else grasps the once ridiculed notions of Demokritos and Leukippos? How long might it be before some Roman or Renaissance Italian or Englishman or Frenchman seizes upon the same outrageous notion as Einstein or Oppenheimer? Throughout the ages, man has always been the same: once he has an idea in his head – good or bad – he will see it through. Perhaps," suggested Tom resignedly, "the destruction of the Great Library of Alexandria did nothing more than buy mankind two thousand years of extra life."

At last, it began to dawn on Alex why they had come to the library. His face began to turn ashen – shock welling-up inside him.

Tom looked directly into the bitterly disappointed face of the boy. He dipped his hand past the many small scrolls and into the bottom of his satchel. "Alex... that is why I brought this – not to open the temple doors." He brought out his fist, opening it to reveal the cheap, disposable lighter that he knew would keep the world from destroying itself faster than it must.

"Al-lex," Tom choked, "I have had my whole life to muse over this. Perhaps this is why I was miraculously chosen to escape the clutches of Zeus – this self-obsessed, self-proclaimed voice of a claimed almighty power. Perhaps this is why I had to endure the extraordinary wasted journey that has been my life. Surely, only someone who has personally experienced man's destructive future could know how dangerous the knowledge stored in this library really is. Perhaps that was the true benefit of my father's wonderful invention? Perhaps that was why the Hippo-Chronos was created? It must be done. Tell me Alex, you do understand, don't you?"

Alex looked back at his neighbour, shock still in his eyes. Then he looked around again at the library. He couldn't bring himself to say it, but he realised the sense of Tom's speech and so he nodded his capitulation. So this was how the destruction of the Great Library was to come about!

Tom confirmed, "Tonight, after dark, when Kyrros and my boyhood self are taken away from here, it is my duty as Kyrros' son to make sure that no more of this wonderful body of knowledge – this amazing pool of information – is misused. I will wait for you to return to the Hippo-Chronos, and then I will burn this beautiful monument to the genius of mankind to the ground!"

Alex choked at both the profound senselessness and the absolute truth of what Tom had said. But most of all, the boy balked at the idea of leaving his new friend – his grandfather – behind to do it all alone. "Then if you must do it," he said simply, "I'm staying with you."

Tom listened to the boy, but did not reply.

Before long, voices grew outside – all Latin. Gradually, more and more soldiers were assembling at the order of Caesar himself – to report for fire prevention duty. Now Alex heard what were obviously the tall ladders clacking against the wall. Outside, the soldiers drew lots as to who would go up on the vast roof. The height, let alone the prospect of having to haul up the buckets of water made it a thankless task – especially as the library was not even on fire.

In due course, Tom stayed down low as Alex poked his head out from behind the shelves, to confirm that the urgent Greek voices inside were indeed those of the librarian, Kyrros and Lio. Alex watched as the librarian was despatched to find the sheets and blankets to collect the works up in, whilst the engineer and his son ran up the ladders and began to throw down the scrolls. All the

369

while, Tom stayed as far from the young Lio as possible. At one point he even scurried away on his hands and knees as the boy threatened to get closer.

"EUREKA!" came Kyrros' shout as he pulled out the heavy wad of scrolls and brought them to the ground. Another short conversation followed, but then there came the Latin shouts that betrayed the fact that the librarian had returned with the Roman guards. From where he stood, Alex could see Kyrros' back. He saw him drop the scrolls into the mound that had been piled roughly into the middle of the floor. There was another short exchange of words as the librarian apologised to his colleague for betraying him, and together, young Lio and Kyrros were marched out, leaving the librarian alone. Without waiting, the librarian started to pick up the scrolls one by one.

"This is it," whispered Tom, "time for you to leave."

Alex looked shocked, "What about the librarian?" he returned.

"Don't worry," reassured Tom. "*I* have no intention of hurting him," he looked earnestly at the boy.

"Okay," Alex whispered, "but I'm staying here with you."

"No," Tom whispered urgently.

"Yes," Alex insisted. "And there's no time to argue."

Tom took a deep breath and started to walk towards Alex to attempt to physically drag him to the door, but Alex backed away.

"Go," Tom whispered urgently, "please!"

"No! I won't. Now, get on with it."

Annoyed, Tom shook his head in frustration and pulled out one of the scrolls in the pigeon hole beside him. He fumbled nervously with the lighter, only to drop it on the floor with a sharp 'click'.

"Who's there?" came the librarian's voice. Both stood quite still, knowing that the librarian would certainly give the alarm to the soldiers outside. "Who is it?"

A shadow crept slowly across the floor toward them as the pair got ready to jump on him and force his silence. As the shadow touched the lighter, the librarian stooped to pick up the curious amber coloured object. But then, as he stood up with it, the ground started to rumble. It wasn't an earthquake and it was not the noise of the Hippo-Chronos. Straight away, Tom knew exactly what it was. The deep booming rumble could be only one thing. It was the only vehicle in the world capable of producing such a powerful, all encompassing noise. Alex also knew only too well from Tom's description that the nightmare machine he had been warned of was about to materialise!

CHAPTER 40:

The Hippo-Tempus!

Dropping the papyrus scrolls and the lighter, the librarian scurried away in shock at what was to him the beginning of another natural disaster. Tom instinctively put on the Ray-Bans for his own protection. Both covered their ears as the deafening roar continued to rise, shaking all of the shelves and sending more of the scrolls cascading down. The walls shook, as outside, the soldiers clambered down off the ladders. They fell into the surrounding area to run as fast as they could – for cover from the intervention of Jupiter himself. Then the shelves came crashing down and the heavy roof tiles began to rain down in sections. A hot blast was simultaneously felt as they saw the slowly developing ball of intense light. Now, it became a hot glow in the centre of the room. Alex and Tom dived for cover beneath the fallen shelves. Then came the final, deep, intense boom.

As Alex poked his head above cover, he pulled down the goggles. All he could see was a cloud of smoke and steam filled up with red and orange flame. Four enormous blackened iron legs touched softly down. Then, as the air cleared gradually, he saw the colossal bulk of the horse's metal and timber body settle down inch by inch. It nestled against one of the main ceiling pillars, pushing it out of kilter. The clearly visible snorting head of the contraption breathed flame and smoke as the machine came to a stand-still. Finally, it ended with a deep, whooshing hiss and the unmistakable radio whine which was the only feature that the machine seemed to share with its original Greek cousin. Alex and Tom stood up to watch as a carpet of blue sparks emerged from it to wiggle their way out across the floor and disappear outside.

Together, they removed their respective eye-protectors and looked at the Hippo-Tempus in all its monstrosity. As the hatch in the centre of its back was opened, a purple and white plumed helmet appeared through the still clearing smoke in the roof space. Then, another soldier appeared behind the repeating ballista and immediately trained the powerful weapon on them.

At the same time, with military precision, the four small, square hatches on each side of the body were thrown open. From each of them, smaller and more portable ballistae – crossbows of a sort – were shoved roughly through. Gauging that the coast was clear, two larger hatches then opened to the side, and rope ladders were rolled out to the ground. Together, two, what at first appeared by their uniforms to be Praetorian guards – if it were not for their similar striped plumes – climbed down together and stood to attention at the bottom. One further figure then emerged to descend more slowly. A heavy purple cloak hung down from his own black uniform. In place of a helmet, he wore on his head a golden crown of laurel leaves – but this was not Caesar!

All Alex could do was watch, as the slight figure that he had heard so much about turned and, carrying his thin stick, walked unevenly towards them. "You two, he called to another two of his men descending the ladders, go and get the technician." Making straight for Tom, Zeus looked down at the spiral stick – the zigzag bolt of lightning that he'd not seen since that night on the temple square. He called out face to face: "so, we finally get to meet – the King's Engineer and the soon to be King of the World" – he said in self-congratulation. "And all thanks to you – and to your adopted son…"

He stopped dead, and tilted his head back to look down his nose at Alex. Narrowing his eyes he said, "You're not the priest's boy!" Looking puzzled, he considered the boy's face. "Same hair, same dress – but not him. Wrong face and… yes – wrong eyes. Now, who are you?" Zeus pondered aloud, holding up his hand to silence Alex. He turned his attention to Tom, looking him up and down and fixing his gaze on the different shaped 'goggles' that once more obscured his eyes. He walked right up to him to remove them and check their colour. Then, as if greeting a long lost friend, he said mockingly, "No, it never is, is it? Then you *did* manage to take the original horse. And, let me guess, you finally found the missing key. But by the look of you, that task took long enough," he laughed. "Oh, time's not been kind to you, has it? Where did that young, athletic body go? That self-confidence when we last met only a few days ago and you explained the code to me?"

Tom didn't answer.

He turned back to Alex. "Then you must be…?"

"Lio's friend," Alex answered boldly in excellent Latin.

"Oh, for a moment there I thought you might have been related. But where's the engineer and his boy?"

No one answered.

"Ah Yes," He looked around for the librarian's body but didn't see it. "I understand – I'm not too *early*, I'm too *late*. Kyrros and his boy have already been arrested, haven't they? Well, in that case, my old self clearly hasn't arrived yet – though I should be arriving any time now. Now *that* should be interesting – two of me! This time-travel stuff is all very complicated, isn't it?" Turning back to Tom, he said, "Never mind, I still owe you a debt of thanks I suppose. After all, it was *you* who gave me half the world – even though it's the world of the past. You do know that someone rigged my masterpiece so that it can't ever go forward again. I realised that much, as soon as I tested it, by taking it back to just the day before. I couldn't get back – but there again I only had to wait for twenty-four hours to get back to my 'home' again – that's those technicians for you, always slacking, always trying to prevent me from getting the job done. I've already killed the man responsible for it, of course." Changing tack he said, "But you do know why I'm here, don't you. I'm going to round him up again before he leaves in the morning – this time with his family – and persuade him to make a few necessary adjustments. Then the world will be truly mine: The King of All Time," he smiled, boasting at the pair. Zeus turned and paced up and down. "Now, what will I do with you both?"

"Let the boy go," said Tom.

"Why should I?" Zeus played with his stick. "*You* can't help me anymore, whether I let him go or not. You don't know anything about these technicalities: you're useless to me now." He took the thin sheath off the steel bladed stick, ready to get rid of Tom, when Alex spoke up.

"What about Troy?"

"What about what?" Zeus asked uncomprehendingly, twisting-up his mouth at the corner.

"What about Troy?" Alex repeated – "Ilium – Wilusha?"

"What about it? True, I'm planning my next trip there – but what's that got to do with you?"

"I know where the best of the treasure is," chanced Alex, "leave Lio alone and I'll show you."

"How would you know?" Zeus asked suspiciously.

Alex calmly announced, "Because I was born in the future, two thousand years from today – I learned about it in history. The best of the treasure gets discovered hidden in a wall, in about eighteen hundred years time. And there was an escape tunnel found below the palace."

"What? Make a note of that," Zeus called over to his commander. The Sicilian seemed genuinely impressed alone by just where and when Alex had travelled from. "Nearly two thousand years! And I'd have given the world no more than a couple of hundred years at the most." His eyes started to light up. "This opens up much greater horizons. Two thousand years of plunder – I'll look forward to that. Just think of the weaponry that will be available then," his eyes started to glaze over with greed and lust for power. "I really could be the ruler of the whole world – forever!" Zeus looked at the boy anew. "Actually, I think I will bring you with me after all," his eyes narrowed, "I'm sure you'll be a mine of information – given the right stimulus." He stroked the steel rod delicately.

"Then only," Alex bargained, "if you take us both."

Zeus thought for a moment, stroking his face. "You aren't attempting to make a deal with me are you?" he narrowed his eyes. "Well… I suppose we could squeeze one more aboard if it saves me time… you wouldn't dare lie if I held your old friend, would you? Go on then, I suppose I am a man of my word," he narrowed his eyes more slyly. Calling out to two of the guards, he said, "Take them on board, I have a task to perform… and send someone after the other two, surely they've found the technician by now, I've told you exactly where we found him the first time."

Tom whispered to Alex as they stood and waited to be tied up by the guards: "You do realise, don't you – that if we get in that thing, we'll not be getting out alive."

"Yes," Alex answered, "I know, but what can we do?"

Zeus strolled casually toward the pile of documents. He kicked the papers around loosely, then looked down to where the heaviest roll lay. "Good, they are still here then," he sniggered at the old man and the boy. "Just a thought: this time around I might save myself some time and money – instead of waiting to retrieve the sunken horse from the bottom of the sea. I'll just hand these straight over to me when I arrive home." Now, both Alex and Tom realised together that they were in deeper trouble – the task of making the Hippo-Tempus would be much faster and easier. And, forewarned this time, he knew enough to prevent the technician from limiting the horse's travel to the past only. In the past, he must have seen Kyrros drop the roll containing the plans, but hadn't retrieved them… which in turn meant…

"Now I understand! Now I know who you all are…" The second silky voice ran out from the opposite side of the library. A helmeted figure in black stepped out and crossed the room. "I've been standing watching you all. I couldn't quite hear you, but I'm right aren't I" he smirked at his older self, "you *are* me." His eyes lit up, "I must have made it after all." He stepped toward the three. "How marvellous to meet me." He picked up another discarded scroll and wiped the blood from his unsheathed stick. Behind him, the legs of the librarian poked out from behind the shelves. Staring at the later version of himself, and at the golden leaves on his head, he said simply, "Well, well, I have done rather well for myself, haven't I!" He studied the other figure, "A little older – perhaps more distinguished – but worth the wait?"

His other self nodded, "Absolutely, it was indeed," he agreed with himself.

"But wait," he pondered, "does that now mean that I can just take this machine and go without having to wait – how many years?"

"Six," his other self answered.

Surely, thought Alex, *that would cause a paradox*: if he didn't take those years to build the Hippo-Tempus, then as soon as he left with it, it would simply cease to exist. Tom looked at Alex hopefully, both of them willing the high priest to attempt the shortcut.

"No, perhaps not," said the helmeted Zeus. "We wouldn't want to risk losing everything just to save a few years, would we?"

"Certainly not," the crowned Zeus agreed, "not when we've already won. Shame though," he murmured to himself.

The guards finally arrived back, pushing the familiar technician roughly into the room before them. "Oh good," The crowned Zeus said, "Just in time – time to go then."

Again, Alex and Tom's hopes were raised, if the technician was taken away on the Hippo-Tempus now, the machine couldn't be completed by his younger self – therefore it still couldn't exist – another paradox!

"Wait a moment," said the helmeted Zeus, "I need him."

"What?"

"I need him to make this," he pointed to the horse – "Without him, it can't be made."

The crowned Zeus blinked. "Of course," he agreed. "Just as well we realised in time," he said, turning his gaze on Tom. At last the familiar vicious streak came out in his voice as he growled. "And *you* would have let it happen – WOULDN'T YOU!" He stormed over to Tom. "Do you know, just for that, I'm going to change my mind." He held the point of steel at Tom's throat, drawing a drop of blood.

The two guards still stood behind Alex, so that Alex wouldn't have dared move – for his friend's sake. The helmeted Zeus also stormed over, changing his own stick to his other hand and holding it also to Tom's throat, so that they stood in a triangle facing each other. Alex looked up at Tom with the two sharp blades at his throat, blood trickling into his white beard.

The look of wickedness on both the faces of the figures holding the sword sticks was identical. "What do you think?" They asked each other at the same time – simultaneously grasping the same idea. As if looking in a mirror, with their free hands, each formed a wizened fist. Then, each held out their hand toward each other, both holding out their thumbs horizontally level. "Is it to be life?" they said together, turning their thumbs up… "Or is it… DEATH!" Both grinned, then they looked back at Tom, savouring their moment of victory. Now, together, they jerked their thumbs quickly down.

It was at that instant that the idea came to Alex. He reached toward Tom, snatched the bull's pizzle from his hand and stepped forward to gently push the crowned Zeus with it. The high priest's body swayed to his side. For the briefest of moments the two thumbs touched together and a tiny blue spark of static seemed to leap slowly across the gap with a 'Bzzzt!' The crowned Zeus kept the blade to Tom's throat while the other, who had seen Alex push his other self, swung around to point his blade directly at the boy's face. "What do you think you're doing?" he challenged. Alex gulped, waiting for something to happen, but nothing did. Now, Zeus dropped the point of the blade and held it directly at Alex's throat. "If you dare ever touch either of us again…" he threatened between clenched teeth.

Alex looked at Tom's face and followed his eyes to where Tom was staring, flicking his eyeballs repeatedly toward the crowned figure that still held the stick at his throat. Gradually, almost imperceptively, the colour in the face of the crowned Zeus started to drain and the figure started to turn pale grey. Not just his face and arms, but the black uniform too, started to turn grey. He turned toward the helmeted figure that now began to stare. Alex heard shouting outside. At long last, Caesar's troops had realised that the source of the commotion minutes earlier had come from inside the library. They had arrived to investigate.

The two guards behind Alex began to stare, mouths open.

"What are you all looking at?" demanded the greying figure – "Stop it." Then he noticed the odd colour of his own arm holding the stick. He lowered it to stroke it with his other hand. Backing away from everyone, he shouted – "Guards!" Nodding toward the soldiers arriving in the doorway, he said: "Take them." As he did so, first his eye, then his face twitched. A cohort of soldiers started to march into the room – "Stop them," repeated the helmeted Zeus. The soldier manning the large ballista looked confusedly from one to the other wondering who was in charge, waiting. "Stop them – now!" both yelled at once. The ballista bolts shot into the cohort in a steady stream, the 'Toc – toc – toc', scattering the normally well disciplined troops. The commander called reinforcements, so more Romans rushed into the library, only to be cut down by the smaller ballistae.

Now, a small spark – like those that had emanated from both the watches and the machine – wriggled from the crowned Zeus's thumb and up the arm of the rapidly greying figure. Then another lone spark followed. Another appeared to dance along the metal stick in the other hand and arm as he looked on incredulously. "Stop it," he called futilely to the sparks, his arm twitching. Now another wriggled across the floor and up his leg. The sparks seemed to be attracted by the now totally grey figure. As they collected, he tried to brush them off like insects. "Stop this, I command it!" the grey figure insisted as the sparks began to automatically root-out what should not by rights have been there. He tried again to kick and brush them off his arms and chest as more and more began to appear, crawling down the bookshelves from the ceiling and back in through the doors. "Help me!" He commanded his other self, gawping back at him in horror as he backed away. The two guards turned and ran back to the Hippo-Tempus as the machine noise started again and more soldiers crept towards its head.

But then, from inside its wooden cabin, a lever was depressed and a blast of flame from its nostrils shot into them. It scorched the soldiers and began to incinerate the shelves and the bone-dry papyrus scrolls. The two guards turned and raced into the machine, followed by the others, as the escaping technician ran out through the back door of the library.

Now, the whole body of the figure in front of Alex and Tom seemed to writhe with sparks as he began to plead with them to stop. As he opened his mouth to do so, the sparks crawled inside his mouth, nose and ears – fizzling as they went. Alex pushed the spiral stick into Tom's hand, then took his arm and led him cautiously to the wall. As he did so, the younger figure of Zeus took off his helmet. He looked around him, assessing his sudden predicament and then began to skirt around the soldiers to head for the foyer. The screaming figure of the crowned Zeus dropped to his knees where he was being eroded away. Bit by bit, the sparks stripped away patches of the grey clothes, then the grey flesh from his greying bones. Now he writhed in agony. "MAKE THEM STOP!" Was the last thing he screamed at the top of his voice.

Alex and Tom began to make their way around the machine, but then came the sound that told them that the Hippo-Tempus was about to escape as they knew it must, en-route to Troy. The grey skeleton dropped forward onto the floor and began to turn to dust as Caesar's troops rushed towards the ladders – only to be cut down with swords as each reached the doors. The noise began to grow louder – smoke and flame building in the machine's chest – flames again belching from its nostrils. It caught more of the scrolls around it, until the flames in the bookshelves spread across each shelf in turn. Now the fire crawled up their edges, toward the ceiling.

"We're too late to stop the machine Tom," cried Alex. "We'll have to go."

Tom gritted his teeth in exasperation, "Then I've failed!"

"No Tom, you haven't, you've still achieved your goal – look." Alex pointed at the retreating troops, dragging out their dead as the flames engulfed the interior – leaping up the shelves. The red stained, white uniformed body of the librarian was dragged across the floor and out of the door as roof timbers and door lintels started to ignite. "Quickly," shouted Alex, "before it's too late."

Tom clutched his chest, hardly able to stand in the intense heat and smoke. Then, Alex grabbed him by the arm, to lead him along the walls and toward the rear door. As its door hatches were closed and the wooden shutters dropped, clouds of smoke now billowed from the Hippo-Tempus. The monster rose a few inches on its legs, a trail of steam coming from its nostrils. It was then that the whole world seemed to shake and tremble as Alex and Tom tapped his way through the door with the stick. And as they did, the almighty blast of the machine tore-off what remained of the roof of the Great Library.

In an explosion of orange flame, the Hippo-Tempus disappeared, scattering the small pile of grey dust to the eight winds. At least one version of the High Priest of Zeus had at last reached his own ekleipsis!

CHAPTER 41:

Carpe Diem

Rain began to fall outside the Great Library, but still the flames grew out of control. Alex coaxed Tom to hurry away from the place as fast as he could, staggering along with his stick. While they attempted to hurry, behind them, the sky burned red. How, wondered Alex, Caesar and Cleopatra could fail to hear the Hippo-Tempus and miss the burning of the library this time was beyond him. But now, at least everything should be back on track.

It took hours, and many long exhausted rests for Alex to get Tom back to the Serapeion. Tom laboured on, his chest heaving in the downpour as they finally started to climb up the steps of the temple again. At the top, Tom sat exhausted, propped up by the pizzle. With a mixture of sadness at the catastrophic loss – and absolute relief at what they'd managed to achieve – they once more looked out over the rooftops of the city at the already rapidly dying flames. The fire had begun to burn itself out, but far too late. Getting his breath back, Alex glanced across at Tom. He looked dreadful.

"Why don't you take a pill, Tom?" he suggested.

"What pills?" he answered, patting his sides in demonstration that he didn't have the satchel any more.

"Oh," said Alex, immediately grasping the gravity of the situation, "then we'd better get home as soon as we can then – you'll have spares there, won't you?"

Tom nodded exhaustedly.

"Where's the lighter then?" asked Alex. "I'll need it to open the inner doors."

"It's in the library," Tom nodded ironically toward the red glow in the distance. But first, we have another problem – the main doors cannot be opened by 'prayer-power' – they were, after all, locked automatically when we left here earlier."

The boy frowned. "So how do we get back in? There must be some other override device."

"There is," said Tom nodding painfully – "inside."

Alex face dropped. "But how?"

"Without disturbing the priests? There's only one way I can think of now. One of us will have to head further on, to the market place... the water well there... climb down it."

"And follow the water supply," finished Alex.

Tom nodded, the pain increasing in his chest.

"Then which way do I go?" asked Alex.

"I was hoping you'd volunteer," Tom managed a painful laugh, "I don't think I'm up to the task myself anymore. I only planned for you to return anyway."

Alex had no intention of leaving him. "I'll be back for you as quick as I can," he promised. Then he left Tom on the step and followed the short, deserted street southward, toward the canal. Thankfully, before long, he came to the well. Without waiting, he climbed carefully down into the black hole, going deeper and deeper. Then, without warning, he slipped and plummeted with a loud echoing splash, into the deep, freezing cold saltwater below. He instantly took a mouthful. Almost in panic, he tried to stand, his feet just managing to touch the bottom before he calmed down. Catching his breath, he stood on tiptoe, gauging the fast flow of the water. Cautiously trailing his left hand along the wall to ensure he took the correct route, Alex moved forward. Eventually, judging by the echo, it seemed to open out into a cavern; but then he stumbled and fell under the water again. This time, he began to flounder around, groping for the wall. But then the right side of his head struck the sandstone walls of the waterway. Shaking his head, he got to his feet. Slightly dazed, he stood, a little disoriented. Shortly, he moved off again.

So far, Alex had walked for twenty minutes in the fast-flowing current. It was too long in his mind, given that it had only taken a few minutes to walk to the well on the surface. He began to doubt that he was on the right trail. But then he came to a heavy metal grille blocking his path. This was obviously not the way he should have taken, *but perhaps*, he thought, *it might be another way out into the Serapeion*. He could hear voices arguing nearby, just ahead of him, and he began to realise from the echo that beyond the grille lay a large chamber of some sort. In the sparse light that lay ahead, he peered through it – a kind of portcullis, divided into large squares. Each square was just big enough to get his head through, but not his shoulders. He stroked his hands around, feeling the stonework to see how it opened, but he couldn't find a catch. Now he went right up to it to peer through, squeezing himself against it and hauling himself up a little further out of the water.

The stench was appalling – like rotting meat – and worse. In the dim light, he placed his head between the bars and stared through. It appeared to be a room – a cell flooded with water – with a steep staircase leading up to a door. This was definitely not what he'd expected – not at all what Tom had described as the entrance to Alexander's tomb. Something made him look again. From the centre of the water beyond the grille, there came a slow, deep, rattling primeval vibration. He saw the water shimmer. Tiny droplets erupted into a patch, seeming to bounce and hover for a few seconds above the water's surface. Then, as his eyes grew further accustomed to the sparse light, he began to make out two figures higher up, standing against the walls. Two men stood there, bickering with one another, one on each side of a door – one short and one tall. Both were spread-eagled, smack flat against the stone walls, standing on a tiny ledge.

Just as he finally realised that he was looking into Cleopatra's dungeon, the water in front of Alex erupted. The jaws and teeth of a huge Nile crocodile snapped directly at his face, making him jump back instantly. Its teeth just caught the front of his garments though, and the croc pulled him back against the bars as he struggled to escape. Another lunged at him, but mercifully missed. Then another caught the front of his clothes. This time the combined tug of both of them pulled his face against and through the bars. Alex took a deep breath and heaved himself back with all his might – just in time. Another huge croc snapped viciously at his face. He still couldn't tear himself free though. As the crocs continued to roll over and over, they twisted the heavy shirt tighter. It began to knot around his neck. Slowly, he was being strangled – garrotted. He felt his face and neck grow hot as the blood pressure increased. Now his eyes and ears burned. Within a few seconds, he was struggling to breathe. He could feel his consciousness drifting. He was about to give in – he wasn't going to make it!

But that was when he thought of Tom waiting somewhere above him. A sudden shot of adrenalin coursed through his veins, and for one last time, he pushed back against the bars. This time, the seams of the fabric tore under the strain. His body shot backwards and under the surface. He took a couple of mouthfuls of the sweet tasting saltwater again, before he spluttered unsteadily to his feet to catch his breath. Now he could hear echoing laughter around the chamber. He didn't go back to see the figures that seemed so amused. Instead, Alex turned and ploughed his way steadily back against the current, thinking of nothing more now than getting back to Tom as quickly as he could – his mistake had already wasted far too much time.

Once more getting to the cavern, this time he retraced his steps to the only in-flowing stream. Then he turned fully around and stepped decidedly to his left. Eventually, thankfully, he at last came to the place he was looking for, and this time he followed Tom's instructions precisely. Climbing up the short steps, he crawled, groping around, looking for the 'Xi' in Alexander's name. And there it was. As he pushed the button in its centre, a chink of golden light showed around the hidden door. Carefully, he prized it open, stepping into the room. Alex exhaled disappointedly as he realised that the body had already been removed from the huge sarcophagus. Without waiting though, he passed alongside it and ran up the stairs to find the door into the street. Pushing against it, it pivoted open and he ran outside to fetch Tom. Even though the rain had stopped a while ago, Tom was still beaded in moisture. "I'm sorry I took so long Tom, I got lost," he explained.

"That's alright Alex," Tom slurred tiredly, the left side of his face twisting badly downward. "Don't worry, you're here now."

Alex took Tom's now clammy hand, and once more he led him back down the stairs and into Alexander's secret chamber. He closed the door behind them, then he headed back around the heavy sarcophagus and made toward the, spiral staircase which led on further to the temple. "Come on Tom," he turned to see him resting, propping his weight against the empty granite coffin while clutching his chest. Suddenly it dawned on him that Tom wasn't wet with rain, he was sweating profusely and in the grip of a full heart-attack. He had to get him home fast.

Yet, even at that moment, Tom called to Alex, nodding down at the opened silvery-gold object that lay on the other side of the sarcophagus. Alex had nearly missed it: the preserved and properly laid out body of his name-sake – Alexander the Great. "Come, Alex," insisted Tom, "take a look."

"There's no time," said the boy in panic.

Tom looked all-in – about to pass out. "Al-lex, there is always time for a moment like this – a once in a lifetime moment – if you miss this opportunity you will regret it always. 'Carpe diem' – seize the day!"

As calmly as he could manage, Alex came back to gaze in awe upon the golden face for one fleeting moment. Curiously, the face was younger, more peaceful than he'd imagined. Alex took in every detail. It was indeed a once in a lifetime moment that he knew he would never forget.

"Al-lex," Tom said softly, "One more thing, before each of us leave this place… please take this from me. I couldn't help noticing that you were especially attached to it, so rather than trust to keep it in the satchel, I took it out and kept it with me. I know that my old friend would most certainly approve. So here – *my grandson"* – he reached into the folds of his jubbah and produced the worn old map that Poseidonios had made. "Please accept this gift – *from your grandfather!"* Alex gratefully took it from him, though as he did, the map finally fell into pieces. The whole, discovered world of the ancient Greeks was becoming a jigsaw.

"But now," prompted Tom exhaustedly, "I think we should head for home Alex. I'm really not feeling too well at all." Even clutching onto the stick, Tom almost fell.

The boy struggled to prop him up: "Tom, hang on!"

Within a couple of minutes, the map fragments safely in his hand, Alex sat astride the now almost friendly looking Hippo-Chronos machine. "Don't worry Alex," Tom smiled, "we all run out of time eventually. And, after all, this is not a bad way to depart this world!" He looked tiredly at the boy.

Not yet though, Alex thought determinedly. And with a last look at the interior of the Serapeion, the young man finally pushed forward the lever.

A mile away, the figure in the black uniform and purple cloak stood outside the palace, watching the library fire die down. *He who fights and runs away…* he thought. After all, he still had the crate containing the Hippo-Chronos and the full satchel of travel accounts and other papers he had rescued from the library – although he could not find the heavy scrolls he'd seen Kyrros drop behind him. Then, from the area of the Serapeion, came the distant noise that only he paid particular attention to, the sound of rolling thunder, followed by a single bolt of lightning!

Conna's dad kept his head down against the rain while he crossed the muddy grass to Tom's house. Over two thousand years later, he saw the very same flash of lightning from the corner of his eye, accompanied by the oddest sounding thunderclap that he'd ever heard. The evening's weather was one of the worst he'd ever known; he couldn't count how many times he'd heard thunder. But now, at last, he was happy to know that his son was safe and warm, and not outside in this downpour. Finally, he determined to make it up with Conna – no matter how long it would take. He banged loudly on the door as he heard the shouts and cries coming from upstairs. Then someone ran noisily downstairs. It was Maddie who opened the door.

"Thank goodness somebody's here," she said, "there's been another accident!"

At that, Conna's father leapt up the stairs to stare at the very familiar face of the old man lying on the floor.

PART V:
AFTERMATH

IF ONLY I HAD KNOWN,

I SHOULD HAVE BECOME A WATCHMAKER

Albert Einstein 19th century AD

CHAPTER 42:

Message in a Bottle

The day-glo striped ambulance splashed up the muddy road, its headlights flashing alternately. Blue emergency lights reflected off the windows of both Alex's and Tom's house. Standing with the baby at the opened back door of her house, Alex's mother could only watch as, for the second time in weeks, the medics rushed into her neighbour's and came out shortly after with a stretcher. Conna's dad accompanied him, as did Alex. They were followed by the twins, and lastly Conna and Boris. All of them, it looked to her, had been saturated by the rain.

Within a few minutes, the ambulance then pulled away again, leaving the girls and Boris standing in the downpour. Seeing Penny, Conna and the girls thought it best to explain to her all together what had happened – the short version that is. They crossed over the mud to fill her in on what had gone on: that while Conna, Alex and the girls were alright, Tom had been taken ill again, a heart-attack, according to Conna's father. All they could do was wait for news, and in the meantime go and tidy up Tom's place. Penny was too distracted about everything else to get too upset about her neighbour just now, although she promised to ring the hospital later on their behalf. So the three left her and crossed back to Tom's house, followed by Boris. Once inside, Maddie went to make three hot drinks.

Now a little more calmed down after the panic, Bex picked up the apple she'd carried with her from Aegilia and looked at it in her palm. She absentmindedly stroked it with her thumb. "I can't believe it," she said sadly. "After all that, he's having a heart-attack. I never saw him looking so frail as when he fell off the back of that horse. It's a good job your dad was here. Do you think he'll be alright?"

"I wouldn't know," admitted Conna, "but I've never seen anyone look that grey before, he looked dreadful, didn't he." He looked down at his hands, feeling hopeless."

Bex looked guiltily at Conna, "I feel awful, I just wanted to tell him what went on – you know – in case anything happened to him."

Conna nodded in agreement, then he rallied a little. "Dad was good though, wasn't he," he said proudly. "I've never seen him like that before – my dad," he nodded sagely to himself.

Bex smiled in agreement.

"Bex," Conna suggested, "why don't we go to the hospital and wait – overnight if we have to. See if we can get a chance... an opportunity... to let him know."

"Let him know what?" asked Maddie curiously, returning with the drinks.

"Let him know about the other part of our trip," said Bex.

"What other part?" She wrinkled her nose.

"Well," admitted Conna, "it was my idea..."

"Our idea," said Bex, "I don't mind saying it now."

"Okay then, our idea."

"But it was Conna who worked out how to do it all – get the sequence right – without getting into danger of changing any future events," said Bex proudly.

"Well, It wasn't that difficult," he shrugged. "We just had to deliver the message *before* we took Kyrros into his future with his family."

"What message? Asked Maddie, "It's not like you to keep secrets Bex, we *are* twins remember," she pursed her lips.

"Well, I didn't want to make a fool of myself, did I," she admitted, "in case the whole story was just nonsense all along."

Conna and Bex then began to calmly relate the story of their own adventure to Maddie – both leaving out their own 'personal stuff'. Although, Bex fully intended to let her sister know later of how they'd rescued Kyrros and had then made two visits to the cave – et cetera! Maddie left the room and returned seconds later. She delicately handed over a piece of ancient, yellowed paper, along with an empty old bottle – Conna's energy drink bottle. "Here, I found this earlier, when I went into Tom's bedroom to find his spare pills in his bedside cabinet drawer. Be careful" she said, handing it to her sister, "it feels very delicate". On one side, in Bex's own neat handwriting it read:

Miriam – one day, when Lio returns from Sicilia – you must *make certain that he and Ashur stop quarrelling. It will be their one and only chance at passing happiness.*

Below, in Alex's handwriting, was a translation into Greek. Thirdly, below that, was more messy handwriting in Latin. It was badly translated and misspelled, and the grammar and syntax were appalling, but Conna had managed in his own hand to somehow get the second, impromptu message across:

Ashur – Lio loves ~~big~~ muchly you – a man old now ~~are them, they is~~, she am – cannot him come home – two thousand (nearest printable literal translation of his own misspelling of annus) *– 'bottoms' away he lives. Always does ~~they them~~ him love – you alone!*

Then, on the back, in a delicate, more educated Greek hand, and in fading pale blue pigment, was written a short page that no one there could understand. However, they all guessed it was Ashur's reply. By the changes in coloured pigment, it had been added-to at least twice – possibly three times. At the bottom of the note were three strange, further notes. They were made up of rows of spindly, almost matchstick men and women. At least the second row was obviously intended for themselves: the youths who had helped rescue Kyrros.

It was a row made up of a tall, bearded man, then a woman

wearing a dress. They held the hand of a boy between them. Then, beside them, stood another woman. Alongside that, there was a single word – 'EFKARISTO' – with the rho this time deliberately written the wrong way round.

In a different shade of ink, a baby girl had been added along with three more figures below: a drawing of a strange horse with splayed out legs, and a boy and girl holding hands. The girl wore a long coat and goggles, and the boy with a black eye wore a single boot – and a wristwatch.

"Blood…inking – heck! I still haven't found Tom's watch," Conna blurted out.

"Somehow, I don't think Tom will mind," said Maddie, "he must have guessed it would happen all along."

Finally, drawn very faintly on the last line was a boat crashing into a rock. Beside it, stood the figure of a lone woman – her hand in the air in final salute – Ashur? Beside that stood a row of very faded X's – kisses from the family.

The letter and the record of Conna and Bex's own journey had managed to get to Tom down the ages.

"I don't understand. How did this get here?" asked Maddie.

"Beats me," said Conna.

"Me too," admitted Bex. "It's ancient, but it's definitely our note, and the proof that I asked him for – that Lio knew Ashur had borne him a child."

The three stood thinking. "Hang on," said Conna at last. "So Tom knew all along that we would help him… had helped him… were going to… help?"

"Maybe… though how could he know the matchstick figures were supposed to be us?" Bex pondered.

"But if that's the case," added Maddie, picking up the thought, "that means that this was all meant to happen – that we were just doing what we were always meant to do."

"Like taking our place in history," agreed Bex – "though we didn't have to do it."

Again the three struggled to take it in. "So our place in history was to help Tom achieve what exactly?" puzzled Conna, not yet knowing what had happened at the library, or why other than Alex's punchy description of events: 'Things went okay –mostly!'

"I don't know, but it still doesn't explain how the note got back here two thousand years later, does it?" said Bex.

"I hope we find out," said Maddie, and together they thought of Tom lying in his hospital bed.

"Please let him pull through," said Bex solemnly to the window.

"Yeah," Said Conna, lifting his mug of tea in the air, "to Tom," he said solemnly.

"To Lio," sniffed Maddie.

Boris lay beside the Hippo-Chronos and began to whimper, sensing that something was wrong. At the hospital Tom had taken a turn for the worse.

Maddie's thoughts turned back to poor Alex, and why he'd originally persuaded them to get involved with Tom. She knew what a crushing blow it was to him if he could not now achieve his own personal goal – to get his dad back. With that, although it was nobody's fault, she thought of her own aborted attempt to help him. Suddenly she felt disappointment both that her own journey had been little more than a short trip into a desert somewhere – anywhere for all she knew (although she did see one and a half pyramids) – and her failure to bring back the man she had never before met.

When Bex's dad Freddie arrived at Tom's, he immediately hugged his daughters to him knowingly. He had already been in touch with the coronary care ward and understood the situation. Now, he feared the worst. In a huddle, together with Conna, he attempted to prepare them as much as he could.

Tom was critically ill, he advised. He'd had a massive heart-attack and it was ongoing. Only time would tell whether he would make it through the night. His girls and Conna were upset and wanted to go to the ward and wait outside – as long as it took – to see Tom again, so he agreed to take them all. As he, Bex and Conna walked to the top of the staircase, Maddie stood there with the dog.

She suddenly had an idea. Perhaps, she suggested, it would be better for one of them to stay here – for instance her. Just to tidy up and be on hand to collect anything that Tom might require at the hospital. In any case, she argued, four was already enough around a hospital bed. Alright, Freddie agreed, Maddie was old enough, or at least sensible enough not to touch anything she shouldn't, so when the three left in his car, his daughter closed the door behind them.

Now that there was only Maddie and Boris in the house, it took only three minutes per side for the electric drill to wind up the springs of the Hippo-Chronos – perfectly normally. But as she did so, unknown to her, a long splinter of wood that had somehow transferred itself from the corbita, presumably on someone's clothing, lay inside the machine. With the vibration, it worked its way toward the timer mechanism of the Hippo-Chronos. It moved steadily toward the rotating rings that kept the heart of the horse upright at all times and allowed the device to 'tink' every ten seconds precisely. Momentarily, Maddie forgot to blow the machine through and over with the vacuum cleaner. Instead, she concentrated on checking the timer and the coordinates repeatedly this time. All of this accomplished, sitting astride the horse, she clapped her hands for Boris to jump up beside her. And for once, he did. Making sure he hadn't touched anything this time, she pushed the lever forward and prepared herself for her second journey.

As Freddie's car pulled into the familiar hospital car park, the torrential rain pounded down. In the rear view mirror he saw another flash of lightning – the umpteenth that night. He didn't mention it to Bex and Conna, both lost in their own respective worlds, each looking out of their own side window.

It was dark, early pre-dawn on the ancient farm at Drodos, and the sky was still full of stars. It was still a few hours earlier than Tom had agreed to meet his neighbour, Stan – his son – though there was still no sign of him. But Maddie was prepared to wait. This time, as the horse settled into the thin covering of sand lying on the yard, Boris spotted the lone, crowing rooster. The dog jumped immediately down and scattered across the yard after it. The bird flapped and fluttered wildly onto the peak of the gable end of the barn, precisely where the weather vane had been.

Maddie looked around her, but there was no sign of anyone at all. Of course, she remembered, there was always the back-up plan – to go further back in time and pick him up just after Tom had left him there. But that would be to rob him of the experiences that he'd had over the year – whatever they may be. Instead, Maddie steeled herself to wait a while. But at the first sign of danger, she would remove herself and the machine to exactly a year previous and complete her mission at all costs. Entirely happy with the plan, she unfolded the pedals and began the slow trudge to wind up the spring for the third leg of the journey, should it be required. As she pedalled, she occasionally clapped her hands and called out for Boris. But, yet again, he was nowhere to be seen. *Some company,* she thought.

An hour later, as the dawn started to rise ahead of her in the east, a small group of figures appeared in the distance. Maddie felt the click of the spring retainer drop into place – which in turn caused the splinter to drop a little further and come to a rest. At six o'clock in the morning precisely, the wooden particle that had previously invaded the Hippo-Chronos finally projected half-way out of the gap it had found its way into. As it did, it fouled the rotating hand and arm of Kyrros' slow escapement mechanism. This caused the arm to stop. The tiny gold ball suspended on the gold thread, ceased its slow, constant, tink. Now, it became an irregular descending tink-tink-tink… before it stopped. So also, the breathing sound of the tiny spring ceased. Unaware of this, Maddie watched the figures get slowly nearer to her. Then, just in case they were unfriendly, she clapped her hands again for the dog to join her, still blissfully unaware that the heart of the Hippo-Chronos had just stopped.

At that very same moment, 25.9 degrees to her east – in the hospital in Tynemouth, even before the buzzer went off in the ward, everyone knew what had happened. Tom's heart had gone into arrest.

CHAPTER 43:

To the Rescue

Freddie, Conna and Bex arrived at hospital to find Alex sat alone
with Tom. He held the bare arm of the unconscious patient while
he lay breathing noisily through the oxygen mask. Conna's father
had already gone to scrub up, volunteering to stay on-hand to help
his old patient. Only the array of complicated equipment attached
to Tom via tubes and wires prevented him from slipping away. Alex
reflected on Tom's and his conversation in the library, about the
proper use of technology: saving life, not taking it. Freddie, Bex and
Conna waited outside, while he continued his private 'chat' with
Tom.

"Tom, you were right about the library – maybe it's best that it
did burn down and take all those secrets with it after all. And I
understand about Troy. I guess that's where the Hippo-Tempus and
its commander must have ended up anyway, so it's best if it *is* left
the way everyone knows the tale." Anyway, I'm sure everything's
going to turn out alright now." Alex got up to make a move. "And…
granddad," he added for the first time, "don't feel guilty about dad, I
know he would have given anything to visit the past like that – see
the tomb of Alexander the Great. Who knows what other adventures
he'll get up to there? Anyway," he said finally, "just get better – we're
all here – waiting for you to return home." Alex looked back once,
then quietly opened the door to give Conna his own two minutes
to speak privately into Tom's ear.

As sad as it seems, Conna could not think of anything much to say other than they'd managed to save Kyrros and return the torc as agreed – and to tell Tom again how much he'd loved the adventure, and getting spend some time alone with Bex. Then he patted Tom's good shoulder and told him that he hoped he'd get well soon. Before he got emotional, he walked silently to the door, and out into the corridor.

Next, in her turn, Bex held Tom's hand and thanked him for not dismissing her as someone lacking the capacity or imagination to believe in him. Then she told him again about her moment alone with Ashur and how radiant she'd looked with Lio's – his own – daughter. Perhaps it was a nervous twitch, perhaps she just imagined it, but as she did so, Tom's hand seemed to squeeze hers as she finished her report. She ended by stroking back his mane of hair and planting a gentle kiss on the old man's forehead. Please Tom, she pleaded, please pull through... for me and Maddie and everyone.

While Freddie waited outside, the other two returned to the room. Now, all three kept silent vigil. Each of them watched the shallow rise and fall of his chest and listened to the more and more irregular blip. But then the blip stopped, and a constant bleep sounded as the monitor flat-lined.

Straight away, the nurse opened the swing doors and ushered the three to stand aside. The crash team followed her through with the red trolley, Conna's father behind it.

Now once more in the corridor, the doors closed. All the four could do was wait.

The figures in the already shimmering heat haze of the desert now grew slowly into three distinct wavy entities. Maddie watched steadfastly over a period of another fifteen minutes as they grew into three camels and riders, trotting steadily toward her. Again she clapped her hands, beginning, not for the first time, to wish she'd left the dog behind. As they neared, from around the corner of the barn came Boris trotting sheepishly toward her. He panted, his tongue hanging down and a feather sticking out from the corner of his mouth.

"Boris, you didn't!" she scolded, but as if in answer, behind him, the cockerel flapped back onto its perch and began to crow, none the worse for wear. The dog jumped up in front of her and she pulled the feather from his mouth as he sat in front of her. He flicked a glance up at her while she stroked him, patiently waiting for the riders to get closer. Maddie's hand returned to the lever, getting ready, now that the figures became recognisable. The three desert travellers were swathed in thin layers of insulating robes. Each of their faces was covered with a long, loose headdress, wrapped under their eyes and draped over their shoulders. None were recognisable as the man she might be waiting for. About a hundred paces away, she called out a single: "Hello" – a word she knew would be recognisable only to her target – but there was no answer. Again she called out – louder this time, but still there was no reply.

The travellers started to slow down, reaching the farm. Then, one by one, each of the camels dropped to its knees and the riders began to dismount expertly. One last time, she called out: "Hello!" but still to no avail. By their stance, Maddie decided that the two on the outside especially did not look friendly.

That was enough for her! She pushed the lever forward and waited for the whirr as the three walked slowly toward her. She would go to the fall-back plan. But as she waited, nothing happened. She looked down, wondering what had gone wrong. She reversed the lever and jerked it back again, but still to no effect. Boris barked as the middle figure walked faster, stooping and looking from side to side toward Maddie and the dog, weighing them up. But then the two side figures made to pull out their long knives. Boris jumped down and stood in front of the Hippo-Chronos, barking and growling furiously, the terrier instinctively defending Maddie and his territory. His rear end high and forelegs stretched out in front, he threatened to attack the group, until the centre man held out his arms across the tribesmen, urging them to put away their weapons. Then, he brought his hands together with a double-clap and dropped to his knees. "Boris?" he called out, the face cover dropping down to reveal a heavily bearded, pink tanned face.

400

His face, thought Maddie, looked strangely familiar.

"Boris…" he called out again, "…come on boy!" And the dog ran toward him, wagging his tail back and forth furiously. The man he had not seen for a year took off the headdress, revealing his gingery-grey hair. Then the dog leapt up to him, nipped firstly one ear lobe then, as he covered it, the next ear lobe. Then, still before he could react, the dog nipped the end of his nose.

"Stan?" called out Maddie.

"Yes," he said, "but who are *you*?" He looked at the lowered machine – now with strange wooden legs since he'd last seen it. Climbing down off the time-horse, she introduced herself.

"I'm Maddie, Alex's friend – Tom asked me to collect you."

"Who?" He asked.

"Your neighbour," Maddie corrected herself.

"Oh," he said, "my father – Billy – or Lio, if you prefer!"

Maddie smiled and nodded, "Anyway, you've been missing for over a year."

"A what?" he gasped incredibly.

Behind him, as Maddie outlined everything briefly, including the birth of his red haired daughter, the tribesmen darted out of the dog's way as it went into play-attack mode. Boris pulled at their long garments as each of them made growling noises.

After finishing the tale, Maddie added worriedly, "But I'm afraid something's gone wrong with the machine… it just won't work."

Now Stan looked worried. "I may have helped clean and re-build the replica Antikythera key, but that's the limit of my knowledge. I'm afraid I'm not very good with more complicated gadgets," he confessed, "I wouldn't know where to start." He stood and looked at the machine as Boris again came back and began to jump up and bark at his feet, but all he and Maddie could do was look down at the mechanical marvel – completely baffled. Neither had a clue what to do.

Back inside the hospital, the crash team worked in the ward. While outside, the group of friends tried to reassure one another that everyone was doing their part – and that while the various noises squeezed out of the gap under the doors, there was still hope. However, it was a full fifteen minutes later that the busy noises ceased and the silence betrayed the crash-team's unsuccessful result. Inside the ward, Conna's dad packed away the defibrillator, and the nurse called out the time to be recorded as life extinct. It was duly recorded on the patient's chart. She reached over and turned the white shouldered knob in the wall, and the hiss of the oxygen supply to his mask ceased.

It was Conna's dad, and not simply his father that came out of the room to deliver his son and his friends the bad news. Taking Conna to one side, he finally confessed to him: "I'm sorry I've ignored you so much. I'll make it up to you from now on – I promise." With that, Conna finally got the hug that he'd awaited so long. He smiled back sadly at his dad, hoping that he meant it, now that his abusive mother seemed to be out of the picture.

Immediately afterwards, the adults walked to one side to let the youths talk amongst themselves and console each other. Dejectedly, each began to try to come to terms with the fact that they would no longer see their newest, oldest friend alive. Each tried not to crack – now keeping a brave face for one another's sake – although a few tears managed to squeeze out from each of them. No one spoke, but this time it seemed an entirely comfortable silence, until the same nurse came out to commiserate with the few she knew had tried to help and befriend him for weeks. It was only then that Bex began to sob, clutching her in place of her twin.

Alex turned to Conna, "Maddie will be devastated when we tell her."

"Do you think we should call her?" asked Conna.

"No," said Bex, blowing her nose. "I think it would be better coming straight from us, face to face. Let's just go."

"Don't you wish to see your friend one last time, alone," asked the nurse, "you may if you wish?"

"Yeah," said Alex, "if that's alright?"

"Yes please," said Bex.

"Well, okay," said Conna, a little more reluctantly.

One by one they returned to Tom's bedside.

By now, at Giza, Maddie and Stan had gone through everything they could. They had, between them, stripped out both keys, one by one. They checked carefully that there was no sand clogging anything up, and then they replaced them. Each in turn then combed the entire machine for signs of any damage, but still to no avail. Both now began to realise the full peril of their situation.

Trying not to worry one another, each pretended to go on looking, whilst their minds wandered-off back home. Maddie opened the chest hatch in the machine and stared at the arrested mechanism, wondering again about poor Tom and how he was doing, while Stan busied himself examining something at the other end. The girl's eye roamed slowly around the interior: around the circular rings and across the red jewels, past the tiny blue spring and the spindle that held the arm with the ball suspended from it. She was about to close the hatch again, when she spotted something foreign – non-metallic. Not part of the horse, but something else – it obviously didn't belong there. Slowly, tentatively, she reached inside. Between her outstretched middle and forefingers, she managed to delicately grip the piece of wood. And as she carefully withdrew it, the arm swung around – a full revolution this time. As the ball reached its small momentum, it dutifully wrapped itself and the thread around the pin. Now, it unwound once more and swung through its proper half-revolution, to wrap around the opposite pin. Once again began the slow tink… tink… tink, along with the breathless sound of the spring. At that, the main spring motor began to unwind. Of course, it was probably just a trick of the light, perhaps a couple of the jewels inside the cranium managing to catch the strong overhead sun, but at that moment, Maddie could have sworn she saw a brief glint in the horse's eye.

"That's it," she shouted. "We've done it. Quick, jump on," she called out excitedly before closing the chest hatch. As Maddie settled into place, Alex's dad leapt on from behind and clapped his hands for Boris. The two tribesmen who had crouched down to play with the strange woolly animal looked at the even stranger object, now beginning to think again about their friend, the odd, pink-faced traveller and his entertaining tale about flying horses. As they stood up, Boris dashed over to sit on the ground beneath the horse's muzzle. The dog barked as the noise grew.

"Boris," shouted Stan, "come on boy." But the dog wouldn't budge this time.

"Boris, quickly," shouted Maddie, clapping her hands over the howl of the machine. The dog looked askance at them both. Then Stan had an idea. He reached into the satchel he had carried for a year and pulled out a small, unopened, cellophane packet. He ripped open the top and jiggled it in front of the dog, so that the glorious smell of quite stale dog treats blew towards Boris's nose. Immediately, as the tribesmen covered their eyes against the sand and backed away, the dog leapt between the passengers. Unfortunately, as Stan pulled out the packet from his satchel, his diary fell onto the sand.

It was only a moment after the machine had disappeared, that each of the tribesmen realised they had in fact been in the presence of 'Orryth', a legendary, mysterious and ancient god of the desert. It was only their friend, the foreigner's strange accent that had thrown them. Each stood in fear and trepidation as the dog's horse carried the deity and Estam noisily into the stars. Though of course, neither one would mention the incident ever again – in fear that they would be stoned to death for their sacrilege in daring to attempt to tease and play games with him.

As they retreated, unseen, Stan's account of Ptolemy's last battle was eaten away by a carpet of blue sparks.

Within minutes, in her house on the Spanish Battery, carrying the sleeping baby girl as she answered the knock on the back door, Penny was taken aback to see the heavily bearded figure now stood there. Not that she instantly recognised the man as her husband – she did not – but because she had not long since taken the phone call from Conna's dad. She knew now that Tom had just passed away – and yet, there was almost the image of him right in front of her. It gave her quite a start. But if that was her mistaken initial reaction, it was only when Boris appeared from behind the figure to sit obediently at his feet, as he did with only one person in the world, that she knew her husband had come back. She opened her mouth to speak, but couldn't, now completely overwhelmed by her feelings. Then she stared at him and tried to speak again. Falteringly, in trepidation, she asked, "Stan… is that you?"

He nodded, "Penny," he said softly, "I've come home."

At that, his wife burst into tears of pure relief. Against her own belief, he had indeed returned. Stan wrapped his arms around her and Rachel, *his* girl.

"Where have you been?" She sobbed.

"Let me in," he said in answer, "and we'll tell you, won't we Boris?" At least enough to get Tom finally out of her bad books – though perhaps not the full version.

CHAPTER 44:

Eos

One by one Alex, Bex and Conna filed back in to stand by Tom's bed. Each of the boys placed an arm around Bex's shoulders, and together they looked sadly at the lifeless shell that had contained Tom. Suddenly, for the first time, the face really did look like that of a much older man; the deep lines and crinkles around his eyes seeming to finally betray a deep secret. It was matterless now though; each tried to think happy thoughts for him – and of their adventure of a lifetime.

In the final few minutes since Tom had been pronounced dead – as hackneyed a phrase as it was, the old man saw his entire life flash before his eyes: his childhood on Rhodos and in Alexandria; his youth in Antikythera; and his all too brief time with his young wife. But it was one memory in particular that stayed with him now. It was the distant memory of the first time he had left Britain since he had arrived with a bang – in the short, missing period before he had tried for the *second* time to settle in Tynemouth with Catherine – while he was still known to everyone as Billy the Greek. It was in many ways the key to his life:

Toward the end of 1962, in the aftermath of being questioned by the hospital about his sanity – for obsessively climbing the rock face of Pen Bal Crag – a storm had been literally brewing outside. 'Billy' was desperately aware that if he stayed in Tynemouth, there were likely to be more questions he couldn't answer – his memory had still not returned to him at that time. He did not want to be detained there, as the hospital had warned him he might be if he refused to explain his fascination with the rock face. Reluctantly then, he decided to head elsewhere – anywhere!

He had packed a few things from the bag hidden in the shed and had walked out into the stormy weather. But he had not used the Hippo-Chronos on that occasion. Instead, he had made directly for the quayside. It did not take long to find a ship heading out that night – as luck would have it, a Greek vessel. In that inclement weather and in the dark, it had been easy to stow away; no one stood properly on guard. Once out to sea, he immediately gave himself up to the captain. He took pity on his fellow countryman with the crude, island accent. The young man told him simply that he he'd had an accident – fallen on hard times. As a result he had been stranded in a foreign country – England. It did not take long before the boy had proven his worth to him, turning his hand to many odd jobs. The captain was only too pleased to keep him on board as casual crew. Billy stayed on board the vessel for the journey to the Port of Amsterdam, then Sicily and finally to Piraeus, the vast and polluted port of Athens. There, after another week, he found a second ship leaving for various Greek Islands. A few days later, in the early hours of the morning, Billy stood on deck gazing up at the stars. The ship sailed steadily across the wine dark sea, toward the somehow very familiar outline of a small rocky island. However, as the pre-dawn began to colour the sky, the young man was immediately troubled by the experience.

From the moment he saw the island's dark silhouette, until the old steam boat passed the twin pinnacles and headed gently into the harbour of Potamos, Billy began to shake with apprehension. For some unknown reason, his heart began to heave. Nevertheless, once inside the harbour, he began to settle down again – at least, enough to unload the ship's small cargo there as dawn broke more fully. As he worked on deck, he watched fascinated at the scattered herd of goats that precariously grazed the cliff face.

Afterwards – killing time – he decided to take advantage of the steadily warming sun. It was something he'd not experienced for a long time. Late in the morning, he strolled up the steep hill from the harbour and onto the gorse scrub of the promontory. The place was studded with abandoned stone houses, coarse, dry-stone walls and terraces. The young man became fascinated with the island's strangely familiar geography: the panoramic view down into the deep harbour; the pebble beach at Xiropotamos; and even the scant ruins of the tiny temple – little more than a stone footprint. It was as if he had been there before. He mopped at his brow.

Moving on, he wandered along the coastline, over gorse covered hills and down into valleys, wading knee deep through rivers and streams. While crickets chirruped their chorus around him, he stopped to rest on a rocky outcrop at the edge of the treacherous coastline. There, he stared around him at the alien terrain. Temporarily blinded by the intense light reflecting off the sea, for a short while, he closed his eyes and began to spare a moment for the lives of all of those who had passed that place before. Eventually, he turned his back to the high escarpment, to head back along a gentler slope and to see what else he could find. That was when he stumbled upon an old, whitewashed church.

Again, the place seemed familiar to him, although the building was not. Distractedly, he approached the cliff edge and its spectacular vista. Standing alone in the intense heat of the midday sun, he looked around him. He watched the seabirds swoop down below him. Then, mysteriously, his mind began to descend into a very dark place. As the mood took its grip, he became overwhelmed by the deepest imaginable feelings of horror, regret and loss. Unable to fathom out why, tears streamed down his face. Within moments, completely overcome by emotion, he stepped perilously close to the edge.

As he did so, an elderly voice called out a well timed: "**Yas**sou, o filos mou – Hello, my friend."

Billy gave a start and stepped back from the brink, "**Yas**sas," he automatically returned a polite reply.

"May I help you young man…?" the older man sensed his pain.

"No," he replied. "It's just that... I think I may have lived here many years ago – as a young boy."

"Ah yes," the old man smiled sadly at the coincidence, "So many memories. I left this place at the end of the war too..." tears began to glisten in his bright eyes. "I was the lighthouse keeper then – I took over from my father. I was here on that fatal day: 7th May 1944 – the single day that the fascists cleared the whole of the island population. All, that is, except for the few of us who were kept here as their personal slaves.

I can still recall seeing their SS commander revelling as his henchmen herded people onto the Nazi boats... men, women and children. I will never forget watching as he used his cane to prod and poke one 'undesirable family' in particular – an adopted, mixed race family – refugees who had fled here from Alexandria. Though I never did find out their fate... "

The older man rallied a little. "I have tried all my life to forget the many things I witnessed that day, but now I have come back here to remember. Please..." he held out his calloused hand, "people call me Gallo." The two shook hands before the older man continued: "Since then, I have lived out most of my *very* full life on the opposite side of the world. Sadly, all alone – despite all of those girls I knew in my youth..." he raised an eyebrow. "But now that I have retired, I have come back to stay." The young man immediately took to him – the conversation kept his own thoughts and regrets at bay.

"Do you know," the old man reminisced, "once, when I was a young boy, just down there," he nodded toward the harbour, "I fell in love for the first time. She was a young archaeologist's assistant," he smiled. "It was during the winter that I found some pieces of old bronze at the end of the dock. Of course, I may only have been a child, but it was, in a way, real love. She was the most beautiful woman I ever saw! A German – beautiful blonde hair, incredible eyes. Like mine and yours," he couldn't help but notice the strong coincidence. "She was a creature of complete wonderment to me. As young as I was, I will never forget her and the time I stole a kiss from her," he dreamed. "Since then I have lived through two world wars. I never stopped searching for someone like her all my life, but no one even came close to that impossible ideal – how could anyone compete with an ancient memory?"

Billy listened in fascination and in complete silence as the older man went on to describe the recovered statues, and how he had linked the fragments of the 'carriage clock' to his father's rambling story:

'*The Tale of Eos,*' he told the younger man, was 'a Greek tragedy,' a daughter's tale of her mother who had lived many, many years ago. It was a tale that spoke of high priests and eclipses, of fantastical ancient machines and philosophers. It told of Caesar and Cleopatra, and Ptolemy and Alexander the Great. It told of travels around the ancient globe and of time stolen away by the wickedest man in the world. It also told of a 'Time-Horse'. And… of the young mother's lost love for her husband of only one day. The mother's name was Ashur. More importantly, all of the tale, the older man assured him, was completely true! The young man did not argue – inside, Lio knew it to be so.

Gallo told the shortened tale faithfully, right up to the point where the husband had left the island, never to return – although it was always said that one day he must. The young man could not speak. He stood stock still throughout, listening until it was nearly dark.

Finally, finishing the tale, the older man offered: "It's time for me to go now, but if you wish, please help yourself to a drink of fresh water – over there, it isn't locked." With that, he raised his hand and bade the visitor good night – "kali**nikta**."

"Nikta," returned the young man. Turning to look for the place where he could get a drink, he saw the one thing he had earlier missed, the thing that had been successively built over for many generations – now transformed into a small, but solid, whitewashed stone building – the ancient well of Andronicus!

He called out to see if there was anyone else around, but there was not. Cautiously, he opened its door and crept in. He stood gazing at the deep pool, just as he remembered doing so before.

Tentatively, he reached up to where the remains of the original door hatch had been – and into Miriam's hiding place. He scratched around vaguely in the loose sand and pebbles that it had been filled with, knowing the exact, deeply tunnelled-out spot. That was when his fingers came into contact with something that he did not expect. He retrieved the glass bottle, and peeled off the red wax seal. Inside it, he found the note, written in a learned hand – though on very faded paper and not papyrus. It read:

My husband Lio, I know that we are destined never to meet again and that fills my heart with sadness, but at least I now know that you are safe. Know in return then, that you now have a child whom I have named after the dawning of the sun. Do not worry for us; she is both beautiful and healthy. I will live the rest of my life here in safety. And I will raise her into womanhood with the help of Kyrros, Miriam and their own son Andros.

I will not be regretful – only thankful for the life that you have given me – in many ways. It is my fervent wish that you, in your own time, are able to keep us in your heart, but trust that you will make the most of the life that has been afforded you. I will keep our story alive for all time, by handing it down through our family – beginning with our daughter.

Each morning, Eos and I will together watch the sun rise, and each evening I will alone watch the sun go down from our hill. I will think of you in another time and place, and remember you for all eternity. Thank you for everything that you have given me – my husband – my life, Ashur.

Astounded once more, Lio wondered how it could possibly be true. He wondered especially about the reference to Kyrros, but then he seized on the deliberate mistake with which Ashur had completed the note: the Rho in "EFKARISTO" had been written back to front. It was proof to him that the note was genuine. Now, he at last knew that, just as he had suspected for many years, history was indeed repeating itself.

Next, for the sake of completion, he checked the secret stash again. Even deeper inside the hiding place, he found another object. What he now found though, threw him completely. Lio's hand

411

touched a small lead box, so he dug out the sand that had been compacted around it. As he clawed it open, inside, he found a wooden box. Inside that, was a block of wax. And inside that, what appeared to be some sort of intricate wristwatch such as he had never seen before. There was however, one slight imperfection in it: a small dent, just beside the winding crown. Lio crouched down to sit cross legged on the floor. Unable to fathom any of it, he replaced the note in the bottle and placed both items in the pockets of the jacket given to him by Catherine.

Now late in the evening, Lio emerged from the cave. He again walked directly to the spot where he had stood earlier. This time, he almost felt the presence of his young wife behind him – felt her arms around his waist. Buoyed up by the experience, he inhaled the sea air deeply into his lungs. These revelations once more drove him perilously close to madness, wondering how it had all managed to come about, and what he was meant to do about it. But that was when he thought again of the written message. And that was when he decided never to take time for granted. In future, he would live on for all those he knew who were not given the chance to enjoy this most precious gift of life.

From the harbour, there came a few short blasts on the ship's steam-whistle. It awoke the young man from his daydream, and he made his way hurriedly back to Potamos harbour in a daze, to catch the boat back to Athens. There he stayed for another few weeks, wandering around the ancient sites and museums, whilst still trying to fathom it all out.

Eventually, he decided to return to his new adopted home in England.

Sometime later, when, after his row with Catherine he'd leapt forward again – this time into the eighties – he had stumbled upon the newspaper article regarding the now very familiar Antikythera device story. That was also when he'd decided that he would make everything in the letter happen – no matter how long it took. Terrified that if he spoke of these years ever again he would be locked-up over this madness, he in turn locked the event away in his subconscious. It would forever remain a 'great secret' known only to himself and Ashur.

In his hospital bed, these memories faded and the world turned dark. Polaris called.

Tom's three young friends stood by the bed, slowly coming to terms with what had happened. "Come on" said Alex, "I think we'd better go."

Conna and Bex nodded.

It was at that precise moment in Egypt, that Maddie plucked the splinter from the mechanism, re-starting the heart of the Hippo-Chronos. And, at that same instant in England, for some inexplicable reason, her twin sister Bex felt compelled to say good-bye to Tom – by placing her hand over his broken heart. Strangely, as the boys looked on, they both noticed the tiny, slow, blue spark of built-up static that might somehow have been originally generated by the defibrillator. With a familiar 'bzzt', it seemed to jump from the palm of Bex's hand to Tom's chest. It then divided into four. Each spark then wiggled away. "Did you see that?" asked Bex.

"Yeah," asked Conna, despondently, "static."

A lone spark reappeared and started to multiply over Tom's heart. "I don't think so," said Bex.

The sparks now covered the centre of his chest. Alex's eyes narrowed, recognising the bizarre effect: "You're right!"

"What's happening?" asked Conna, unsure that he was seeing it himself.

Tom's chest suddenly rose as he breathed in.

"That," said Bex, as the blip started suddenly on the heart monitor.

The three burst out into the corridor, shouting simultaneously.

"Help!"

"Nurse!"

"Dad!"

Against all logic, Tom had come through his ordeal. Obviously, he had not run out of time after all!

The traffic lights of the Pelican crossing changed from flashing amber to green as Freddie's car turned into the busy morning village high street. It passed the flower beds as the gardeners busily replanted them in evergreens. The saloon headed on, up towards the twin promontories. Inside it, the three hopeful friends were now happy enough to want to report to Maddie: Tom was out of immediate danger again. Jumping out of the car, Bex asked Freddie, "Dad, give us some time together and pick us up in a couple of hours would you please?"

"Whatever you say girl," he agreed, "You sort yourselves out and gimme a call," he offered, happy at long last, to go home and catch up on his sleep and spend time with his wife. The rain had now stopped and the three walked together towards Tom's house. Alex pulled out the key that he still had with him. Letting the others in first, they started to climb up the stairs when Maddie awoke from her snooze on the sofa to hear them coming. Jumping up immediately, and running to the top of the stairs she asked, "How is he?"

"He's still got a long way to go," said Alex. "But the doctors – and Conna's dad especially – seem a bit more hopeful now. They said to ring later to give us an update." Alex followed Maddie into the room, eager to see the Hippo-Chronos once more and be able to complete the mission to collect his dad.

He looked at the badly dented heap lying on its side, the wooden trestle, or legs, now smashed to pieces. His hopeful expression dropped, along with his shoulders. "What happened?" he asked disappointedly, "what's wrong with the horse?"

"Well," she confessed. "I had an accident – I went back myself."

"You didn't?" scolded Bex, "not again? Not on your own!"

"Look, I survived didn't I?" Maddie protested.

"So, what happened?" asked Conna on behalf of Alex standing there silently, fearful to know the outcome, knowing that the horse was now unusable.

"Well," she looked at Alex, proud of herself, "I went back to the farm, and this time he was there."

414

Alex perched himself on the edge of the sofa as Maddie went through the short series of events, including much to everyone's astonishment, her description of restarting the horse's heart.

"What are the chances of that happening?" asked Conna.

"I have no idea," wondered Bex softly. "But if you'd told me that yesterday morning I wouldn't have believed you."

"So… about dad?" Alex finally plucked the courage to ask. "Is he… okay?"

Maddie smiled radiantly. "Of course he is, silly."

"So, he's…"

"Next door, yes, he went home last night with Boris. I saw him first thing this morning, taking him for a walk."

Alex's heart leapt, though he still didn't let his emotions show, desperate to believe the news but terrified to accept it in case it was somehow untrue – a silly wind-up."

"Maybe I should go," he suggested, standing up.

"I think you ought to" said Maddie. "Good luck."

"Yeah, good luck mate." Conna clapped him on the back.

"Go on then, go find him," urged Bex.

Alex opened his mouth to speak to Maddie but couldn't.

Maddie stood and looked at him. "Well, run along – do as you're told boy," she smiled.

Alex stepped toward the girl and hugged her briefly in thanks.

"Hurry," she said, "go and see for yourself."

Suddenly reanimated, he turned and almost leapt down the stairs. Then, banging the front door closed behind him, he ran up the already drying path directly to his own front door. Grasping the key, he shoved it into the lock, and burst into the hall. Boris barked wildly at him and followed him as he ran up the stairs to his mum and dad's bedroom. "Dad?" he called out, knocking before he entered. His mother was sat up in bed, smiling at Rachel. "Where is he?" asked Alex. Then, not waiting for a reply, he ran almost in panic back downstairs, through the passage, into the sitting room and then the dining room. It was there that the smell of the frying bacon hit him. Alex stood stock still. Looking on, as he turned slowly around from the cooker, Alex saw his dad's clean-shaven face, more or less exactly as he remembered him – though with a pink tanned upper half.

"Dad" he almost whispered, "I thought I'd never see you again."

The man took a deep breath and held his arms wide, a look of massive relief on his face to once more see the young man that he'd dreamed of and missed for a year. "Alex," he said simply, "I'm sorry for all the worry I caused you – if I could only turn back the clock in some way... I swear I'll never leave you or your mother again."

Alex smiled at the thought and stepped toward the man he loved most in the world. "It's good to have you home again dad," he blurted out.

"It's good to be home sunshine," he replied. "It feels like a lifetime since I last saw you.

CHAPTER 45:

Many Blissful Memories

In the ward, only a few days later, Tom, as he insisted everyone still call him, sat surrounded by his young friends, comfortably propped up in bed in a nest of pillows. Each was happy to have played a part, and each had learned something from the experience. Of course, the four had already privately shared most of the information, especially each other's successful conclusions. Everyone knew especially what had happened in the library – and to the older Zeus.

As far as they were all concerned, for now, although not everything had gone like clockwork, most things had. The Hippo-Tempus itself had been halted from wreaking havoc for all eternity. Wherever and whenever it had finally gone, the changes it had made to history were already done. At least, as Tom pointed out, due to a rather obvious design fault (it did have a tendency to accidentally incinerate things around it), the ancient knowledge held in the Great Library had been removed from the hands of the Romans and thus prevented from being used against early humanity. Kyrros – his father – had been saved as Lio had promised as a boy, so that he could live out the rest of his life in peaceful isolation, and help bring up Ashur's and Lio's daughter, Eos. And, (if ever they should need the reserve) the torc had been rightfully returned to Miriam. Nevertheless, even when questioned directly, Tom was never able to share the tale of how it was that he had come into the possession of Ashur's letter or the watch. That secret was now locked away forever.

Now, in answer to the latest question – this time from Alex – "I can only assume," ventured Tom, "that the sparks between the watches actively challenged which one had the right to exist, before deciding both did. The two versions of Zeus patently did not have the right to co-exist… and they solved that paradox naturally. "Who really knows?" he concluded. "The younger Zeus, on the other hand, will forever be destined to build the same war machine – but only to lose it when it travelled without him to Troy. I cannot conceive of a way for him to escape this endless circle."

"And your chest," asked Maddie, "how is it?"

"Oh, it's fine now – getting better all the time." Tom explained: "If the Hippo-Chronos had returned me home on time to begin with – a year earlier – the doctors would not have perceived the wound to be such a big a problem anyway. After all, to me, the operation is only a few months old. But there again, if the horse had been on time," he mused, "perhaps we would not have all met and become such good friends.

Tell me Alexander, for the painful year that you thought you had lost your father, would you wish it not to have happened – if all of your memories of that year, and what we have learned and achieved together could be removed permanently?"

Alex was ahead of him, "No Tom," he looked around him and at the others. "I wouldn't have missed it for the world," he said honestly.

"And you Conna, perhaps it was not such a happy ending for you, but at least the problems of your family life may begin to be changed now that your father and mother have been forced to deal with their situation. And, not least, that you and your father are now lodging in my house."

Conna nodded acceptingly. He glanced over at Bex, then he shook his head. "I wouldn't have missed it either Tom," he thanked him.

"Maddie, Bex, before your mother took ill and you flew here from the Caribbean, would either of you have imagined that you could find such adventure and true friendship in a small, seaside town like this?"

Maddie smiled from Alex to Tom. "No Tom," she said, "I'm glad we came – and you'll all have to get used to us being around now – while mum continues to get better."

Bex shot a sideways glance at Conna. "Okay, me too," she admitted.

"Then thank you," said Tom. "Thank you all for helping me – from the bottom of the heart of '*This Old Man*'," he smirked.

The four couldn't help but smile, knowing that Tom had guessed the origin of his nickname all along.

"No apologies necessary – anyway, as I said… I like the name. And, I now realise that I have spent far too much of this short life living in emotional isolation. From now on, I will try to be more outgoing; no man is an island.

You realise of course, that in those moments you shared with me, it was you who brought back the world from the brink of perpetual enslavement. It was in those moments that you yourselves became the sentinels of time!"

Tom looked at each of the four in turn. "Not that your work is over," he cautioned. "Your own generation has many new challenges ahead. Mankind stands at a new dawn in technology. Nanotechnology, genetic engineering, biotechnology and synthetic biology – between these things alone, we now have the potential to grow things to our own design at atomic level, just as Mother Nature does. We will shortly have the opportunity to repair body and brain cell tissues – or cure and even prevent disease by targeting defectively coded DNA." Tom looked into their eyes as he spoke. "But will these projected new fields of study be used for good or bad? Will they be used for our benefit, or subverted instead, to develop hitherto unimagined and insidious weaponry? For instance," Tom continued his caution, "to create diseases targeted to attack specific DNA code: the DNA of those people deemed 'less worthy' to share this Earth? Remember the many regimes who have claimed the Earth for themselves. Just think what would happen if some modern fascist-like dictator got to hold the secrets of this new technology in their own nefarious hands!" Tom nodded sagely. "It seems only time will tell.

It is your generation who must ensure that this new power is used only for the deliverance of man, and not his downfall. That is the legacy of knowledge and responsibility left to your generation by Alexander and Ptolemy Soter – but I am sure that in time you will all rise to the challenge. And, in time, warn others!"

Alex looked around at his friends, each in turn silently accepting the charge. "Don't worry Tom, we won't forget."

They all nodded.

After a short pause, Maddie asked a little awkwardly, "But Tom, there's something else – something that no one's mentioned…"

Tom looked at her directly. "And what is that?" he asked.

"I'll say it." Alex picked up the obvious question. "What about you and Ashur?"

"And your daughter, Eos!" added Bex.

"Ah… alas that seems destined never to be. I am locked here. As much as I would dearly love to be back in Aegilia with my wife, and as much as I have longed to see my daughter at least once in my lifetime, long ago, I resigned myself to the fact that that time has passed away.

Bex cajoled Conna to speak up about an idea they'd had between themselves. Still unsure, he asked: "but Tom, what if you could get the Hippo-Chronos working again? What if one of us travelled back in time to meet you when you first arrived here – when you were eighteen? I mean, what if we took you straight back to Aegilia?"

Tom looked doubtful. "Assuming that the machine could be repaired, if I was immediately taken back home, how could I have met you all now? Surely that would be a paradox… and surely, then, Alex in particular would cease to exist!"

The disturbing thought hadn't occurred to anyone before – except Alex.

Alex tried out an alternative idea. "Then if you're too old to return to her now, couldn't you at the least return to a time when both of your ages are closer together – when Ashur is older too?"

"And risk crashing sideways, unannounced, into the life she may have built for herself since our youth?" Tom spoke philosophically. "Who knows, perhaps she took up with the Cretan boy who was so obviously taken with her, perhaps she is happily married with more children – even grandchildren? After all, that is what I wished for her – to live out her own life in full. And if that is indeed what happened, I am most happy for her. Surely to go back and attempt to find her now would be quite wrong."

"But what about Eos?" argued Bex. "Surely you could at least return to see her!"

Tom looked directly at her. "At my age, what use would I be as a parent – I would be far more of a liability. I would certainly not wish her to spend her life looking after me," he glanced at his hospital surroundings. "No… some things are better left alone," he offered resignedly, "the reality would be far more disappointing than she imagined her hero father. "And for my part, at least, now that you have described her to me as an infant, each morning as I watch the dawn rise, I can picture her properly."

Alex still wondered about Ashur, although he accepted that Tom was right. "But if you ever found out there was no one else…?" Alex's final question drifted out, "…that somehow she was still there alone, waiting for you…"

Tom breathed a deep sigh. Suddenly reanimated, he said: "Then, I would fly immediately to her side. Wild horses would not stop me! But, realistically", he mused, "how could I ever find out whether the time was right for us to find each other – it was all such a long time ago?" Taking off his sunglasses, he turned his bright eyes on them all. "And, as most people in the world agree – we cannot turn back time." He managed an ironic smile. "Don't worry. In the meantime I can visit my beautiful young Ashur and our daughter, Eos whenever I wish. I simply close my eyes… like this."

Tom relaxed and dreamt about an idyllic day on Aegilia. He stood alone on the hill at his house, looking out to the indigo sea and a clear blue sky. As he basked in the warmth of the sun, a distant pelican flew lazily below the cliffs. To his left, an old couple pottered around in the garden, whilst to his right, their young son played with a wheeled, clay horse. In Tom's arms, his beautiful little daughter giggled and laughed up at him. Now, from behind, he felt a pair of arms slip softly around his waist and embrace him. Neither spoke. Eventually, he turned to gaze at Ashur's serene smile. He looked once more into her beautiful brown eyes, remembering her face in full. And Lio smiled.

Unable to fault the logic of his argument, or fathom out a solution to Tom's personal dilemma, the four friends regretfully made their way out of his room, to let him dream on. However, they would, for certain, they all agreed, make sure that Tom would not slip back into obscurity or loneliness. Instead, he would forever become one of their own closest circle of friends.

CHAPTER 46:

The Removal of Evidence

A few weeks later, the small dining room of Alex's house seemed packed. It was late in the afternoon, just before dusk. One by one, Tom's new friends piled in from the living room and took their seats around the extended table. They did not have to be reminded that they were forever sworn to secrecy about their recent adventure. Though frankly, they all reasoned, no one would believe them anyway. Their parents would never understand – adults tended to be far too logical.

However, everyone knew they owed an enormous debt of gratitude to Tom for well… all sorts. Alex's mother sat at the back with Rachel on her knee whilst next to her sat Bex, then Conna, then Maddie. Next to them sat Freddie and, looking bright and cheery, though still in her wheelchair, sat his striking half-French wife. "My lady Helena," as he introduced her romantically; but "just Helena," she smiled, shaking her head. There was a space left for Alex, then sat their guest of honour, Tom.

He was not dressed in his usual off-white jubbah, but now, instead, he wore a pair of baggy canvas trousers and was enormously brightened by a Caribbean shirt – get well presents from them all. His beard was trimmed neatly and his hair now tied back in a ponytail – Bex's idea – it took years off him. He stood gazing at the old map that Alex's father had had mounted for his son, and which now had pride of place in the dining room. Tom was well on the mend, his arm now healed, he had been secretly exercising. The overall result of this effort was a transformation. If not quite athletic, he at least looked and felt fitter than he had in years. There were another two vacant seats completing the circle: one for Alex's dad, who was still in the kitchen, and one for Conna's dad, who'd promised he'd be there barring emergencies.

"Dig-in," said Stan, coming through the door.

"Sausage rolls, brilliant," said Conna, making a lunge at the plate before Bex slapped the back of his hand playfully.

"Calm down boy," she reminded him and he still didn't blush.

"Would you like a sandwich Tom?" asked Maddie politely.

"Certainly, I would, thank you," he held out his tea-plate as the conversation buzzed around the table and Rachel bounced up and down on her mother's knee while she bit on a stick of celery with her four new teeth.

There came a rattle at the front door and Conna's dad walked in, flustered. "Hi everybody, I'm sorry I'm late," he said, hanging up his coat on the doorknob. "I was held up." He took his place at the table, took a drink of tea and one of the sausage rolls. He smiled comfortably across at his son, whilst out in the kitchen Alex's dad turned to his own son.

"You know Alex," he said, "all that time I was away, all I really wanted was to come home to you and your mother – and see the baby of course. I'll not be going away any more," he assured.

"Really? Alex sounded astonished. But dad, going into the field is what you do – that's who you are, you bring the past to life, don't you?"

"I suppose so," he smiled, "but it's not healthy to always live in the past."

"No," agreed Alex, "I suppose not, but we do enjoy it, don't we. Anyway. I've talked things through with your mother, and I've decided to teach from now on. I think I'll enjoy working with people your age – you and your friends."

Alex didn't argue, entirely happy with the decision.

From Conna's dad's coat there sounded an urgent bleep. "Not again," he said, getting up to check his phone. He looked apologetically at his son and the rest of the table.

Conna smiled, "Just go dad," he said. "Go on, hurry – someone might be counting on you."

Tom smiled at his new lodger, the man who helped save lives. "Don't worry," he said, "we'll bring you something back, won't we Conna?"

Conna nodded happily.

"Sausage rolls maybe?" his dad suggested. "Sorry everyone," he left abruptly, knowing that everyone understood.

After twenty minutes or so, once more back in the kitchen, Alex and his dad finished placing the few candles on the home-made chocolate cake. Just then there was another bleep, this time from Stan's pocket. Retrieving the iPhone to read the message, he called out into the dining room next door. "It's from your dad Conna – Falcons just scored again."

Conna swallowed. "Yes," he punched the air, this time managing not to spray anyone with food.

Alex's dad clicked a few buttons, and then laid the iPhone on the bench in front of his son. The boy frowned as he looked casually down at the screen, and at the image on it.

It was very dark, pixelated and quite blurred, an ordinary enough photograph of a sleeping face. But Alex was almost certain that he recognised the golden face of the man whose name had been handed down to millions. "Where did this come from dad," he asked.

His dad smiled conspiratorially. "Hmm, oh… it's just a holiday snap," he answered, "someone I bumped into in the desert! I had written a whole account of my travels across the ancient world – and the people I met – but somehow I lost it. Maybe it just wasn't meant to be."

Alex looked at the iPhone again, then back to his dad, wondering.

"It's just something I wanted you to see – in case you didn't get a chance yourself," his dad admitted. Of course," he reminded his son unnecessarily, "it is strictly herkoose odonton. Maybe it's time to delete it… okay by you?"

"Absolutely", said Alex and watched as his dad pushed a few buttons. Within a few clicks, the image and the evidence had gone.

The boy looked at his dad again. *Maybe we should talk about what had happened sometime, but not just yet.* "Oh," he said, "by the way dad, this is yours," he unfastened the wristwatch.

Stan looked at him. "You don't want it?"

"I've kept it long enough," Alex looked at him, "it's far too precious dad. And it's not really my time to own it *just yet* – thanks anyway."

Stan looked at his son with pride, "Okay, I'll take it back – but some day it'll be yours." He strapped it on. "Then instead, how about a swap for now?" he offered, taking off the sun wheel pendant he'd found years ago in the garden.

"You're a good lad sunshine, come here," he put it around Alex's neck and rubbed his mop of hair. "It's still okay to do that?"

"Of course dad," Alex grinned back at him, "I'm just a *little* older."

When he returned to the dining room, Alex showed the token to Tom. Tom smiled easily. "Good," he whispered. "I'm glad it was found. After all, it was an ancient peace symbol long before it took on a darker meaning. And I'm sure Poseidonios would approve of my grandson wearing it now."

Just then, Stan walked in with the cake decorated with the words, *'To our friend Tom – welcome home'*. He brought it through to the table with its dozen lit candles.

Seeing it arrive, Alex's mum called to him in the deepest voice she could manage, "Okay Alex, how about this one… 'Smoke goood… fire baaad!"

"Easy," butted-in Tom, "Boris Karloff – Frankenstein – 1931."

Penny laughed: "Okay," she said, "And take an extra point for the date. After all, it's a bit before your time isn't it."

"Oh," said Tom inconsequentially, "perhaps I was born earlier than you think!"

Eyes were raised, but no one commented. As they smiled and applauded Tom, Alex took his place beside Maddie. "I'm glad your mum looks okay – she's very pretty isn't she," he complimented.

"Very," Maddie smiled across at her mother while Helena talked to Tom. "She'll be fine, I *know* she will, she's tough. Anyway," she changed the subject, whispering into his ear, "I know Conna and his dad are living with Tom now Alex, but do you ever think he'll feel truly at home here when he's got somewhere else to live?"

"I don't know," replied Alex. "Maybe someday, if he repairs the horse…" He shrugged. "Who knows? Anyway, thanks again for helping with dad," he squeezed her hand beneath the table.

Maddie smiled comfortably back at him in reply.

At that, while Penny cut up the cake, Tom got up and excused himself. Using the pizzle as a precaution only, he left the room steadily. Alone, he made his way through the living room and out toward the front of the house. There at the opened door, he stood looking at the darkening skyline as he had done almost every day of his life. On the horizon, two RAF trainers flew close to the water. Tom closed his eyes – and Lio saw fishing birds skimming the surface. "Sleep safely Ashur – and you Eos, my daughter," he mumbled under his breath. "Perhaps it will not be too long before we are finally together…" Then the old man opened his eyes again.

Only a short while later, inside the dining room, the occupants heard a growing roar. Boris jumped up to bark at the window, and everyone stopped eating. The noise grew louder and louder reaching a painful level as the sonic boom crashed out and faces around the table looked at each other worriedly. Then, with one voice they shouted, "TOM!"

Opening the passage door as both of the jet trainers roared over their heads, Tom asked: "Yes, what is it?"

And this time, nobody spoke. But together, they all heaved a sigh of pure relief.

Beneath the dining table, Boris settled his head on his outstretched front legs. He snorted noisily, stretching out his cat like nails. Then, lazily, he rolled onto his back, instantly asleep again and whimpering noisily as he dreamed of who knows what!

EPILOGUE

[From the Greek: *epi* – after, and *logos* – speech]

CAN WE EVER HOPE TO FIND THE RIGHT WAY?

I ANSWER WITHOUT HESITATION THAT THERE IS,

IN MY OPINION, A RIGHT WAY

AND THAT WE ARE CAPABLE OF FINDING IT.

I HOLD IT TRUE THAT PURE THOUGHT CAN GRASP
REALITY,

AS THE ANCIENTS DREAMED.

Albert Einstein

The Legend of the Desert

Giza, Sometime in the Third Millennium BC

In the scorching heat of the sun, a place of reception had been carefully prepared on the on flat top of the unfinished pyramid. The area – now swept clean of all building rubble – was carpeted and an elaborate banqueting table had been prepared. A golden cloth covered it and hung down to the ground. Much exotic food and drink had been brought to the site by the portly architect, in case his royal client would wish to refresh himself after his long journey. Another, smaller table sat just off the centre, another cloth covering an obviously geometric shaped object beneath it. The architect was confident that it would astound – it was his latest work of genius.

His slim assistant stood behind him, and together, both peered down at the slowly ascending procession of priests and guards leading the carried royal palanquin. All other workers were dismissed for the day, lest the noise of construction work should annoy the King. Sat beneath the cloth canopy, the walnut skinned Pharaoh was furthered steadily up the final stretch of the long ramp that wrapped around the pyramid base. The line of two abreast parted at the top and made way for the four bulky slaves who continued to carry the king toward the top. Now, from his throne, the middle-aged, gaunt looking Pharaoh clapped his hands twice – loud! In response, the four carriers carefully placed the carriage down onto its short legs and stood to attention beside it.

Two even more muscle-bound guards stood to its sides, each carrying a ceremonial golden machete-axe, while the bare-chested

431

Pharaoh Khafra stood up confidently. He wore the double crown of Upper and Lower Egypt: the white gourd shaped headdress surrounded by the gold band. Too hot and heavy for outdoor use, the crown had made him tired and irritable over his long journey here. His hang-dog face with its charcoal-painted eyes and the recent affectation – the blue-dyed and tightly plaited white goatee beard that was supposed to disguise his growing age – looked resplendent in the sun. He sucked-in his stomach and looked down at the now kneeling architect and his assistant. Again, he clapped twice: "Stand," he commanded, his overlong tongue betraying a slight lisp.

"Your majesty," the architect fawned, "some refreshment perhaps?" He pointed to the table. The Pharaoh looked irritated. "I have not come all this way to dine," he advised, "get on with it. What is it that is so important that you could not have presented it to me at my palace – that you had to drag me all of the way out here to see?"

"Your majesty," grovelled the architect, wringing his hands, "if it pleases you, I have brought a scale model of the design which I have prepared for your own tomb, here in the company of your ancestors." Again he held out his hand as if to present the king with the obvious flat site at the base of the two pyramids.

The king ignored him and looked across at the second table. He sighed frustratedly. "And this model that you speak of: 'the unique monument that you alone among architects can provide…' The monument to my memory: Khafra, King of Upper and Lower Egypt. The one thing you told me would last for five thousand years or more – the thing that will tell the future world of my greatness."

"Yes your majesty," the architect smiled, self-satisfactorily.

"The thing that needed to be presented to me personally in the sweltering heat of the desert's edge…" he went on. His shaven chest glistened with sweat, "it wouldn't be yet another pyramid – would it?" He glared at the suddenly unsure man.

In the uneasy silence that followed, the architect squirmed. However, as he did, his assistant's attention wandered as he watched a commotion develop on the ramp. The double line of followers parted mysteriously. Distracted by the mumbling, the servant wasn't listening properly as the architect told him to take the covered model away. "Now!" commanded his master. He snapped out of his inattention and crossed to the square table. Then, just as practiced – with a flourish – he ceremoniously removed the dustcover. With that, he revealed the model pyramid, bowing low as he did so.

The once physically powerful king shifted his weight, now standing with his legs slightly apart, wearing only the golden kilt and heavily bejewelled necklace. His belly suddenly sagged as he sighed more deeply. Irritably, Khafra removed his crown and handed it to one of the slaves. Then, with the back of his wrist, he wiped the sweat from around his eyes, smudging the eye make-up down his face. He clapped again. Without turning to the nearest bodyguard, he held out his hand. The smirking bodyguard stepped forward proffering the heavy machete axe. Taking it from him, the king asked the architect, "Would you like to explain this 'unique' design to me?"

"Your majesty", he continued in trepidation, "this pyramid is unlike the other two because... unlike the others..." he floundered "...it is different!" His mouth now dried, he struggled to come up with an excuse. "For instance, he suggested... it will not be topped with electrum... it will be topped with... *gold?*" He floated the impromptu idea.

The pharaoh stepped up to the model in exasperation, his shaven head sweating profusely. Crossing his arms, he closed his eyes and twitched distastefully.

The architect's assistant's attention wandered back to the commotion in the ranks.

"So," said the king pointedly, "after taking my money for the past ten years – to develop this unique idea of yours – you are now suggesting that my tomb, the house where my own mortal remains will be kept on earth as my soul journeys into the night sky – to Sirius – will indeed be a pyramid after all. Though, your pyramid will not attract the life giving lightning through its sacred cap of electrum, as my ancestors' pyramids. Instead, it will be replaced by a gold cap?" The architect swallowed uncomfortably as the king

433

continued. "A golden magnet which will attract the thieves of the world to constantly disturb my peace: by attempting to rob from me – throughout all eternity." He thumbed the edge of the sharpened machete.

That was not how the architect had thought of it: as long as he was well paid and well out of it, he hadn't considered how it would look or perform much into the future. Now, he gulped.

In the background, his assistant saw something move. An animal, something small and blue-ish-grey trotted through the double row. It was not a lamb, nor was it a goat. It passed behind the guards and the king and finally disappeared beneath the tablecloth that covered the refreshment table. From the far distance, he heard a girl's voice call out – a shouted name that he couldn't quite make out.

The architect dropped heavily to his knees. "Your majesty I can explain," he gabbled, his head bowed.

The king ignored him. "And you," Khafra challenged the assistant, "would you like to explain also?"

The slim man looked back at The Great Pharaoh. He breathed-in triumphantly. "Yes…" he said confidently, "Yes, your majesty, I would." He cleared his throat. "Your majesty, what my partner wishes you to know."

"PARTNER?" spat the architect.

"Full partner!" emphasized the assistant, pausing for acceptance of his terms.

The architect looked again at the sun's rays glinting on the edge of the machete and nodded his head rapidly.

"Then, what my partner wishes you to know," he repeated, "is that this pyramid," he pointed to the model, "is intended only as a decoy. It will be built on the other side of the site, closer to the Nile. And," he made it up as he went along, "out of respect for your majesty and his ancestors," he assured, "built smaller than these two."

The king and the architect listened intently.

"The real reason your majesty was required to visit here, was to show The Great King the inspiration for your own resting place, an animal so rare, that it is said not to exist." He swanned over to the table and took hold of the edges of the cloth. Your majesty, let us present to you 'Orryss', he blagged shamelessly, 'The Legend of the Desert'. With that, he deftly flipped the front edge of the tablecloth back over the food, revealing the mysterious animal beneath.

Boris lay insulated against the heat in his light woollen coat. His head once more held haughtily aloof, his fluffy headdress, with the long-tasselled ears hanging out and down the sides of his face. Front legs straight out, back legs tucked up against his sides and his thin, shaven tail curled around him. The animal looked cool and resplendent in the hot sun. Snorting briefly with boredom, Boris moved only his eyes. The *sphinx* looked directly at the king and woofed loudly once, dead on cue.

The king was taken aback – genuinely moved. He grasped the architect's expertly conceived concept immediately. "My soul will be guided to the dog-star, while the stone image of this mysterious woolly-haired beast named Orryth – a panther – no, a lion..." the thing changed and grew in his imagination as he spoke. "With the tail of a snake – no, an ox – the voice of a dog and the lightweight headdress that will be the new symbol of royalty, it will forever guard my body and those of my descendants." The architect was an absolute genius!

Without looking, Khafra casually tossed the machete back over his shoulder at his bodyguard and as he commanded the architect to stand, there was a short painful grunt from behind him. Then he beckoned the 'genius' and his new business partner forward nervously, to be hugged by the king – and kissed on both cheeks repeatedly.

While all of this happened, the tablecloth blew back down and Boris stood up unnoticed. For no special reason, he suddenly shot straight out of the back, clambered down the steep, rough side of the unfinished pyramid and down to the ground. As the Pharaoh celebrated on high, the dog bounded back over the hot sand, then the dry earth and finally over the grass to the farm of Drodos. He stopped briefly to sniff at, and then water the Oak tree. Then, he disappeared as mysteriously as he had arrived.

Boris, the dog of Northumberland, had skipped lightly out of the desert, and into history. Orryth, a new legend of the desert had been born.

In Homage and Apologia

Please take the time to read this. After all, the truth is often stranger than fiction!

Regarding the facts of this book.

The vast majority of what I have written about here is, as I promised you at the beginning of book one, based on what has been rediscovered recently. In order that the truth is not obscured from view though, I have a few 'slight confessions' to make.

Firstly, regarding Kyrros: Andronicus of Cyrrhus, or Andronikos of Kyrros, did indeed exist, although the dates given for his life and work would indicate that he lived to an incredibly old age – around two hundred years! His combined works in the Tinos sundial and the Horologion certainly seem to have astounded his peers. His complete disappearance from the pages of history therefore astounds me.

Also, the ancient technologists and inventors did produce the variously described machines, gadgets and weaponry, perhaps with the exception of the giant wheel of Ptolemy: (although, Alexandria's water supply was massively polluted by Ptolemy somehow). Even Caesar cites this in his own histories. I would venture that this wheel is at least theoretically possible.

Of the two battles I have depicted, the sea battle for Alexandria is, I believe, in the main true. However, although the burning mirrors of Archimedes (and further ingenious weaponry) were said to have been used earlier against the Romans at Syracuse, no one has claimed their use since then. Their effectiveness is *hotly* disputed. Neither are there any reliable records of how the battle of the Nile was fought and lost, nor how the boy king Ptolemy XIII actually died. Contemporary accounts of him – written from the Roman standpoint – describe him, unsurprisingly, in less than glowing terms – little more than a spoiled child.

Regarding Cleopatra, despite popular myth, there are remarkably few verifiable details of her – especially contemporary details – only a handful! Most accounts of her were written several generations later – as highly opinionated popular Roman legend. Truthfully, historically, she effectively remains a blank canvas. These facts alone account for her often being portrayed as the beautiful, intelligent and resourceful commander of her country. However, her actual murderous record (especially of her own family rivals) and her abandonment of her country for a life of luxury in Rome, paints an entirely different, more scheming and selfish picture – rivalling that of many modern dictators. Regardless, I find the excuse that she was only doing what many men did in that brutal world, hardly laudable. But, as I have previously said, no doubt, she will continue to be held aloft in some circles, depending on the agenda of the viewer.

By contrast, I repeat: the career, coldness and vanity of Caesar are well documented – even to his belief in omens and his prickliness toward his thinning hair! The symbolism and signs Caesar used in his First Reich, including the swastika, the *faces*, the black uniforms and the outstretched arm salute, were eventually to become the same symbols that were adopted by the twentieth century's most infamous dictator, Hitler.

As for the swastika itself, clearly, this paradoxical sign remains one of the most potent symbols of hatred and intolerance in the modern world: so much so, that attempts have been made to ban certain forms of it outright. However, it should be remembered that originally, the sign of peace and good luck existed many centuries before even Caesar. The sun wheel remains a revered symbol of faith for many eastern religions; just as the Crucifix, the Star of

David and the Crescent Moon are revered elsewhere. Its use is a dilemma, is it not? Perhaps then, it is the intention of man, and not the symbol which is the true problem.

With regard to the whereabouts of the mortal remains of Alexander the Great, although it is not known, I find it difficult to believe that a relic prized so highly might have been accidentally destroyed or 'lost'. (There is one later account of Caesar Octavian – later given the title Augustus, or Revered – damaging the intact mummy, after which it finally goes missing.) I am therefore quite certain that Alexander lies purposely hidden somewhere, waiting to be rediscovered – perhaps someday soon? perhaps even inspired by someone reading this book!

As if to back up my own scatological opinions, some expert credence has recently also been given to the idea that Britain was indeed an alternative source of tin since the time of Wilusha's destruction – a theory which first entered my head in the mid eighties, after watching various TV documentaries, made by the historian Michael Wood in particular. Truth, it still seems, is sometimes stranger than fiction.

Regarding the burning of the Mouseion and Great Library of Alexandria, it is almost entirely shrouded in mystery. Caesar's own short personal account of the siege of Alexandria and the sea battle does not mention it, but there again, would you admit to being the cause of such a calamity – either accidentally or purposely?

Archeologically, of the sites on Rhodes, Athens, Tinos and Antikythera especially, many of the places described still remain. Even after thousands of years, they may still be visited. They lend great insight into temple life at that time: from the steps leading to the acropolis of Rhodes (Monte Smith), to the temples and hidden accessed cellars and corridors below them. Even to the fossilised seashell in the marble, all are still there! (Please note though, my version of this ancient acropolis of Rhodes pre-dates the accepted founding of the present ruins – circa 400BC.) I would recommend that if you ever have the opportunity, you should go there – or somewhere similar – just to sit and ponder all of the ordinary lives of those who have shared this small planet with us for a short while – many thousands of years before us.

As for the two diving scenes, the first, using the Siebe Gorman equipment is, I believe, reasonably accurate, although rumours abound concerning what may have been stripped from the site before it was reported to the authorities. Regarding the second, ancient description, it is known that skandalopetra were used in ancient pearl and murex diving, and there is at least one account from Aristotle himself, that describes diving technology using an upturned cauldron. (More details are discussed in **The Hippo-Tempus – Appendix 3**, posted on the **time-horse.com** website).

Regarding the more modern event which is touched upon latterly – the single, Second World War event I speak of regarding Antikythera – this is also true. When I first visited Crete, many years ago, I remember having a short conversation with a man whose family had escaped there from Antikythera – 'the island of ancient pirates'. He was a jeweller, and I was looking at a remarkable, but vastly unaffordable watch in his window. It was his casually related story which first alerted me to the existence of the island. Until then, I had not heard of the place. He told me that the whole population of that strategic island was brutally cleared within a single day – for spying and passing information on naval movements. It seemed such a cruel event to me, although, I have no doubt that the islanders would have been perfectly able and willing to pass information to both ELAN – the free Greek navy – and the British, their allies and past protectors of the strategic island's freedom. The tale stayed with me ever since. When I got home, I decided to look the story up in a regional library, but couldn't find it. It was then that I first discovered an account of the 'Antikythera device'. It was written by Professor Derek de Solla Price. Now, I do not wish to rake over the recent past unnecessarily, the subject of the Second World War event is, I suspect, still very sensitive – even raw – for many reasons. But during the many visits I've made to Greece since then, unsolicited, I have picked up several accounts of Nazi atrocities committed there at that time. Knowing the modern German people as I do, I still find it incredible that, for a time, the psyche of a significant part of their whole nation could suddenly be subverted by such a staggeringly evil and vengeful ideology. Does that mean that, given similar economic and social circumstances, it could happen to anyone? But it especially frightens me that, even since then, many similarly intolerant ideologies have risen around the world – and many are still seemingly fuelled by fanatical and ancient allegiance to one or another deity. As Lio's grandfather or even Tom might say – where will it all end? Anyway, when I finally visited Antikythera, part of my purpose was to clarify what happened there all those years ago. However, finding the island so quiet and peaceful now, and being accepted so readily by the people I met, I decided that to bring up such a subject would be quite impertinent, potentially painful and perhaps unnecessary after all. For that reason, I have not embellished it. Perhaps that account needs to be documented properly by a 'pukka' historian? Nevertheless, it was this WWII story which first sparked my own tale: mechanical discovery; primitive beliefs; pirates; the First Reich; time repeating itself – et al.

And finally, regarding the speculative dates of the Antikythera shipwreck, or device: In fairness, most archaeologists have until now believed either that the ship went down earlier, or that the computer was made earlier, perhaps in Alexandria or on Rhodes. However, even now, these dates are being re-examined. There is no proof positive – like a specific coin which may date the event definitively. Over the time it has taken me to write this short saga – over four years – the accepted speculative dates for both the wreck and the mechanism have been changed at least three times. I freely confess that when I started, the places I chose for my story were entirely speculative – my own personal hunch. However, I have recently read that the computer may well have been constructed either in Alexandria, Rhodes or now, even Syracuse. Additionally, various candidates for its design now include Sosigenes of Alexandria, Andronicus of Cyrrhus and even

Archimedes of Syracuse – much earlier than previously mooted.

As for the computer's exact purpose – well… who will ever truly know the full extent of the genius of the Ancients?

The next time you hear a particularly loud crash of thunder above. The next time you imagine Zeus hurling one of his zigzag bolts to earth in anger, you might also spare a thought for the first scientists and technologists who sought to explain our universe properly. After all, as Conna would say, theirs truly was – a brilliant story!

M.R.

Acknowledgements

As in my first book, I'm afraid I have largely the same confession to make regarding the sources of the material I have used for this one. That confession being that those sources are still so many and various that I could not justifiably single out any one of them – perhaps with the exception of the historian, Michael Wood. Nevertheless, I will again, at least, group them into six.

Firstly, I would like to pay tribute to the schoolteachers who opened my eyes to this whole subject all those years ago – and to school teaching as a profession.

Secondly, the excellent accredited Greek tourist guides who have not only given me the official historical story, but quite often, the less well known and admittedly more controversial line. I still can't help wondering at what point speculation actually becomes accepted as history. (I am certain that Heinrich Schliemann faced the same resistance to his romantic beliefs.) This is especially true of the very helpful staff of both the Acropolis archaeological site and the Athens Museum of Ancient Antiquities. Thankyou then, to the many professional guides who have shared with me the benefits of their considerable collective expertise.

Thirdly, the many ordinary local people I have bumped into on both my older and my more recent travels in particular. Some, by what I will still only allow myself to say, share the most incredible and coincidental interests, have been able to lead me down new avenues of research. Again, in this respect, I would like to thank a certain Athenian sculptor and designer who, after only one short straight conversation – during which he was astounded by the repeated coincidences I outlined to him – helped reconfirm my own view, and spurred me on to re-write my tale – because somehow, this book was meant to be!

Fourthly, to librarians and archivists, keepers (and often interpreters) of knowledge.

Fifthly, penultimately, I would once again like to thank my whole family and friends who have unselfishly contributed in a very real sense, spending many hours of their time in getting personally involved.

And, once more, as I admitted previously, I am certain that I have, over the years, absorbed much from books and TV: and the **BBC, The History Channel**, and **National Geographic** channels in particular. Through them, I began many years ago to connect the seemingly unrelated events as I have. Years later, as I mentioned elsewhere, I am delighted to learn that the same private theories that I would not dared to make public at the time are already quite well accepted by professionals. No doubt, there will be many who will recognise something of the themes of their own work in these pages. In some cases I have borrowed from these shared themes, in others, both details and learned explanations. I trust that I have not overstepped the mark. If I have, I hope that interest in these fascinating previous documentary works and theories will be rekindled as a result, but they are again, too numerous to list.

Again though, if I really had to pick out one overall source of both information and especially verification after all, there is still one selfless and learned body to whom I would like to pay particular homage. This truly amazing organisation advocates the freely accessible and uncensored education of the whole planet. Eventually, I am still confident that this enlightenment may very well be the saviour of us all. I refer of course to **Wikipedia.** Please then, once again accept my heartfelt thanks and continued support – to all of its contributors.

THE FUTURE

[From the Latin: *Futurus* – 'about to be']

STRIVE FOR TRUE KNOWLEDGE,

TRUE PEACE AND TOLERANCE –

TRUE LOVE AND FORGIVENESS

– FOLLOW YOUR CONSCIENCE

AND YOUR HEART!

Lio's grandfather, 585 BC

Hand In Glove

Alexandria 48 BC

On the square directly outside of the conflagration that had been the Great Library, flames continued to leap into the sky. They sent a shower of hot sparks high into the night, like tiny stars making their way back to the heavens. Remarkably, the atmosphere seemed entirely peaceful now that the immediate danger had passed.

Roman soldiers lay dead and dying as the army medics were rushed in to see who could be saved. The smoke-blackened troops coughed and moaned as they were sorted into three separate piles: the dead; the dying (and therefore, to be 'dispatched'); and the salvageable. The white uniformed librarian that had been thrown unceremoniously into the first pile was picked up and removed under the instruction of a guard, before being dragged toward the palace. The centurion in charge spared not more than a fleeting thought for all of the works he had seen littered across the floor, now virtually all gone. All, that is, apart from the few rolls that he'd kicked through the door himself during the 'tactical withdrawal'. *What had been contained in them*, he wondered fleetingly, *and where have they gone – especially the heavy one?*

Not that he cared that much. He had far greater things to worry about. He began to count his troops and prepare the statement he would need to give to Caesar himself. And yet, how could he possibly tell Caesar that a fire breathing horse had appeared from nowhere, burned down the library, killed his troops and disappeared. Best not mention the horse then! It really was time for him to retire as soon as he had enough money. As he struggled to collect his worried thoughts, a black uniformed Praetorian guard approached, tossing a small grubby ochre bag of coins in his hand – it was going to be the centurion's lucky night after all.

The troops began to finally get the fire under control just as the rain started, dampening down the sparks. As this happened, a lone, gloved hand picked up the roll of papers, taking them under cover to look at what had been found. Unfurling it, the examiner looked briefly at the features of the machine that bore a resemblance to a horse of sorts, although perhaps a rather ugly one. Assessing the documents' value before rolling them up again, the finder wondered who amongst the rich and powerful, might be willing to pay the most for what had been rescued!